Alternative Energy

By

Marc Gregory

Copyright © 2021 by Marc Gregory
First Edition - June 2021

ISBN
978-1-7776468-2-0 (Paperback)
978-1-7776468-3-7 (eBook)

All rights reserved.

The characters and events portrayed in this book are ficticious.
Any similarity to real persons, living or dead, is coincidental and not
intended by the author.

Published by:
Stand Publishing Inc.

www.facebook.com/mgregoryauth

Distributed to the trade by Ingram Book Company

Other books By Marc Gregory

Alternative Energy

Alternative Energy II - Blow Me

Price Per Barrel

Quantum Avidya

1

How will it be now? I wonder, as I watch my sons walk away from me on that rainy day, hand in hand with my recently ex'd wife in the graveyard where we just buried my father before his time. Workplace accidents had become a plague in my life, as my mind recalled a time many years passed, in the blink of an eye. They're still so young. I haven't had my time to show them the side to me that was more than leaving for work early and coming home late. Sifting through the bills and cracking a beer to sit on the couch and watch the fights. I never had it… or never took it? *I wonder how it will be now?...Not the same.*

As I drove home the rain subsided, and islands of blue sky began to form between the heavy clouds. I walked inside my new-to-me, sparsely furnished apartment in the lesser desired part of town. I threw my jacket over the chair, loosened my tie and kicked off my shoes as I grabbed a cold one from the fridge. I stepped out to the slanting deck and sat in the single chair. I took a swig, closed my eyes, and let the weight of the last couple months buckle me forward to watch tears pool on the faded deck between my feet.

This is what life has become for me as my experience builds to 40.

There'll be a new man in their lives soon. Probably with cool tattoos and a fast car. I'll be the guy working every day to pay alimony and child support in the wake of a divorce I never wanted. She just got bored… we all got bored… of me. Even myself.

I sit back in my chair and look up at the now clear sky, to see the tail of exhaust trailing behind a jet passing so far overhead.

I remembered then… it was so long ago. Lifetimes it seemed. Almost lost beneath the ash in my mind. The burning of the past to clear room for the new. But it was still there. That time, and the stories I held sacred. I felt the urge then to let it all go, before I fade to the background of their life. To make record of the time when I wasn't so boring.

But what is most important for me, is to show them there is an alternative to this. An alternative to the traffic lights and the tax filings, the divorce lawyers and social workers. An alternative mindset, an alternative lifestyle… An alternative energy.

So, here it is boys…

2

Twenty-ish years earlier.

At 6:00am Monday morning, my alarm clock celebrated my survival of yet another binge weekend. The instant my eyes opened and the pain of my hangover kissed me good morning, I promised myself I'd never drink again—or not 'til at least Wednesday. My work shift didn't actually start until seven, but I'd set the alarm for six to convince myself I was a responsible adult. And yet, the drunk adolescent in me hit the snooze until six-fortyish. I jumped out of bed, and the sudden shock of movement caused the room to spin vengefully. I almost puked up the six or eight excess beers I'd drank the night before. I rushed into the bathroom and did my best to brush the evidence of the festivities from my breath before throwing on the same dank work clothes I'd worn the previous Friday.

I eased my way through town in my early eighties, white four-door Honda Civic "sex machine." The sun was rising in the clear blue summer sky. The blinding rays reflecting off the puddles left by the last night's rain excited my headache. The weather forecast set the current temperature at 20 degrees, predicting 35 for the afternoon. Combined with the humidity from the uncommon summer moisture and I could anticipate hot sauna conditions.

It's a good thing I had called it a night when I did. Hangovers are much worse on a hot day. I stopped for the red light beside Connaught golf course and watched as the sprinklers threw their tall arch of refreshing water onto the fairways. I got lost in a daydream. Thinking of how nice it would be to head out for a round, instead of busting my sorry ass at the sweatshop. I found peace momentarily as I admired the serene landscape, wishing I could spend the morning rubbing my battered forehead on the cool, freshly pruned turf. The light turned green and the horn from the asshole behind me revived the pounding in my forehead, wrenching me from the dew-covered grass to the reality of the workday ahead. I hated Mondays, and so my mood decayed the closer I got to work.

As usual, when I pulled into the parking lot, the only spot that remained was in front of the dumpster. All employees at DJ's had their own designated parking space but me. I had asked several times, but my request was always ignored. So, I'd park in front of the dumpster, the garbage truck driver would later find me blocking his access. The garbage man would piss on Dick, and Dick would piss on me. I'd explain the situation and again asked for a proper parking stall. Dick would scratch his head and mumble something that sounds a lot like "fuck" then grump back to his office and slam the door behind him. Dick was the owner of DJ's. A company passed down to him by his father. Richard Jerkins was the legal signature on his passport, but to me, he was just a dick!

Every week, the same thing happened like clockwork. It was incredible to think it had been going on for at least six months now. We didn't support evolution at DJ's, only repetition.

I parked the car and rushed inside, just in time as always. I headed to the change room, which I'm pretty sure was originally a closet that was later upgraded to a change room large enough to accommodate no more than two people at a time. My check for a clean stack of coveralls on the top shelf of the cabinet came up empty. So I threw on my last week's set and headed to the lunchroom.

I was the last to arrive as expected. Dick was waiting with his clipboard in hand, ready to give out the day's marching orders. I scanned the room. Everyone was present except for Donny. I figured he must have gotten caught up partying all weekend again and blew his shift. Donny was the slackest of the crew. He only got his job because he used to be a big local hockey star, and the Jerkins were big fans.

Dick turned to Trevor, the field foreman, who by some strange coincidence was married to Dick's sister. "Okay Trevor, you and Brent head out to the mall expansion and continue erecting the shit out there. I want that complete by the end of the week. Corey, we got a big order to build permanent ladders for the base. Hundred and three to be exact." He handed Corey a roll of blueprints.

4

"Here's the prints. Set Brandon up to cut the material for you. Frank, keep on with what you were doing last week." Dick finished with a commanding nod and headed straight back to his office.

We scrambled out of the cramped lunchroom into the shop and separated into our designated groups. I followed Corey over to his worktable, thankful that I'd been placed with him. He was the only guy of the bunch I really got along with.

He spread the prints out and began his review. "Hundred and three, fuck me. This is going to be a long one." He pointed out the obvious. "I'd feel sorry for you having to cut all this shit, but then I'm the poor bastard that has to weld it together. Whatever, all the pieces are the same size. There's just going to be a lot of them."

"Fucking Monday," I moaned.

3

Corey took time to do some calculations on the table. "All right, let's get you set up on the chop saw."

I followed him over to the saw, not that I needed direction. I knew where it was well enough, though I hadn't worked with it much over the last few months. It was the next rung down on my continual demotion. Corey found a pile of round iron for the ladder rungs and grabbed the first of many twenty-foot lengths. He placed it on the chop saw guide, measured out the length, and set the material under the blade and the stop to the tip of the piece. For those who have never worked with this equipment before, the stop is…well…the stop. It's a guide so that you don't have to measure out every piece. You just measure the first and set the stop at the end. So for the rest you just butt the material against the stop and cut. Easy, and mindless. So, he set the stop, made the first cut and double-checked the length of the finished piece.

"Perfect," he turned toward me, the look on his face told me he was excited to hand over the reins. "Think you can handle it?"

I nodded with a jaded expression.

"Good. So just do that fifteen hundred times."

My jaw hit the floor, "Fifteen hundred? As in one-thousand-five-hundred?"

"Ah, an educated man, eh. That's right genius, fifteen hundred." His laugh echoed through the shop as he headed back to his worktable.

Fuck, I shook my head as I turned back to the dreaded saw. *Fifteen hundred.*

It's gonna be a long week. I grabbed the next piece of steel, fed it under the saw to the stop, and began counting in my head, *One, two, three…*

The morning dragged on. It's one thing to be stuck at a monotonous job all day, but having a clock right over your head so you can watch the second-hand crawl through its laps is worse. *Cut…tick…cut…tock…cut…*

I followed the beat of the ticking hand all morning through lunchtime. The 12:00 pm bell rang, announcing the arrival of our allotted half hour to feed and water ourselves before the afternoon shift. I finished the piece I had in the saw, then shut down my one-man assembly line. I removed the soiled rag from my back pocket and wiped the sweat from my face, while overlooking the pile of completed rungs. The count at an even one hundred. *Only fourteen hundred and life to go.*

Not interested in making small talk with a group of assholes, I avoided the lunchroom during the break and made my way out back to the steel yard to fnd a spot to sit in the shade. Because I didn't have time to pack my lunch, I used the break to rest. *Only forty more years. If I don't die before then,* I thought. *The cutting and welding fumes oughtta cut that time in half. At least.* I'd seen the result: a thirty-year-old man looking like he was sixty. Missing teeth and fingers, and an alcoholic. It seemed like he was living the life every night as he returned to his usual pub, waving his money around like he hit the jackpot. Gambling on the VLTs, tipping the young waitresses way too much in some hope that he could buy their love and attention. He stayed at the pub 'til closing time. The only place he could get a small ounce of respect, even if it was paid for. He had nothing to go home to. It was a look at my life in the future.

The bell rang again. I pushed my sorry ass up from the ground and dragged my feet back to my workstation. I exhaled in self-pity. The fun and games of lunch now over, I placed my safety glasses back on my face and hit the big green button. Shocking my assembly line back to life. *Only four more hours. Four more hours and you'll be off until tomorrow. Tomorrow will be better because…because…*

The afternoon ticked by second after second. The hand on the clock called to me as if it had finally found an equal in life. Someone who understood its pain of doing one robotic motion after another.

The mood in the shop was obedient. Each welder hid beneath his helmet. At 2:00 pm, Richard the Dick came out of his office for reasons unknown. Boredom, most likely. Internet porn had probably seized his computer again. He made his rounds at all the stations, checking up on each crew member. Stopping for a chat and a laugh with some. When he got to Corey's station, he stood over Corey's shoulder before stopping him and pointing at something on the ladder he was currently building. I couldn't quite make out what he was saying. Suddenly he unclipped the tape measure from his pants, measured one of the ladder rungs, and threw it back down on the table in disgust. Then he marched straight to my station. Corey followed behind with a troubled look.

I watched the action through the corner of my eye. Continuing my work. Pretending not to notice. *Maybe they'll pass by, maybe it has nothing to do with…*

"Get out of the way!" Dick came straight at me. Pushing me away from the saw with no concern for anyone's safety. He grabbed a length of round iron from my finished pile and measured it before turning to me, hands on his hips, beet-red face beaming over me like he was the bloody sun around which my whole world revolved. "What the fuck!!" his voice boomed across the shop. Everyone else stopped their own work and flipped up their helmets, looking over in my direction to see what I had screwed up this time.

That's right, boys. The fuck up fucked up again. Go ahead, laugh it up. I looked up, way up, and met Dick's bulging eyes staring down at mine. "What's wrong?" I asked meekly.

"What's wrong? What's wrong? Have you got shit for brains or something? I give you one job and you fuck it up. So I give you a different job, and you fuck it up again. What do you want me to do? I'm trying to keep you around. I try to find something you're good at. I give you the easiest job in the shop. And now, I don't know. I just don't know what to do with you."

I lowered my head in shame, my face flushed at the public belittling.

That was Dick. Outside of the shop he had no friends. No one gave him the time of day. Not even his wife or kids. But in this shop, he did whatever he wanted, as it was his signature on our paycheck. "You're useless!" he yelled. Then straightened his posture and looked around the suddenly quiet room. His chest pressed out with pride at what he had just accomplished. The son of a bitch was even grinning. He turned and began to walk away.

"Wait!" I yelled after him. "Are you going to fucking tell me what I did wrong, or what?"

He turned back with a snort. "If you can't figure that out yourself, then pack up your shit and go home. No one here can help you." He stormed into his office and slammed the door behind him.

As I stood at my station with a piece of iron in my hand, I heard someone muffle a cough. I looked around at the others who quickly turned from me. Pulling down their helmets, they continued with their work. Doing their best to pretend they hadn't noticed. Corey was busy measuring random pieces in my finished pile.

"They're too long," he said. "The first ones are good, and then somewhere along the line something went wrong. The stop must have moved." Corey reached over and pulled down the saw. He measured the distance from the blade to the stop. "Sure enough," he concluded as the tape snapped back into its case. "Shit, that's my fault Brand. That stupid homemade piece-of-shit stop. I should have warned you. It has a habit of moving. Sorry man."

I stood there quietly while he continued. "Well, it's not so bad. You cut them too long, so it's not like there's a lot of wasted material. It would have sucked if you'd cut them short. Anyway, just go through 'em again and nip off any excess. It's not that big a deal. Everyone in this shop has been through this more than once. Though I'd never seen him be such an asshole about it. Guess he likes you." Corey smiled and gave me a friendly shot to the shoulder while I continued to stand mute. Adrenaline from the encounter caused a slight tremor on my nerves. "Don't sweat it man, it's Monday. He's probably pissed because his wife slapped him around last night."

"Yeah, I could see that," I finally replied. His joke eased the tension, somewhat. I picked up the first piece from my pile, measured it, and reset the stop. I really wasn't paying much attention to Corey. I was stuck in a trance, looking at the saw. *Just walk into his office and punch the asshole right in his face!*

Corey started back toward his workstation. He called over his shoulder, "It'll all be forgotten tomorrow."

4

At quitting time, the bell rang. I looked up at the clock to confirm the time and gave a slight nod of farewell to the second hand. I released the saw handle from my grip and flexed my now stiff fingers to get the circulation flowing again.

Despite the shitty day at work, the beautiful summer weather brought a smile to my face as I made my way to my car. Monday was over, *thank fuck*. My car was hotter than hell after a long day of sitting under the sun. I started the engine and quickly rolled down the windows. Air conditioning made me sick. With six months of winter on the horizon, I welcomed the warm summer breeze.

Pulling away from work, I checked my phone for any messages. "Hi sweetie, it's just after four. Call me please." I hit the speed dial.

"Hey Mom, what's up?"

We got into the usual mother-son chitchat. We hadn't gotten together in a while, so she invited me over for supper. She and her husband Bruce had some steaks marinating.

It didn't take long for me to come up with an answer to the invite. Bruce did cook a good steak, and their fridge was always stocked with cold beer. I looked forward to a little pampering after the day I'd had. "I'm on my way," I said, as I hung up and adjusted course for my mother's house.

I pulled up to the house and headed around through the side gate to the back, where they sat listening to the radio and gossiping about their neighbours.

"Hi honey," Mom smiled and opened her arms as I made my way up the back steps.

"Hey guys," I walked over and greeted her with a quick hug. I turned to Bruce who was busy working the grill. "Hey Bruce, how's it going?"

"Hey Brand, it goes well. I'm still above ground." He smirked. "There's beer in the fridge bud, help yourself."

"Right on, I need it. You got any Clam?"

"Picked up a brand-new bottle just after work. The spicy stuff."

"Sweet." I went through the back door to the kitchen freezer where I grabbed a nicely frosted mug, then down to the fridge where I found myself a cold Coors Light. I rummaged around some more 'til I found the new bottle of Clamato juice. Then, I mixed up about two-thirds beer to one-third Clam, my own secret recipe. Taking my beverage, I returned to the deck and settled into my usual reclining patio chair, complete with cup holder. I took a sip and leaned back, *Ahhh, that's good.* My problems at work seemed long behind me then. Until, that is, Mom began her nosing around my business just minutes later. She never was a woman to waste time.

"So, what's new with you hon? How's work?"

Sonofa … Dammit! Why'd she have to ask? Knowing she had a sharp skill for reading my facial expressions, I leaned back farther in my chair and turned my head away. "Oh, work's work, you know how it is," I replied, with less enthusiasm than I should have, knowing she'd pounce at any sign of instability.

"What honey, is there something wrong? What now? Tell me." Her voice took on the same concerned tone along with the hint of accusation she always had whenever the subject of my work came up. Only being out of high school for a few years, I had already retired from five different companies. Each time bringing my mother to the edge of a heart attack.

My mother herself had been a nine-to-fiver since the day she left school. She'd found a desk job at a local insurance company and stayed there ever since. I tipped my hat to her for sticking it out. But the sad thing was, she hated it. She hated the work, and she hated the people she worked with. But it was all she knew, and that's how it went in her world. Get a job—any job—and stick it out no matter what.

"Ah nothing Mom. Just had a shitty day."

"It's a paycheck Brandon. You'll never get ahead if you keep jumping around from place to place you know."

"Yeah right, I know. It's good, I just had a bad day. Tomorrow everything will be good again." I looked over at my mother and gave her my best reassuring smile. When it came to work, I did my best to assure her everything was all right at all times, so we could move away from the subject before getting in an argument.

She seemed satisfied…for the moment. The tension from her body lifted as she felt she had accomplished her job, and her son was still in line with reality… her reality, at least.

Bruce poked his head out the back door. He was wise enough to avoid the whole conversation. "Supper's ready!" he announced.

We all dished up and gathered around the kitchen table to enjoy the meal. We kept the conversation light. The weather, some sports, yadda yadda. I finished another beer over supper, and when I was done eating, I cleaned my plate at the sink and grabbed another cold one from the fridge before retiring back to the deck.

Mom and Bruce were still inside cleaning up while I found my chair and kicked back into recline. Stomach full of steak, I relaxed and breathed in the warm summer air. The sun was beginning to set, leaving an orange tinge to the leaves on the trees. A reminder of the coming autumn season. It was nearing the end of summer and, although it was a scorcher today, the weather could turn on a dime now. The sun set a little earlier every day, and the nights began to feel cooler. I was drifting off into a daydream somewhere far away when my phone rang. I snapped back to the present, sat up in my chair, and scrambled to pry the phone from my jeans pocket.

"Hello?"

"Brand, how's it goin' eh?"

"Good, good. Uh, who is this?"

"Ah, c'mon man. I guess it's been a while, so I'll forgive you this time."

"Steve…man…Is that you?"

"Hey, now you got it buddy. What's goin' on?"

It was my cousin Steve, on my father's side. He was a few years older than me and lived up in Calgary, the big city. We used to see a lot of each other and hung out together when we were young. We were almost like brothers.

"Ah well, not much, working, drinking, same old…You?" It was a nice but completely unexpected surprise to hear from Steve.

"I'm good man. I'm good. You know, I started that job working the oil rigs what, about … shit, I guess it's been about five years already."

"Oh yeah, right, I almost forgot all about that. Jesus, you still working there? That's a long time to be in one place."

"Well, still working for the same company, but never in the same place. We move around a lot. It's almost like starting a new job every week. Where are you now, at your dad's? You still living there?"

"Oh yeah, you know it. Riding the gravy train."

"Shit, you're kidding me. You ever going to leave the nest?"

"Don't knock it man. Rent cuts into my lavish lifestyle."

"Yeah, and living with your old man cuts into your getting laid!"

"Oh no, I got it figured. I just drag home whatever's passed out on the floor at the end of the night. A grown man who lives with his parents has no morals."

"Whatever gets you off, I guess. Anyway, you at home now?"

"No, I'm just over at my mom's for supper."

"Oh yeah? Well tell her little Stevie says hi. She always had a soft spot for me," Steve chuckled. "And hey, I'm coming through town bud. What are you up to for work these days?"

"Me…nothing really. Sweatshop shit, the usual."

"So, nothing you're really attached to?"

"No. Why, what's up?" I sat up in my chair with a sudden curiosity as to Steve's line of questioning.

"I'll be at your house in half an hour—if I remember how to get there. Meet me there and have some cold ones ready in the fridge. I may have an offer of interest to you."

"What… what?"

"See you in half an hour," he chuckled and then hung up.

Slightly dazed, I flipped my phone shut and replayed the conversation in my head. Just then, my mother joined me out on the deck. "Who was that honey?"

"It was Steve."

"Steve? Your cousin Steve? God, it's been a long time since I've seen little Stevie. How is he?"

"Good," I managed to say before raising the last half of my beer to my mouth for a power chug. "He said to say hi." I let out a large nasty burp that caused my mother's face to clench in disgust before quickly jumping out of my chair, rushing back inside, and placing my empty mug on the counter. I shouted goodbye to

Bruce, then headed back out to the deck past my mother and down the stairs.

Mom stood up, confused by my sudden urgency. "You going already? Why the rush?"

"Yeah, sorry. Thanks for supper. It was great. Steve is coming through town, wants me to meet him at Dad's."

"Well, that's a surprise. It'll be nice for you to see him again. What brings him to town?"

I hesitated slightly with my reply as I continued toward my car, wondering if I should get her wound up. "I think he's got a job offer for me, on the rigs. Gotta run, see you." I sprouted a rebellious grin while I pictured her jaw dropping, as I closed the gate behind me.

Once in my car, I raced straight for home. Driven by hope and the promise of good things to come. My mind reeled with possibilities.

5

I arrived home to find my father leaning over the kitchen sink cleaning up some dishes. He looked up as I shut the door.

"Hey Dad, did you get a call from Steve?"

"Steve…no…Steve who?"

"Cousin Steve."

"No, Christ, I haven't heard from him in years. What makes you think he'd call me?"

"Well, he's coming over. Should be here any minute now." I took a quick peek out the living room window to see if there were any unfamiliar vehicles out front. Last time I'd seen Steve, he was driving a miled-out Chev half-ton. I guessed he'd probably upgraded since then.

"He's coming here?" Dad responded with shock. "Does he even know where we live?"

"Yeah, he's been here before. Said he'd call if he has any trouble finding it." I paced the floor, glancing out at the driveway every few minutes.

"So, what in the hell brought on this sudden, surprise visit?"

"I'm not sure. He just called me when I was at Mom's and told me to meet him here."

I passed by the window again and noticed some movement on the street. I pulled back the curtains and saw a brand-new, silver Dodge truck. One of those mega-cab, four-door, diesel models, pull up to the curb in front of our house.

Sure enough, cousin Steve hopped out of the driver's seat, threw a backpack over his shoulder, and headed for the front door.

I opened it just as he was coming up the front stairs. "Stevie, how's it going man?" We locked hands with a manly shake.

"Good, good. Nice to see ya. Been a long time, eh!" Steve glanced over my shoulder to my father standing in the background. "Uncle Ross, what's up!"

Dad greeted Steve with a big smile, joining us at the door and giving his long lost relative a friendly punch to the shoulder. "Holy shit, he even remembers my name. Good thing you showed up, I was just about to drug-test the boy when he said you were coming."

"Hey fuck you, you got a phone too!" Steve defended, laughing.

Dad put his arm around his nephew, pulled him inside and closed the door. "Well, come in. I got you here now; I'm not letting you go. Say, what's the bag for, not planning on staying, are you? I mean we have to ease into all this socializing stuff," he joked. "C'mon there's beer in the fridge."

We moved into the kitchen, Dad dug some beers out of the fridge, and we found spots at the table. The conversation broke out with the usual chit chat. The weather, the last time we'd seen each other, blah, blah, blah. All I really wanted was the juice on the proposition Steve had mentioned. The suspense was killing me, but I didn't want to seem pushy or too anxious by jumping right in. I was playing it cool. Giving Steve a chance to bring up the subject on his own. He sure was taking his sweet-ass time. He had been there now for at least three minutes. I felt like jumping across the table, grabbing him by the shirt and shaking him, screaming, "Tell me! Tell me! For the love of God!!!" Then good ol' Dad, who was ignorant of the situation, stuck his foot in the door.

"So, what's new? What cha been doing with yourself, Steve'o? Your dad tells me you're some kind of hotshot oil rigger or something?"

Steve gulped down his mouthful of beer. His grin was subtle, with a lingering hint of cocky. As if the son of a bitch knew he found the pot of gold but he played it as if it was no big deal.

"Ah yeah. I started with this oil drilling outfit about five years ago." The smirk on his face grew broader the deeper he got into the story. "And it's been going good. Really good, actually. I've moved up the ladder really quick. So they tell me anyway. I'm up to driller already. Bought myself a nice house, some nice toys. Makin' some good money. Can't complain."

My Dads' eyebrows peaked. "Really…Driller, eh. Yeah, I know some guys who work the rigs. They make damn good money." I caught my father's gaze as he turned toward me. I could see his suspicion growing. "They're not home very much though. They spend a lot of time on the road, work some pretty long hours."

"Yeah, we work out of town a lot, but we do get some time off during spring. I'm not saying it's the best job in the world. You work bloody hard. But you also get paid for it, and you get paid well. If I'm going to spend most of my life working, I may as well get compensated for it." Steve countered, and shot a subtle wink my way.

I listened intently to the conversation, nodding in agreement, as if I knew something. But really, the rigs were foreign to me. You'd see them in town, the rig workers. Throwing money around the bars, tying one on. All the information I had about working the rigs was from local legend: You made a shitload of money, but the hours were long and the work was physically exhausting…and dangerous. It was no profession for some small-town pretty boy like me. It was a "real man's" work.

"Yeah, that's right, I suppose. Gotta do what you feel is best." Dad ended the debate with a swig of beer and a change of subject. "So! What the hell brings you down here anyway?"

"Well, my rig's down for repairs for a couple weeks. So I'm on vacation, actually. Meeting some friends down at Flathead Lake in Montana. Supposed to be nice. We rented a cabin right on the lake, buddy took down his new ski boat, supposed to be kickass. Sounds like it's going to be busy this fall, so I better get some recreation time in while I can. Anyway, since I was passing through town, I thought I'd stop in and stay the night, if that's okay?"

"Yeah, you bet. You can stop in anytime," Dad welcomed.

"And also," Steve continued. "Well…see…we've been having trouble finding a good roughneck for our crew. We just fired the third one in six months this last go-around. Anyway, my foreman asked if any of us on the crew knew someone who would want to give it a shot. Guys with experience are few and far between these days, so we're just happy to find someone who can get out of bed in the morning and is willing to learn. I never really gave it much thought. But as I was coming up on town here, I thought of Brandon." Steve shot a quick smile my way.

Although I'd been waiting for the moment when Steve actually laid the offer on the table, I found myself choking on my beer.

Dad cut in. "Well, I don't know Steve. Brandon's never had a job like that before." He scratched his chin. "He must need some qualifications or something?"

"No, nothing specific really. And Brandon's worked on the tools for a while now. He's got more experience than the guys we've been getting." The excitement grew in Steve's voice. "He needs some basic safety courses, and all the gear is supplied. I know Brand's worked some construction jobs and shit, so he's not totally green."

"Well…Steve…this is all pretty sudden. Does he have some time to think about it? When would he start?" Dad asked.

Steve looked at me, seriousness drowned his enthusiasm. "You've got two weeks, Brand. Think about it, and think hard. This is a big opportunity. A lot of guys would kill for it. But it's not something you go into and fuck up either. I'm sticking my neck out for you here."

I sat up at attention, trying to match Steve's weighty mindfulness. I was excited to get a job offer, but going out of town to work the rigs may be a little too much adventure for me. But I didn't want to turn it down right away and let Steve think I was a pussy. Humouring him was the least I could do. "Yeah…yeah, I got it. I'll think about it. I won't screw you over man. Thanks for the offer."

"It's no problem Brand. I just want to make sure you realize this isn't something to take lightly. I know it sounds all good, but carefully consider all the pros and cons. You need to understand what you're getting yourself into, okay? It's a demanding job, a lot different than the nine–to-five punch clock stuff. But it has big rewards."

"Yeah… sure, Steve."

"Okay, so he has something to think about for a while. Let's change the subject," Dad cut in, having his fill of the topic.

We cracked some more beers and the night grew on. Finally, after drinking his share, Steve announced that he was calling it a night. He wanted to get an early start for his vacation the next day.

Steve went to the spare room downstairs. I climbed into bed with my head spinning, partly from the beer and partly in disbelief at the proposition handed to me. *The rigs…is he fucking nuts! Working at DJ's isn't a dream job, but the rigs are beyond me. More money would be nice, but what about my friends? Why would I want to leave Medicine Hat?* Even with my mind made up, I found myself tossing and turning for much of the night. Until finally, thanks to all the dedicated employees at the Coors Light factory, I succumbed to my heavy eyes.

6

I found myself inside a large, cube-like room that was continually tilting and shifting on an unseen fulcrum in the middle of the floor. The walls and floor were tiled with what looked like computer microchips. The only other thing in the room with me was a purple ball that was rolling around in response to the shifting of the room. Avoiding the sphere was challenging, not because of its speed but because of its incomprehensible ability to change size from that of aerobic exercise ball to over 10 feet in diameter. At times, I had to push it off in order to escape, but it had a surprisingly thick gel-like texture that molded perfectly to any part of my body it contacted. Somehow, I continually dodged it as the room shifted, until I found myself trapped in a corner, the floor so steep it was impossible to crawl up. The ball moved toward me at an incredibly slow pace, despite the steep pitch of the floor. As it got closer, it continually inflated until I could see only purple. I sensed my end with no chance of escape, and soon the giant ball was against me, slowly applying its suffocating weight. I punched and pushed as the mass devoured my limbs and pressed in on my face, cutting off my air supply. I forced one last, mighty kick before complete darkness took over!

I woke on my bed, struggling for air, only to realize that I had just escaped and successfully defended myself against…my Star Wars comforter? I leaned my head up against my outstretched palm, elbow on the bed, blinking and rubbing my eyes, gathering my thoughts and placing my surroundings. Seeing my blanket on the floor, I pulled it back to its rightful place. I returned my head to the pillow and stared up at the ceiling, replaying the dream in my head. *What the fuck? Right now, every other guy in the world is dreaming of having three-ways with hot chicks, and I'm dreaming of giant killer gel balls.* I checked the time on the nightstand, 5:12 am. I debated going back to sleep, but my brain was way overstimulated.

My mind quickly drifted to the job offer. *I wonder if he's up yet?* I listened for any sign of movement in the house and heard nothing. *Well…it is only five o'clock…he probably wouldn't be up this early…not while he's on vacation.*

Resigning myself to the fact that rest was no longer an option, I quietly got out of bed and made my way to the bedroom window. Steve's truck was still in place.

I tiptoed down the hall to the bathroom for a leak, then went back to bed again hoping that the relief on my bladder would relax me enough so I could fall asleep. But I just laid there, staring, unblinkingly at the ceiling. *Wake up Steve!* I couldn't stay still any longer. My mind was a blizzard of thought. I got up again and went to the kitchen for a glass of water.

"Dude…what the hell?"

I turned toward the voice. Standing at the top of the basement stairs wearing nothing more than a T-shirt that stretched down far enough to spare me witness to my cousin's body parts that I prefer to remain a mystery. He stood yawning, rubbing his eyes and scratching his balls. His hair was a mess.

"Oh…shit…Steve…did I wake you up? Sorry man."

Steve stared blankly at the floor for a few seconds. I could see his mind brushing away the cobwebs. "Whatever man. What time is it?" He pushed his arms up into a mighty stretch that lifted his T-shirt high enough to reveal a pair of leopard-print skimpies.

"Oh, it's only five thirty." I fumbled over the words, somewhat distracted by his choice of undergarment.

"Well…I'm up…might as well hit the road."

"Yeah right, get going on your vacation. Enjoy it while you can, eh." I watched as Steve turned back toward the stairs.

"Hey, Steve, before you go…this job…roughneck…what is it? Just out of curiosity"

"So, you're considering it?" He turned back with a grin.

"Well…I don't know…maybe."

He shook his head with a light chuckle. "Roughneck is the entry position to the rigs. Basically, you're the bitch. You help everybody and do the shit work. Listen, Brandon," His expression stiffened, "working the rigs isn't a dream job. It's cold in the winter, and we're never home. There's a lot of bad stories going around about working in the oil field, and for the most part, they're true. But it really depends on the company you work for. And our company is one of the best. People are dying to come to work for us. The guys are top-notch, we pay well, and we have the best benefits. This is a big opportunity for you, for anyone. If you work hard and do a good job, you'll move up fast. There's a lot of money in this industry and a lot of demand for skilled people. The possibilities for the future are endless. The thing that worries me is, well, I know you haven't spent much time away from home. You'll have to move to Calgary, closer to the crew. I don't know how you'll handle it. So please man, I am taking a risk for you. If you're not ready for this, don't take it. I respect honesty, but if you take it and end up quitting a month down the road, I'll be pissed. Got it?"

I looked my cousin in the eye and nodded. "I do get it. I'll think about it, really."

"Good," Steve nodded back and his smile returned. "Now seeing as you fucking woke me up, I'm gonna brush my teeth and get the fuck out of here."

7

Friday night, I left the shop and the weight of the work behind me. All that week I had toyed with the idea of taking Steve's offer, it was nice to have something to daydream about. He said he'd call me, yet I still hadn't heard from him. So, I kept the job offer to myself. My mind was racing with possible scenarios. Something must have happened; otherwise, he would have called by now. Maybe the job got filled? Or perhaps the company had crashed? Most likely, Steve was having too much fun to stop and pick up the phone. I had only a week left to entertain the idea, and the only other person who knew about it was my dad.

That Friday night, I picked up the phone and hit the speed dial. Joey answered on the second ring, likely waiting for my call. "Hey buddy, what's up?"

Joey was well known on the party circuit in town. An ex-junior hockey star, it seemed he knew everyone in Medicine Hat. His former dreams of being in the NHL had faded, and his new career of driving a water hauler for the city was well underway. Which allowed him to focus his energy in a new direction, partying. Joey would start drinking on Friday evening and often didn't stop until early Monday morning, sometimes going without any sleep at all. He was that kind of animal. Though he held no official title in our group, pack leader would be a suitable description. Loyal to the last drop, he'd never let you drink alone and he was the one who kept the order. If you ever needed to know where the action was, he was your man. If you ever had a problem, he would be there for you one hundred percent…with a bottle of forty percent.

"Not much. Just pulling away from the pit," I replied.

"Nice, I wish I could get off that early," Joe growled.

"So, what's on the schedule for tonight? Talk to any of the guys yet?"

"We're meeting at Roscoe's around six. I'm just going to rip home after work for a quick rinse and head over. Then we'll see what the word is on the street, see if there's any big event going on anywhere. Man, after the week I've had, I could just plop my ass down in a plush chair and pound them down through a funnel and hose."

"Right, sounds good. I'm heading to my mother's for supper, so I might be a little late. But I'll keep you updated."

"Sounds good man. Check ya later, eh."

Okay, that's done. Now for Mom. Steve`s job offer still weighed heavily on my mind, even though accepting it wasn't even an option. Move to Calgary? That's crazy talk. Yet it was fun to consider it and I did promise Steve I'd think about it. Part of me wanted to run the idea by my mother to get her thoughts, even though I already knew what they would be. I'd just have some fun with her. I always held onto a glimmer of hope that maybe I'd be able to sit down and have a sensible conversation with the woman.

I gave her a call and invited myself over for dinner. She knew something was up the minute she answered the phone.

"What's going on Brandon, is something wrong? I usually have to call you for a visit." I felt my blood pressure rise as I imagined her back beginning to arch and the claws coming out. I could just see her there, teeth bared, ready to take me on and put me back in my rightful mind.

"No…nothing, really. Just need to talk is all." I could keep nothing from that woman. I still stuttered around her like I did when I was ten.

"What…did you quit your job?" Her tone was harsh.

"No, no… Christ, don't worry about it. I'll talk to you later."

"All right, fine, I'll see you later." The chill in her voice literally cooled the phone in my hand.

Dammit, I hate it when she uses that tone with me! I got in my car, cranked up the tunes, and slammed my foot heavy on the accelerator.

8

I got home, cleaned myself up, changed into some casual bar clothes and messed up my dark hair just the way I like it. After calling out a quick goodbye to my dad, I got in the car and headed over to Mom's. Leaning back against the headrest, I stuck my hand out the window and let the wind whistle through my fingers. I reached over and cranked up the tunes, catching the beginning of Stone Temple Pilots' "Interstate Love Song." *Leavin' on a southern train uh uh ya ya ya.* My hand tapped to the beat on the windowsill.

I took a deep breath and exhaled my tension. The combination of good music and late summer air blowing through the window eased my stress. That is, until thoughts about my mother resurfaced. She was obviously upset. I already regretted the idea of wanting to talk to her about the job. *I'm not taking it! Why the hell did I get her all worked up about nothing? Why not just go to the pub, park my ass in a plush chair, and start pounding them through a funnel and hose? Idiot!*

After all, I was not what you would call a worldly man. I had taken a couple of trips with my family, shopping in the big city. Along with summer vacations out west in British Columbia. They always insisted I keep my passport current, which I never understood, as an expired passport makes just as good table coaster as a current one. Then my parents divorced, and all of the adventures, if I can call them that, just kind of stopped. From that time, all I knew was Medicine Hat and me and my friends boozing it up. Shit, I'd rarely even seen a black person in my lifetime, except during baseball season. The Hat was not exactly a mecca of cosmopolitan activity, and so my exposure to different cultures and people was extremely limited. In Calgary on the other hand, there was no limit to what I could encounter, and I wasn't so sure that was for me.

I pulled up in front of my mother's house and turned off the car. The music stopped, replaced by the sound of lawnmowers and children playing. My stress level took another step up as I got out of the car and began walking toward the front door. It was time to face the music.

I gave a quick knock before entering just to be considerate, in case they were making out on the kitchen table or something. *Ugh, scratch that thought please.* I stepped in the door to see my mother standing on the upper level, leaning over the open phonebook. She looked up as I entered, flashing me her motherly smile and doing her best to conceal any indication of concern. It was her trap. I'd fallen for it many times before. She acts unconcerned and carefree so as not to discourage me from spilling my guts. Then, when she gets the full story, she unleashes.

"Hi honey, you made it. Well, come on up. I'm going to order pizza. But I was waiting to see what you wanted."

I hopped up the stairs. "Right on. Where's Bruce?" I looked around, noting his absence.

"Oh, he went out to play a round of golf. Left us to fend for ourselves."

I suspected my mother had set this up so she and I could be alone for the news I was about to drop on her.

We finished placing our order over the phone. Then came the awkward silence. She waited patiently, lovingly, the wolf in Mom's clothing.

"So, what's up, what's this news you have?" She asked, trying her best to sound uninterested. I knew so much better though.

Normally, I would have danced around the question. But time was running and I wasn't planning on spending Friday evening arguing with my mother. There was this part of me that dared myself to take the job just to piss her off.

"Well, I haven't quit my job." Even though I didn't verbally complete the sentence with a "but," my voice and body said it for me, in blinking neon.

"But?" Her voice was strong and threatening. "So, what's the problem? What the hell are you—"

"I've been offered another job!" I cut her off, which I rarely did, but like I said, I was not in the mood. I raised my voice over hers, causing her to pause in a moment of awe.

It was surprising how lost for words she was. Usually, I just bowed my head like a stunned fighter backed in the corner as she rained down with blows. I knew the way she worked. She had put together a full speech while waiting for my arrival. But the effectiveness of her assault was dependent on my usual silence.

"Phfft, another job! Really, where's this one?" She turned back on me, slightly gaining her composure and leaning over the counter with a growing expression of intimidation.

"It's a job working on the rigs."

"Oh come on Brandon. Who's going to give you a job on the rigs? You know nothing about the rigs." She began to pace the kitchen waving her arms.

"Well, I can learn. Cousin Steve offered me the job. That's why he stopped in town last weekend." My voice stayed strong.

I continued with the story before she could begin her cross-examination. That way, if the situation got too ridiculous, I could just walk out having said what I needed to say. "He's on vacation for a couple weeks. His company's been having trouble finding a decent guy to fill the position, and so Steve mentioned me. His boss said if I want to give it a try, it's mine. They don't care if I have experience, as long as I'm willing to learn. Steve's giving me 'til his vacation is over next week to think about it. The only thing really stopping me is, I'll have to move to Calgary."

I finished, keeping my gaze trained on my mother's face and waiting for her usual retaliation, but there was none. She held her position, looking concerned? disappointed? For once, I couldn't read her emotion. Usually it was black or white, but now she just seemed scrambled. I was tired of the whole tug of war with her. I couldn't recall a time when she ever supported me. Having said my piece, and reaching the end of my patience with this never-ending battle, I decided I wasn't in the mood for pizza anymore. I exhaled, then got up and left the table, headed down the stairs and out the front door. She never once made any attempt to stop me.

9

My conscience battled an army of guilt threatening to turn my car back in the direction of my mother's. I hated leaving her like that. She had pissed me off, but she *was* my mother. I decided it was best to leave her be. *She'll live. The best thing to do right now is get my ass over to Roscoe's.*

Truth is, the farther I got from my mother's, the better I felt. So, I made my way across town as fast as legally possible. I opened the door to our favourite pub, took my usual chair and placed my usual order with April. It was a well-established routine.

Conveniently, as soon as my face and hands were covered with hot wing sauce, my cell phone chimed to life. I scrambled for napkins, wiping myself down before retrieving the phone from my jeans pocket. I checked the display. Finally, the call I had been waiting for.

"Steve, hey, what's up?" For a second all I could hear was Steve mocking and laughing in the background.

"Brand, you there?"

"Yeah, I'm here. What's going on?"

"Hey buddy. Just living the life bro, living the life. The weather's been fantastic. Met some of the local ladies. So far, an awesome vacation." Steve's speech was badly slurred.

"Yeah, right on. I've been waiting for your call. What's up? Is the job still open?"

"Well, I just talked to the boss this morning, and he's waiting for an answer. You thought about it? You want it or not?"

"I've been thinking about it all week. I'd like the job Steve, don't get me wrong. The money'd be awesome, but really man, I haven't got a clue about working rigs. And, well, this moving up to Calgary thing, is it really necessary?"

"Sorry buddy. The move is a must. I know we work out of town all the time, but the company wants us to live reasonably close to each other, and our manager lives in Calgary. So, it makes everything easier. That's it, no rocking the boat. Take it or leave it."

"Well, I have one more week to think about it, right?"

"One more week Brand, it's good. I'm glad to hear you're thinking it through. But really, the quicker you can let me know, the better."

"I know Steve. I just want to make sure this is what I want."

"You got it buddy. See you in a week. You've got one week left." He finished with his best drunken gangster impression.

I flipped my phone shut, and placed it gently on the bar. *One more week. It's all happening so fast.* A bright flash from the corner of my eye caught my attention. I turned to the door and saw the first member of the crew arrive, Joey. He gave a quick salute on his way across the pub to the seat beside me. I greeted him with a friendly slap on the back. "Haha, you made it on time, eh? I never doubted you for a second."

Joey caught April's eye, held up one finger, and she quickly delivered his favourite poison, a double rye and Coke. "Ah, nice," he turned to me. "Yeah, yeah, I made it. What's up with you Brand, how was your week?"

"Work was the same old shit, you know how it is." I kept thinking about whether to tell him and the others about the job. I didn't know how he or my other friends would react, but in all honesty, I could use all the help I could get in making my decision. "But, well, I, uh … got a new job offer."

Joey choked on his drink a little. "A new job? Well, what is it this time? Same shit, different pile?"

"Actually, it's a job on the drilling rigs."

Joey's jaw slackened, as he focused more on what he was hearing. "The rigs. Really? How the hell did you hook up with that?"

I gave him a quick version of the story. One that would cater to his short attention span.

"No shit, eh? The rigs. The big bucks. Right on, so when do you start?"

"Well, Steve's stopping in town next Sunday to pick me up. If I decide to take it that is." I kind of trailed off toward the end of the sentence, realizing that I had forgotten to mention the move to Calgary.

"Well, why wouldn't you take it? Big bucks, right? And it'll get you out of that shit hole you're working in now." It took him a moment to catch up. "Wait, what do you mean pick you up? Pick you up for what? Where is this job?"

"Well, they recommend I move to Calgary. You know, more central location. Closer to the crew."

"What the … ! You're leavin'?! Fuck man, what the hell! You can't leave. What about the rest of us?" The news struck Joey hard, as I knew it would. He lived for the gang, in denial of the day when we would have to part ways. Our guys, we were solid, like three musketeers. Except that we were five, following a slightly altered "all for one and every man for himself" sort of motto. Joey held up another finger, signalling April for another round as he polished off his first. I sensed it was going be a long and raucous night.

"Yeah, it's a bitch. I don't know what to do. I don't want to take the job and leave all you guys. But I can't keep working in that dead-end sweat shop. This is my break, the job I've been waiting for. Still, I hate the idea of moving."

Joey slammed his glass down on the table and paused in thought, looking down at the bar. "Son of a bitch, that's a bunch of shit! You can't leave dude. Calgary—fuck. Man, you'll never make it up there—gangs, murders, rapes! Sure, there are probably lots of girls, but they're all gold-digging bitches! It'll change you man. I know some guys that moved up there, they kept in touch for a while, then one by one, they each turned all too good for everybody back here!" He took another long draw from his glass, shaking his head.

"Yeah, I know Joe, but what's the alternative? Stay here and keep working for the Dick?"

"Well fuck man! A job's a job. I don't like my job, but this is what it's all about, right? Hangin' out with the crew, having a couple a bevies." Grasping. He was grasping for excuses, and he knew it. And he knew that I knew it, and that pissed him off even more.

I could also detect resentment, though it was hard to read what exactly he resented: The thought of losing a friend, or not being the one with the option? He kept his gaze on his drink, swishing the ice around in his glass.

When he spoke, his tone and expression were steeped in sarcasm. "But, I guess you gotta do what ya gotta do. Don't worry 'bout us man, we'll be here where we belong."

It was the argument I expected from him. Joey wasn't the one to sit down and discuss this with. Clearly, he was one-sided. "Well, I haven't made a decision yet, so no need getting all worked up over it, right?" I lifted up the rug and swept frantically, wanting to bury the subject before it could escalate. Best not have Joey in a foul mood at the start of a whiskey binge.

Joe lifted his head slightly, looking past me to the entrance and nodding. The door to the pub opened, letting in a faint breeze, and with it, the rest of our brethren. Kent first, followed closely behind by Aaron and Curtis.

Joey and I moved from the bar to a table to better accommodate the pack. Joey quickly reverted to his usual routine, plunking some money in the jukebox and picking an assortment of our favourite windup songs.

We started in on the usual conversation about the week's events, laughing and putting the drinks back. It didn't take long for Joey to announce the biggest news of the week: my job offer. The effects of his previous five drinks were becoming more apparent as he explained to the guys—and me—why I shouldn't leave. His words got progressively cruder and louder. A couple of the guys quietly congratulated me, but for the most part, everyone simply shied away from the discussion, letting Joey speak his mind. They knew that to counter his attack would only add fuel to an already blazing fire.

Finally, having had enough of the conversation, Curtis tapped Joey on the shoulder and pointed to a little hottie making her way over to the jukebox. That was all it took to shift Joey's train of thought. Sometimes I was thankful for his ADD. With the topic altered, we were allowed to enjoy the rest of the evening.

The night went on just like the countless nights before. We ate wings, drank beer, played our music. And toward the end of the night, like clockwork, Joey, pissed to the gills, proposed yet again to April. And to none of our surprise, he was denied yet again.

The dating situation in Medicine Hat works like this: been there, done that. Not that it's just one big orgy or anything. But you do the one-night stand thing a few times over. Usually after the bar closes down, and neither person is in any shape to satisfy the other sexually. From high school to young adulthood, most of us had slept with our share. And because we were always drunk, that's as far as it went. Sleeping with someone never turned into anything more than that. The ones you hadn't slept with yet had slept with your friends, and there were all these complicated rules of engagement around that. Needless to say, untapped supplies of women in town were limited.

That night at Roscoe's was as good a night as any, but Joey and I kept our distance from each other. It sucked, the awkwardness between us, and I was beginning to wish I hadn't brought up the job offer at all. The booze began to do what it does, and as the night wore on, my mouth was thick with a dry with a sticky aftertaste. I decided nothing new and exciting was going to happen, and that the same old Friday night rerun just wasn't worth the hangover. I was the first to pull the disappearing act.

10

The next morning, I awoke and took a minute to analyze my condition. I had learned through years of extreme hangover experiences not to be too quick to jump out of bed, as I may not be able to stick the landing. So, I laid in bed and thought about the previous night's events. When I had happily concluded that I had managed to make it through the evening without making a complete ass of myself, I decided life was worth getting out of bed for. I turned my head and checked the clock on my nightstand. Six thirty. *Son of a bitch! Why so early?* But I knew exactly why. One week. One week left to decide on the biggest decision of my career, of my life. I was restless.

I wandered out to the main area of the house to find my father in the kitchen cooking breakfast. As I rounded the corner, I hit the familiar squeaky spot in the aged hardwood and scared the shit out of Dad. He turned on me with lightning-fast reflexes, arm outstretched, spatula in hand. Everything would have been fine if it hadn't been for the crack of some internal back component that echoed through the kitchen, followed by a deafening scream as my father fell to the floor. He released the spatula, and sent it spinning through the air like a ninja star, connecting with the spot right between my eyes. I braced myself against the fridge, hand over my forehead, wincing in pain. As I shook it off, waiting for my vision to clear, I heard faint moans coming from my father. I moved around the counter. There he lay in all his glory, spread out, leg twisted under him in an awkward and completely unnatural position, his body sprinkled lightly with hash browns and scrambled eggs. Jesus it was funny, and I couldn't help but break out laughing.

"There you are, Chuck Norris and Chef Boyardee in one crumpled package."

"Don't be a smartass. Help your old man up."

"Well, I don't know, are you all right? Should we try moving you, or should I call an ambulance?" I asked with honest concern, but I was still laughing

"Shut up and help me."

I leaned over and dragged him along the floor until his leg straightened out and then made a pathetic attempt to help him to his feet. In the end, he was better off doing it himself. I was no fireman; I'd had no official training in senior rescue. Shaving Joey's eyebrows when he was passed out on the pub floor was the closest I'd come to any paramedic-type activities.

Somehow, my old man eventually made it up on his own. Hunched over at first, he slowly straightened his back, making sure no serious damage had been done. He eventually made his way to a fully vertical position, slowly examining all of his attached limbs to make sure everything still worked.

"Goddammit Brandon, it's six thirty Saturday morning. Shouldn't you be sleeping it off? You scared the shit out of me."

"Yeah, well, I didn't really get that drunk last night. Came home reasonably early—for me anyway. But I can't sleep, so I got up."

Dad raised his eyebrows. "Really? Ah, I guess you got a lot to think about."

I didn't usually open up to my father about events in my life, but I was running out of time. I'd already heard everyone else's thoughts on the subject, and they were all pretty negative. I guess I was ultimately looking for the elusive straight up yes or no. While at the same time, I knew that in the end, this decision was all mine. "Yeah, it's been a challenging week."

He smiled sympathetically, leaning back against the counter. "So, I'm guessing you haven't made a decision yet?"

I shrugged my shoulders and turned my gaze to the floor.

Dad turned to the stove to survey the disaster. "Well, I usually only cook for one, but it'd be no problem to slap on another couple of eggs."

"Yeah, why not. I'll have to move some things around on my schedule, but I can make room for family." We gave each other a smile across the room, and got to it.

Dad cleaned the previous breakfast mess from the stove and began a new round. For an extra treat he threw in some bacon as well. This was, after all, not something we did often. I busied myself cleaning the mess from the floor and getting the plates set. It was a nice change, being up early minus the hangover, to enjoy a decent breakfast. We had filled our plates and sat down at the table, and Dad returned to our conversation.

"So, what's up son, what's the trouble?"

"Well, on the one hand, I've got this awesome job opportunity, something I've been waiting for my whole life. But now, if I take it, I have to move away. It's not fair. And Mom's no help, of course. She thinks I'm crazy to even think about moving to Calgary, leaving DJ's. Then the guys—well, Joey anyway, he's pissed. Gave the whole drunken speech about how friends are forever. Made me feel like a shit head that's breaking up the gang. And Calgary is a dangerous place I've heard." It felt good to get these thoughts out into the open.

Dad reacted with a smirk. "I'm not a well-travelled man son, but I've been around a bit. Number one, I don't recommend listening to your mother, unfortunately. She loves you and she just worries about you. But the truth is, she's never done anything extraordinary with her life. She's content with that, and that's fine for her. Doesn't mean you've got to follow in her footsteps. As far as Calgary being a dangerous place, I don't doubt that it can be. It's a million people big. But like anywhere Brandon, you just gotta use your common sense. Keep your head on your shoulders, steer clear of any of the troublemakers and you should be fine. Besides, you'll be living with Steve. He's been up there awhile now and he's still alive. He'll wise you up as to what to do and where not to go." He paused then he set down his fork and looked me in the eyes. "As for your friends, look at me son. Do you see me hanging out with all my old high school buddies? Life keeps moving on Brandon. You've got to know that. And ask yourself, if Joey got the same offer, do you think he'd stick around?"

I chewed my mouthful of breakfast and mulled my father's speech. Of everyone I'd asked, he was the only one who somewhat approved of me taking the chance. Then I thought about something else that had been troubling me. Dad noticed my hesitation.

"What is it?" He looked on caringly.

"Well, nothing. It's just … you. What would you do if I left?"

"Haha," he chuckled. "It's nice of you to be concerned son, but honestly, don't worry about me. I promise I can take care of myself. The point I'm trying to get through to you right now is you have to do what you feel is best for you. Why listen to your mother or Joey when it comes to working the rigs or living up in Calgary when they've done neither? How do people know they won't like something until they try it? I'm not telling you to go or to stay. I'm just saying this is your decision, and you have to make it. Okay?"

His answer sucked. How dare he leave all the responsibility with me? Yet, I knew he was right.

"Hey, you got any plans today?" The twinkle in his eye had father–son event written all over it.

"Nah, the guys will probably be in recovery mode all day."

Dad's face shone with a look of brilliance, like he had just invented time travel or something. "Let's go golfing. C'mon, whaddya say?"

I looked out the window. The sun was breaking out into a cloudless sky. There were few days like this left with the change of season. I pictured Dad and I on the course, and smiled. Jesus, we sucked at golf. If there were ever two men who had no business being on a golf course, it was Dad and I. But we sure had a lot of fun whenever we played. Our favourite spot was an 18-hole, par 3 course with a creek running through it. No pros behind you cursing your name after your fifteenth stroke. Dad looked so excited. I couldn't refuse. Who knew when we'd get to play a round together again?

"You're on, let's do it."

We wasted no time piling the rest of our breakfast into our mouths, leaving our cleanup for later. We went to the garage and dug out our clubs from underneath the pile of other rarely used sporting goods. I checked the golf bag pockets and removed the beer cans left over from the round I'd played. We threw our stuff into the back of Dad's truck and headed for the course.

The morning air blowing in the truck window carried the scent of summer's end. I guessed the temperature to be in the mid-teens already, and with no wind and no hangover, it was going to be a beautiful day. We turned off the main drag and headed down into the coulee to Paradise Creek Golf Course. It was a nice spot. Set down in the valley, with an abundance of trees that sheltered it from the strong winds that blew over the area more often than not. The prices were reasonable, and there was a refreshment cart making rounds if one should get thirsty. It would never host a PGA tournament, but it was the perfect place for a little father–son one on one.

We pulled into the near-empty parking lot and found a spot close to the course entrance. As soon as Dad parked the vehicle, I hopped out and grabbed my clubs from the back, anxious to be first on the course. It was a feat I had never accomplished before, unless you count that time I'd woken up drunk and half-naked on the number 3 green.

Unfortunately, Dad's back injury had stiffened on our ride down. I peered around the corner of the truck as the driver door opened, just in time to see my proud old man roll out of his seat. He landed on his feet, which I considered a good sign. He stood hunched over for a moment with his hand on the rail of the truck bed. It was sobering to see a man who, when I was a child, possessed godlike powers now struggle with simple everyday life.

"Hey, you gonna be all right? We don't have to do this you know. I don't want you to screw your back up any worse."

Dad placed his hands on his lower back and stood up straight, slowly but surely. "No, no, we're playing. The worst thing I could do is sit around all day nursing it. Look how stiff I am after a short truck ride. Don't think you're getting out of the ass kickin' I'm about to give you."

"Pfft, ass kickin'. Yeah right. I'm going to have to rent an extra pull cart just to wheel your sorry ass around the course."

He mumbled something under his breath that sounded a lot like "ass hole," then grabbed his clubs out of the truck and slung them over his shoulder, playing it cool to any discomfort he might be in. "That's it. It's go time!"

We set out for the clubhouse, crossing the wooden footbridge that spanned the creek. I took in the morning scenery as the sun crested the hills and the birds chirped out of the leafy trees. Sadly, when I looked on long enough, I could see the faint telltale hint of yellow to the foliage straddling the deep green fairways. *This is good. A perfect way to spend the day....* I paused in that thought for a moment as a distant lonely reality brushed my subconscious. I'd never really thought about it—about my dad, or my mom. To this point, I had really only considered my friends. About saying goodbye to them and all the crazy days of drinking and partying that would consume what could be my last week at home.

We got to the clubhouse and checked out the action on the tee boxes. There was a group on the back nine already. It always seemed to be the more popular spot, but the front nine was empty. We rushed inside, paid our fees and grabbed a couple bags of used balls. We lost too many to justify paying for new ones.

We snatched a couple of pull carts outside and went over to the first tee box. There was no one in front of us, and no one behind. Perfect. That morning, it was just the two of us.

Hole one presented an obstacle I had never noticed before. A sprinkler spouting an arching rooster tail of water over the fairway about halfway to the green. I set up to tee off, fully expecting that my next swing would be taken with high-pressure water shooting at my ass. I shivered at the thought. To my surprise, the ball shot straight and clear past the spray landing just short of the green. I could usually count on one decent shot a round, and I was happy to use it up on that hole. I turned to my opponent with a cocky smile and waved him to the mound.

Dad shook his head at my luck, set up, and duffed the ball right into the sprinkler.

Grabbing my cart, I kept my gaze on the ground to conceal my jeering smirk, and began my journey down the fairway, saying nothing. Even though the urge to taunt singed the tip of my tongue. I pulled my cart down in front of the spray just short of Dad's ball. He positioned himself beside me, dropped off his cart and grabbed his club of choice in silence, then began the walk of shame through the sopping grass. He stood proud as he looked to the green and lined up his shot, pretending not to notice the stream of water pummelling the side of his head. As he bent over, the arch of spray lined up perfectly with the curve in his back, forcing his shirt up to his shoulder blades.

He stood unfazed, totally focused, at one with the shot. Eyes burning into the ball in front of him, he drew back his club and—CRACK. I watched, breathless, as the ball flew straight over and past the green, hit the tree on the far side and bounced back to its final resting spot. Ten feet ahead of where my father stood. I pushed at the bruise with a proper golf clap as the brave warrior stepped free of the wash. He wiped at the water on his face with his wet shirtsleeve. Moments after he stepped out of the water, we heard the pressure drop and the sprinkler retreated back beneath the surface.

I struggled to maintain balance and not fall over while holding my stomach, shaking from the laughter that consumed me. Only so many moments in life are so brilliant, so spectacular, and I was here to witness this one. On any other weekend, I would have spent the better part of the day in bed. But, for coming home early and getting up at the break of dawn, I had been amply rewarded.

My father exhaled, then looked over at me. "Why the fuck couldn't you have just stayed in bed?" He was unable to finish the sentence without smiling.

We finished the front nine then restocked our ball supply before continuing on to the back nine. The weather behaved and the course remained sparsely populated. It was just one of those rare occasions that made me glad I was sober enough to enjoy it.

After a second round on the front nine, we collapsed into a couple of chairs in the clubhouse.

"Well son, thanks. I needed today."

"Yeah, it was great. A perfect day." Expressing the fact that I sincerely enjoyed spending the afternoon with my father made him swell with pride. I even caught him blush. The smile on his face made me wish I could turn back the clock, even just a little, and exchange more of my foolishly wasted time.

11

Monday morning came again, and I awoke to the alarm clock hangover free. My third day in a row. I couldn't remember the last time I held such a record.

At work, it was the same old bump and grind. They definitely weren't giving me a reason to stick around. I was handed another job cutting a ridiculous number of components for a project. The exact same routine as the week before. Every cut, every piece brought me closer to the realization that there was never going to be anything there for me. Lost in my thoughts, I brought the blade down to the steel and it grazed my glove, cutting instantly through the almost leather and into my finger. The cut wasn't deep, but it stung like hell and the bleeding was relentless. I wrapped a rag around it before anyone could notice and make a big deal out of it. I pushed the steel through and grabbed the saw handle to continue. And suddenly, that was it. I paused for a second, looking at my station and feeling the pulse in my throbbing finger. *All for what, minimum wage?* That was the turning point, the moment I knew my decision was made. It was time for a change. I felt an odd combination of terror and release.

I had done what Steve had asked. I thought long and hard about the job. And after considering all there was to consider, I was sticking with my decision. There remained only one last obstacle. I turned to my work and remained focused on my task, working as diligently as possible and avoiding eye contact with the clock. Before I knew it, Friday had arrived.

By Friday afternoon, I had finished my project. I had worked hard over the week and after a small internal debate I decided that I deserved my last afternoon off. I cleaned up my station and walked straight into Dick's office, without knocking. Dick looked up, a little surprised. He was going over some paperwork on his desk. Half of a lit cigarette hung from his fingers.

"What is it?"

I opened my mouth to say what I'd wanted to say for months, but he interrupted me and what he had to say really spoiled my moment.

"I know why you're here. Don't think I haven't noticed. You've really turned over a new leaf kid. You've been givin'er all week, and I think this is the first time I can remember that I haven't given you shit for fucking something up. Good work Brandon. Keep this up and I'll be looking to … I don't know … move you up or something. Let's wait to make sure this week isn't just a fluke, then we'll talk more seriously."

I paused. My mouth hung open while I absorbed what I'd just heard. Dick noticed my "hard work." I had been so consumed with finishing my project so I could get the hell out of there and he had mistaken the effort for my wanting to further my career at DJ's. *Hmph, I'll be damned. Maybe Dick isn't as much of an asshole as I thought.* I looked at Dick and shrugged. "I quit, Dick." I turned and left his office, closing the door behind me.

12

I spent the rest of the afternoon driving around. It was stupid, really. I thought about how I could have stayed at work for just another two hours and made a few more bucks instead of driving around aimlessly and burning gas.

After extended consideration, I decided to take the plunge and call my mother. She was stressed, I could pick it up in her voice. Yet she surprised me by being supportive, or at least holding back the verbal lashing I'd anticipated. She invited me over for supper, and somehow, I was glad to go.

It went better than I expected. Bruce wasn't around again. He was out golfing with some buddies. So, it was just me and her, which usually meant the conversation was going to get ugly, but this time it didn't. It seemed she had given up fighting with me now that I had made my decision. This came as a welcomed relief.

My phone vibrated. I checked the display. It was Joey. *Ah, shit. Here we go.* I debated leaving it, I didn't really feel like getting into it with him, but I had to face the music sometime. "Hey Joe, what's up?"

"What's up with *me*? What's up with you and this job thing, Brand? Let me guess, you're taking it?" His voice carried a false sense of acceptance.

"I just quit DJ's this afternoon, totally out of the blue. Are you pissed?"

"Ah, whatever man, I warned you. It's your funeral. You'll be back, I have no doubt, but it's a good excuse to go out and get shit-faced drunk. I'm putting together a plan as we speak."

It was a better response than I had expected. "Sounds good buddy. Let's rip it up!"

"Nice, where you at now?"

"I'm at Mom's, just finishing up some pizza."

"Oh, Mom's house. You ask that sexy bitch if she misses me. Tell her I'll be over later tonight, and she better have her freak on."

"Go fuck yourself!"

"Brandon! Watch your mouth!" Mom yelled from the background. My mother loved the guys, especially Joey. If she only knew.

"That's right Mrs. Baker, you tell him," Joey shouted. "For shame Brand, you kiss your mother with that dirty mouth?"

"Shut up! C'mon man, what's the plan?"

"How long 'til you're back home?"

"Well, I wasn't really planning on going home. I got all done up before I came over here so I could just head over to the pub after. Is that where we're meeting, Roscoe's?"

"I don't know," Joey's voice had the tone I'd learned to fear over the years. "We kinda wanted to mix things up a little tonight. You know, broaden our horizons."

"You're not going to tell me, are you?"

"We'll pick you up at your house in twenty minutes." That was all he gave me before he hung up.

Mixing it up a little, hmph. Yeah, what could that be? Some new place that just opened up? Or maybe they've organized a city-wide pub crawl? Or they're renting a limo and hired some strippers to ride around with us for the night?

The last thought prompted me to say a quick goodbye to Mom, as I explained that the guys were picking me up at home so I didn't have to worry about driving that night.

"They are good friends to you Brandon. I don't know what you're going to do without them looking after you."

"Yeah, yeah. I'll have to manage somehow. Bye Mom, thanks for supper." I gave her a peck on the cheek and headed out the door, waving as she watched me climb into my car. As I drove away, I realized it was the first time in a long time that I hadn't left her house pissed off. It was a good way to leave it.

On the drive home, my phone started to vibrate in the console. I expected it was one of the guys calling, wondering where I was. I grabbed the phone and checked the call display. It was Steve. It would be my luck to go through all the mental stress of making the decision I'd just made only to have him call the whole thing off.

I took a deep breath and answered the phone. "Hello," my voice cracked like a pubicly challenged teenager.

"Brand? Brand?" while I hadn't spent a lot of time with Steve over the last few years, I was willing to put money on the fact that he was right trashed. He sounded like he was falling over. There was some crashing in the background. I could hear a combination of guys and girls laughing and carrying on above the music.

"Brand, what the fuck man?! Sounds quiet there. Aren't cha fuckin' partying? Man, don't tell me you're going to chicken shit out of this."

"Steve. Jesus Christ man, you scared the shit out of me. I thought you were calling to tell me it was all off."

"Off…what the fuck, eh? I told you you've got the job if you want it. Get it in your head man. I had to call you dude," Steve dropped his voice to little more than a whisper. "I had to call you, you're not going to fucking believe this. We picked up these five chicks today in the boat. They're from out east somewhere, I think, got some accents. They're smoking hot buddy—sexy little bikinis, I've never seen anything like them before. They're all standing on the deck right now, and two of them are topless!"

"Shut up!" I was relieved to hear that everything was still a go.

"I ain't fuckin' kidding cuz. Anyway," Steve raised his voice again and cleared his throat like he was trying to get everyone's attention. "I was just bragging to all the girls here about how my little, good-looking, single cousin is coming to work with me next week. So, you made a decision yet? You gonna man up, or puss out?"

I could hear all the girls in the back in unison, "Hi Brandon!"

I just about drove off the road, picturing the half-naked women hanging out on the deck of a lakefront cottage. My life was really going to be like a beer commercial.

"I'm in buddy. Can't wait!"

"Thatta boy! Now quit fucking around and get out and party. It's your last night in that shit hole man. On to bigger and better things."

"I'm on my way now man, thanks for the call. Tell the girls I'll see them next year. And I'll see you real soon."

As I hung up the phone, my foot pressed down a little harder on the gas pedal. I pounded lightly on the steering wheel, excited about my future. Reality was sinking in and it felt good. It felt damn good. I raced home to meet the guys.

13

I pulled up in front of the house. Sure enough, the guys were there, parked out front and leaning up against Kent's mom's minivan. *So much for the limo and the strippers.*

I hopped out of the car with my arms in the air, "What the fuck boys? We takin' the kids to soccer?"

As I got closer, I began to notice how I was dressed to kill and they were dressed like a bunch of homeless guys. Each of my friends was sporting a heavy coat and a toque, complete with pom-poms on top. Joey was wearing coveralls. The heavy, cold weather deals. It was late summer and the nights were already cooling off. We could expect frost anytime now, which led me to the conclusion that we weren't going to Roscoe's, or anywhere else indoors.

"Get in the car Brand," Joey ordered and waved me toward the van.

"But, if you … I'm not dressed. I thought we were going to Rosc—."

"Brandon, shut up and get in the fucking van. We packed some warm gear for you."

I surrendered, ducking my head as I got in through the sliding door. All the guys were there, each one with a beer cracked. Except for Kent, who was driving. Kent turned to me from behind the wheel, "Welcome aboard Brand man. Booze is in the back, help yourself."

I turned to check the selection. If it was booze I was looking for, I'd found the mother load. I grabbed a beer, popped the top and took a long swig. "Ah, okay boys, let's do this right." The tires on Mrs. Morgan's seven-star, safety-rated minivan chirped slightly as we pulled away from the curb.

"Don't you want to know where we're going?" Aaron called back from the front passenger's seat,

"What am I, new? To the fucking tower!" I shouted and everyone raised their beers in celebration.

The tower was a place discovered by Joey and myself when we were about fifteen, riding our bikes down by the river. We had come across what we figured was an old drilling tower. It had a large pit sunk into the earth right next to it, which was perfect for bonfires.

In Medicine Hat, it had always been a battle for us young rebels to find places where we could be free to indulge in the poor choices we were rightfully entitled to. There were a couple of designated fields where kids would get together every so often, secret places passed down from generation to generation. After some years, the secret wasn't so secret anymore, and the cops would usually bust up the parties before they even started. Being in the middle of a bald ass prairie, most of the fires could be detected from town. But this place was different, better. It was just on the outskirts of the city. So we didn't have to drive far, but it was sunk down in the river valley, so no one could see the fire, or hear the childish rants of our revolt against society. The only way to enter it was through a farmer's gate and down a dirt road. The road wasn't the best, but you could easily navigate it in a compact if you took your time and it was reasonably dry.

We weren't in a compact though. We were five, now fully-grown males, some of us packing on a little extra weight since our high school years. Add in about another hundred pounds of booze, and that resulted in the bottom of our love boat scraping and banging every rock and rut along the way.

"Shit, I don't remember it being this rough," Joey noticed as he adjusted his beer can with the sway of the vehicle, ensuring that not a drop was wasted.

"Yeah, well, I don't remember your ass being that big last time either." Curt called out.

"Son of bitch Brandon, I asked you if my ass was getting fat! You told me it was fine."

"It's not fat buddy, just more ... curvy. And curvy's in now big guy. Think J'lo." I tried my best to soothe his booty complex.

"Hear that Curtis? Curvy's in, fucking flat ass."

We laughed as they traded shots at each other down the bumpy road to our destination.

We piled out of the vehicle and took a minute to stretch our legs after being cramped in with all the gear. Then we instantly fell into the old routine, and it felt like high school again. Joey wasted no time getting a fire going in the pit. Within minutes, the flames stretched six feet tall and climbing. While Joey committed arson, the rest of us got the booze and lawn chairs out of the van. In about ten minutes flat, we had the full party zone assembled.

I sat down in my chair and cracked another beer. "Ahhh, I gotta say, I definitely wasn't expecting this. I was dressed to go dealing with some women tonight. Thought you'd be taking me out and getting me laid for my last hoorah."

Curtis cut in, "Laid, what the hell would you want to do that for man? You're done with this place. Next weekend you'll be chasing some exotic tail up in the big city. Do you really want to risk going out tonight and finding some honey that ends up tying you down in the Hat? Besides, tonight's about us, the guys, one last time. Who knows when we'll all be together again."

Joey started in, while monitoring his burning masterpiece. "Yeah, this is how it all starts. One leaves, then the other one gets married. Some of us manage to still get together on holidays and long weekends. But it'll never be the same." We sat silent, hypnotized by the dancing flames. He was right, and we all sensed the change coming.

The night continued with us guys sitting around bullshitting. Being at the tower brought back old memories and stories. Some of which we had actually forgotten. We took turns venturing out into the cold to hunt for wood that we delivered to Joey. He would then assign each piece to a special spot on his offering to the gods. He took pride in his blazing architectural design.

Slowly but surely, the stash of booze diminished as the fire grew larger. Joey threw an empty can on the fire, cracked another open, and handed one to me. "Whaddya think Baker? You still got what it takes to make it up the tower?"

"The tower!" I swallowed hard, looking up at the condemned structure.

It was a rusted-up steel pillar. A two-foot-square column of trusses and cross bracing rising straight up fifty, maybe sixty feet with four cables coming off the top anchored to the ground. We'd all climbed it before, grasping the ladder rungs covered in bird shit, trying to avoid the nests all the way up. At some points on the climb, the birds would fly out at you unexpectedly, something that you could

48

never really prepare for. Sober, I would never even consider climbing it, but after a couple of beers, a man feels the need to prove himself.

"You bet! One last time, eh."

Off we went, the two pioneers pushing common sense aside one last time, for old times' sake. We got to the base and I wasted no time being the first to grab hold, knowing that the only way it was going away was to just get it done. In case climbing an abandoned tower drunk in the dark wasn't challenging enough, we always felt the need to hold a beer in one hand. And that night was no exception. Of course, we'd be wearing most of it by the end.

Rung after cold, dirty rung, we made the slow ascent. As the first up, I got the pleasure of flushing out all the birds. I'd made the journey up many times before, so I knew to move slowly and to pick my hand and foot placement carefully, keeping no less than three-point contact at all times.

About ten rungs up, the nests started. The tower was stuffed full of straw, sticks, grass and whatever else the pigeons could pack in there. It was almost impossible to get a good foothold. All was quiet so far. I could hear the guys talking and laughing around the fire below. But no birds.

"Mother fucker," Joey's voice called out from below, muffled by the frantic beating of wings. "What the fuck, you're first. You're supposed to flush them out for me."

"What do you want from me? I'm climbing the fucking ladder." The yelling and commotion spooked out two more birds right over my head. Joey and I both stopped climbing and held on, waiting for the assault to dissipate.

"Hey, you guys all right?" Kent yelled up from the ground. "Get any shit on ya?"

"If any more birds fly out, you might be the one getting shit on, and it won't be from the birds," I replied.

I waited a minute longer, taking a couple of sips of my beer. Finally, convinced that the nests were cleared, I scaled on. The climb was endless. It seemed to stretch on forever. And the farther I got, the more I began to second-guess our decision to climb the rusted pillar in the first place.

Finally, at the top, I pulled myself up onto the platform, which was about four-feet-square. Enough room for about three full-grown drunks, comfortably. Joey arrived right behind me. Breathing a little heavier than when we'd set out below.

"Shit, that seemed a lot longer than last time," He wheezed.

"Last time, hell, when was the last time we were up here you figure?"

"Jesus, I don't know. Four, maybe five years ago."

I took the final swig of my beer and tossed the empty can toward the fire below, earning myself a "Hey, fuck you, guys!" from the party down below.

I opened another beer I had stashed in my pocket and leaned back against the railing, taking in the view. It was fantastic: moonlight shining off the river as it wound through the valley, towering cliffs straddling either side, unobstructed natural beauty all around us. Only a few brave and intoxicated souls would reap these rewards.

"Son of a bitch man," I said, looking out over the dark countryside. "It has been a long time since we've been up here." I pointed toward the new artificial lights in the not-too-far distance.

"Yeah, I know," Joey followed my gaze, "That's the new Ranchlands development. It's only the first phase right now. There's three more to come. This place will be a strip mall in a couple of years. They'll probably have a restaurant up here," he grinned. "Looks like our secret place ain't so secret anymore, eh? I guess we got what we needed out of it."

"Yeah…and one last hoorah tonight," I leaned over the railing looking down at the darkness below. It was so dark that if the fire hadn't been nearby, you wouldn't even know there was a ground.

Joe tossed his empty can over the side and opened another. "So, Calgary, eh, makin' the big move?" It was the conversation I had been dreading. Even in Joey's congratulations, there was a hint of resentment.

"Yep, guess so. Shit," I shook my head in disbelief. "It doesn't even seem real, you know, moving and all. Guess I'll believe it when I see it." It was kind of sad, being there, at the place we had discovered together. Me and my best friend.

"Yeah, it's gonna be a big change. Lots to do up there. Working the rigs too. You'll be making the big money. Good for you man. You deserve a break."

"It's too bad though. Hey, you know what," I looked at him with a glimmer of hope. "You could come. Yeah, just give me a month or so to get my feet planted, then I'll get you in. You can move up. We'll get a kickass place downtown!" It was an empty suggestion; I had no pull in the company. I could fail miserably myself and be back to town in a week. The expression on Joe's face said he knew it was drunk talk.

50

"I don't know man. It sounds pretty sweet, but I got a pretty good thing going here. Probably be stupid of me to throw it all away on a chance."

Joey was right, if one wanted to think sensibly. But I could never recall anytime previous when he had a sensible thought. I knew he didn't like to leave his element. He was comfortable in his hometown. He had his friends. He was popular. Beyond the city limits, he was just another face in the crowd. And that wouldn't work for Joe.

"Yeah, you're right. I'll just have to go this one alone, I guess."

"Cheers," Joey raised his beer. "Good luck to you Brand." He turned from me and leaned over the railing, and we fell silent.

That was it. No hugging or sloppy goodbyes. Just the sloshing of two beer cans against each other. Men—young men, stuck on a rusted, condemned tower in the middle of nowhere, drunk beyond reason. We stayed up there a while longer, telling stories about the good times we'd had. When we ran out of beer, we headed back down.

The way down was always a lot quicker than the hike up. Mostly owing to the fact that we were out of booze and chilled to the bone. At the bottom we rushed over and found spots close to the fire. I turned to Kent who was searching for a refill. "Hey buddy, grab me a beer, eh."

"No. No more beer for you," Joey ordered. The light from the fire dancing off his face, flickered a devilish glow. "In fact, everybody's on whiskey for the rest of the night."

We all groaned. We liked whiskey, but the thing with us and whiskey was that at least one of us would get out of hand.

And get out of hand we did. Joey went off the deep end with the fire and soon it seemed the flames would exceed the height of the tower itself. But we continued to cheer him on. Curtis assisted by throwing on a log that was too big for one man to handle. He ended up throwing himself in the fire along with it. He escaped with mostly just burnt pride and we laughed our asses off. The last thing I remembered from that night was standing, barely standing, in front of Joey, with my eyeballs floating on a swell of liquid courage. I poked him in the chest and told him how it was going to be. He then placed his hand on my forehead and, with as much force as it would require to push open a door to a bathroom stall, he put me on my ass.

14

I woke up just as Joey had left me—on my back. Only now I was shivering as the morning light started to appear on the eastern horizon. My face, the only part of my body not bundled in winter clothing, was covered in what would have been frost if I were an inanimate object. I stared at the sky for a moment, trying like hell to stop the world from spinning. I placed both palms on the ground and tried my best to hold the world steady, but found it had little effect. *Please, God, please let me make it through this. I'm finished, I'll never drink another drop, pure health from now on, water, apples.* I opened my mouth and took in a big gulp of cool air, only to discover how dry and disgusting my mouth was. It was a strain to open it. It was coated with a film of dried-up sugar. Combined with a burning in my throat from the whiskey. *Oh, God. ...*I rolled over just in time, before the bulk of the puke exploded to the ground. My collar got hit somewhat, but the majority cleared past. I welcomed the purge, like an exorcism, casting the demon spirit from my body. If I'd been offered death right then, I would have seriously considered it.

I lay twisted on my side for quite some time, heaving out what remained in my stomach as my body rejected the poison. When it ended, I remained on my side, my body limp like road kill. I thought I felt a little better. From there, I scanned my surroundings. Trying to piece together the events leading up to my lying shit face drunk in the middle of the prairie. It took a couple of blinks to recognize where I was exactly. Through my blurred vision, I saw the rusted brown landmark stretched against the morning sky. The sight of it jogged my memory, and I remembered the tower, the guys, the booze. *Why God, why?* And then I remembered why. If I survived the morning, I would be leaving for Calgary with Steve. Life as I knew it would be different.

I watched as a narrow stream of black smoke rose silently from the embers that remained from our fire, rising straight into the still morning air. From where I lay, that was all I could see. I remembered driving down the dirt road in the minivan, but the spot where we'd parked was not in my direct line of vision. I would have to roll over, and in my current state, an acrobatic move like that could prove fatal. I listened hard for the sound of other survivors, but all was silent. The thought of turning over scared me, but the thought of turning over and finding the van no longer in its spot, scared me even more.

Don't be stupid. They wouldn't actually leave you here. Would they? Surely they would realize that left alone out here in my drunken state, I could possibly die. Right? But it would be funny. They like funny things.

I couldn't think anymore, it made me dizzy. Hell, lying motionless on the ground made me dizzy. I would just have to turn over and face what lay on the other side. I took a deep breath, focused, counted to three and

I pushed off the ground with my hand and made the roll. Quick, tight, stuck the landing. *Nice, hold it, hold it…shit!* Bluuuugh!! More puke shot out onto the ground, and some splattered back at me. I had puked myself into a corner. I was surrounded by my own vomit; rolling over was no longer an option. I laid there with a trail of drool stringing from my mouth to the regurgitated pool; eyes clamped shut, my foot pressed down hard on a brake pedal that didn't exist in an attempt to halt the swirl of madness that held me captive.

Gradually, the tremors faded and I opened my eyes slowly. The spinning lessened and my vision began to clear. The vomiting, although painful and raunchy, had cleaned some of the filth from my system. Little by little, I gained back control.

Driven by self-hatred, disgust, and vengeance for what I had done to myself, I slammed both hands against the cold ground and heaved myself up. Gathering my feet beneath me, I scrambled to a shaky but vertical position. *Ha! Good work Brandon!*

I raised my head with a feeble smile, proud of my accomplishment and feeling bolder by the moment. Off to my left, right where we'd parked it the night before, sat our shining steed.

I went straight for it, stumbling and dragging my feet, arms swinging loose and wild in every direction. I hit the side of the vehicle with a thump, welcoming the feeling of the cold metal against my cheek. I grabbed at the handle on the side door and pulled back. It didn't budge. They had locked the doors. I peered in through the window and there they all were. Kent passed out in the reclined driver's seat, while Aaron and Curtis were sprawled out on the middle and rear bench seats. I couldn't see Joey, but he had to be in there somewhere.

I pounded on the side of the van—THUMP, THUMP, THUMP. "C'mon guys, let me in! I'm freezing my fucking balls off!" I screamed.

Kent sat up in his seat and looked around, fumbling for the button to unlock the doors. I heard the lock pop and threw open the door, jumping in, I slammed it behind me. "Please, turn the van on and get some heat going before I die!"

"Holy shit man! You all right?" Kent looked at me in disbelief as he struggled to find the ignition, finally bringing the engine to life.

Aaron stirred in the back, "Brand, dude. You fucking reek."

"No shit assholes! What do you expect! You left me out there for dead! I've been laying in my own puke!"

"Left you?" Kent stepped in. "Fuck that man. We tried to get you up and into the van. Each time we tried to move you, you took a couple of swings at us and told us to fuck off. So, that's what you get."

I had no response. I just sat, holding my hands in front of the vents, waiting for the heat to come. Thankfully, it came on quite quickly and soon I was able to gain control of the shivering. "Hey, we got any water?"

Aaron passed me a bottle from the back seat. I pounded it back rinsing the putrid filth from inside my mouth. *Ahhh, water. Giver of life.*

I pressed my head back against the headrest and took time to breathe. I had reached the point where I felt like I had a fighting chance of survival once again. It was quiet, too quiet.

"Hey, where's Joey?" I turned toward the back of the van waiting for a head to pop up.

Kent shrugged, as if missing a buddy wasn't that big of a deal. "Oh shit, who knows? After you two got into it, he said he was going home and started walking off down the road. We tried to convince him that he was an idiot, but that's the challenge with trying to talk sense to an idiot. So, we let him go. He was being an asshole. You know how he gets."

"What the fuck? You let him go? He'd never make it, not in his state!" I couldn't believe what I was hearing.

"What do you want man?" Aaron piped up from the back seat. "Joey's Joey. He's going to do what he wants. We weren't walking after him, and none of us could drive. He's all right."

I looked over at Kent, my eyebrows raised. "What the fuck man! Let's go. He could be dead! You all right to drive now?"

"Yeah, I'm all right." Kent reached over his shoulder, grabbed his safety belt and clipped it in. He threw the van in reverse and—BEEEEEEEP—the dash emitted a loud, high-pitched tone.

"What's that man? Shut that fucking thing off!" Curtis shouted from the back seat.

Kent sat staring at the dash, confused by the gauge cluster. "It's the backup alarm. Something's behind the van." He looked in the rear-view mirror.

I looked over my shoulder through the back window, "There's nothing behind us but bald ass prairie. C'mon, let's get the fuck going."

"Fuck that, man. Get out and check. This is my mom's van dude. If I wreck it, you're coming down with me. Get out and have a look."

I looked at him in stunned disgust.

"Get the fuck out of the van and have a look! I'm not moving until you do." Kent insisted.

"Fine. Son of a bitch." I opened the door and staggered quickly to the back of the van, looking around for anything that might have set off the alarm. And there he was. Snuggled up in his camping gear, whiskey bottle in hand, as cute as a drunk in the gutter.

He was a true poster child for minivan safety features. "Stop! Stop the van! Put'er back in park. I found him!"

The engine stopped and the van doors opened. The guys hustled their way to the back of the vehicle.

"Holy shit!" Kent took a step back, realizing what could have just happened. "That dumb son of a bitch! What the fuck was he thinking? I just about ran him over."

"Relax buddy, this van doesn't have enough balls to get over his dumpy ass," Aaron made a pathetic attempt at putting Kent's mind to rest. "Good thing too.

We'd be high centred for sure."

It's sad, but we all shared a laugh at the mental picture of the minivan high centred on an ass-up Joey. It was ridiculous, really, the number of times one of us had come close to death throughout our high school years, and the way we'd laugh it off as if it was no big deal. Curtis picked up a stick and began poking Joe. "You think he's still alive?"

"Hey, Joey." Too sick to bend over, I began kicking him lightly with my foot, looking for any sign of life. "Hey, Joe!" I kicked him a little harder. "Wake up man, let's go."

Aaron screwed the lid off a bottle of water and slowly tipped it till it dribbled lightly on the side of Joey's head.

Suddenly, without a curse or a yell or any sound at all, Joey stood up. He didn't take time to sit up and rub his eyes and look around. He just stood up silently. He looked straight ahead, off into the open prairie, no acknowledgment that any of us were there with him.

We in turn stood silently watching him, shocked by his ability. Then, with a robot-like motion, Joey bent over abruptly, right at the waist and puked, a long and wholesome puke. One heavy, "get it done" episode. As soon as it was over, he returned to his upright position, wiped his mouth on his sleeve, and took a look around, as if nothing had happened.

"What the fuck's up, eh?"

We were speechless.

"Joey, dude, you all right?" Curtis looked at him as if he had just returned from the dead, and it was totally possible that he just had.

Joey looked back at him with the exact same look of concern. "I'm fine man. What the fuck is wrong with you?"

Kent explained, "Joe, buddy, you passed out under the van. I just about ran you over."

Joey turned around to where he had lain only moments ago. "Fuckin' lucky you didn't. You'd have got high centred."

Our shocked expressions turned to smiles. We had all survived another bender. Barely, but barely counts.

"Say, is there any beer left? I feel like hell. Gotta wash the shit out of my mouth." Joey spat on the ground. "Any of you guys fucking hungry? We should go hit some steak and eggs somewhere." He trailed off as he walked surprisingly well toward the door of the van. He reached inside and dug around till he found a beer he most likely had stashed the night before, just for this occasion. Joey believed that the best thing for a hangover was more booze, and he had a list of scientific theories to back it up.

The rest of us turned to each other, shrugged our shoulders, and made our way around the camp, picking up any stray bottles and chairs and packing them in the van. Satisfied with the cleanup, we piled ourselves in and took off back to civilization. No doubt, we had lived to do it again another day.

15

"Brandon … Brandon, wake up!"

I opened my eyes. I was in my bed. Dad was leaning over and shaking me with one hand while holding the phone in the other.

"Brandon, holy shit, you're alive. Here, Steve's on the phone."

Steve … Steve? It took a minute to bring myself back to what was happening in my life.

Finally realizing where and who I was, I quickly sat up and grabbed the phone from my father.

"Steve, what's up?" I tried to sound calm and collected.

"Brand, dude, you're still fucking sleeping? Must of did 'er up good last night? Right on man, might as well get 'er done. Got your rocks off one last time on home turf, I hope."

"Wha—? Oh yeah, yeah, you bet." I looked down to see I was still wearing my winter camping gear.

"Good stuff. Listen, I'm on my way. Been on the road for a while now and I should be there in about two hours. You all packed up and ready to go?"

"Yeah, no problem. I packed up last night," I lied.

"Right on. Get up and get ready. I'll see you in a bit."

"Right, can't wait." I hung up the phone and checked the clock.

Three o'clock…shit, shit, shit. Well, at least I got a decent sleep. I still got two hours. I can do this, no problem. I exhaled and fell back into my bed.

When I rolled over and opened my eyes, the three on the clock had turned to a four. *Mother fucker!!!* I always did like to challenge myself when I was hung over.

I jumped out of bed, got out of my smoky clothes, and hopped down the hall into the bathroom. While I was in the shower, I reviewed the situation. It was too late to do laundry so I would just have to pack my clothes as they were and deal with them when I get there. The shower gave me new life, washing off the old and leaving a clean canvas for the new. Having survived a forty of whiskey and countless number of beer, I felt I was being given a second chance, and I was ready to take on the world.

I finished in the shower and checked my shit out in the mirror. It was good to see all my good looks still intact, with no major damage. Not counting the loss of brain cells. Satisfied, I wrapped up in a towel and headed back to my room where I found my dad laying out piles of my freshly cleaned clothes on the bed.

"Ah shit Dad, I'm sorry. You didn't have to do that."

"It's all right son. I know you had other priorities. It's no problem. Besides, you have the rest of your life to do your own laundry."

"Thanks, really. You saved my ass."

"Just remember, up there, I'm not going to be around to save your ass. And I'm sure your cousin Steve has enough ass of his own to look after. So it's all up to you now, all right?"

"Yeah, I know. Thanks." I turned to him and pulled him in for a big ol' hug, catching him a little off guard. We didn't usually show each other much affection. Maybe I felt I had some time to make up for. I thought of all the years I had taken for granted. Thinking that he would always be there for me if I needed him, and now, I was the one that wouldn't be there.

"Pack your things. I'm going to head out and get some chicken for us to eat. Can't send you boys off on an empty stomach."

I had never packed for a trip of this calibre before. The vacations I had been on were with my parents, and they had handled the packing, for the most part. Any of the short road trips I'd taken with the guys were easy to pack for; we just needed a box of beer and a hat or a toque, depending on the season.

So how in the fuck do I pack for this? Technically, I am moving up there. So, should I take everything? What's Steve got for a bed up there? I should probably take some rubbers. Yeah, I'll be needing some rubbers. I hope I need rubbers.

My mind was racing as I tried to get organized. I did my best to keep my thoughts pure and focused on the task at hand. Besides, the only rubbers I had were long past expired. I tried different ways of packing my things, made some adjustments, then second-guessed those adjustments before realizing that my head still really fucking hurt. So, I just grabbed a random pile of clothes and tossed them into a single duffle bag. I stood for a moment considering the really important items, making sure I had included them.

I dropped my bag by the front door together with my coveralls, hard hat, and work boots. As long as I had those, I'd be fine. I could just buy the rest. I looked out the front window just in case Steve was making better time than he thought, but there was no sign of him yet.

I paced around the house a couple of times. There was nothing I could think of that would help me kill time. I was expecting Steve within the hour, but every minute that passed seemed like ten. Then I remembered something, and it was a good thing, too. She was probably waiting by the phone.

"Hello, Brandon?" My suspicions were confirmed as my mother picked up the phone before the first ring was even complete.

"Hey Mom. Yes, it's me. How are you?"

"Well, I was wondering what happened. If you got home all right last night, or if something bad happened to you. I was worried."

"I know, I know. Sorry I waited so long to call. I've been busy packing and stuff."

"That's all right sweetie, I understand. I'm glad you made it home safe and sound. Have you heard from Steve yet? Do you know what time you're leaving?"

"Yeah, he called a couple of hours ago, should be here any time. Dad went out to get us something to eat before we leave."

"That's good of him. It's too bad we won't have time to see each other before you go. You take care of yourself dear. Call me when you get there, okay? And say hi to Stevie for me."

I could hear the distress in her voice. Like she wished there was something else that she could do. She had motherly instincts clawing out of her and no way to satisfy them other than nurturing through the phone.

"I will Mom, I will." Our conversation seemed short for the large life change we were both about to undergo, but I couldn't think of anything else to say. It would have to end sometime. "I love you."

"I love you too dear. Bye, honey."

I could picture the desperate expression on her face and the tears in her eyes as we disconnected. I returned to my pacing and barely made one lap before I heard a vehicle pull up. I hurried to the window. It was Dad. I watched as he explored several options to get the big bucket of eleven herbs and spices and all accessories from the truck to the house. I ran out to give him a hand.

"Thanks, son. No sign of Steve yet?"

"No, I—"

I stopped in mid-sentence as Steve's oversized truck pulled around the corner with a couple of toots on the horn and a wave from the window, announcing his arrival to the neighbourhood.

With our arms full of KFC, Dad and I continued on to the house. Steve got out of the truck and hurried to catch up. "Nice, you guys read my mind. I'm starving."

"Yeah, Dad figured you would be. How was the trip?"

"As good as can be expected with the hangover I'm nursing. It's been two weeks of hard partying."

"Yeah, well, that makes two of us man. It'll be a long trip to the big city."

"Yeah, you are looking a little rough there cuz. You packed up and ready to go?"

"You bet. After last night, I can't wait to get the hell outta here."

We dumped the grub on the kitchen counter and I began getting out all the fixins while Dad set out the plates and cutlery.

"So, break any hearts on your vacation, Steve'o?" Dad started.

"I definitely broke something." Steve recounted the wild vacation he'd just had. It made me happy to think that now, with my newfound wealth, I would be able to go off on similar erotic adventures. Instead of passing out in the middle of the open prairie with no sign of a woman for miles.

We plowed back the chicken. Steve kept insisting that I fill him in on my last night out in town. After several attempts at dodging the question, I finally gave in.

"That's the shittiest thing I've ever heard," Steve replied. "Are you fucking joking?"

"No, I'm not."

"So, you didn't get laid or anything?"

"Not that I'm aware of. Unless some stray animal had his way while I was passed out, or Joey. But I'm sure I'd know, right?"

"Fuck buddy, it's about time you moved on."

After we finished eating, the three of us sat around the table laughing at each other's stories, waiting for our stomachs to settle.

"So, what's your plan?" Dad turned to Steve. "Are you heading out right away, or did you want to stay the night and head out tomorrow?"

"I don't think so Uncle. Thanks for the offer though. I think we should pack our sorry asses up there tonight and get a good sleep. Tomorrow I can show Brand around a little, get him settled in."

"That sounds like a pretty good plan," Dad nodded with a look of both understanding and disappointment.

Steve turned to me. "Well kid, whaddya think? You ready to say goodbye?"

"As ready as I'll ever be, I guess." My cheeks puffed wide as I exhaled. I lifted my head and took a last look around the house and at my dad. Reading my insecurity, he smiled and gave me a nod of reassurance. I faced Steve, "Let's do it. Onward to bigger and better." I was excited about the move earlier in the day, but with the hangover taking its toll, combined with some greasy chicken, I'd of been happy to just return to my familiar bed.

"Let's move out then," Steve slapped me on the back as I followed him to the front door.

Dad and Steve occupied themselves with some idle chitchat in the entrance way as I loaded my stuff into my car. "I hope I didn't forget anything."

"Work boots, coveralls, and your hard hat. If you've got those, the rest you can buy when you get there." Steve smiled.

"All right then. I guess I'm ready to go," I announced.

"Okay man, I'll lead the way, just follow behind. You got my number in case we get separated?"

"You bet."

"All right, I'll go start the truck. Say your goodbyes, but make it quick, eh. See you, Uncle Ross, thanks for everything." Steve reached out and shook Dad's hand.

"Thanks Steve. Take care of my boy, okay?"

"Will do." Steve gave a last wave then headed down the front steps.

I turned to my father. "Well, I guess … here I go?"

"Don't worry son. You'll do fine. Call me if you need anything." He hugged me.

I had to work a little to hold back a tear, and with a final pat on the back, we broke it up. "Thanks Dad. Thanks for everything." The last awkward moment was over with. I turned and walked down the driveway toward my car. I gave one last wave to Dad who stood in the open doorway as I followed Steve down the block and around the corner and out of sight.

We made our way out of the crescent, then out of the neighbourhood and onto the main drag. I watched the passing landscape as I drove. Memories of the old town crowded my mind. It was in my past now. We took the last turn onto the number one highway toward the Wild West. The big city, my soon-to-be new home. I pushed the pedal down and brought the car up to cruising speed. I couldn't remember the last time I had driven that fast. We passed beyond city limits, and I was filled with a new sense of freedom and uncertainty.

16

Anyone who has driven the number one between Medicine Hat and Calgary has had the pleasure of travelling the flattest, straightest and most monotonous stretch of highway in the world. The minimal attention required to navigate the pancake-flat route leaves a traveller with a lot of time to think. As I followed Steve, I thought about my new place, the job I'd be doing, the new friends I'd make, the girls I'd meet, and the new clubs I'd party at. I was forging a new path, and for the moment, that left me no time to think about what I'd left behind.

As I passed through town by town, mile by mile, I felt myself being pulled toward a giant unseen star in the distance. Finally, it appeared, like a glowing halo on the horizon. The radiant hue from the city beyond stretched high into the night, a beacon for all who had places to go and things to do.

Entering the city limits, the highway turned into Sixteenth Avenue and stretched four lanes wide. There were overpasses, underpasses, and signs for international airports and hotels. All the action and the mesmerizing blinking colours were overloading my senses. I made sure to follow close to Steve, hoping he would give lots of notice before he turned. There was no telling what would happen to me if I got lost in the vast forest of light.

I snapped to attention as Steve's right indicator announced he was about to make a turn. I couldn't see past his truck to where he was taking us, but some signs suggested we were merging onto Deerfoot Trail. I'd heard of it before. People who had escaped from Medicine Hat years ago would return for holidays and family visits, transformed into alien-like beings. Those people who used to drink beer, wear muscle shirts, and belch out conversations, returned wearing sweater vests, drinking warm ale, and telling witty stories about Deerfoot Trails and 17th avenues.

We took the off-ramp onto Deerfoot, and I fought for my rightful place in the heavy traffic. It was chaos. Something I'd never driven in before. Reaching speeds well in excess of the posted limit, the cars were so close that if the person ahead of you even thought about reducing their speed, thousands of motorists would surely die.

Steve, the maniac, drove like it was a fucking frogger game. Left lane, right lane, back and forth. His truck tilting violently with every lane change. I was doing my best to follow, sitting so far up on the edge of my seat that I might as well have been on the hood of my car. If I died a sudden death in a violent crash, the cops would have no problem identifying my fingerprints embedded in the steering wheel.

I felt myself growing significantly older with every weave down the expressway, until Steve finally turned right and led me to an exit out of the endless autobahn. We continued moving to the right, which led us around a curly, pigtail sort of exit, and we ended up heading west on what I could best make out as Country Hills Boulevard. At this point, I didn't give a shit what the name of the road was, as long as it didn't contain any animal parts.

The traffic was still thick, but had slowed down so much that we were now inching along the roadway. In one turn I had moved from the raceway to the parking lot.

My phone rang. I had to dig for it beneath the passenger's seat, where it had fallen partway through the trip.

"Hello?"

"How you doin' back there?" Steve laughed.

"What the fuck was that? There's no way I could do that again, especially not on my own."

"Ah c'mon, the first time is the worst. Once you get used to the pace and get to know your way around a little, you'll love it. Everybody has the same experience their first time on the Deerfoot. Consider it your initiation into the big city."

"Initiation? Can't they just beat me on the ass with a wooden paddle or something?"

"Actually, if you're into that, there's this club downtown."

"Fuck you!"

"Just hang in there a little longer. We're almost home. I promise the pace will be more relaxed from here on."

We hung up and I turned my attention back to the line of clogged traffic ahead. We had progressed a total of one whole car length in the past three minutes. We continued at slower-than-walking pace until we passed the root cause of the jam: a truck that broke down. Once we cleared past it, the traffic instantly lightened.

We drove onward through a few sets of lights. I knew I should pay closer attention to where we were for future reference, but I was tired of driving in the mayhem. I just wanted it to stop. I noticed a mall on our right side, along with some theatres and a string of restaurants. Figuring we were passing through the downtown area, I looked excitedly for the Calgary Tower landmark, but was unable to locate it.

We continued driving through the lights. The city seemed to be a never-ending jungle. Then Steve put on his left blinker and moved into the turning lane for the intersection ahead. I followed him off the main drag and into a residential neighbourhood, which I hoped was a sign that we were nearing the end of our trip. Then we took a right and a left and another right. By this time, I had lost count and direction. We turned finally into a dead-end crescent.

Steve pulled off to the side of the street in front of what I guessed to be his house. I parked behind him and got out of my car. My legs were stiff after being cramped for over three hours. I gave a quick stretch as I made my way to the truck.

Before I made it to his window, Steve stuck his head out. "Hey that's my place there," he said, pointing to the house. "Can you give me a hand unloading this shit from the truck?" He motioned to the pile of gear in the truck box.

"You got it."

We worked together, moving two weeks' worth of party gear out of the truck into his garage.

"This neighbourhood isn't bad for crime compared to the other parts of the city, but if you get lazy or careless with your gear, there's a good chance you'll lose it. Best not to keep anything of value in your vehicle if you can help it."

It was going to take some getting used to. Back home, it was not at all unusual for me to leave the house and car unlocked. Sometimes even with the keys in the ignition.

With the truck unloaded, I returned to my car and grabbed my bags, doing a quick once-over to ensure anything of value was out of sight and the windows were closed.

Steve's house was a respectable place. It wasn't too big, but it was big enough for a guy to do what he wanted, whether it be bach'n it or raising a family. A split level with a detached garage. Everything was done up in a basic white siding with grey trim. I headed up to the front door, dropped my stuff in the landing, and closed the door behind me. It was a relief to have the drive over with.

"Welcome to the pad," Steve said, standing at the top of the stairs. "C'mon up, I'll show you around."

I followed Steve up the stairs and straight into the living room. It was just the right size and done up to the tens. Hardwood floor, leather furniture, and a huge entertainment system including a big, flat-panel TV and a stereo that suggested its owner might be compensating for other lack.

"So, we can share the upstairs. We'll figure out some grocery system, just see how it goes. Your room is downstairs," he nodded back to the stairwell.

I followed him back down to the landing, picked up my gear and continued on down to the basement.

It was pretty plain, with basic carpeting and some well-worn furniture in the main room. But it was more than livable. There was an old model TV—the big-box, bulky style, which was plenty big and would do the trick. Down the hall was a room that doubled as a laundry and utility room, a bathroom with a shower and two bedrooms at the end of the hall.

"Take your pick," Steve smiled. "You get the downstairs all to yourself. Like I said, we can share the upstairs, but we still have our separate floors just in case we need our own space, right?"

"Right," I agreed.

"Get yourself settled. I'll be upstairs sorting my shit out. Come on up when you're done and we'll find something to eat."

Alone and on solid ground after all the driving, I took a moment to stretch and try to let my nerves settle. I looked around the basement, trying to get the sense of hominess I was hoping for. I didn't feel it, but the place did have potential—I was just going to have to work at it. It was the bed I had chosen to lay in.

I ended up taking the room at the far end of the hall for what I figured would be added privacy. It was a simple room with a queen bed, a small closet, a wooden dresser, and a nightstand. I spread out the comforter I'd brought from home to make it feel more familiar. I finished unpacking and headed upstairs. Although Dad had fed us before we left, my stomach had been rumbling for the last hour.

Too lazy to cook anything ourselves, we ordered pizza and even found the stamina to slug back a couple of beers while watching a football game. After the last night I'd had with the boys back home, it didn't take much to get me back to a semi-plastered state. At which point I said goodnight, and made my way down to my new room. I crawled dizzily into my new bed and quickly passed out.

17

I awoke to find the sun peeking through the curtain of the small, lone bedroom window. Powered by the excitement of getting out and exploring the city, I hopped up and made my way to the bathroom. The usual morning routine had a new spin to it while I adjusted to the new arrangements. The toilet didn't have a problem sucking down last night's pizza and beer combination, which made me breathe a sigh of relief. There's nothing worse than visiting someone's house and finding things don't run as downhill as they should.

I finished up the morning cleansing routine and returned to my new bedroom to figure out the right combination of clothing for my big city début. After testing out a couple of options, I went with a simple pair of jeans and a navy blue, button-up shirt casually untucked. Let it hang and hang with it, I always say.

I went upstairs, and to my surprise Steve was slaving over a hot stove. Cooking a full breakfast spread, bacon, eggs, hash browns, and toast.

"Holy shit man, you been drinking already?" He jumped a bit as I snuck in.

"Yeah, fuck off smartass," he said. "I like my big weekend breakfasts."

"I'm sure I'll like your big weekend breakfasts too." I said, pulling up a chair at the table. "So, what's on the schedule for today?"

"I thought we'd check in with the guys from work. We usually get together for lunch on our Sundays off. I'm sure we'll be getting together today and getting our marching orders. It'll be good. You'll get to meet the crew."

"Right on, sounds good." I got up and made my way to the fridge, pouring myself a glass of Sunny D.

It was fun to imagine the fast cars and girls waiting for me in my new exciting future. With all the thinking I had invested toward the fun things, I put little thought into the reality of the job that would make my rock star lifestyle possible. Steve's announcement of meeting the crew today sent visions of big greasy oil workers reeling through my mind and caused my palms to sweat slightly.

Truthfully, I don't fit the rig worker stereotype. Clean cut, with a decent fashion sense and a slim build, I had everything to be nervous about. But going home wasn't an option now. I'd worked around big, ugly, greasy Dicks before. So no matter what, I had to make a go of this.

We finished up our breakfast and cleaned up the mess. For a bachelor, Steve was remarkably disciplined at keeping a clean place. He wiped the last few crumbs off the counter and said, "Grab your shit and let's get going. We meet the guys at the Rooster's Den at noon. It's a pub just over at the shopping centre."

"Sounds good," I ran downstairs and grabbed my phone and keys and then double-checked myself in the mirror to make sure I wasn't looking too pretty. I was going for a delicate balance between looking rough enough to impress the crew while still looking good enough to attract the ladies. This would be my first time in a big city pub, after all. I headed back upstairs and met Steve at the front entrance. He looked over and tossed me his keys.

"You can drive the truck. You have to get used to driving in this town. Just be fucking careful with it."

"Uh—" I stopped myself from telling him that I really wasn't comfortable driving his truck. I did need the experience driving in town and Steve's truck was way sexier than my Honda. So, I kept the keys and we headed out.

As I fastened myself behind the wheel, I was overcome with a sense of awe. We sat high in the jacked-up diesel. With plush, leather heated seats, a sunroof, and dashboard switches I could not explain. I had yet to ride in such a glorious steed. I never realized how much I was missing out on. How could I ever pick up a decent chick in my Civic when there were other guys driving around in these? As I began considering my competition, I quickly sold myself on the belief that if I was going to amount to anything in life, I would have to get a truck of my own.

With a turn of the key, the monster machine sprang to life. And what had taken Mother Nature millions of years to create, was puked out of its four-inch exhaust pipe in a great plume of black smoke.

70

I followed Steve's directions as we made our way out of the neighbourhood. "The area we live in is called Country Hills. It's the newest area on the north side of town."

"So, was that downtown we drove through last night?" I asked.

"Downtown what? Where?"

"You know, that big shopping centre. The theatres and all the restaurants we drove past."

Steve chuckled. "You mean the shopping centre just over there? No man, that's just for this area. There's a mall, couple of grocery stores, some pubs, and some theatres. Everything you need really. No, to get downtown you have to get back on the Deerfoot and drive like an hour south of here."

"You're shittin' me. An hour, really?"

"No shit man. When you're downtown, you'll know it. We'll go party down there when we get a chance. I have a good buddy that lives downtown."

Everything was so different. It was going to take some getting used to, but I was eager for the change. We drove to Rooster's Den Pub and parked out front. I could feel the adrenaline beginning to pump when the truck came to a stop and I turned off the ignition. It was time to meet the crew.

18

As I followed Steve to the pub entrance, I understood that I no longer just wanted this opportunity; I needed it. I was going to go in with a smile and a firm handshake, and just be a man. Nobody was going to spoon feed this to me. Steve had done as much as he could. The rest was up to me.

The Rooster's Den was bigger than anything we had back home. There was a family-oriented dining side with booths and then there was a get-drunk-and-eat-some-chicken-wings side. Steve made straight for the chicken wings. He scanned the joint until some guys at a table in the corner waved us over. He held up his hand as we made our way over.

Just smile and nod, strong handshake. Here goes.

"Hey guys, what's up," Steve greeted the group while I stood in the background feeling swallowed by his shadow. After everyone said their piece, Steve pulled up the only remaining chair, leaving me to stand solo with an awkward smile on my face and a slight sweat breaking on my forehead.

Steve looked back up at me, "Oh Brand, sorry man." He took a quick look around and then pointed to an empty chair at another table. "Yeah, just pull that chair over. We'll make some room." He motioned to the guys to make a shuffle.

I grabbed the chair and squeezed in.

"Hey guys," Steve stood up for the announcement. "This is my cousin Brandon from Medicine Hat. I'm sure you've all heard that he's going to be starting with us this next job. He's worked in a lot of industrial fabrication shops but never on a rig. So, we've got to watch out for him 'til he gets his balls wet."

I stood awkwardly beside Steve smiling and nodding while he discussed my wet balls with complete strangers.

Steve continued, "So, I'll get everyone introduced. Over on the left here we've got Brian, he's the rig manager. And then Dave here's our motor hand. And last but not least, our senior 'do it all' man, Smokey."

I reached around the table as Steve introduced the guys, greeted each of them with a polite smile and a handshake before sitting back in my chair. Thankfully the group wasn't as intimidating as I was expecting. They were all quite welcoming really.

With the introductions complete, Brian started in with his speech. "So, I was just beginning to fill the guys in here. We were supposed to start this week but it has been pushed back again. I know nobody wants to hear that. But it's good in that it gives us more time to prepare. Steve, I may be calling on you this week to give me a hand with getting some things ready. Brandon, this actually works out better for you because you have some safety courses you've got to get done before you can work on site. I've got you booked in starting tomorrow at First Safety out in Airdrie. Steve, you know where that is, right?" Brian looked at Steve, who nodded. "Good. Class starts at eight tomorrow. Don't be late." Brian shot me a stern look. "With any luck, we'll be balls to the walls starting next Monday."

That was it for the work announcements. Everyone broke off into groups. Steve and Brian had some sort of important business to discuss, which they did in their little corner. Dave jumped on me right away.

"So, Brandon, you're from the Hat, eh? I've done some work down there. Nice place." Dave was an eager sort. Like an excited puppy. He seemed to be a jolly, mid-thirties guy who was well fed and watered judging from his excessive waistline.

"Yeah, it's not bad, but I've kind of had enough of it. You know, hometown and all."

"Yeah, yeah, right. So, have you spent any time up in Calgary?"

"No, none at all. Other than shopping trips with my parents."

"Well, let me tell you little buddy, you are in for a treat. If I was your age and single, I would be living here man. This place is packed full of sexy little things running around, just dying to meet a young man like yourself."

"Now that's what I like to hear! What about you Dave, you single?"

"Nope. I'm married to my high school sweet heart. So, you'll have to settle for second best buddy. She moved down here a few years back to go to nursing school. I couldn't move down until I found a job. So, I kept driving all the way here every chance I got to hand out resumes. I'm from the Leduc area." He paused, sipping on his beer. "I eventually lucked out and got on with these guys. Tough to beat the pay, but it seems I'm out of town more now than when I actually lived out of town." He scratched his head and chuckled. "Been hitched a few years now, and we're expecting a little one in the spring." His face glowed with pride.

"Awesome Dave, congratulations. I can already tell that baby's going to be one lucky kid to have you as a Dad." Dave blushed. He was as red as I've ever seen a man. I liked him immediately. He was one of those people who were always happy and excited, and he was all about family.

With the ice broken between me and Dave, I set my focus toward Smokey across the table. "So, Smokey, where are you from?"

Smokey put down the chicken wing he'd been gnawing on, seemingly taken aback that a young buck like me would show any interest in him at all.

"Me? Oh, I'm from way out in central Manitoba. That's where I was born, anyway. Otherwise, I've been here in Alberta for most of my life. Worked in the Middle East for a while." He was a bit of a quiet talker, but I got the impression he was just being a little shy around the new guy, so I kept on him.

"Wow, you've been around a little then. It'll be good to learn from someone with some legitimate experience." I caught a slight smirk on his face as he leaned back coolly. I could tell he was flattered with my remark.

Dave leaned over to my ear. "Hey Brandon, here comes one of the local hotties now."

It was the worst thing he could've done, as I'm not a man known for subtlety. Excited by the news, I immediately turned my head around to the waitress walking in our direction. My laser vision locked on and scanned her fully up and down in deliberate appreciation. Leaving no question as to my intentions. She looked older than me, mid-twenties maybe. With dirty-blond hair tied back in a ponytail. Her breasts were a bit bigger than my liking, but they looked fantastic in her tight uniform, which included a short skirt that showed off her sexy legs.

She acknowledged my visual harassment with a glare that told me she was not impressed and I would be dealt with in time. After she finished delivering her tray of drinks to a group nearby, she made her way back over to our table.

74

Her pace suggested she had business to take care of. I was actually scared. And if I'd had quick access to an exit at that very moment, I would have used it. But I didn't, so I turned around in my seat to face the guys. I slunk down in my chair a little with a wild hope that she might dismiss the little exchange we'd just shared.

"Hey Ashley," Dave called as she stepped up to the table.

"Hi Dave. What can I get for you today, honey?"

"Hey Ash, this is Brandon." Dave announced loudly as he turned toward me. I wanted to disappear under the table. "Brandon just moved up here. He's going to be working with us."

"Is that right?" Ashley replied, leaning toward me with her well-endowed bosom. She talked softly, but still loud enough for everyone at the table to hear. "Well, Brandon, welcome to Calgary. I'm gonna guess, judging from the way you were mentally undressing me a moment ago, that you don't have many, if any, women back where you come from. So, let me be the first to clue you in. On top of looking incredibly sexy in this outfit, I am also an amateur kickboxer. So be warned that if I ever catch you groping me with those beady little eyeballs of yours again, you'll need a surgeon to remove my shoe from your ass. Deep in your ass. Got it stud?"

My jaw was slack. Only the ripest tomato on the vine could match the colour of my face that moment. And if anyone looked closely enough, they'd have noticed my chin quivering like that of a scolded infant.

She turned abruptly and walked away from the table. Her chest pushed out and her confidence pulsing with every sideways thrust of her hips as she moved across the floor.

Sounds of coughing and choking engulfed the table as soon as she was a comfortable distance away. Beer dripped from noses. Eyes streaked with tears. The guys were laughing so hard they were clenching at their guts.

Brian, the rig manager, wiped his eyes on his sleeve. Laughing hysterically as he held his beer up to me in a toast. "Welcome to the big city kid. She can be a tough one."

For the rest of the afternoon and into the early evening, we sat around bullshitting, drinking beer, and satisfying our hungry appetites with pub food. Eventually, Ashley and I made peace with each other, and laughed things off. Steve and I left for home at about seven. My first meet up with the crew was a success. Once we got home, I went straight to bed. I had safety courses starting first thing in the morning and I wanted to be in top shape.

19

The long week of safety training included things like learning that H_2S is a poisonous gas found everywhere, sure to kill off the whole human population in good time. And our chances of exposure to this substance during rig operation is so great that it is mandatory for us to wear personal monitors at all times. Then there was something called "Fall Arrest," which taught me that it was a waste of time to go through a long and dramatic fall when I could die much more quickly by hanging from a harness. I also learned that in this world I was about to enter, I could sign away any chance of laying charges against my employer for any work-related accidents. Halfway through the first day, bored out of my mind, I entertained the idea of sucking on poisonous gas just to put an end to my boredom.

But I stuck it out as I was getting paid a shitload of money, and I made a promise to Steve. He explained that in my new job, I'd be starting out at over twenty bucks an hour. With double pay for time worked over so many hours. Along with pay for travel time and expenses when driving to the site. I had dollar signs dancing through my head all week as I sat through the training sessions. I daydreamed about all the toys I'd be able to buy for myself once the paychecks started rolling in.

On Thursday, I could feel the end of the week coming, along with the urge to call the guys back home to see what was up for the weekend. Although it had seemed like a long week sitting in class, the days had actually passed by quite quickly. Plus, I'd made more money sitting in class that week than I would have in a month at my old job. I was feeling the urge to gloat just a little.

I hadn't talked with anyone back home except for my mom and dad all week. I suddenly felt an urgency to go back for the weekend and share my adventures with the guys. The instructor told us that we could expect to get out the following day at around 1:00 pm if everything went smoothly and we worked through lunch. I planned to pack my stuff that night and leave right after class the next day. I spent the rest of the day thinking about returning home for the weekend and convincing myself it was a good idea.

So, with my mind made up, I returned to Steve's on Thursday after class and began packing. He had been gone most of the week, getting things ready with the rig. He was not usually home until late. But that night, he was home early. I heard the front door close, followed by his call.

"Brand, you here?"

"Yeah man, just packing up."

Footsteps thundered down into my room. "What's up?"

"Not much, just packing up some basics. Think I'll head back to the Hat for the weekend."

My decision did not sit well with him, which I had expected. I had been hoping he would work late that night and that I could just sneak out of town.

"What? Why would you go back there?"

I was armed with only a couple of pitiful excuses. "I don't know. It could be the last time for a while, since we're heading off to the site next week."

"Don't be a bitch. You're running home to Mommy and Daddy and your warm blankie," he laughed.

"Fuck off," I said. Though I couldn't help but laugh along. "What do you care anyway? You're working."

"No, dude. I'm done for the weekend, as of right now. I called my buddy Nate. He's the one with a condo downtown. Downtown man! Party central! I told him about you and that I wanted to take you out on the town. He said to bring you the fuck over! You'll love Nate. Everybody loves Nate. We'll meet up with some chicks, hit some clubs. Brand, you can't miss this dude."

"All right, I'll stay." I heard myself saying, though the words came out reluctantly. I began the dizzying process of redirecting my mind. Although I'd been looking forward to going home, Steve was jumping up and down and yelling about the things we would see and do. Like a kid that was promised a trip to the amusement park. He made a convincing argument for staying and playing in the big city.

"And this other place, man, they set drinks on fire. Oh … and wait until you … the waitresses there, man …" Steve led me out of the room while he went on about the weekend to come. I reached over to the wall beside the door on our way out and switched off the light. Leaving behind my half-packed suitcase.

The next morning, to my relief, Steve was still sleeping when I left for class. He had kept me up until ten the night before, going on and on about the things we were going to do. Though it all sounded good and I was excited, strangely, I felt less excited about it than I had been about going home. I had no idea what to expect that weekend. Even after listening to Steve rant and rave for all that time. All he said seemed to intimidate me more than excite me.

That day in class, the instructor looked like he had just as long a week as the rest of us. He breezed through the remaining material and handed out our tests before noon. I completed the ten multiple choice questions before the rest of the class woke up.

The sun shone brightly in my eyes. It had been a long week, but I'd made it through, and I was now legal to work. Plus, I was getting paid for eight complete hours even if we were dismissed after only four. Life was pretty sweet.

On the way back to Steve's, I held onto a sliver of hope that I could go back to the Hat. I decided that if Steve wasn't home when I arrived, I would give him a call. And if he didn't answer, it would be a good enough excuse for me to head out and carry through with my original plan. But when I rounded the corner to the house, I saw his truck in the driveway. I wasn't going anywhere, but downtown.

"All right! I knew they'd let you out early." Steve greeted me at the top of the stairs. "The best thing is, you're still getting paid man. There's nothing like partying on company time. Go get ready. I already called Nate, and he's on standby at work. I'm supposed to call him as soon as we're on our way, and he'll sneak out early."

He wasn't even going to give me ample time to pout. I sucked it up; there was no getting out of it now. So I decided to make the best of it. I took a deep breath, accepted my fate, and did a complete one-eighty. Looking up at Steve, I shouted. "That's right man, company time. You got any fucking beer in this place?"

Steve was a little surprised by my change in spirit. "Wha— yeah, man, I got some beer."

"Well, what the hell! How the fuck can I get ready without a beer! Let's get this fucking party started!"

He caught up with the program, running to the fridge. "All right buddy! That's what I'm fucking talking about!"

"Fucking right! Giddyup!" I cheered. Steve returned at the top of the stairwell and tossed me a beer.

I snapped off the top and gulped down half the can in one shot. Burp! "Ahhh," I looked back up at Steve, he was wearing no more than a shirt and a pair of boxer shorts. He looked far from ready. "What the fuck, man! Are you ready? 'Cause you don't look like you're ready!"

My aggressiveness had good old Steve'o fumbling again. "Well, I just gotta …"

"Don't worry about me," I said. "I'll be ready in twenty minutes. You better be fucking ready!"

"I'm on it." He took off running down the hall to his room like a little kid, shouting back over his shoulder. "Meet you back here in twenty!"

Having set Steve in his place, I took my beer and went downstairs. Our little exchange had gotten my blood flowing, and I was feeling better prepared for the experience ahead. It was to be my first Friday night out in the big city.

After showering, I took a little extra time to get ready than I would have back home. Keeping in mind the higher class of women I hoped to get acquainted with. Looking at myself in the mirror now that the beer had begun taking its effect, the young stallion reflected in the vanity gave me a wink and headed upstairs.

I jumped up the last step into the living room. Steve was nowhere in sight, but I could hear the tap running in the bathroom down the hall.

"Hey Stevie," I called out.

"Holy shit man, you all ready?"

"Time's a wastin' buddy, get moving."

"Yeah, be out in a couple of minutes bud."

I made my way to the fridge and cracked open a new frosty beer.

"So where are we off to tonight?" I yelled.

"Ho, never fear my friend. We are going to show you a good time. Once we get to Nate's, he usually has everything planned out for us, and he likes to fucking paaaarty!"

I sipped my beer and casually paced the floor in the living room, looking at the framed photographs on the wall. Pictures of good times. Lakes, ski resorts, women—life appeared as one big beer commercial to these guys. I couldn't be one hundred percent positive, but judging from some of the tales of past adventures Steve had told me, I was pretty sure I had picked out this Nate guy in more than one frame. He looked fairly tall, over 6 feet, pig shaved dark hair, good shape, and took care of himself. Just as Steve described him. He had a rare photogenic quality that rode the thin line between boy next door and porn king. An aura that could earn him a portrait on the classy condom dispenser in the men's room.

20

After twisting and turning, weaving in and out of the strings of high-speed streams of light, I caught my first glimpse of the legendary downtown Calgary skyline. Massive towers stretched against the clouds. In the background, the even mightier peaks of the snow-covered Rocky Mountains lent a *Lord Of The Rings* feel to the occasion. I wondered what was going on beneath that skyline at that very moment. Was there an office worker putting in overtime behind locked doors away from his spouse? How about a young lawyer snorting rails in an upscale bathroom stall? Or a seventeen-year-old who ran from home, forced to turn tricks in an alley? As I breathed in deep, my pulse quickened, and I realized for the first time how far outside my comfort zone I really was.

I once again lost track of how many turns we took or in which direction we were headed. I was entranced by the giant city core as it sucked us in like a lone ship being pulled toward a giant star.

As we neared downtown, I looked out the window, twisting my head in an attempt to see just how high the buildings were. But no matter how I contorted my body, I couldn't see the top. Pedestrians made their way on the sidewalks. Some wore business suits, trench coats, and fancy dresses. While others ambled along in multiple layers of tattered rags, some pushing rusted carts full of personal possessions. A group of girls primed for the evening festivities walked arm in arm, wearing heels and designer dresses, laughing with each other. In the shadows and the crevices, the sudden glow of a red ember signalled someone taking a drag of a cigarette, or maybe a pipe. Perhaps it was a dealer, a thug, or a lady of the night.

I turned to Steve who was navigating the street traffic and smiling at my wonder. "So, whaddya think? Pretty wild, eh?"

"It's fucking crazy," I replied. "How in the hell do you find your way through all this?"

"Ah, you'll find your way when the time is right young Skywalker." He joked, with his best Yoda impression.

I turned back to the window, wanting to take it all in. "So where are we going? Where does Nate live?"

"17th Avenue, the south side of downtown. One of the city's trendiest areas. His balcony literally overlooks 17th. there's no better place to be on a Friday night. Fast cars, fast ladies." He flashed a toothy grin.

We turned off the main drag onto a side street and then took a sudden left turn onto a downward sloping driveway that led to an underground parking garage. Steve pulled up beside the bright yellow pin pad and entered a number. The door opened magically before us.

"I rent a parking stall in Nate's building. Parking in this area sucks. If one thing's certain about downtown, it's that your vehicle is sure to get broken into at least once."

We made our way to the stall, Steve's truck's antenna bounced off of every ceiling truss we passed. I was surprised his truck even fit in the garage, which seemed tailored more to accommodate compact cars rather than large diesel trucks. But then, this was "Cow Town."

After parking, we crawled out of the truck. I stretched and scanned the dimly lit parkade. I saw vehicles ranging from two-door compacts to luxury sedans, Honda, Lexus, and BMW.

Steve came around the end of the truck pointing to the jet-black Honda Accord in front of us. "That's Nate's ride. I bug him about driving a pussy vehicle, but it doesn't bother him none because," Steve smirked, "he really does pick up a lot of pussy. C'mon, let's go in."

We went toward the elevator and waited for it to come down to the letter "P" on the illuminated floor banner.

Finally, the flashy brass doors opened wide. Two very sexy ladies stepped out. One was a blond, the other a brunette. Both dressed to kill in outfits that emphasized their slim yet sculptured figures. I had thought the girls back in the

Hat dressed up to the nines, but what I saw in front of me that night took things to a whole new level. Level ten. The ladies seemed to be in a hurry, and in their haste they bumped into us, sending them stumbling off balance.

Steve, obviously feeling less out of league with these women than I, called out. "Hey, you girls are going the wrong way. The party starts up at Nate's."

To my surprise, the two women stopped and turned around. The brunette replied, "Oh, you guys are going out with Natey tonight? You tell that big stud to come and meet us over at Melrose, okay?"

Steve, the idiot, played hard to get. "Yeah well, we've got a pretty full schedule, but I think I can convince him to fit you in."

The girls found this play more humorous than I did, rolling their eyes at Steve and giggling before continuing onward. Their laughter echoed through the underground cavern as they walked away.

Steve's face broke into a cocky grin, as if he'd just scored the winning goal in overtime. "Yeah, they'll do, eh?" He nudged me with his elbow.

I remained silent with a sheepish nod. It was embarrassing for me, really. Hard to believe he didn't realize how not sexy he was. Maybe he did know; he just didn't care.

Other than Ashley at the Rooster's Den, this was my first "up close" encounter with the female species of this concrete jungle. Truthfully, the experience almost made me sick. The women reminded me of models in a GQ magazine. I suddenly felt like the guy who shows up at the Playboy mansion party, with a fruitcake.

With those thoughts running through my mind, I grew mildly nauseous as the elevator floor pressed up on our feet lifting us to the next level of the evening: Nate's place.

21

The elevator chimed, announcing the end of our ascent. Steve led us onward, stepping out of the elevator doors and turning left down the hallway. He stopped in front of a door marked with the golden numerals "321". The door resonated audibly to the music cranked in Nate's apartment. Steve tried the knob. Finding it locked, he began banging hard on the door.

After several attempts with no success, we heard the stereo fall silent. Steve seized the opportunity and gave one last series of desperate blows to the door. I felt a slight pounding on the floor as footsteps from the other side drew closer. Finally, the deadbolt disengaged and the door swung open.

Standing before us was Nate, wearing no more than a towel wrapped around his waist and a smile only a porn flick producer could love. He looked identical to the pictures in Steve's living room.

"Bitches!" he greeted us with open arms. "What's up?"

Steve and Nate clashed hands in a "high five," then Steve announced, "Nate, this is my little cousin Brand, Brand this is Natey." He walked straight past Nate into the apartment.

"Brandy!" Nate shouted at me. I cringed somewhat at his choice of nickname. I immediately knew there was no way to get by Nathan without a Goose and Maverick "need for speed" high fiver.

After the primitive greeting, I was accepted by the Nate man who, with a manly near naked embrace, welcomed me to his lair.

Once I'd shed my shoes at the entrance and took a few steps inside, Nate shut the door behind me. To our right, Steve appeared from out of the kitchen with a round of beers in hand.

Nate started his welcome-to-the-pack speech. "Brando, any cousin of Steve's is a bitch of mine. Make yourself at home. There's beer in the fridge, AC/DC on the stereo, and if you look down from the deck at this time, the street below should be filled with tits and ass."

I didn't mind AC/DC music at the right time and place. The view from his deck sounded pretty inviting too. So, I followed Steve out and found a comfortable spot leaning over the railing to check out the nightlife below. Natey was right; there were girls everywhere. The deck was the perfect height—high enough to scan a wide range, but low enough to carry on a conversation with your choice of pedestrian.

As I looked over 17th Avenue, I was awestruck. The street was literally crawling with people dressed in everything from suits and ties to hard-ass punk gear or western cowboy and everything in between. Some of whom I couldn't even label. Behind me, also taking in the sights and sounds from below, was Nate. Still sporting just a towel around his waist, he shouted out to a girl he knew.

"Hey Stacey! Ooooh! Oooh!" Nate cheered to the sidewalk below. He pressed his hands up in the ultra-popular "raise the roof" gesture.

Everybody on the block looked up, searching for the source of the mating call. Then from within the crowd, the call was answered by none other than Stacey. A nice-looking blond standing directly below Nate's deck. She was wearing a shirt that emphasized her substantial cleavage, which was accentuated even more by our aerial view.

"Hey Natey! Get that big horse cock down here, stud. Oooh! Oooh!" she called back.

"Oh yeah!" he replied with the primitive grunt of a great silverback gorilla in heat. "I'll bring it down there and shove it between those big titties!"

"Dirty boy," she laughed. "See you later Daddy."

This amazed me. Nate was one of those guys. The type that can say anything to any girl and have them laugh it off like he's just a sweet little boy in need of some attention. Me on the other hand, if I would have spoken to Stacey like Nate just did, she'd have surely scaled the side of the building to kick me square in the nuts.

Returning inside, Nathan turned the music back up so people on the street would know where the party was. "I'll just be a couple of minutes, then we'll hit the town boys." He disappeared around the corner.

I followed Nate back into his place, casually taking in the pad. It was a simple, two-bedroom apartment but nicely finished and, like Steve's, it was very neat. Everything seemed to have its place and everything was in its place.

Nate returned to the living room, towel replaced with a stylish pair of jeans and a button-up shirt, which was unbuttoned low enough to show a little chest hair and snug enough to highlight the finer points of his physique. "Another round guys?" he asked, walking straight to the kitchen.

I looked at my two guides for the evening, now standing side –by side. I recalled the ladies from the parking garage and with some quick calculations concluded there was no way this was going to work. Steve was just wrong; our encounter in the garage had confirmed it. The girls had laughed hysterically at him. In his mind, he was sexy. And Nate, I was sure I'd seen him in a porn somewhere before, I just couldn't place it. There was no way I could see sexy girls like the ones from the garage ever getting hot for this posse.

We cracked our beers in unison and Nate raised his up in a toast. "To Brando, welcome to the club." We clashed our cans together then tipped them back.

"Okay, let's get this show on the road." Nate shut the balcony doors, turned off the stereo, grabbed his keys, and led us to the exit.

While putting on our shoes, Nate dug into his pocket and handed me a piece of paper. "Keep this on you Brando. It has my address and cell phone number on it, in case we get separated in the chaos."

I took the paper, somewhat concerned that the precaution was necessary. I hoped they didn't plan on ditching me later.

Nate took one last check around the place as he opened the door, then we all filed out into the hall. "Okay, Brand, we're going to hit a lot of spots tonight, so stay close. And if you pick up any chicks, you have to share with me. Oh yeah, Oooh! Oooh!" As Nate's voice echoed down the hall, I questioned my choice in guides for my first night out in the big city.

22

We made our way through the main lobby and poured out onto the street. The air was cool but one couldn't complain for the time of year; it could be a lot worse.

People were packed on the sidewalk. Like cells in a living vein, we were swept away in the current. We couldn't move without bumping someone. For me, it was quite uncomfortable at first. Back home, everyone had their personal space, and invading that would more often than not result in a physical confrontation. Especially with the redneck types, which was pretty much everyone. Convinced I would be in need of their support before the end of the block, I made sure to follow close behind Steve and Nate.

I was admiring a passing Porsche when I got a heavy shoulder on my left side that spun me around so that I stood facing the bully. There before me stood a large man with a nipple ring poking through a rip in his Iron Maiden T-shirt. My pulse increased as I looked up, way up, until I made eye contact with the giant heavily decorated with tribal jewellery hanging from his lips, nose, eyebrows, and likely other places I'd rather not imagine. Primitive instincts advised me to not make eye contact with the beast. As soon as I did, I braced myself, praying for Steve and Nathan to stop looking at girls long enough to notice that my life was endangered.

"Hey dude, I'm really sorry 'bout that. You all right?" The now seemingly tender giant laid a caring hand on my shoulder.

My eyes blinked in disbelief as I faced the monster whose expression was of sincere concern. "Ye … yeah, you bet, man. No problem." I stammered, trying to collect myself, feeling suddenly embarrassed of my ignorant stereotype.

"Shit man … dude, I am such a fucking klutz man. I'm always running into shit. Again, sorry 'bout that."

"No, don't worry about it man, I'm fine. Thanks."

"Right on buddy. Have a good night," he gave me a comforting pat on the shoulder before continuing off down the walkway.

After my encounter with the friendly hulk, I began to relax. The strangers on the street suddenly seemed less threatening. I kept my head up now, watching their faces and most of them shared a friendly smile as they passed. I wondered how I must have looked with my head constantly twisting from side to side, appreciating the countless attractive women that we passed. I was flattered to see how many of them turned their own heads to check out all my assets in exchange, ending with flirtatious smiles all around. It was nice to see all the new, unknown faces. I began to feel in tune with my surroundings.

Nathan gave me a stiff slap on the chest before he ran to catch the next crossing signal. Steve and I followed him to the other side of the street where I was pulled into our first stop of the night, Morgan's Pub.

I winced slightly to the rawness of the live band finishing up a cover of Led Zeppelin's, "Tangerine." The pub was dimly lit and wasn't big enough to provide room for an actual stage. Some tables and chairs had just been cleared away to accommodate the band on the right-hand side of the room. They were good, loud but not retarded, death-metal loud. They played a lot of cover tunes, mostly alternative stuff. To the left was the horseshoe-shaped bar. The back area catered to the billiard crowd.

This was a lot different from the pubs back home where groups would be clearly separated, with punks at one table and preps at another. Here, the crowd was mixed. Just as they were out on the streets. Seeing people intermingling was a refreshing change. I lost the guys temporarily as I checked out the scene. I scanned the crowd for Nate's head, then the familiar mating call "Oooh! Oooh!" led me to the big guy who'd found himself a spot at the bar. He was being tended to by a good-looking brunette.

Nate caught sight of me through the crowd and reached his hand up high in the air, waving me over.

"Brand! Hey, Brando! Get the fuck over here man!!"

I raised my hand in response in case someone in the bar didn't realize who he was yelling at. I made my way through the crowd over to him and Steve who was talking to a pretty blonde.

"Jackie," Nate nodded toward the bartender. "Jackie, this here is the Brand man, the third horseman."

She acknowledged me with a flirty smile. "Hi, Brand Man."

"Hi Jackie, nice to meet you," I smiled.

"Brando, here man!!" Nathan thrust a shot glass of brown liquor into my hand. "A shot of Jager to start off the night. Oooh! Oooh!"

We all tapped glasses before tipping the shots to our mouths.

Nate turned back to Jackie who seemed to enjoy his attention. The mischievous grin on her face, left no doubt of the less-than-Christian compliments Nate was whispering into her ear. It baffled me how such a seemingly sweet and beautiful girl could be charmed by such filth.

Steve wrapped his arm over my shoulder and handed me a pint of beer, then fanned his hand across the crowded room. "So, little cuz, how do you like the big city so far?"

I noticed two lovely ladies near the wall dressed for action and looking in our direction with unmistakable interest, whispering to each other and smiling. I made eye contact and returned the smile. "I think I like it very much, big cuz." We tapped glasses.

I contemplated an approach. What opening line would be the best for the two young ladies? They weren't the best-looking specimens I'd seen that night. But they were still way above the standard I'd left back home.

Ready to make my well-planned move, I turned away for a moment, took a deep breath and a healthy chug of ale, then turned back toward the girls. To my disappointment, good old Stevie already picked up their vibe and had already slid in beside them to work his magic. I considered assisting as a wingman, then picked up on the ladies' body language, that they were less than impressed with Steve. In fact, I was surprised he wasn't dripping with the girls martini's from the head down. So I stayed back and chalked it up as a loss.

I continued surveying the club, looking for other contestants. Unfortunately, although I was good-looking enough, I was not much for approaching women. I was hoping that things would kind of just get thrown my way as Steve and Nate introduced me to people throughout the night. But at that moment, they were both preoccupied, and my interests were not their main concern.

I drew deep from my glass. The promise of a good time began to fade as I felt more and more alone and out of place. A sudden bump to my elbow caused my drink to spill down the front of my shirt. Luckily, my glass was almost empty, so the damage was minimal, and I was experienced enough to choose a dark blue shirt for just such an emergency.

"Oh, shit. I'm sorry, I'm so sorry," said a playful voice. A set of feminine hands reached out and rubbed a bar napkin across my chest where the drink had landed.

I followed the hands up the arms to the torso, where I was greeted by a very nice set of breasts wrapped in a casual yet form-fitting grey shirt with pink "U of C" lettering. I found myself staring at the breasts longer than any man should ever stare at a set of unfamiliar breasts. Unless he is paying for the privilege. The pert nipples pressing subtly against the fabric commanded my attention like a maestro's baton.

"Um … hello? Excuse me." A hand very rudely waved in front of my eyes, disrupting my concentration.

I broke from my trance, realizing I had just been busted with my hand in the cookie jar. Flushed with guilt, I looked up from the breasts to the face above. "Oh, I'm sorry, really. I'm not like a pervert or anything." I struggled with my recovery, then finally accepted my inevitable fate and braced myself for a slap to the face.

"Well, you look innocent enough," she smirked. "I suppose I could let you go this time. Actually, it's kind of flattering. I suppose I'm feeling a little neglected. My outfit lacks the glitter of most of the competition."

"That is true," I agreed, as my gaze dropped back toward her chest.

"Okay, now you're starting to worry me." She placed a finger under my chin and raised my eyes back to her smile.

"Yes, pushing it a little," I replied with a blush. "What kind of world must we live in that a beautiful girl has to spill a man's drink to get him to notice her breasts?"

"I know," she laughed. "I'm so sorry about that."

"Not a problem at all. It was my pleasure," I said. "How 'bout we call it even?"

"Done," she smiled, tapping my glass.

With the ice broken, we fell into an awkward silence. I swished my glass and tried to think of a witty remark, but I was drawing a blank. My palms broke out into a slight sweat. She was stunning, but not like the girls in the garage. She wasn't sporting a fancy dress or any of the bling. But what she was wearing suited her. Casually dressed, with her hair tied back in a ponytail. Her allure was subtle next to the neon signs of the competition, but I wasn't fooled. Through years of girl-watching, I could tell that beneath her simple outfit there was a kickass body.

"My name's Kaitlin, or Katy if you want." The introduction gave me hope that she might actually have some interest in me.

"I'm Brandon, Brandon Baker." I grasped her hand in a polite greeting.

"Very nice to meet you Brandon," she smiled in exchange. "So, are you from around here?"

"No, no. I'm actually from Medicine Hat. A couple of hours east of here. I just moved up here this week. Had to with my new job offer." I decided to play up the high-paying job. Whatever it took to maintain her interest.

"Oh wow, a new job, how exciting. So what industry are you in?" She leaned casually against the bar, causing a slight arch in her back. I couldn't help but follow every flawless curve with my eyes. She seemed well aware of all my interests.

"Ummm … Oh, the drilling rigs. I'm going to work on the rigs with my cousin. He got me the job. How about you? Are you from around here?"

"No, I'm from Saskatchewan. I'm a small-town girl. I came out here for university. But it turns out I wasn't as dedicated to my studies as I thought. Now I'm pursuing a Ph.D. in my true passion. Which I haven't figured out yet." She grinned, her cheeks flushed slightly. "I'm a personal trainer for the time being. At a gym on the West Side."

"A personal trainer? Hey, there's nothing wrong with that." I drew in a deep breath. Slowly expanding my chest to its full capacity and pulling in what little gut I had. I couldn't let this one get away. My first night in Calgary, and I could hook up with a super-fox. A personal trainer to boot. The guys back home would freak.

"Yeah, I enjoy it. Beats sitting at a desk all day. And it keeps me in shape." She stood up from the bar, stretching her arms back, unwittingly exposing her firm chest. Or perhaps the move wasn't as innocent as it seemed.

"Yes, your shape is very good. I mean, you …"

She laughed, slapping me playfully on the chest. "It's okay. I'm glad you like it. I work hard for it. So, the drilling rigs, huh? I have a couple of friends with boyfriends that work the rigs. Seems they make some pretty good money. Sounds like a good opportunity."

"Yeah, this was my first week, and all I did was sit in a training room. But I've made more money than ever before."

As the conversation continued, I slowly relaxed. Growing more confident that she was interested in me. Whether it was for who I was, or for the money I made, it didn't really matter. All I wanted was her naked. And for the moment, it seemed like a possibility. We were getting well acquainted. Our flirting getting to the point of us playfully bumping and rubbing up against each other. I had almost completely forgotten about Nate and Steve.

"Hey Brando! Oooh! Oooh! There you are little buddy! Wondered where you'd gotten to." Nate's unmistakable voice came from the other end of the bar.

I was a little nervous about sharing my bounty with the big man himself. Concerned that he may tempt her away from me, or he was serious about having to share with him. Steve didn't worry me so much. But Nate just had that way about him. He sidled up to us, and to my relief, I saw that he had acquired a blushing blond of his own, secured like a trophy under his right wing.

"Where's Steve-o?" Nate screamed over the music now blaring through the bar. The band had just started into a new set.

"I don't know." I leaned closer to Nate to muffle our conversation from Katy, in the hope of diverting his attention. "Last time I saw him, he was over at the corner working some girls."

"And you left him! You left your leader, dude?" Nathan turned to Katy with an accusing glare.

"Oh, yeah. Nathan this is Katy, Katy this is Nathan."

Nate held his hand high to Katy's, slapping hers with a strong high five, "Oh- hoh … Katy. Now I see why Brando's ditched us." He winked at her before turning back to me and placing a hand on my shoulder. "Can't blame you Brando, she's a little fox but we must find Stevie. Time to move the show along my friend. Say goodbye to your little honey there, or get her to come along. We're off down the street to the Melrose, I think. Unless we're tempted to stop in somewhere else along the way. The night is young, and we have many places to visit." He turned into the crowd, placed a hand to his mouth, and gave the call. "Oooh! Oooh!!" Across the bar, a lone hand shot into the air. "Haha! There's Steve-o. Hey Steve-o, buddy, it's time to move!"

Panic set in. I didn't want to leave, not yet. I couldn't just leave her like this. Would I ever see her again?

I turned to Katy who surprisingly looked just as disappointed as I felt. "Well, I … Are you here with anyone else?"

"Yeah, I've got my roommate and some friends over by the pool tables." She pointed to the billiards area at the back of the bar.

"Brando! Come boy, it's time to MOVE!" Nathan called as he shoved his way through the crowd toward Steve.

"Listen, I've got to go. I really don't want to, but … well, this is my first time in Calgary, and they're my friends. So, I guess we're going down to Melrose. Do you know where that is?"

"Yeah, it's down a few blocks. It's nice. A bit trendier than here, but you'll like it."

"I'm sure I'd like it a lot more if you came with me."

She blushed again. "Well, I'll try, but I can't promise anything. You know how it is."

A strong hand poked back through the crowd and grabbed hold of my arm. "Brand! It is time to go! Now!"

A yank finally separated me from Katy, pulling me through the sea of people. "Bye, " I called out to her. "It was nice meeting you. Hope to see you later." I watched as the mouth of the crowd closed behind me and erased Katy from sight.

I pushed out the door and into the fresh night air. Nate came up to my right and clamped a heavy arm around my shoulders, while Steve pulled up to my left to get in on the conversation as we moved down the sidewalk.

"Listen, Brand, buddy" Nate began. "It's okay. This is your first time in a place of this caliber. But you have to be careful dude. You just about got sucked in man."

I didn't have a clue what Nathan was talking about as he shook his head at my confused expression. "It's our fault just as much as it is yours. Stevie, we have to pay more attention to the Brandinator here. He can't be trusted on his own right now. There's too much temptation."

These guys are fucking crazy, I thought. I'd had enough. "What the fuck are you talking about? Aren't we supposed to pick up chicks? Isn't that what this night is all about? I was doing good back there. She was hot."

"Oh my God. Phew! Nice catch Nate. I didn't realize how sucked in he was.

Listen to me Brando. Man, we are your friends, okay. I understand you're new and unexperienced. Nate is right."

I stopped, suddenly furious at the bullshit the guys were giving me. Why would they take me away from her? "Would one of you fuckers tell me what the fuck is going on? What the hell are you talking about?"

"Whoa! Whoa, boy!" Nate settled his hands on my shoulders, holding me firmly in place while looking me square in the eye. "Listen to me, Brand. I'm your friend. And that's your cousin Steve over there. He's your friend too, and family. Remember he got you that kickass job."

"Of course I fucking remember you idiot!" I was emotionally deranged, caught somewhere between rage and fear.

Suddenly, Nate's open palm came out of nowhere, landing straight across my face and nearly knocking me on my ass.

"Holy shit, Nate, he's delirious." Steve whispered in Nate's ear as the two looked at me with dumbfounded expressions.

Nathan continued to hold me in place. After the slap he'd just delivered, he had my full attention.

His voice boomed down the sidewalk. Demanding the attention of more than one passerby. "Now you listen to me Brandon! Me and Stevie are your only true friends down here. You have to put complete faith in our guidance! So listen up, because I don't want to have to hit you again!"

"I'm all in favour of that," I replied.

"All right then. Now I need you to understand that this is not the small town from which you came. That girl back there, the first one you met tonight—you think she's the one? Don't be a retard, young Brando. Look around you," he motioned with his hand. "How many women do you see?"

I turned my head quickly from side to side and then returned my gaze to Nate before I got another beating. "I don't know, twenty maybe?"

"Exactly. You see, what happened to you in there is common with newbies. We just don't want to see you go down like that man. Okay?"

I nodded slowly in acknowledgment even though I still understood nothing.

"So many guys come here, fresh from small towns, and they meet a girl at the first bar they walk into. And next thing you know, they're in the mall carrying shopping bags for their girls. And walking those little pussy poodle dogs, with the life sucked right out of them. Is that what you want Brando? Huh? You don't want to spend your time walking poodles and picking up poodle shit in little plastic baggies, do you?" Nathan's huge hands shook me back and forth violently.

"No! Of course not!" I said whatever it took to make him stop. Finally, Steve grabbed on to Nate. His familiar touch soothed the madness. "Whoa, big guy, take it easy. I think you got to him."

Nate let go and stepped back, thanking Steve for the intervention.

"Listen Brand," Steve cut in. "It's just that, there's so much pussy walking around down here. You owe it to yourself to at least look at the menu. Look at you man. You dress well, you got some style, you got that look to you. I see big things down here for you buddy. Well, not big chicks, but you know what I mean. Unless you're into the big ones that is, and I'll back you on that. Some of 'em really give a hundred percent."

"No, no man. I'm not into the big ones."

"You know what I mean though, eh buddy?"

"Yeah. Yeah, I get it." I said, rubbing the side of my face.

"Just take some time man. The city is crawling with women so don't get hooked on the first one you see. Did you tell her we're going down to Melrose?"

"Yeah."

"Well, if she's really interested, she'll meet you there, right?"

"I guess."

"Right on then. Forget about her, and let's keep moving." We stepped up the pace and continued in the direction of Melrose down the crowded sidewalk. I couldn't help but sneak a peek back behind us when Nate's attention was elsewhere, in hope that Katy may be following. But she wasn't.

23

Melrose was a trendier place, just as Katy said. But it wasn't a snooty place as one might expect. Yes, there were people dressed up in suits and ties and drinking martinis. But martinis are a wild and crazy time when sucked down a funnel and a hose. It was another first of many for me that night.

"Oooh yeah!" Nathan announced upon entering. Some of the patrons recognized the call and looked up in excitement. A girl in a tight skirt getting to the bottom end of a hose took her lips off, accidentally spilling some of the drink down her cleavage before placing her thumb over the end.

"Natey!" She yelled, throwing the hose at the bartender, who struggled to cap it before its contents soaked the surrounding crowd. Some guys with suit jackets removed and ties hanging loosely around their necks, turned toward Nate and raised their glasses in welcome. While the sexy little hose sucker came running into his arms.

"Hey baby. Nice form on the hose, you dirty girl." Nate turned on the charm.

She pushed herself away from him slightly and giggled, slapping his cheek teasingly. "Jealous, Natey?"

"Pamela, this is Stevie. You remember him, don't you honey?"

"Hello Stevie, very nice to see you again." Pam leaned her head against Nate's chest, addressing Steve with her fluttering long eyelashes that made Steve's face turn pink.

"And this here baby, is the newest member of our entourage. Meet Steve's little cousin, Brando."

"Brandon, actually, but Brando will work." I said as I lightly grasped Pamela's hand.

"Oooooh, he's cute" She winked. "Can I keep him?" She giggled, running a suggestive finger up the centre of my chest and toying with the buttons on my shirt.

"Boys, this here is Pamela," Nathan repeated. Calling her by her full name in his best *Borat* accent, which wasn't half bad. "Pamela, let's go get something to drink, shall we? I'll have whatever spilled down your tits." Nathan got another giggle and playful slap as the couple made their way toward the anxious crowd. It seemed Nathan knew everyone judging by the rounds of 'high fives' he received before grabbing the hose from the bartender and finishing off the concoction.

Steve and I followed the reunited lovebirds to a round of introductions. There was a Mike, a Dickie, a guy they called Hanso, and another Steve. For the females, there was a Melissa and a Jen. They were all downtown workers of one type or another—an accountant, some computer nerds, a legal secretary, and a bank worker. They were good-time people, blowing off some steam after a long week. Dickie slapped a large pitcher of rum and Coke into my hand and the rounds kept coming.

In about half an hour, I had a new best friend. Hanso was a regular guy. A pencil pusher, whose hair and shirt were in shambles. His coat and tie were nowhere to be found. He was a drunk accountant with something to say. He leaned on the bar beside me, arm over my shoulders, explaining an important part of his day. Apparently, everyone else in the crowd knew to avoid him at moments like this, so I was his sole audience. His words came out violently slurred. The excessive spit coming from his mouth forced me to protect my drink with my hand over the top of my glass. Hanso never did catch the hint.

"So I said, 'Fuck you Dave'." Hanso went on with his story. Repeating that one line of his tale for the fifth time in a row due to the many digressions he got caught up in. Causing him to skip like a broken record. He never did explain who Dave actually was.

"So I said, 'Fuck you Dave. You can't write that shit off!' People just don't understand Brando." A severe case of the hiccups now added to Hanso's slurred speech. I could see that even he had lost interest in his own story by this time, but he still went on like a true rambling drunk. "You can't just do that shit. They don't get it," he continued, slamming down his glass in frustration and splashing his drink all over the bar onto our clothes and the floor below. "Ah, fuck. I'm sorry about that man. Shit. I'm really sorry about that. Hey, bartender, can I get a rag down here? HICC—"

I remained at the bar with Hanso. The level in my jug had hardly shallowed. The rounds of shots we'd consumed since arriving now took their toll, placing me into a depression. What with all the booze and Hanso's uplifting story, the excitement of downtown Calgary was diluting. All I could think about was Katy and how someone had probably moved into my spot beside her. Laughing and flirting, which I wished I could be doing.

While Hanso fought the bartender for a rag, I monitored my fellow horsemen. Steve-o was working his magic on Melissa in the corner. Nate meanwhile, busied himself by sucking a lemon wedge from Pamela's cleavage. Everyone was having fun. But I had to get away from Hanso. I liked the guy, but he was bringing me down. I started toward a casual escape, but good old Hanso returned before I could complete my getaway. I found myself a captive audience yet again. "Hey man, I found a rag." He began wiping randomly at the wet spots on the bar and my shirt.

"No man, really, it's okay. It's a dark shirt, it won't show once it dries."

"Ah yeah, right," Hanso put his arm around me and leaned over the bar once more. "Hey, you're all right man. I like you. It's like we just click, you know. Hey, look at me, Dude, let me tell you something."

I tried to avoid eye contact with Hanso, since I was somewhat embarrassed for him and I worried that he would misinterpret it for interest in his story.

He grabbed my face and forced it toward his, looking me directly in the eye. "Dude, man, I really like you, you know that? Hey, you know what?"

What I did know, is that I didn't like the look in his bloodshot eyes at that moment. The twinkle made me uncomfortable. Suddenly, my new best friend Hanso wrapped his hand around the back of my head, closed his eyes, gave a slight pucker to his lips, then leaned in.

As my mind worked diligently to decode exactly what was happening, an arm grabbed me from behind and pulled me from the line of fire just in time. The sudden loss of support sent Hanso stumbling across the floor to land on his face. To my relief he apparently decided to take advantage of this down time and have a little power nap.

I turned to thank my tall pig shaven buddy for saving my virgin lips. He really was a good guy after all. But to my surprise, it wasn't Nate who'd come to my rescue.

"Shit, Brandon, I have to say I'm a little insulted. I'm in way better shape than he is. You're just full of good times for everyone, aren't you." It was Katy.

I was so happy to see her that I pulled her in for a strong, heterosexual embrace. I ran my hands up and down her back, pressing her perfect female breasts to mine. I'd never been that forward before. But at that moment, I found myself desperate for the touch of a woman. She felt good, so very good, and she wasn't fighting off my desperate attempt to confirm my sexuality. So I held on a little tighter, for a little longer..

"Whoa, party boy! Listen stud, you gotta decide which team you're playing for. I don't mind some experimentation, but that's a little too much freak for me." She struggled to maintain the serious expression on her face, which eventually failed to laughter.

"Holy shit! Am I ever glad to see you! Thank you." Feeling the need to justify what Katy had just witnessed, I looked back down at Hanso in disgust, as he remained passed out on the floor. "Jesus. Anything goes here in the big city, eh? That fucking guy. Doesn't know when to cut himself off, I guess." I laced my response with a hint of anger, hoping to reassure Katy that Hanso wasn't my type.

"Seems I arrived just in time, Brandon," she winked. "I believe that man had full intentions of plucking your flower."

"Jesus, don't say shit like that," I shuddered. "Well, do you want a drink?"

Katy examined my drunken condition and again started to laugh. "I think you've had enough." She scanned the group, noting everyone's attention focused elsewhere. "Hey, how 'bout we get you out of here?"

I looked behind me at Steve and Nate who were having a good time and who most likely wouldn't even notice if I left. Then I remembered Nate's speech, and getting slapped in the face. "I don't know. I better not. I can't find my way back to Nate's. You can stay here though, can't you?"

"Well, it's not really my crowd. Come and let me show you a different side of the city," she said, putting her arms around me and pulling me in close until I could feel her breath on my neck. "It'll be fun, I promise. Oh hey, look," she pointed down to Hanso, who appeared to be coming around. "Your boyfriend's waking up."

I grabbed her hand and pulled her behind me toward the door. "Let's get the fuck out of here!"

24

We busted out onto the main street, greeted once again by the cool night breeze.

"Phew, that feels good," I said following Katy down the sidewalk. Simply having her hold my hand made leaving my friends worth it. *Don't leave the team. Yeah, right. They're making out with chicks while I get molested by Hanso. Fuck that. Besides, I got my cell. They can contact me—if they even notice.*

"Where are you taking me? You're not going to drug me and harvest my organs then sell them on Ebay, are you? Cause I heard that shit happens up here." I joked, kind of.

"Yeah, right. I can see the ad now, 'well used liver for sale. C'mon, we've got to get you a drink," she laughed. "But I'm done with booze for tonight. And guessing from your little sexual experimentation back there, you've had way too much."

"Hey, I was the victim back there. You know that, right?" She was right, I had had way too much to drink. But what else was there to do on a Friday night?

I let Katy have her way. Dragging me, zigging and zagging past the other pedestrians, while we took in the sights and sounds. Then she turned a hard left into some Hawaiian-looking coffee shop. It took my eyes a second to adjust. The bright canary yellow paint on the walls reflected the light from an overhead, fluorescent bulb. It wasn't at all where I expected Katy would take me on our first date, but then I'd only known her for about two hours. Small yet charming, the shop's service counter spanned the length of the room. The patrons followed a fashion I could best describe as 'hippy alternative', some with long dreadlocks and loose colourful clothing with beaded accents. Maybe it was a Jamaican coffee shop?

Behind the counter stood a large man with a dark complexion. He was dressed in standard restaurant kitchen apparel: white pants, white shirt, and a white apron with coffee stains straining around his very large waist.

Katy continued to hold my hand while we waited in line for our turn and then stepped up to the imposing figure at the counter. "Hey Sammy," she said.

The man behind the counter grunted with a single raised eyebrow. His way of asking for our order.

"My friend here needs a very large bottle of water. Then I'll get two extra-large, extra specials to go please," she said.

Sammy made his way around the brew station like he'd done it thousands of times before. He first went to the cooler and tossed over a large bottle of water to Katy who immediately cracked the lid and handed it over to me. "Start chugging," she ordered. "We gotta make sure you can last the rest of the night."

I followed her command and drank. It was just what I needed, I felt the cold water make its way through my dehydrated body, reviving my organs, slowly restoring life and diluting the toxins that had invaded my bloodstream.

I paid attention to the "extra special" good old Sammy was brewing up in our extra- large cups. My knowledge of coffee bars was limited to the drive through window at Tim Horton's. There was a lot of popping, hissing, and steaming. Along with a couple of small explosions, which Sammy took completely in stride.

Our order complete, Sammy passed the drinks to Katy. I quickly stepped forward, offering money for the service. The total amounted to more than any bottle of water and two coffees ever should. I followed Katy outside, where we took a right back down the sidewalk. I offered to take my coffee from her, but she quickly refused. "After you finish your water!" she said, which I didn't understand, but had the feeling I wasn't supposed to either.

"What happened to your friends?" I asked, in attempt to break the silence.

"I don't know. I left them back at Morgan's."

"So, you're out wandering the streets by yourself?"

"Don't let the big city horror movies fuck you up. I feel safer here than in a lot of the small towns. There are some areas to avoid, but once you learn, it's pretty easy to stay out of trouble. I like it here. You can be yourself. Nobody judges you.

No matter how weird you can possibly get, there's always someone weirder. Back home in Saskatchewan, everyone had to walk a straight line. But most of them were just good actors."

She was original, in an interesting way. Looking around, I could see what she meant. There were no boundaries here; anything went. In downtown Medicine Hat, you're pretty much guaranteed that everyone will be dressed roughly the same. No wild or unusual hairdos or outfits, just the same ol' blah.

"You going to fill me in on where we're going, or is it a secret?" My head filled with the vision of a warm room, candles, a bed laced with fresh rose petals, and the two of us crawling all over each other. Exploring our naked, sweaty…

"No, it's a secret."

Oh ho! A secret spot, eh, you sexy little…

We came to a park. Toward the middle of the park, where it was a bit darker, we took a seat on a bench. I looked around to find that the park was only a block long and maybe half a block wide. From where we sat, one could easily reach the other side in about ten long strides. It wasn't for muggers, or serial killers to hang out in. Just a nice break in the concrete. Some large trees created the illusion that we weren't surrounded by giant cement structures. The interior foliage was broken with cobblestone paths lined with the occasional park bench. In the space around us, people lay, hanging out on the grass. One guy was playing some bongos while another was blowing softly on a sax. Rather than scary, the place was actually quite relaxing.

"This is it, your secret spot? You prefer this to the bars?" I asked.

She looked at me with a grin beneath slightly raised eyebrows and a cocked head. "Well, if you're good at keeping secrets, I'll be honest with you. I hate bars. I can't afford them, and I hate hanging around people who get all dressed up to get drunk and make asses of themselves. That's all we did back home, get drunk. Spent a fortune making ourselves sick. Wasted the whole next day in bed, and then did it all over again the next night. I just got tired of the whole scene, you know."

She lowered her head, fidgeting with her coffee cup. I sensed she was waiting for my response. Whether I would accept her crazy views, or flee to the nearest overpriced establishment, never to be heard from again.

I swilled back the rest of my water. "Ah, well, no morning hangover sounds like a pretty disturbed way to start the day. But what the hell, I'm into new things."

I leaned back and stretched my arm along the bench behind her, before using my other arm to reach for my coffee sitting between us. Again, she yanked it away.

"What the— C'mon, I finished my water. I'm feeling pretty sober now. What's the issue here?"

"Easy Romeo, first things first." Then she did something unexpected. Something I hadn't considered up to that point. But when she did it, everything began to make sense. I reviewed the short time we'd spent together. The things she'd said, the places she hung out at, and it was all so obvious. I mean, a cup of coffee in the park on a Friday night?

She pulled out a fatty—a joint, that is. To my hometown crowd, it was also known as "devil weed." The only true poison for a redneck was booze and not the pussy stuff either; we're talkin' beer or whiskey. Marijuana, on the other hand, well, that was fucked-up flower child shit. It made ya go all weird, and once you did it, you'd never be the same. *"No son, just stick with the good old alcohol,"* fathers would caution their young. *"It's what's right."*

The look on my face said that this was not a normal event for me.

She wasn't shy about flashing it around either, holding it up to my face and waving it around like a legal substance. The park was dimly lit, but not dark enough to hide our secret … and illegal doings.

She held the doobie up in the air like a beacon in the night, sending me into panic mode. "Ah, Katy, I know I'm new to the city and all, but should you really be waving that thing around like that?"

"What's wrong?" She giggled. "Don't panic, stud. Look around you. Everyone here is stoned; nobody cares. Here, look," she reached out to a couple relaxing on the grass beside the bench and slapped the guy lightly on the leg. "Hey, buddy," she said, while he glanced up at her with a friendly smile. "Sorry to bug you, but my friend here is a little new. Do you smoke grass?"

Our new friend took notice of me peeking around the side, nervously awaiting an answer.

"Phfft! I'm high right now." He laughed. With his telltale squinty eyes, I'm pretty sure I'd seen his face on a wanted poster back home. "We got some more if you need some," he offered.

"No, thanks. We're good." Katy left them to their business, turning back to me with a know-it-all smile on her face. "See, I told you. Nobody cares. Let me guess, you're not into this kind of thing."

I tried my best to be casual and blend in with the rest of the junkies in the park, but this was definitely on the dark side of exciting for me. I'd heard it all before. How it wasn't addictive, and how it was a lot better than alcohol. But whose word do you trust, the drunk's or the stoner's? It was an intense moral battle.

"Brandon, relax. I know this is probably a little out of the ordinary where you come from, but up here it's a pretty regular thing. Look around. See over there, those people have one going right now, and nobody's even looking twice at them. Really, Brandon, it's no big deal."

I took a deep breath, leaned back on the park bench and looked around at the other park dwellers. At first, I didn't even realize how relaxed and unusually mellow everyone was. Sure enough, looking more closely, I noticed the blazing red embers being passed around and a faint, sweet smell of cannabis in the air.

Don't get me wrong. I'd been around the stuff before. Heck, I'd even tried it once. Though I'd been too drunk at the time to tell if it had any effect. But stoners—I was sitting in a park surrounded by stoners. I go to downtown Calgary for one night and look what has become of me.

Katy let the pressure off my hand, sensing I wasn't going to run away.

She continued giggling. "I'm going to make a wild guess here. You've never done this before, have you?"

I was at a loss for words. This whole situation had come from out of nowhere. Katy was so perfect, sexy, funny, and great to hang around with. I felt we were on the same page, had so much in common. And then she turns out to be a park junkie.

"Listen," she continued, "back home in high school, it was booze. Grass was a drug for losers. We drank the school years away. A couple of friends died from driving impaired, you know that old story. Then I moved here. One night, I went to a small get together with some new friends I'd met and there was no booze, not a drop. Instead, they whipped out joints and started passing them around. It scared the shit out of me at first, but I had been hanging with them for a while and everyone seemed really nice and sane—you know, down to earth—so I tried it out."

"And?"

"Now, I prefer it to alcohol. I mean, see the people around you. Do you see anyone out of control? Everyone's just mellow. It's a totally different drug,

Brandon. All those people who badmouth it are wrong. It's cleaner than alcohol, and safer. It's nice."

"Yeah, but I got drug tests for work y'know."

"Have you been tested yet?"

"Well, yeah."

"Brandon," she grabbed my hand again, looking up at me. "I'd never force you to do something that you don't want to. But I promise that nothing bad will happen. In fact, I bet you'll have the best night of your life."

She was a hell of a spokeswoman for the pro cannabis movement.

Her speech ended, and now it was time for business. She placed the joint to her lips, took out a lighter and sparked it up. Just like that, in the middle of the park.

She took a long drag and then passed it over. It was judgment time. Either I smoke up or I run. I exhaled hoping to deflate some of the built-up anxiety. Her eyes sparkled with encouragement. I placed sin to my mouth and began sucking hard. If I was gonna do it, I may as well do it right.

She cheered me on from the sidelines. "Good, good."

I stopped and pulled the joint from my mouth.

"Okay, hold it. Hold it as long as you can."

I could only bear a couple of seconds before the giant plume exploded from my lungs. Followed by a hacking, heaving cough. *Oh shit! What have I done?*

25

After the smoke cleared and my hacking stopped, I leaned back on the bench again and began a mental tally of the damage. I heard Katy giggling and clapping. The guy she had spoken to earlier was now sitting up and looking over the arm of the park bench, cheering me on. "Bravo, man. That was huuuuge! So, how do you feel?" he asked, excited for the tale of my awakening.

"How do I feel?" I repeated slowly. *How do I feel … how do I feel. What a strange question*. What I expected to happen didn't happen. There was no sudden onset of horrible paranoia, no rocking in the fetal position and muttering nonsense words to myself. There was no rubber band around my arm, no needles, no pool of vomit on the ground beneath me. I wasn't foaming at the mouth while begging for another hit, and Jesus wasn't communicating to me via someone's dog. *Television's full of shit man.*

Instead, the dim park brightened. The bongos found harmony with the sax. Suddenly, everything was … easy. My foot began tapping, my head bobbing in time. I felt relaxed yet curious. Keen to observe new colours and experience new sensations. I was wide-eyed, taking in the scene as my mouth arranged itself in an overzealous smile.

"I feel goooood man! Really good!"

Katy and the stranger joined together in a moment of celebration as they clasped hands in honour of my coming into junkie-hood. I was okay with that. I was okay with everything.

"How's your mouth?" Katy asked.

My mouth, why would there be anything wrong with my mouth? I drew my tongue back in, smacked my lips a bit to investigate the possible reason for her odd interest.

"Mmmm, dry. Really, really dry." For no reason at all, I burst into gut-wrenching laughter.

"Here, you can have your coffee now." She handed me the warm beverage.

Excited to finally taste the mysterious coffee, I took a sip. Finding it had cooled to the perfect temperature, I took a larger gulp.

"It's good. What's in it?"

"It's half special blend coffee and half cappuccino with a shot of espresso."

"Well, it is indeed extra special." I took another swig. The invigorating ingredients rushed through my body, amplifying my senses. I stood up. Full to the brim with confidence and cannabis, I had a sudden urge to mingle. I looked down at Katy, grabbed her by the hand and pulled her up from her seat, while she giggled excitedly.

"You brought me here. So let's mingle with the locals."

We walked around the end of the bench and joined our friends on the lawn, introducing ourselves and settling into the mix. It made sense now to relax peacefully and hang out with a bunch of people in a dark park. As opposed to being smashed out of my mind, blowing hundreds of dollars and hoping to pick up women in the bar.

The scene was totally different for me. Katy and I spent the following hours meeting new people. One person would introduce us to the next, and on it went until I shortly lost count. We lay in the grass absorbing the music and the various stories people told. Occasionally, a freshly-rolled joint would get passed through the crowd. No one ever got violent or even the least bit hostile. At one point, a bike-mounted police officer rolled slowly through our gathering, hardly batting an eye at the smoky haze. And what were we doing, really? Would he take us in for relaxing on the grass and playing bongo drums in the park? There were far bigger crimes taking place elsewhere in the city. This bust was hardly his ticket to the front page of the local paper.

I found, in this little park, people not only from all over Canada but from all over the world. Switzerland, Brazil, Australia—all in this amazing little park. People with different stories, different cultures, and languages were all around us.

It reminded me of those misfit groups back in high school that became outcasts because they just didn't fit in. All that time, we missed all those stories and all the great personalities out of sheer ignorance. Back in the bar, everyone was probably so drunk you wouldn't understand anything they were saying. But here, in magical story land, I was glued to my spot, taking in all the tales of adventure from exotic lands.

The people I spoke with seemed far removed from the everyday stresses of work and life, at least of the ones I knew. Some spoke of strange jobs like spending summers out west in the sun picking grapes by the bucket and then stomping on them barefoot in large wooden tubs to harvest the juice for wine. Others recounted tales of travelling through foreign countries with nothing more than a backpack full of clothes and a few dollars in their pockets. It was wild stuff.

There were none of the drunken bar legends from back home of working sixteen-hour days covered in grease. Battling temperatures of thirty below, while holding frozen tools and risking frost bite. I just listened. Somehow, my upcoming adventure of working on the drilling rigs for good coin just didn't fit in.

Katy and I sat comfortably listening with perma smiles. She wrapped her arms around me and leaned her head on my shoulder. It was good. The whole experience was like a dream.

Riiiing! Riiiing!

It took a minute for me to recognize the sound of my own phone. I pulled it from my pocket, checking the display. *Steve. Shit.*

"Steve, what's up?"

"What's up Brand? you all right? Where the fuck are you man? We've been lookin' for you for the last ten minutes."

Steve's words came out slurred. I could feel the spit through the phone. In the noisy background, I could hear Nate repeating some primal chant.

"Ten minutes? Dude, I've been gone for like three hours." I had to yell into the phone so he could hear me over the noise in the bar.

"Well, where the fuck are you? You're missin' out! We got some hotties!"

"I'm with Katy!"

"Who?"

"Katy. The girl from Morgan's, remember?"

"Oh, that sexy little thing!"

"Yeah, well, she ended up at Melrose and picked me up." I heard Steve explaining the situation to a hyped-up Nate.

"Oh, yeah, suck it Katy, you dirty bitch!" Nathan yelled into the phone.

"So, are you all right man?" Steve cut in. "You need us to come getcha?"

"No, no. I'm fine. I've got my phone and Nate's address. I'll meet up with you guys later."

"All right, man, if you're sure. You give me a call if you need me, right?"

"You bet. Talk to you—," Steve hung up before I could finish. He was truly concerned for my safety.

I didn't care. I was having the time of my life in the park with my new girl. Away from the drunken limelight. Eventually, our new friends began leaving the park, moving onward with the night. The weed had taken its toll and my eyes were squinted to tiny slits.

Katy and I decided to move on as well. Having both developed a serious case of the munchies, Katy wrapped her arm through mine and led me down the street. While we walked along, I realized how cold I was. Katy was too, as she snuggled in closer. I began wondering where I was going to stay for the night. I didn't really want to go back to Nate's and deal with the afterparty crowd. Unfortunately, I knew Katy wouldn't be inviting me to share a bed with her. She didn't strike me as the type. But she didn't seem like a park dwelling pothead either.

"Hey Katy?" I said. "Where the hell do you live? Are you staying down here?"

She looked up at me with tired eyes and a relaxed smile. "Actually, I rent a place with a couple of friends out in the West Side. But for now, I'm house-sitting for my uncle who has a condo not far from here. He travels a lot for work. So he lets me stay at his place while he's gone. It's nice, gives me some alone time." She examined my expression, reading between the lines.

"You can come and stay over if you want. But I'm not going to suck it, as your friend Nathan would put it." She grinned slyly.

I blushed, not realizing she had overheard the earlier phone conversation. "Well, suck it or not, I'd be stupid to turn down the invitation."

She stopped suddenly, turned and threw her arms around me then pressed her lips to mine. It was totally unexpected and completely fucking awesome. Her hips moved slightly as I pressed myself against her. She giggled at my enthusiasm and then pushed me back. "Naughty, naughty." She grabbed my hand and we continued down the street to an all-night pizza joint.

By the time we reached the Pizza Baron, which sold pizza by the slice, I was starved like never before. Given the number of slices I was able to devour, it would have been cheaper to buy the whole restaurant chain. I made a complete pig of myself. It would have been embarrassing if I wasn't so high, but at the time I didn't care. Katy, despite her slight build, managed to keep pace.

After the feast, I was ready for a warm, clean, comfy bed. "Take me home and have your way with me, please." I smiled.

Luckily, her uncle's place was only a few blocks away. More posh than Nathan's building, its high-speed elevator stirred the pizza in my belly. We entered the suite laughing and stumbling. The place was amazing, but I was too tired to take it all in. Katy led me to one of the bedrooms, turned on the TV and disappeared into the ensuite. I imagined the sexy lingerie she was putting on for the occasion, but when the door opened, she appeared wearing baggy sweat pants and an oversized T-shirt. It was all right though. She still looked incredible.

We lay together and watched television for a while. I can't remember what was on, but it didn't really matter, since a few minutes later we were both sound asleep. Snuggled in each other's arms.

26

When I awoke the next morning, as soon as I remembered where I was, I rolled over and quickly searched for Katy. To my relief, I found her lying in bed beside me. We had separated during our slumber, each claiming our own personal space. I searched the room for a clock. The one on the nightstand read 8:02 am.

I rested my head on the pillow and recalled last night's events. Nathan, Steve, meeting Katy, Katy rescuing me from the oddly-named, bi-curious drunk. Then the coffee and the park—and the weed. I checked in with myself and realized I had no headache, the room wasn't spinning, and I felt well rested. The only thing uncomfortable at the time was a dry mouth. I remembered Katy saying this was her uncle's place and that he was out of town on business. That meant we were alone. I looked over at her. She was peacefully asleep. I hated to leave her side. I couldn't remember when or if I'd ever felt this comfortable with a woman before. Usually, I woke up trashed from the night before and then tried to silently sneak out of the house before whoever I had spent the night with woke up.

This morning was different. I wasn't hung over. I remembered everything from the night before, including who I had come home with, and I was happy to be where I was. I had absolutely no regrets. I was still concerned about the effects of the cannabis, but so far, so good. I wasn't out giving blowjobs in the alley for another hit like in the commercials.

I leaned over and ran my hand down Katy's back, and her ass, just a little. It was an accident. Really. Then I lightly kissed the back of her neck. It was a ballsy move, kissing a girl I hardly knew on the back of the neck when she was passed out. *Score! You go, Brandon!* I slowly crawled out from under the covers on a quest for water.

I walked through the sunlit hall to a fantastic living room beyond. The morning light beamed in through the giant floor-to-ceiling windows, which led to a full balcony. I continued on through the kitchen to the dining room where I found a water cooler standing in the corner. I gulped down a couple of glasses, a stream of water trickled down my chin. I filled the glass again and took myself on a tour.

There was another, smaller guest bedroom and a large main bathroom with a fancy steam shower. After walking around a bit, I was back in the grand living room. It was stylishly decorated with hardwood floors throughout, a large flat-panel television set attached to the far wall and a sophisticated stereo system. I looked out at the view beyond the deck. Wow! What an awesome sight! We were way up high. It must have been a hundred floors, or at least it felt like it.

I was leaning against the glass overlooking the morning skyline when I felt her warm arms wrap around me, followed by a soft moist kiss on my back. "Good morning," she whispered softly in my ear. "How're you feeling?"

"Great. I feel amazing." I turned toward her and our lips naturally drew together with desire.

"Thanks for last night," I said when we broke. My hands slid daringly down beneath her sweat pants to that sexy ass I'd been waiting to get my hands on. She didn't even flinch. "You were right. It was the best time I've had."

Her smile changed slightly as I lightly bit her bottom lip. I felt her own hands slide down to my ass, while a glint of hunger flickered in her eyes.

She started kissing my neck, running her tongue lightly up to my ear. "I'm really glad you stuck around this morning because I think the best way to start the day after a great night is with a great fuck."

I sprung to attention so fast I almost ejaculated on my own face as she grabbed both my hands and led me toward the steam shower.

She pulled me into the bathroom, slammed the door behind us, and cranked on the hot water. She then reached down and started tearing open the buttons on my pants.

It was all the permission I needed to start ripping into my present. Lucky for me, Katy was wearing sweats, I simply slid the elastic waist over her firm ass and they fell in a heap around her ankles, revealing a sexy pair of pink lace panties. Not quite a thong, but goddamn close.

I knew exactly which direction I was headed but she was still fumbling with the buttons on my pants, obstructing my path. I shoved her back and ripped my pants off Ron Jeremy style. I left my underwear for her to take care of—they were buttonless! I yanked her shirt over her head to find her naked breasts. There they were, finally, just as I had imagined: perfect, round, firm. Her small nipples stood erect.

I pulled her to me hard, simultaneously sliding my hands down to her underwear, prying them off and kicking them to the side. Our naked bodies pressed hard together and our open mouths began to explore. As the head of my shaft spread her moist lips below, she moaned into my ear, anxious for penetration. I forced her back against the sink, her back arched, and my tongue found its way down her neck to her breasts. I slipped a nipple between my lips and then continued downward toward her stomach. Unable to detain myself any longer, I dropped to my knees and lifted her leg over my shoulder, her essence called to my primal needs. She was dripping wet. I closed my eyes and breathed her in deeply, again and again. I held back as long as I could. Wanting to savour the scent of her pureness before soiling her with my lust. My fingers clenched hard to her thighs and saliva began to trickle down my chin. I had lost sanity. Another moan clinched the trigger and I surrendered fully to my sexual instinct, bending under and taking her swollen lips in mine. I collected every drop from her weeping petals.

She responded. Groaning loudly, she lifted herself fully onto the counter, spreading herself wide, then grabbed the back of my head and thrust her hips forward. Our bodies became slippery with sweat as the hot steam filled the room. Her salty essence funnelled into my open mouth and I drank down all that was offered.

After a few minutes, her ass grew sore from sitting awkwardly on the counter so we broke position. She pulled me into the hot shower and pushed me to the wall. Her tongue chased the streaming droplets down to my throbbing shaft, which she took deep in her mouth. I held back my release, both fighting my natural urge yet craving her touch.

After a while, she was taking on too much water so we broke position again. She stood and turned, quickly pressing one hand ahead to the wall then reached back for my cock with the other, pulling me in behind her. I again held myself back but she'd had enough foreplay. In response to my resistance, she thrust herself back, forcing me inside. The warmth of her around me had me begging for mercy. Her wet pussy pulsing, her body undulating, she persisted. Moaning loud, she left no time for me to catch my breath. *Hooooly fuuuuck! Don't blow! Don't blow! Think of something unsexy. Breathe, breathe! Five times five is … fifteen? Holy shit, holy shit!* I tried, God how I tried distracting my mind off the miracle bent before me. But Katy remained relentless, grinding harder, deeper, twisting and turning, wet and groaning.

I couldn't stop myself anymore; the intensity and the steam were suffocating. I was about to burst but I told myself I couldn't have it, not yet. I pulled out, opened the shower door and pushed her out, causing her to slip on the tile floor and fall hard on her ass. I rushed to help her up, afraid that her mood might be ruined. But she remained unfazed with full intention of continuing.

As I flung open the bathroom door, the air outside cooled our steaming bodies. I breathed in deeply, grasping for rejuvenation. I grabbed Katy and led her into the bedroom, throwing her wet body down onto the bed. I pounced on top of her and thrust myself inside her. She moaned with satisfaction, spreading herself acceptingly. I stayed on top, pounding on her harder and harder until finally she gave me what I wanted. Her back arched, and her legs quivered right down to her curled toes. I felt the river of warmth flow over my pulsing dick as she held herself for as long as possible until finally, her body relaxed. She lay in a euphoric state as I slowly continued sliding myself in and out, kissing her breasts softly. Without warning, she flipped me onto my back and climbed into full mount. She rode me hard; she had a mission and she dedicated herself completely to it. She fucked me hard and long, working to get it out as I simultaneously worked to hold it in, a battle I was destined to lose. Finally, clawing into her firm ass, I pushed up into her as fiercely as I could. We shared one final explosion as I came deep insider her, our combined tonic spilled out down her thighs to the sheets beneath. At last, our mutual needs fulfilled, we pulled up the covers, curled into each other, and snuggled in for an after-sex morning nap.

27

I woke to the ringing of my phone. I rolled out of bed, tracing the noise to my pants in a crumpled pile on the floor.

"Hello?"

"Brandon! Where the fuck are you, man?" Steve sounded as ugly as I'm sure he felt.

"Steve," I rubbed my hand over my face, allowing a moment for my brain to catch up. I looked at the clock on the nightstand. It was 11:00 am. "Steve, I'm at Katy's."

"Katy? Who the fuck is Katy?"

"Dude, we've been through this. Katy, the girl I met at Morgan's. She came and picked me up at Melrose, remember?"

"Man, I don't remember shit! Oooooh, my fucking head!"

"Little rough this morning buddy?" I chuckled. It was nice to hear the suffering of another's hangover.

"Oh Jesus, man, I just got up. I'm still trying to piece together what happened last night. All I know is I woke up this morning on Nate's couch feeling like a bag of shit. Couple of used condoms on the floor and some leftover pizza. My mouth tastes like shit. I'm pretty sure it isn't the pizza."

"Haha, nice buddy."

"No, man, I don't think she was nice at all."

"Don't let your friends see you!" I scratched the wound.

"Yeah fuck! So anyway, where the hell are you?"

"I'm not sure. Downtown, somewhere not too far off seventeenth."

"Well, we should get our shit together and hit the dusty trail."

Just as Steve was suggesting it, I felt Katy's soft lips from behind on my bare ass. She reached around front and started stroking my shaft, which immediately stiffened to her touch.

"I don't know man. I was thinking maybe I would hang out here a little longer," I turned, looking down at Katy for approval. "Possibly another night." She nodded then continued with her project.

"What? You know we're leaving for work tomorrow, right?"

"I know, I know. I'll be ready. What time are we leaving?"

"I'd like to get on the road about noon at the latest."

"Yeah, I'll be ready. Katy will make sure I get back either tonight or at the crack of dawn, I promise." There was a long pause on the other end.

"All right buddy. She must be some lay. You're a big boy, I guess. You better be ready to go by noon tomorrow or I'm gonna kick your ass something severe. Don't fuck this up."

"Don't worry Steve. I promise I'll be ready by then."

"All right buddy," the concern in his voice eased. "Enjoy yourself. I'll keep my phone with me at all times. Call me if you need anything!"

"I will man. Thanks." I hung up as Katy spun me around and pulled me down on top of her naked body for round two.

The second round was just as amazing as the first and had stirred up quite a hunger. I went to the kitchen and rummaged through the fridge, finding enough ingredients to whip up a couple of omelettes while Katy rinsed off in the shower. We ate our breakfast, then she convinced me to join her out on the deck for a morning joint. Dark clouds rolled in over the western mountains and gave foresight to a coming rain.

We got ready. It pained me to watch her get dressed but she was insistent on spending the day showing me around downtown. By the time we hit the street, the rain had already started. We kept sheltered as much as possible, running across the streets and ducking beneath the awnings. We spent the day going to the small shops, then to the pubs where we experimented with exotic ales and various live music of all types—Jamaican, African, Irish—all the while unable to keep our hands off each other. It was the perfect day. And as much fun as I was having cruising the town, deep down I couldn't wait to get her back to the condo.

Katy was amazing. I've never been one on one with a girl for that long and had such a good time. I was falling quick. I caught myself daydreaming about our possible future together more than once. I wanted to spoil her with my newfound wealth of money. Set her up in a nice place of our own and provide for her all the luxuries she deserved. The only issue being dragging my ass away from her to go to work.

But that's how it goes with infatuation, and my newfound love for her made me all the more eager to succeed at work so I could provide for us. I would go away for a week or so, make lots of money, and come back to spoil her. Thoughts of all the money I would be making and all the things we could do rolled in my head as I started recalculating my wages. It didn't take long for me to add up new motivation for going to work. Still, it wouldn't hurt my feelings if it got postponed another couple of days.

As enjoyable as the day was, however, there remained a continual nagging at the back of my mind about work and how I was going to get back to Steve's. I knew his place was a distance away, and I was fairly sure Katy didn't have a car. I didn't want to spoil the mood, but I knew I had to ask. "Katy, how the hell am I going to get home?"

"Home? You're not leaving now, are you? I was hoping you'd stay another night."

She placed a hand on my chest entrancing me with a saddened gaze.

"Well, I'm all for staying another night, and every night for that matter. But I have to leave town tomorrow for work. So, I have to be ready to leave first thing in the morning." She lowered her head disappointedly.

I felt like the love boat we were sailing on was starting to sink. So I searched frantically for a paddle and dug in deep. Holding her chin, I pulled her eyes back to mine.

"Hey, listen. I don't know where this weekend is going. Neither of us knows much about each other. But I had an awesome time and, well, I'd like to keep seeing you." I blushed, turning away in doubt that she felt the same. For all I truly knew, this could be just another weekend dope smoking sex romp.

It was her that turned my head back this time. "Brandon, of course I want to keep seeing you. What did you think, I do this type of thing every weekend with random guys?"

"No, I mean," I started tripping on my words. "I just want you to know that it wasn't just a one-nighter for me. I really like being with you. And I don't want to scare you away, but this whole thing is pretty serious for me." It was a true battle of brain versus penis to avoid using the mighty "L" word. In the end, the two powers agreed that it was too early and using it would most likely result in the three of us going home very much unsatisfied.

She smiled and pulled me in to her sweet lips. "Quit taking my lines." Then she pushed me back. "And just in case you took me for something I'm not, Mr. Baker, I don't do this thing all the time. And you better damn well call me every night that you're gone. And this better be serious for you, or I'll kick your ass!"

I smiled, glad to hear we were both on the same page. "Sounds good to me." We wrapped our arms around each other and pulled together. A little closer it seemed that time.

Day turned to night. We continued hopping from club to club, ducking into the odd alley or park to quickly smoke some more reefer. The Saturday night crowds started coming out of hiding, rested and recovered from their Friday night battles only to fall again.

We had a great time, finding booths in dimly lit corners of all the low-key night clubs so our public exhibitionism was shielded by the cloak of darkness. In between the making out, we also found some time to get to know each other personally. But mostly it was making out.

I was expecting to hear that she came from a family with lots of money. I was used to the college girls from Saskatchewan with rich farm parents. Living off Mommy and Daddy while doing whatever they wanted. But that wasn't her case. She was what she said she was—a failed student who, for the time being, was just doing what she loved. She lived with a couple of roommates on the West Side. It wasn't her ideal setup; she didn't really care for them, but it was what she could afford. She didn't have a car or even a cell phone. All she had was the bare essentials.

Admirable in a way, I suppose, but it wouldn't do. My girl shouldn't be living the life of a minimalist. Things were going to change for her in a big way, I would see to that.

The day turned to evening and the substances took their toll. Our minds grew dreary and tired so we decided it was time to head back. I had an excellent time around downtown, experiencing a whole new style of life. But truthfully, as the man I was, my thoughts never left her pants.

We began the cold trek home. Katy had to stop in quick at Morgan's bar again to check in with her friends for something. It didn't take long till we were back at her uncle's.

Inside, cold and damp from the rain, she went to the kitchen to boil some water for tea. Drinking tea was a little out of character for me, but then so was smoking my breakfast. She then went to the bathroom and turned on the steam shower. I'd never been more aroused by the sound of water sprinkling from a showerhead.

She returned to the kitchen where she removed from her pocket a small plastic baggy, the apparent reason for checking in with her friends on the way back. It looked like a bunch of small dried-up sticks. She split the group in half and placed what I guessed to be my half in my open palm.

I looked down at the small pile then back at her, puzzled. "Uh, they're beautiful, thank you?"

She giggled. "They're mushrooms."

"Mushrooms?" Hearing her explanation only confused me more.

"Yeah, you know, magic mushrooms."

Magic mushrooms. The term meant little to me. I had heard it mentioned on a movie before, and even heard a tale of some kids back home that had experimented with them many years ago. Apparently, it screwed them up pretty bad. Some urban legend about a mass murder spree before they disappeared into the wooded river valley. Once every couple of years, rumours would surface in the schools about sightings of the crazed mushroom killers.

"What do they do?" Another drug. I was beginning to feel burdened with over experimentation. I had already smoked the weed. What did it take with this girl? But I liked the weed. She was right about that. And then that other naked stuff that we did, that was neat too.

"They're like a hallucinogenic. Make you laugh a lot."

"Listen, Katy." The brain wedged itself between my cock and the girl insisting on some answers, "I've got to ask. Now don't get me wrong, I've had a great time with you. But … how many different drugs do you do? I mean weed the first day, mushrooms the next? I'm not going to wake up tomorrow with a rubber band strapped around my arm, am I?"

She laughed at my virginity. "No, no. I guess I can see how you would think that. So I'll let it go. Don't worry, I'm not a meth head or anything. I just stick with the natural stuff—weed, mushrooms, hash sometimes. Nothing hard. I'm a nature girl." She sung playfully, bobbing her head side to side.

"Well, is this shit going to fry my brain or something? I'm a little concerned. This is a lot of substance abuse in a weekend."

"Brandon.," she frowned. "I'm not forcing you to do anything. They're just mushrooms that grow in the forest. The high will last about four hours, then you'll be back to normal. They're a lot of fun as long as you don't take too many. Some people take too many and they get a bad high. But they don't fry your brain. I hardly do them at all. But I like to have some on special occasions."

"Special?" I looked at her quizzically.

She smiled, reaching behind me and pulling her body close. Her scent seduced my senses, bringing back memories. She whispered in my ear. "Have you ever had sex on mushrooms?"

My jaw fell slack as she backed away. "I've had mushrooms on my burger."

She laughed then leaned in 'til I could feel her breath in my ear. "I highly recommend it." Her moist tongue tickled my lobe.

That's it. She had me figured out. She untangled the complex puzzle that was me. I quickly got into the groove. "Okay, how do we do this shit? Shoot it, snort it, shove it up my ass, what?"

"Well, I'm not sure about any of that. Some people put them in their tea but that just gives me a body stone. Others put them in their food, but I think that interferes with the high. Bottom line is, they taste like shit! But I just shove them in my mouth, chew them quick and wash them down with some juice. It's quick and you get the best bang for the buck, I think."

I looked down at the grungy pile of spores. Having trouble believing all the life changing experiences I'd had in the last twenty-four hours. *Oh, what the hell, why stop now?* I looked up at Katy. "See you on the other side." We raised the mushrooms to our mouths and chewed frantically. It took all the willpower I had to shove them down my throat. She wasn't bullshitting about the taste. I finally took a huge swig of my juice to finish them off.

"Ahhhh," I let out after downing what was left of the juice. "Well you were right about the shitty taste!" I waited for a bit, holding on to the counter. I had no clue what was coming my way. "I don't feel any different."

She giggled and grabbed my hand, leading me toward the bathroom where

122

the hot steam shower waited. "Don't worry, it's coming. They take a bit of time. Let's warm up quick with a shower."

"Now that's what I'm talking about," I reached down playfully into her pants.

"Uh-uh, you have to wait," she slapped my hand away. "This is strictly a warm-up shower. Don't worry, we'll get to the good stuff."

And she meant it. We got into the bathroom and closed the door. She let me help her undress a bit and play a little touchy feely in the shower, but that was it. She knew it was killing me. I was rock hard the whole time. I eventually forced myself to relax and let the warm water wash away the chill from my body. From time to time, I would concentrate hard on whether I was high yet or not. Wondering when the magic would begin. It had been a while and I almost forgot that we took them.

Warmed up nicely, Katy turned off the shower then rushed out. Grabbing a towel, she patted herself down quickly and hurried out the door, closing it behind her. "Take your time and dry off, I'll be back to get you in a minute." She called as the door closed.

I did as I was told, slowly getting out of the shower and thoroughly drying off, waiting for her return. *What the fuck is going on here? What is she doing out there? This is getting a little too weird. Whew! It's hot in here, fucking hot! Hard to breathe!* I began rubbing my hair dry with the towel with my head bowed to the floor. *Hey, fuck me, that's some nice tile buddy's got in here. It looks kinda like a mountain, but I mean it's not a mountain, obviously, cause it's right here in the bathroom. You can't put mountains in a bathroom. It's a pretty big bathroom though. Hey, look, it's like one big piece of fucking tile. How's that even possible?*

Fascinated with the flooring, I got on my hands and knees to examine the tile and all its wonder. Then it hit me. *Wait a minute, what the fuck, Brandon? You're on your hands and knees molesting a bathroom floor. Something strange is going on here.*

With impeccable timing, the door flung open, banging into my side. Katy forced her head in the door to witness me in my glory—buck naked, ass up, feeling up her uncle's floor.

"Brandon?" Fully ashamed of the act she had just walked in on, I kept my head down and remained still. Hoping she would lose sight of me if I quit moving. "Are you all right? You're not getting sick are you?"

"Katy," I called back, my eyes held to the floor. "Are you high?"

She giggled, "I might be starting to feel something."

"Well, I think I'm high."

"Why are you feeling up the floor?"

"I guess I really like it."

"Okay, well how about you save some of that loving for me, tiger?" she dropped her towel and bent over to help me up.

I stood up straight. Both of us were naked. "Look Katy, I'd like to explain what I was doing down there, but I can't remember." I couldn't help what was coming. I no longer had the controls. "Isn't that funny? I can't remember."

"Haha, you are fucked, aren't you? C'mon." She led me out of the bathroom. Both of us were laughing hysterically down the hall, bumping back and forth off the walls naked.

We made it to the living room. Just as soon as my laughter started, it stopped as I took in the changes that had transformed the living room.

She had laid out a large comforter and pillows in the middle of the room, flickering candles placed sporadically. In the background playing on the stereo, I recognized The Fragile album by Nine Inch Nails. I never liked their music pre-mushroom, but I suddenly found it a lot catchier. The balcony curtains were drawn wide. I ventured over to take in the sparkly of the city lights. Forgetting about my complete nakedness, I stood bare for the world.

"Fuck me, this is awesome!" The choice of decoration perfectly complimented the high. Even distracting me from the sex, momentarily. Katy came up behind me and wrapped her warm arms around me. My skin tingled to her touch. I breathed in deep and exhaled. My body relaxed, and blended in to my surroundings like a chameleon. I gave up control to the vibe of the moment.

"You like it?" Katy whispered to my ear.

"Like it! I love it! I've never had anything like this before!"

She turned me away from the windows. "C'mon, let's sit." She led me back to the plush leather couch and handed one of two mugs from the coffee table filled with herbal tea. I took a sip. It was warm and replenishing. I could feel the mystical liquid tingle through my every vein.

We sat back in the couch with our arms and legs entangled, drinking our tea and talking about everything. The conversation was interrupted occasionally by uncontrollable fits of laughter. My eyes would water from too much laughing. I bent over, clutching my gut, my stomach and face clenched to the point of pain.

Time no longer existed, and the high suddenly turned in a new direction. The conversation stopped. We both took a moment to look around, familiarizing ourselves again with the surroundings we seemed to have distanced from while distracted in conversation.

The haunting music filled the room and mingled with the aroma from the candles while the flames pulsed to the beat. Then my nakedness and her nakedness became very real. As if she could read my thoughts, she reached over to the table again where sat another cup full of steaming liquid. Floating in the liquid was a small bottle. She removed the bottle and brought it to the couch, popping the lid open she squeezed some of the warm silky oil onto her palm. She rubbed it between her hands, then glided around and positioned herself behind me, wrapping her legs around my waist. I could feel the warm pulse of life through her breasts pressed to my back as she began rubbing the oil on my shoulders.

It was hot at first, then tingly, then cool and refreshing. She continued, getting a little more carefree and splashing it sporadically on my body and on hers. Then we fell off the couch to the blanket on the floor. She continued to give me the full body treatment, sculpting me erect with her hands.

The flickering of shadows awed my sense of vision, and the sliding of her hand with the pulse of the music excited my sense of touch. As she grew more aroused, her scent pushed through the saturated air to my nose. Instinctively powerful, it informed me of her desire, commanding my attention like blood to a shark. The hallucinogen had erased any trace of evolved being leaving only primal need. I grabbed and forced her to the blanket. I reached for the oil, splashing it on my live canvas, rubbing deeply, every finger a probing microscope, massaging, exploring. She lay with her back gently arched, moaning softly. I had no desire to end it quickly. Holding back from simple penetration. I needed more. It was incredible. She was incredible. Her body a true work of art, and I wanted to inhabit every inch.

The ritual bordered on the line of good and evil and continued for what seemed like hours. Never once stopping the touching, smelling, and listening. Then the music changed. A steady, deep bass shook the floor. It grabbed hold of my strings, guiding me at its will. A master puppeteer. Grasping her legs and spreading them wide, I closed my eyes, following the source of her scent. Breathing in her beauty, I pressed inside her my soul, charged with a sense of power that I was given the opportunity to possess someone so brilliant. At first, I followed the slow pace of the music, long deep strokes, as her nails dug strong into my back.

I had never felt so alive—the mind distorting music, the bass of her moaning and the sweet stink of our sex hung like a thick smog. It lasted for hours. My stamina seemed supernatural as I held tight inside her through every orgasm. Lusting for the feel of her body in ecstasy.

I finished, pulling out and showering her with my pollen. It shimmered on her young hard body.

We were exhausted with little left to say. We lay beside each other, motionless on the floor. Until we built enough energy to blow out the candles and hit the steam shower once more to rinse off. Too tired to even tease the idea of a round two, we curled up in bed together. Passing out almost instantly.

I was climbing a cliff face. I was by myself. The face of the rock was straight vertical and I hung off the side. Looking below, I couldn't see the ground and I couldn't see the top, just a straight endless cliff face. On the horizon, I could see the countryside. Rolling hills, mountains and lush green fields in the distance. There was no sound. Not a bird, or a breath of wind. As if the world had become void of all noise. I yelled out, expecting an echo. But every vibration seemed to be absorbed by an invisible nothingness. Everything was dead still, until suddenly, the wind picked up fast and strong from out of nowhere. Blowing powerfully, I clutched at the rock and clung as tightly as I could. Trying to flatten myself out so the wind could not grab me. But it was no use. The harder I fought, the harder it blew. It wasn't just the wind. There was something powerful driving it. As if it were alive. It taunted me, whispering in my ear and daring me to let go and surrender to its will. I fought and fought only to realize my defeat. It was a seemingly never-ending powerful force. My fingers slipped one by one, and accepting my fate, I let go.

28

Unlike the morning before, when I woke, I was immediately aware of my surroundings. Of Katy lying naked beside me. There was no other place I wanted to be but right there next to her warm body. But I knew it was time for the weekend romance to end. Time for the reality of work.

I rolled over to check the time. It was 6:30 am. Still early, but I knew I had a long trip to Steve's house to pack my stuff for the long shift of work ahead. *Two weeks minimum. Two weeks without Katy. Will she be here when I get back? Will she move on and find someone else?* Even though we had only spent the weekend together, the thought of losing her killed me.

I kissed her shoulder and silently rolled out of bed. Finding my clothes, I dressed up then walked over to the bedroom window to watch the sun rise on the unbelievably quiet city below. I didn't want to wake her. But I really wanted to wake her.

I heard the blankets rustle behind me and turned to see her leaning up on her elbow, blinking frantically as her eyes adjusted to the morning light.

She yawned and saw me fully dressed, standing by the window. "What are you doing?"

I left the window and made my way over to the bed. Sitting down beside her, I rubbed her back underneath the covers. "I have to get going."

She rolled slightly looking at the clock. "It's not even seven yet."

"I know, but I have a long ride and I still have to pack all my stuff. Steve wants to be on the road by noon."

She flopped her head on the pillow, disappointed. "Where do you have to go?" She asked.

"I don't know. Somewhere up by Cold Lake, I guess. Wherever that is." I leaned over, placing my head in my hands and wiping off the cobwebs.

Katy sat up and motioned me out of the way as she got up and put on her sweats and T-shirt. "Well, you gotta do what you gotta do." She smiled and leaned over for a comforting kiss. I followed her out to the kitchen. "So how long are you going to be gone?"

"Well, Steve said the usual shift lasts two weeks. Then we get a week off. But he also said that sometimes we have to stay longer." She frowned at the last part. I felt that she needed some reassurance, so I went over to her as she was filling the coffee pot and wrapped my arms around her. "Listen, I hate to leave you. But … I'm going to make a lot of money. I mean, a lot of money! So, I'll go work for a couple of weeks and when I get back, we can go spoil ourselves stupid. What do you think?" I smiled convincingly.

"Well, that sounds nice." She eased, leaning into my embrace. "What kind of spoiling did you have in mind?"

"I don't know. Why don't you think of some things while I'm gone?"

"Hmmm, think of ways to spoil myself. Yeah, I think I can do that." She kissed me.

I let her finish putting the coffee on, then got her to call me a cab. She poured me a cup to go. A few minutes later, the dreaded door buzzer rang. She went to the intercom and told the driver I'd be down in a minute.

She walked me to the door and watched as I slowly put on my shoes. Goodbyes were hard, especially this one.

When I straightened up, she latched on to me with a big hug and a long kiss. She held close and scolded me. "You better be good up there!"

"Good? What do you mean?"

"No going out to all the bars at night and picking up the local girls!"

I laughed at the suggestion. "Oh, yeah! Well, the same goes for you!"

"Pffft, yeah right! I'm sure you'd be really upset if I brought another girl home from the bar," she joked. She handed me a piece of paper with some writing on it. "Here, I don't have a cell phone, but here are some numbers you can reach me at. If I don't answer, whoever does will know how to get a hold of me. Call me as much as you can."

"I promise." We shared one last goodbye kiss, then I turned into the hall and closed the door behind me.

With the finality of the clicking latch, I exhaled sadly. I made my way down the hall into the elevator and pressed the button for the main floor. The two weeks would pass quickly. I was extra excited about the increase in cash flow as I imagined all the things we could do.

29

Steve and I headed north on the number two highway. He quizzed me up about the weekend. I told him as little as possible. Leaving out all the drug details, as I was pretty sure it wasn't his thing. I called Dad and let him know I was all right, and fed him some bullshit story about the weekend. I hung up then turned back to Steve.

"Hey, how far of a drive is Cold Lake?"

"Ah, I don't know. Six hours or so, I guess."

Running out of things to talk about, Steve turned up the tunes. I relaxed in my seat and stared out the window. Watching the flat prairie landscape slowly transform to rolling forest hills, as we headed to the Northeast part of the province. We stopped at small-town gas stations every couple of hours to refill gas and beef jerky.

I must have fallen asleep in my seat. The next thing I remember was my head bouncing off the side window as Steve jerked the wheel hard to wake me up.

"Haha, wakie wakie, cuz." I rubbed my head and noticed the city lights on the nighttime horizon. "Welcome to your new home, Cold Lake."

We breached the town limits and slowed accordingly. Steve seemed to know his way around and quickly pulled up in front of the Super 8 Motel. We grabbed our gear and checked in. I was under the impression that we would be sharing a room, but Steve said Big Johnson was one of the only outfits that supplied separate rooms for their guys. It was a relief for me; even though Steve was my cousin and all, I wasn't looking forward to sharing close quarters with him for weeks at a time.

I slid my card through the slot in the door. The green light flashed and I pushed it open.

The room was as nice as could be expected. With a single queen bed, television, and a fridge. I pulled up a seat on the bed, found the controller and turned on the television. I thought about unpacking my stuff but that was as far as I got.

I kicked off my shoes, stripped down to my underwear, and slipped under the covers. Cell phone in hand, I thought about calling the guys back home and telling them about my weekend. I hadn't checked in with anyone back there all week. I couldn't help but feel somewhat guilty, but I was too tired to go through the guilt trip. So I called Katy instead.

I let her know I'd arrived all right. We lay in bed talking about everything long into the night. Some of it dirty. We did eventually run out of stuff to talk about. I told her I was pretty nervous about my first day on the job and she assured me that I would be fine. We said our goodbyes and hung up. God, how I missed her. It didn't help that the smell of her still clung to my clothes. Worst of all my underwear. I picked up the hotel phone and called the front desk requesting a 5:00 am wake-up call. Then I turned out the light and fell asleep.

Five o'clock came way too early. A wake-up call from the front desk is no way to be dragged from a subconscious sex romp with your new, sexy hot, fitness trainer girlfriend.

I rolled out of bed, went to the window, and pulled back the curtains to the parking lot. All was quiet, except for a couple of diesel trucks running. Steve's was among those, which meant he must be up. Or up enough to push the button on his command start. The exhaust from the trucks billowed out into the still morning air to form a hanging cloud of smog. The scene confirmed one fear: winter had come to northern Alberta.

It was my first time this far north. By Canadian standards, we weren't that far north, really. Just a little past the central mark, about five hours straight north of Medicine Hat. Even with that minimal change, the prairie had been transformed to forest, and the daylight hours were noticeably shorter.

I started to mentally prepare myself for the worst. Usually, I didn't shower in the morning before work. But this morning I figured I'd best have a nice warm rinse since it could be a while before I would feel warm again.

I met the rest of the crew in the hotel lobby for our complimentary continental breakfast. After we had our fill, we all gathered into the vehicles and began the great Big Johnson truck convoy from the hotel to the site. Stopping only once at our choice of gas station. A migration that would take place every morning at the same time, throughout the winter season.

"Okay dude, you dressed warm enough?"

"Yeah, I got the woollies on," I answered. Showing Steve my winter jacket and toque.

"Good man. It may not seem that cold out yet, but wait 'til you work in it for a couple of hours. I got some extra warm gear in the back there if you need it. Head into the store and grab some food. Remember, we're working twelve hours…twelve long hours. So make sure and get enough."

"Gotcha!"

We got out of the truck and Steve stayed back to fill his steed, while I went into the store.

There was really nothing there with any true nutritional value. I shopped around, observing what the others were picking up. Smokey picked up a couple of chocolate bars. I didn't see Brian pick up anything. And Dave ended up with two very full bags. I didn't really know what I could buy at a convenience store that could tie me over for twelve hours. So I got a little bit of everything: some chips, chocolate bars, beef jerky, pop, and vitamin water. The first day would be chalked up as a learning experience.

Everyone finished up with their supplies and then got back into the convoy. As we drove, I began to get nervous. I had no idea what to expect, and I didn't know anything. I hoped they wouldn't want me to do a lot on my own. Brian seemed like a hard-ass that way. So I wasn't sure what the day held in store.

We stayed on the main highway for about an hour, then turned left onto a gravel road, which then turned to dirt. Finally, we pulled up next to a tall, skinny steel structure, visible only by the top marker lights. We parked in a line beside the rig and hopped out of the vehicles.

"All right kid, let's go." Steve yelled, throwing the truck into park.

I got out and grabbed my gear, then followed the line of guys to a portable trailer. Inside the trailer was a lunchroom to the right, another door to the left led to the change rooms. I was assigned a spot to hang my coat and coveralls, and a locker to store any valuables. Everyone got dressed quickly before Brian came in with his hard hat on and a clipboard in hand.

"All right guys, this should all be routine for you now. Steve, man your usual station. Brandon, you will be assisting whoever needs assistance. Stick with Smokey for now." Brian turned and looked sternly at Smokey. "Smokey, the kid is your responsibility. Make sure he doesn't get killed!"

Smokey nodded his head subtly in response.

So, there's a decent chance I could get killed today. That's nice.

Brian followed the speech up with a list of chores. All of the talk was foreign to me. When it was over, we went out to our stations. It felt like it had taken forever to get to that point. But the time was finally here, and I was sure that I wasn't ready.

The day started off thankfully easy. The rig was running strong. I followed Smokey around the grounds, and we just kept ourselves busy doing a bunch of rudimentary tasks. We'd run into Dave occasionally. He'd start into a story, we'd listen for a bit, then Smokey would lose interest and we'd move along. That's how the day went for the most part. We moved some shit around—piping and stuff. Some of it was heavy, but really no big deal. I was quickly forming a conclusion that all this tough guy rigger nonsense was a bunch of shit. These guys were up here making all this money for doing next to nothing. We took our breaks together. The guys taught me some card games, and the afternoon went by.

Then at about five o'clock, the rig made a very sudden, loud, eerie grinding noise. Shaking the ground slightly and finishing off with a bang and a puff of smoke. It came to a stop, and all fell silent. Brian opened the trailer, stuck his head out and yelled at Steve. Steve yelled at everyone else in turn. Dave went instantly into panic mode, while Smokey didn't even flinch. He actually grinned slightly at the chaos, then he turned toward me. "So, you ready to be a rig worker?" he asked, giving a sinister chuckle. We headed out from the tool shed toward the rig. He knew where he was going, so I did just as I was told, and followed.

Something had happened to the mud pump, which pumps mud down the hole for some reason, and then something else had happened to the drill rig motor. All I know for sure is that it was a scramble. We ended up working well past our twelve hours, focusing our effort on the pump. At first, they had me running for tools. Which would have been fine if they had been tools like hammers and screwdrivers, things that I knew. But packing pullers? Impact guns?

Pipe stretchers and metric crescent wrenches? It was nice to see everyone having fun with the new guy.

"C'mon, kid, this thing ain't going to fix itself. Mommy ain't here to do it for ya." Smokey yelled. The comment about my mom really pissed me off. Smokey could make a decent living as a motivational speaker.

It's true what they say: everything's good when the rig is running. But when it goes bad, you don't want to be anywhere near it. After the guys' tool list ran out, I stood by for a bit, watching Smokey work on the internals. A rod bearing had seized. Luckily, we had enough replacement parts on site. Smokey was headfirst, waist deep in the crankcase. I was back behind him holding a flashlight, trying to get a look at what he was doing. Finally, he pulled his head out. What a sight he was. His face, hair, and coveralls were covered in oil, and frost fringed his moustache.

"Okay kid, you're up. I need a break."

My first instinct was to hand in my resignation right there and then. But working the rigs was the decision I had made. It was what I had signed up for. So I went in.

I felt cold like never before. My clothes soaked down to the skin. Smokey stayed with me, holding the light, guiding me through the process. My gloves got so saturated and slippery that I eventually removed them and worked with my bare hands, in the cold, with frozen tools. It was a crash course in manhood. I stuck it out; I took the grease, I took the wet, I took the cold. The impact gun was heavy and awkward, with the one-inch air hose hooked up in the cramped crankcase. As I wrestled to get the tool into place and pull the trigger, the gun rattled and wrenched violently in my hands. Twisting and slamming my frozen bones against the crankcase walls, searching for support. To top it all off, the powerful blast of cold air coming through the exhaust valve was full of methanol. Which was used in compressors during the cold months to prevent the condensate in the air lines from freezing. The icy blast exposed my face to subzero temperatures, which kept me both alert, and extremely uncomfortable.

I heard some muffled yelling outside, but paid little attention until the crank mysteriously started to slowly turn over and the weight of tones of solid steel pinned my frozen hand against the case wall. As frozen as my hand was, the nerves were still working, and I screamed out in pain. "Ahhhhhh!"

"Oh shit!" came Smokey's voice from outside. "Brandon! Brandon, are you all right? Didn't you hear me yell "clear" before Dave turned the crank over? Shit kid, you gotta pay attention." He scolded.

Exhausted, I lay my head down in the case, checking my hand for any permanent damage. It seemed fully functional, but it was throbbing. I failed to answer Smokey at first, his words burned in my head. *Pay attention, pay attention! How 'bout you guys pay attention? I'm the one with my fucking head in this thing!*

Smokey called out again. "Brand, you all right? You need a break? C'mon, I'll switch out."

"No, no, I'm all right. Let's keep going." I took a deep breath. I pushed out my frustrations and neutralized my emotions. I couldn't let the job get the better of me.

I took another breath to clear my head, then righted my body. My brain went void of all thought other than completing my task. My hands and limbs weren't mine anymore. They were tools, just like the wrenches and the impact gun. Inanimate objects used to hold and manipulate other inanimate objects.

Much as I told Smokey I'd keep going, I found myself at times ready to throw in the towel. I had made a mistake. I wasn't ready. I saw flashes of the warm shop back at DJ's and my familiar cutting station. Thinking how good it would be to be back there again. But I removed the thought from my mind and focused on my new life and how great it would be. Sure, I was cold and tired. But I was getting paid double. I pictured Katy at home, sleeping in something skimpy in her nice warm bed. Then flashes of our psychedelic sexcapade, and her naked body spread out in front of me. It gave me the strength to power through any obstacle the rig could throw at me.

There were moments during the day when I felt we would not succeed. But sure enough, late into the night, the beastly machine roared back to life.

Everyone satisfied that the unit was back up and running again, we retired to the trailer and began removing our drenched clothing. My hands and toes were frozen. I sat on the dressing room bench looking over my extremities, which were bright red in some areas and glacial white in others. It hurt to clench them. My toes tingled in excruciating pain every time I moved.

I was beat. And the longer I sat in the warm locker room, the more exhaustion set in. I rid my body of some of the wet clothing. But because I failed to bring a complete change of clothes, most of what I had on was still soaked. I didn't care. All I wanted was to climb into the truck, crank the heat, and pass out. I stood up from the bench, grabbed my jacket off the rack, and went for the door. Dave and Smokey remained in the change room, silent and spent. As I walked by them, Smokey raised his head. "Good job tonight Brandon. You stuck in there. It was rough tonight, but there'll be more like it. I had my doubts about you at first. But I give credit where it's due. Good job."

I turned back weakly, looking down at the old timer who was hunched over on the bench. "Thanks Smokey. Thanks for looking out for me. I learned a lot today."

"Yeah, well, you did good. When the shit hit the fan, you stuck your face in it. Did what you were told, and got it done. That's what it takes to make it out here son."

I shrugged my shoulders. "Just doing my job, I guess."

Smokey chuckled and bowed his head, working his socks. "Well, I'm glad you see it like that. There are a lot of young jackasses we get in here that need to be literally carried around the site. It's good to have you on board kid. Keep it up."

"Hoooooly shit!" Dave piped in from the far side of the room. Stripped down to his underwear, his belly hung way over the waistband. "A compliment from Smokey. You must have done somethin' right Brandon. I'm lucky if I get a smack upside the head at the end of shift. Sometimes I feel he really just doesn't care anymore." Dave mockingly scrunched up his face like a sobbing child.

"Shut the hell up!" Smokey laughed, firing his sweaty, rolled-up socks back at Dave.

Dave shot back a cocky grin and flipped his middle finger out. "Really, Brandon, he's right. You did a hell of a job out there tonight. If you can survive that, then I'm sure you're gonna make it."

I admit it felt good to get some acknowledgment. Especially after a night like that. "Right on guys. Thanks. Well, I'll see you tomorrow. I'm fucking beat." I gave a wave and walked out the door.

I hadn't seen Steve since quitting time. Like Brian, he didn't need to change. I figured the two of them were holed up somewhere having a private meeting. I didn't care. Steve's truck was running, so I hopped into the passenger's seat, cranked the heat, leaned back and closed my eyes.

Within minutes, Steve jumped in, slamming the door behind him and snapping me out of my partial slumber.

"Brrrrrr! Fuck dude, it's getting cold out there. Here comes winter!" He

136

rubbed his hands together frantically, then latched his seatbelt. "Let's get the fuck out of here, eh!"

We pulled off the leasehold and out onto the gravel road. Still in a state of exhaustion, I sat in a daze staring out the side window. Then Steve fired up the conversation.

"Well Brandon, I'd say you kicked ass on your first day. Thanks for not making me look like a shithead bringing you out here." He laughed, reaching over and mussing up my hair like an older brother.

I brushed the hair out of my eyes and looked back at him. "Thanks Steve. I really didn't want to let you down after all you've done."

"Well, let's get back to the room and have a cold one. It's already pretty late, so we'll keep it to one."

"Sounds good to me. Cold beer, hot shower, then bed. I'm beat man."

Back at the motel, I followed Steve to his room where he dug a couple of frosty beers out of the small fridge. A couple of minutes later there was a knock on the door. Smokey and Dave joined in.

One thing led to another. We started bullshitting and laughing at some of the day's events. One beer was followed by another, and then another. Luckily, Steve only stocked a dozen, because I could have easily gotten carried away. With the last one finished, we said our good nights and retired to our separate quarters.

I went straight to the shower and cranked it to full heat. I undressed while the water warmed and checked to make sure all of my toes were going to make it. I turned the shower back to a bearable temperature and hopped in. The warm water felt fantabulous, running over my head and down my chest all the way to my toes. Taking with it the cold, sweat, and filth from the day's work and rinsing them down the drain.

I soaked myself for half an hour. Scrubbing furiously to remove some of the stains on my body. Some never did come off. Renewed with warmth and blood moving freely again in all my fingers and toes, I got out of the shower and dried off.

Back in the main room, I put on my pajama pants and sat on the edge of the bed, flipping the TV set on to the evening news, while drying my hair. I slowly felt the full body fatigue settling in. So I threw the towel back in the tub and crawled under the covers. I could have easily passed out right then, but I had some calls to make.

I called Dad and filled him in on my victorious first day. I told him about what had happened, about the major breakdown I'd helped fix. I kept our conversation brief. He finished by saying he was proud of me. But he didn't actually have to say it as I could I could hear it in his voice.

I again thought about calling the guys back home. The guilt was picking away at me. I knew they'd be really pissed by now not having heard from me yet. But I put it off again, making a promise to myself to call them the next day. Hopefully, we'd be back from the rig a little earlier. Katy, she was the priority.

I called her uncle's number, not sure if she was still staying there or if he'd come home. I hadn't a clue what to say if he picked up the phone. I thought it would be best if I just hung up.

Luckily, Katy answered on the second ring. "Hello?" Her voice sounded sleepy.

"Hey sexy, did I wake you up?"

"It's okay. I must have dozed off. But I've been waiting for your call. What took you so long?"

"We had a break down on the rig. We had to work late and then we went to Steve's room for a couple of beers."

"Oh. Well, how did it go?"

I went through the tale again. I was pretty excited, but sensed after a while that I was talking shop a little too much. So I dropped the subject. "So, how are you? How was your day?"

"Pretty lazy, really. Just cleaned up the condo and relaxed. My uncle's due back sometime tomorrow. So I'll probably leave in the morning. I have to be at work tomorrow anyway."

"Yep, back to work with you. Gotta keep up that kickass body."

She giggled. "Well, aren't you sweet." The conversation continued on way longer than it should have. And by the end, I was pretty turned on. I considered returning to the bathroom to take matters into my own hands. My penis said yes, but even it didn't possess the power to get me out of bed. I'd never been that tired before. Once we said our goodnights, I fell into a deep sleep.

30

The rest of the first shift passed quickly. Everything being new to me, I had something different to learn every day. Other rig components broke down over the course of the shift. But as I learned the equipment and procedures, I had a better idea of what to expect and what to do. I soon adjusted to the routine: wake up, have breakfast, go to work, get back to the motel, drink a couple of beers with the guys, shower, go to bed. I called Katy every night and together we counted down the days 'til my return.

Finally, back in Calgary, I hopped into my frozen little shit-box car, with one single destination in mind. The Civic had been sitting in the cold since my safety course. I hadn't ever left it that long, and was concerned if it would start. I was relieved when it sputtered to life on the first turn of the key. What it lacked in sex appeal, it made up for in reliability. I left it running while I removed the foot of snow that had collected on top. A winter storm had blanketed the city while we were away.

I hopped back inside and waited patiently for the needle on the temperature gauge to reach an acceptable level. Every minute seemed like an hour to my manly needs.

As I waited, I remembered that it had been nagging me for a while now, not having checked in with the guys back home. I'd been telling myself that I was waiting for some ideal moment, but it wasn't really that. I just didn't want to deal with it. I'd get the "Oh, hey, finally found the time" sarcasm. And the fact that I had ignored it this long would make the guilt trip that much worse. Then I'd ask what they'd been up to and they'd tell me exactly what I already knew, the same old, same old. Then it would be me talking about all the new shit I'd been doing. I mean it had been weeks already since I left, and I'd done so much. I couldn't do it. I was reluctant to shower them with my exotic tales of life away from my friends.

I needed a situation where I could end the conversation at my convenience and not be totally lying. Joey was one of those relentless guys who couldn't leave well enough alone. If I made the move to say goodbye, he'd be like, "Why? Why do you have to go? Where you going? What're you doing?" So, it would help to have something that required my immediate attention. Life threatening if at all possible.

I took a deep breath and dialled Joey's number. He picked up instantly. "Well, holy shit! Look who took time out of his important schedule to call his lower-class friends."

"Aw, c'mon, man. Don't be like that."

"Well, what the fuck, eh! What the hell have you been doing that you couldn't take time to call?"

I gave him the quick version of my time in the big city and my first week on the job. Keeping out the good parts, except for Katy and how fucking hot she was. I might of mentioned she was a fitness instructor, and that we'd had really good sex three times, maybe four.

"I'm sorry Joe. I've been meaning to call, but I've been—"

"Oh boo hoo. Poor little Brandon stayed up and went partying in downtown Calgary. Spent the weekend spanking some hot fitness model's naked ass in her uncle's downtown penthouse. Hmmm, let's see, what did I do last weekend? Tough to recall. I mean so many things going on. Oh yeah, we went to Roscoe's, stuffed our faces with wings and beer, and in case you were wondering, April said no again. Whew, wild times! Whatever man! It's what's going to happen. I just thought you'd hold out a little longer than this before cutting us off."

"C'mon man, I'm sorry."

"You c'mon! What's it been, two, three weeks?" He paused long enough to calm down and regain composure. "So, when you coming down to visit?"

The question caught me off guard. "I … I guess I'm kind of busy right now …"

"No, I know you're busy. We're all busy."

I'd had enough of the conversation. "Oh, shit! I gotta go!" The urgency in my voice was as honest as reading script from a teleprompter.

"What! What's up? Where you gotta go?"

"Sorry Joe!" *Throw some things around in the car, make some noise. C'mon Brand. Think man. Think!* "I'll call you back, my engine's smoking!" *SNAP* I shut my phone and tried to shrug off the selfish feeling that plagued my conscience.

I checked the temperature gauge on the dashboard and seeing that the life fluid of the car had climbed enough to move, I got the mule into gear and set off to the races. My eyes were on the road, but a vision of Katy dressed in nothing more than a smile fogged my windshield.

She had given me the address to her place on the west end of town. I had looked it up on Map Quest and printed it off for the trip. I told her to stay by the phone in case the inevitable happened. I had driven in Calgary a little, but I was still very much a rookie. But overall, things went pretty smoothly. As I got closer, I called to let her know she could watch out for me. Finally, I pulled up to the address and gave a quick honk. The front door opened immediately and out she came, as gorgeous as I remembered her. In the doorway, her roommates stood. They were the two skinny girls I recognized from the bar. They giggled to each other and waved. I smiled and waved back through the passenger window. I felt bad for Katy, having to pay rent to live in a place with people she didn't really care for. I couldn't relate having never been in that position yet myself. But I couldn't imagine it being pleasant.

Katy ran down the snow-covered walkway as quickly as she could. Taking care not to slip on the ice. When she got to the car door, she found it had frozen shut. After several attempts to yank it open, she gave one last mighty tug and ended up stumbling backwards across the walkway falling flat on her back in the snow bank. Held high in her hand, shining in the streetlight, was my passenger side, exterior door handle.

Fuck me, what a piece of shit! Embarrassed and pissed off, I scrambled out to the sidewalk and helped Katy to her feet. The two ditzs back in the doorway stood laughing their asses off. Katy was unhurt. She held one hand in front of her mouth while the other grasped the former chrome appendage.

"Fuck!" I hissed under my breath. "Stupid piece-of-shit car," I continued muttering. I was too embarrassed to even look at Katy. Surely, someone as hot as her could find another guy with a functioning passenger door.

Katy grabbed me hard by the hand, noticing how upset I was. "Brandon, it's all right, really." She giggled, wiping the snow from her ass.

I looked at her smiling up at me. She really didn't seem to care.

"No, it's not all right." I said, giving the tire a kick. "Stupid car. I can pick you up in something better than this. It's time I traded this junker in. So … I don't know how to go about this now, but—"

"Oh, that's easy." Like it was routine, she ran around to the driver's door and crawled across the obstacle course to the passenger seat. She was full of surprises. Most women would have ended the date and faked an illness as soon as I pulled up in this rust bucket. But Katy—well, I was beginning to think she just liked me. I followed her into the car, taking my place behind the wheel and tossing the broken handle in the back. The tires spun madly, searching for traction as we pulled away from the curb.

When we finally got away, Katy leaned in with a kiss, nearly sending us head-on into a parked car. "I'm so glad you're back. I missed you so much!" she said.

"Not as much as I missed you, sexy! I'm excited for this week together. What's up for tonight?"

"Well, there's this sort of wine, beer, coffee place that's not far. They've got these comfy sofa chairs, and tonight there's a comedian doing stand-up. I've been there before. It's just local talent, but some of them are pretty good. What do you think?"

"Sounds like fun. What's your story for tonight though? Do you have to work tomorrow?"

She looked over at me with a big smile. "No, I took tomorrow off just for you." She giggled and sat back in her seat. "Really though, it's no problem for me to take a day off. They have lots of trainers to fill in for me.

"Well, then maybe you should take the rest of the week off!"

"Yeah, right!" she laughed. "I'd love to Brandon. But this is the real world, and I have bills to pay just like everyone else. I love that you're home, and I want to spend time with you. But I can't lose my head here."

She was right, and I knew it. But all I wanted to do was spend every minute with her. I understood she had to go about her life, but really. I mean, I was making awesome money. I had gotten my first check the previous week and it was more than I had ever made before in a whole month. Shit, in two whole months. I could literally pay her wages for the week and not even notice. And I still had more money coming in from last shift. But like she said, we couldn't lose our heads. I hardly knew her, and it was too early to think about such things.

But it wasn't too early, not for me anyway. As Katy directed me to our destination, a scene rolled over in my head. The two of us set up in a nice condo somewhere. A view of the Rockies on one side, and the downtown skyline on the other. I would come home from my shift, she'd be waiting for me naked, or maybe some little thing on just to tease. We'd spend my time off doing whatever we wanted: travelling, hanging out, smoking drugs, having sex. It would be perfect.

"Hey, Brandon!"

I snapped out of my daydream and turned back to Katy.

"Holy shit, where were you?"

I smiled, a little embarrassed that she caught me in a daze. "Huh? I was just thinking."

"I could see that. The big grin on your face told me you were thinking of something pretty good." She looked at me curiously, then reached over poking and tickling. "C'mon, Brandon, what is it? I know you want to tell me."

I did my best to keep one hand on the wheel while defending the assault with the other. "C'mon Katy, I'm trying to drive here. It's nothing, really, just work stuff."

"Uuuuh! For shame Brandon. How dare you think about such a thing when we're together." She slapped me on the shoulder and flopped back on her side of the vehicle disappointed. "Well, I've got something that will take your mind off that," she said.

I looked over to see her pull a joint from her jacket pocket, a welcome sight. There weren't any all-night runaway drinking binges up while we were working. But a couple beers after work every night, took its toll on a guy. I was looking forward to getting back on the herbal remedy.

Katy pulled a lighter out of her other pocket. "So, Brandon, this is a pretty sweet ride. What do you say we hot box it?"

"Hot box? What the hell you talking about? You want to burn my car down?"

She shook her head with a smile. "Another first time for Brandon. I'll show you," she said and sparked up. "Just don't roll your window down. Keep the smoke in the car, and you have a hot box."

"Oh yeah, I think I've seen something like this on Cheech and Chong." I replied while admiring the sexy awesome girl I had discovered.

We pulled up to our destination. A stall in a newer strip mall built from giant timbers to mimic the ambience of a small mountain village.

We found a parking spot way back from the main entrance. I could barely see through the window, thanks to the hot box experiment. I opened my door and a cloud of cannabis billowed out around me as I coughed and hacked. Once I got out, Katy again crawled her way through the hazy interior to the driver's exit.

The hot box served its intended purpose. I was screwed, and happy to be so. Now that I was with Katy again, life was good. The smoking car scene was probably quite alarming to passersby, but I paid little attention. I stood with heavily-squinted eyes and a broad grin, proudly holding the door open on my smoking piece-of-shit car. But the most surprising part to any bystander must have been the point in which Katy exited the car and filtered from the cloud. No doubt they were wondering how a guy like me in a little shit box ended up with such a hot girl. I'm not going to lie; it felt great to be that guy.

We remained by the car for a minute, leaving the door open to let all of the smoke escape. Not that it mattered; at that point, we probably could have scraped the resin off the seats. I wasn't really concerned about the resale value. We closed the door and proceeded hand in hand to a trendy little pub called the Live Lounge.

We entered with large, contagious smiles, and everyone who noticed us as we came in returned the warm greeting. It occurred to me that we likely reeked of cannabis. We had just been sitting in a human-sized vaporizer for the last fifteen minutes, which lead me to the conclusion that all the other patrons probably drove to the club in their own hot boxes. Normally, such attention would have me heading back for the door, but I was high enough to not care.

31

The spot we'd chosen was dark and cozy, with a single lit candle on the table. The waitress attended to us promptly. Having no idea what to order, I left the honours to Katy. Once our attendant left, Katy kicked off her shoes and stretched her sexy legs over mine.

Our waitress returned quickly with a couple of glasses of red wine. Meanwhile, a lone spotlight flashed to life, illuminating a single bar stool on a tiny stage at the back of the room. We heard laughter from the crowd of people as the comedian did his thing, but Katy and I were in our own world together.

While most of my body was beginning to relax in the setting of the cozy bar with the drugs erasing all responsibility from my mind, the brains of my operation was continually growing stiffer. Eventually digging hard into Katy's side.

She looked over at me with a naughty grin. "Hmmm, what's on your mind, Mr. Baker?"

"Well, I don't like to sound too forward, but I was wondering if you knew of any place around here where we could get really naked and have sex?"

She giggled at my subtleness. "I was thinking about that a little too. Just a little though," she smirked. "I really don't know what to do, both my roommates are home. I don't recommend going there, not much privacy, and my uncle's home, so that's out. What about your place? Or your cousin's?"

"Steve's? Yeah, we could go out there, I suppose. I hadn't really considered that. He's home tonight though. It's not a big deal. I do have the whole basement to myself. But it's still not as private as I would like. We couldn't be truly free with our freakness. I hate to say it about my cousin, but I don't think he's above peeking around corners and snapping pictures."

We took a moment of silence to review all options. "Hmmm … you know, I had a good shift at work, got a lot of extra hours. And I did say we could spoil ourselves when I got back. So, do you know any fancy hotels around here you've always wanted to try out?"

"Mr. Baker, you sure know how to win me over. There is this one place out in the hills just west of here. I'm sure it's quite expensive. But if you think you can afford it, I promise to add in some extra-special perks for my hardworking man." She ran a finger playfully up my leg.

"Oh, I really like the sound of that," I smiled greedily. "You think they have any suites with Jacuzzis in them? And let's not forget about champagne and strawberries while we're at it, eh?"

Her smile grew even brighter at my suggestions. "I'm glad I played hard to get for those thirty seconds. To think I was ready to give it up in the back of your car."

"Well then, book it up sexy. Time for me to spoil my girl a little." I'd let that one slip. I never referred to Katy as "my girl" before. Well, not in front of her anyway. I hoped it wasn't a big deal. It wasn't like I used the "L" word, but they make big deals out of little things sometimes.

Sure enough, I peeked in her direction through the corner of my eye and she had her full attention locked on me. She was wearing a sweet yet devilish look. As though she just jumped a level in our relationship. "What Brandon? What did you just call me?" She came closer, wrapping her arms around my neck.

"What? I don't know, what did I say?"

"Don't play stupid, I heard you," a look of victory lit up her face. "You called me your girl. Is that what I am? Your girl?"

"I don't know, it just kind of slipped. I didn't … " Flustered, I blushed and fumbled out my reply. I didn't want to rush anything or scare her away. But really, that was how I thought of her, or how I wanted us to be, anyway. I just never announced it verbally before. But my concern that moving too fast may scare her off was unjust.

"It's okay, I think it's sweet. Your girl." She ran the tip of her tongue lightly up my neck and sent a shiver down my spine and a surge in my pants.

146

I wasn't sure about Katy, but I was ready to find the hotel. I handed her my cell phone, prompting her to make the call and find out if they had any rooms available. We were in luck, there was one room left but it was an upper scale executive suite. Katy's look of shock as she listened suggested the price was excessive. I was long past the point of negotiating room rates. I needed this girl's clothes off fast. I motioned to her to book it, then signaled the waitress to get us the bill.

Katy directed us to the hotel as best as she could remember, winding our way through the dark forested foothills. We crested a hill and the night opened up to an endless, starlit sky. The moon was full and brilliant. To the west lay the mighty snow-covered peaks of the Rocky Mountains. Then, as we turned a bend, in the middle of a clearing stood a grand, five-star palace.

The hotel had valet parking, but I opted for a spot in the back behind a fenced-in dumpster. We made our way to the entrance. Fancy cars pulled up one at a time, depositing fancy people. The main lobby was a massive hall crafted from expensive marble and large rustic timbers. Dressed in our best jeans and T-shirts, stinking of booze and marijuana, we proceeded in stealth to the front desk.

The desk attendant seemed surprised to find that we were the couple who had booked one of the more upscale suites. But she greeted us with the same courteous manner as she'd surely been well trained to do with all of the guests. She handed us the keys and directed us to the elevator and the top floor. Relieved to finally get to the privacy of our own quarters, we hung the do not disturb sign and latched the door.

While the cost of the room equalled half a month's rent in Medicine Hat, it was an amazing, spacious room with a bed that was at least king-sized, maybe even bigger. I was a little disappointed at first when I didn't see the Jacuzzi tub, until we discovered it out on the spacious terrace. I say terrace because balcony just didn't fit. It was large, as big as the room itself, with a small mini-bar that could be reached from the deep soaker tub. And, just as we'd ordered, on the corner of the tub sat a bucket of ice with a bottle of champagne complimented with some freshly-cut strawberries. I looked over at Katy. Her eyes sparkled in awe as she took in the room that was ours for the evening. Then she locked on me with a look that told me she was going to repay every last penny with rituals far beyond my imagination.

I cranked the hot water in the tub and threw in a block of scented bath salts, likely a thirty-dollar option, but at that point, I had stopped counting.

Between kisses, we managed to smoke two more joints while savouring the champagne and strawberries. With one brain laid to rest, there was little to interfere with alternate desires, and none of them were pure. It wasn't long before Katy started to repay me with the special treats she'd promised. We started in the tub with the majestic snowcapped mountains glowing in the background. Eager to hit the main event, we retreated inside. I hit the switch for the gas fireplace and we crawled into the bed under the thick duvet cover. Our love making continued long into the night and early morning till our animal instincts were satisfied.

32

The next morning, I awoke to yet another strange place. But this one I could definitely get used to, with my beautiful girl snuggled next to me. I lay on my side, kissing her soft skin and admiring our grand accommodations. It seemed that money could buy some happiness after all, as I was very happy at that moment. A month before, I had been living in Medicine Hat working for beer money. Now I was lying naked in bed with a goddess in a five-star castle.

The sun rose slowly, sparkling off the western slopes. It was 7:30 am, the latest I had slept for at least two weeks. I needed it. I felt renewed. It was also nice to know that I could stay warm and clean that day and not have to breathe in any sickening fumes or smash my frozen hands with cold steel.

I walked to the window, opened the sliding door and took my naked body out onto the deck where all my parts were greeted by the cold mountain breeze. It was then that I pondered the true purpose of pubic hair as I found the insulating factor to be quite poor. What began as a great idea quickly led to my manhood being reduced to a small fraction of its normal size. I reversed back toward the room, deciding that I best have a hot shower immediately so I could return all components to their natural size before Katy woke up.

I entered the room, quietly closing the doors behind me, hoping not to wake her, but of course she did. Rubbing her eyes, she looked up at me with my arms crossed around my chest to defend the cold. Her gaze then fell down to my genital area … then she giggled. I frowned in frustration, realizing that I chosen to conceal the wrong parts.

"Good morning handsome. A little cold outside?" she smiled, still focused on my not so flattering manly attachments.

I blushed slightly. It was sooner than I wanted to have to explain or display shrinkage to my hot girlfriend. "Yes, it is cold, very cold!"

She lifted up the blankets invitingly, "Come back to bed poor boy, and let your woman warm you up."

Since she didn't seem too disappointed with the current package, I crawled in and snuggled up close. I found the controller for the television and turned it on. Katy pulled in close to me again. Using the distraction of her body to snatch the controller out of my hand, she flipped through the channels until she found her favourite morning program. It was a pretty girly program, but I had other things I could focus on.

As she lay against me, I ran my fingers through her hair. She was so incredible. I couldn't believe I was naked in bed with her. I wanted things to be like this always. The thoughts rolled in my head. I wanted to ask, but I was scared it was moving too fast. She seemed happy with the relationship, but she was still somewhat unpredictable. I had admitted to myself that I was falling in love. I didn't want to tell her that yet. I guess because I had such strong feelings for her, I was that much more afraid of rejection.

But I couldn't wait anymore; this was just too inconvenient, running around like a couple of teenagers. Why shouldn't we have our own place where we could stay and not have to worry about where we could go to get some privacy? Besides, I needed a place to call home. Someplace familiar, so I could quit all the bed-hopping. But this is what we were always warned about by our parents and friends: moving too fast. We were still so young. Yet there were those couples who could battle past the odds and make it. I had a good feeling we were one of those few. How many guys actually get a shot with a girl like her? One thing I couldn't deny was that whatever it was she was selling, I was hooked; she had her own junkie. Whatever brain part or hormone that held the majority vote in my system at the time voted that she was an absolute necessity. That I should keep her at any cost. I felt less like a man and more like a hand puppet, on the end of a penis.

I began to sweat, and my heart pounded more urgently in my chest. Even still, I felt the time was right. I was just waiting for a cue, an opportune moment to begin.

Katy lay across my chest, watching her show as I continued to fondle her hair. She turned her head slightly and started planting small kisses on my stomach.

"Hmmm, that feels nice!" I moaned. "I could spend every day like this, eh?" I threw the meat on the hook and cast it out into the unknown. Then the wait began.

She bit. "Yeah, I'd have no problem with that," she continued to kiss my belly.

I cleared my throat nervously. "Umm … Katy?" My voice cracked slightly under the pressure.

"Hmmm?" she answered, quite content to continue exploring my body with her soft lips.

"Well, what … umm, I mean, what do … "

My nervous babbling quickly drew her attention. She lifted her head, turning to face me with an expression of concern, "What's wrong?"

"Katy," I raised my voice confidently. "Katy, what do you think about, maybe … getting a place together?"

Her eyebrows rose, suggesting maybe I was wrong to think she may have been expecting this.

She moved off of me and sat up on the bed, taking some time to think.

I remained in my spot, motionless, looking down at the blanket in front of me. I had made a mistake, moved too quickly. I regretted even thinking it. I'd ruined what we had.

She looked at me with a blank stare like she had mentally left the room biting on her lower lip. She didn't seem mad, thank God, just unprepared. She saw the distress on my own face, the fear that I had crossed a line. She reached over to the back of my head and grinned. "I'm sorry Brandon, I didn't mean to act like that. It's just so unexpected. I was beginning to wonder if guys still asked girls to move in with them these days."

Now that she was talking to me again, I did my best to backpedal and fix my mistake. "Listen, Katy, what we have is great, and whether or not you agree to this … I mean, it's really soon, and I know that. I was scared as hell to ask, but bottom line is, whether you say yes or no, I don't want to lose what we have. We move in together, great. If not, we just keep doing what we're doing and see what happens down the road."

"No, Brandon, you didn't scare me, not at all. It's fine, it's just like I said. I wasn't expecting this, not this soon for sure."

"I just really like spending time with you. That's all I want to do when I'm here. All this running around, hopping from place to place is silly, really. Why don't we just get our own place? I mean, I'm making more than enough to get a nice condo or something somewhere. Even out where you are now, close to your work. You wouldn't even have to pay rent or anything. I'll cover all the expenses." I was carrying on and on, trying to counter any reason she might have for getting dressed and walking out.

I could tell she was thinking quite deeply on the subject as she continued chewing her lip and looking out the window to the mountains. I remained silent, giving her the time she needed. Then she finally turned to me with a hint of excitement in her eyes.

"Well, I'm not saying no, but really, is this even realistic? Aren't we just jumping in slightly? I'll tell you what, since you can afford it all by yourself, why don't you get a place? I mean, I can stay there while you're in town, and we'll just see how things progress." She was smiling, thrilled with her brilliance. She was right. We didn't have to officially announce it as moving in together. Her suggestion seemed like a perfect middle ground.

In a way, I was also deeply relieved and surprised. The fact that she hadn't just jumped on the bandwagon made me even less concerned about her being a gold digger. She continued kissing my mid-section, and I revelled in her attention. My breathing eased, and I lay there thinking to myself how lucky I was to have this gorgeous woman in bed with me.

33

As we snuggled together a while longer, I remembered that this fantasy world we had rented for the evening had a checkout time. The clock read 10:00 am and we had to be out by eleven. We reluctantly pulled ourselves out from under the warm blankets and I chased her into the bathroom where we shared a hot, cleansing shower.

I was out and towelled off before her, thinking about where we were going to stay for the rest of the week, hoping we could accomplish something more permanent so as to avoid any more last-minute three-hundred-dollar expenses. I found my clothes and put them on. Pulling my phone out of my pants pocket, I flipped it open and noticed one missed call from Steve while I was in the shower.

Reluctantly, I dialled his number, figuring I'd better see what was going on. He was probably going to try and get me to go on another whore tour with him and Nate. But to my surprise, it was better.

"Hey Steve, it's Brand. What's up?"

"Holy shit, found some time to check in with your cousin, eh?"

"Yeah, I'm sorry man, just been …"

"Tappin' some ass! No problem buddy, just giving you a hard time."

The noise in the background on Steve's end sounded like he was driving the truck, "What's up, where you goin'?"

"Actually, that's why I was trying to get a hold of you. I got a call from Brian this morning; he's still up with the rig. They're going to move it. Just down the road a little, not too far. We'll be in that area for a while, lots of holes to punch. Anyway, he called me up and he wants me there to give him a hand. Kinda sucks I'll miss my days off, but it's big money buddy! All of it overtime."

"Holy shit man! That's awesome. Good for you."

"Yeah. Anyway, Brian kinda hinted that he's probably going to be moving up the chain here soon, company's expanding. So, he mentioned in his roundabout way that his job's going to be up for grabs and he said I'm first in line for it."

"Wow, that's great Steve, awesome! You deserve it man. You'll be a great guy to work for."

"Thanks Brand, sucking up will get you everywhere! Anyway, this could be good news for you too little buddy. If I move up the chain, then my job will be open. And if someone moves up into my position, then there'll be a step up the ladder for you too somewhere along the line. It's not going to happen overnight. But probably by the New Year. So, learn as much as you can over the next couple of months, eh?"

"That's awesome, thanks man!" I said, meanwhile mentally soiling my pants. A promotion, already! Couldn't I just sit and enjoy what I had for a minute? How could I move up a position already? I just figured out where the bathroom was on site.

"Yeah, so anyway, I'm outta here, on my way back to the great white north. So my place is free for you and that chick of yours to get your freak on if you need it," he joked. "Just don't do any nasty shit in my bed!"

"Oh yeah? that's great! Thanks man. Good luck up there, you'll do great."

"Thanks buddy. So, whatever, enjoy your days off. Just make sure you're up there for work Monday morning, eh!"

"You got it boss. Give me a call if you need anything," I closed my phone.

Katy stood by the bathroom door dripping wet, towelling her hair dry. "Who was that?"

"Well, I got some good news. Number one, Steve is probably moving up in the company soon, which might lead to me moving up in the company." She smiled a bit flakily. She never really got excited about my work. It was just a boring rig job to her, which she knew nothing about other than I had to leave her to do it.

"Well, it's good though, right, more money?" she said, doing her best to find a bright side.

"Yeah, more money. But really, I've just started. It's pretty fast to be moving up, although Steve did tell me this could happen. Which leads to the other good news. Steve is on his way back up to site for the rest of the week. So we've got the place to ourselves!"

"Whooo hooo," she celebrated, with a little bounce and a smile.

Her naked bouncing always brought me joy.

That night, back at Steve's, I went into his office and grabbed his laptop and brought it out to the kitchen table so Katy could browse the real estate listings, while I worked on my special Greek Rib supper. The only dish I knew how to make.

Katy surveyed the listings. Continually reminding me that I didn't have to buy over on the West Side just for her convenience. I insisted that it was my favourite area of town no matter where she was living. She knew I was lying, but she played along.

At first, she figured I would like a house that's nothing fancy but something like Steve's. A bit more private than a condo. But with the current housing market in Calgary booming out of control, a house was a little out of range for a first-time home buyer like me, unless I was okay with an old "fixer-upper." But with my job, I wasn't going to have much time for fixer upping.

So, condo it was, and luckily the West Side was full of them. Katy narrowed the search to five units and then found a realtor who had one listed, deciding that she was the right one to show her, or us, around.

We ate supper, which had turned out not too badly. A bit burnt which was usually the case when I was in charge of the cooking. But Katy said it was great. We scrolled back and forth looking at the pictures of all the different places. We were both excited.

"These look great Katy, I'm really excited, but we shouldn't get too carried away here. I mean, I've never owned a place before, and I really don't have much of a credit history. I'm pretty sure it won't be that easy to buy a place."

"I don't know Brandon. I know a few people in town who had bad credit and made a lot less than you and still managed to qualify for a mortgage. So never say never!" She put her arms around me, kissing around my neck the way she always did. She had thrown caution to the wind. Whether she would admit it or not, she was just as, if not more, excited about this than I was. She was simply playing hard to get earlier.

ALTERNATIVE ENERGY

The realtor Katy had emailed called me on my phone, and when I explained my situation, she didn't seem at all discouraged. She explained that she had a mortgage broker that she worked with exclusively. She was confident she could make something work for me, so we set up a time to meet the next day.

Once I was off the phone, the reality of the situation set in. This was no longer talk. It was, by the sound of it, a definite possibility. I felt a little faint. *Me, a home owner.* I wasn't really scared knowing that of all the things I could do with my money, investing in real estate was probably the smartest. But it was all happening so fast. I mean, I had mentioned it to Katy that morning, and then the next day I would be filling out a mortgage application. I paced the floor anxiously in an effort to slow my heart down. Then I looked down at Katy, who was still admiring the pictures on the computer screen like a little girl at Christmas, and it temporarily numbed my doubt.

34

The next morning, Katy invited me in to watch her teach a class at Mountain Fitness. How could I turn down the chance to watch her get all sweaty jumping, bending, and arching. The show was great. I felt like a dork though, hanging around in my jeans watching all these muscle jocks flexing in front of the mirror.

After class, she came over to me while towelling the glistening sweat from her tensed muscles. "So, what do you think?"

"It's pretty fucking intense."

She laughed, "You should come give it a try."

"Nah, think I'll pass on that one. I get enough of a workout on the job."

"All right, but you don't know what you're missing." As she continued towelling off, a large muscular brute of a man came up behind her and pressed the tips of his fingers to her ribs, causing her to squirm and giggle.

"Good class today, Katy," he said. "You really punished them."

"Yeah, thanks Brad. With the extra time off, I felt the urge to really give it to them."

"So, who's your friend here?" He nodded in my direction. "Is this the reason you're taking so much time off lately? You going to introduce us?"

"Oh yes, of course. Brad, this is Brandon, the new man in my life. Brandon, this is Brad. He's the owner of the Mountain Fitness chain."

"New man, eh?" he smiled, shaking my hand with an over enthusiastic grip. Like he had something to prove.

He was large. Over six feet tall and twice my size—all of it muscle, and not an inch to pinch. He had blond wavy hair and blue eyes. All this time I'd known about Katy's job as a trainer, I always pictured her surrounded by oversized women. Never really considering the option of her being surrounded by good-looking chiselled men all day.

"Well, you're a lucky man Brandon. She's a hell of a woman. Hope you can keep up." He gave me a wink, which fuelled my imagination and made me curious about their history together.

With the introduction complete, Brad went back to the workout area.

"I'll go get changed and we'll get out of here." She gave me a quick peck on the lips then disappeared into the change room.

I waited in the car for her to finish changing, having my first bout with jealousy about this Brad guy and his winking ways. Had they shared a past relationship? What was his current relationship status? She hopped in the car. I remained silent, pulling out of the lot on route to the realtor's office.

She noticed the cold change to my mood. "Brandon, is something wrong?"

I tried to play it cool. I didn't want to be that jealous guy, but it was really bugging me. "Huh? Oh, no, it's nothing."

She placed her hand on my leg, sensing now that something was definitely wrong. "Brandon, what is it? Is it the realtor thing? If you don't want to do this, just say so. It's okay."

"No, no, it's not that."

"Well then, what? Tell me, please."

"It's that Brad."

"Brad? From work? What about him?"

"I don't know, just the way he acted in there. Have you two ever … you know. Is there anything there?"

"Anything like what? Oh!" She giggled, finally catching on to my concern. "Brandon, are you jealous of Brad? Don't be silly. There's nothing between us. There never has been and there never will be. He's married Brandon, and his wife is gorgeous. They have two young kids. Even if he wasn't married, he's not my type. Too much of a jock for me. Besides, he's old, like thirty-five or something." She rubbed my leg reassuringly. "He's my boss Brandon, and that's all." She leaned over kissing my cheek. "You're the only man for me, okay?" She looked over for my acknowledgment.

"Okay." I said. My face broke into a smile. Relieved, I placed my comforting hand onto her leg as we pulled up to the office. Everything was going to be all right.

Sandra, our realtor, wasted no time in helping me fill out the mortgage application forms before we discussed anything else. "We might as well find out if you qualify." She flashed her selling smile. "I think two hundred and fifty should cover it."

Two hundred and fifty thousand. Breathe Brandon, breathe. I looked over at Katy who was still bubbling with excitement. *It's all worth it man. Hang in there. Anything to drink in this place?*

"Okay, done," Sandra smiled, happy with her early morning accomplishment. "I'll just fax these off to the broker then we'll be on our way." She headed out the door.

"Excuse me, Sandra. How long will it take for you to get a response?" I asked.

"Could be an hour, but no more than a couple of days. They really don't have much to research with your limited history. So I can't see it taking that long. I'll be right back." She left.

I breathed heavily. Katy noticed, placing her hand on mine. "Brandon, you don't have to go through with this if you don't want to."

I looked into her eyes. She meant what she was saying. It was my decision. I thought it through a little bit and decided that I was going to go for it. I mean, really, what are the chances that I'll be qualified? I make a lot of money, but I've only had the job for a month now.

Sandra came back to the office, "Done, the papers have been sent. So, shall we go have a look?"

It didn't take long to show us all the condos in my price range. In the end, there was one winner that stood out from the rest, in a complex called the Rocky Mountain View Estates. A small place. But a corner suite with a wraparound balcony on the South West corner. A nicely decorated one bedroom, with stainless steel appliances, and an ensuite with a Jacuzzi tub. Not surprisingly, it was the most expensive. But it was also the only one with two underground parking stalls. It was great. Katy fell in love with it instantly.

I was excited, but the more time passed and I had time to think, the more I doubted my mortgage qualifications.

Riiing! Riiing!

Sandra fished her phone out of here pocket then went out to the privacy of the deck to attend to the call. Katy and I stayed put. I had to try and bring her back down to reality.

"Listen, Katy, it is really nice, but I don't think I'll qualify. We have to be—"

The balcony door opened and Sandra returned inside. "Well," she looked at both of us with a big smile on her face as she raised her arms. "If you two like this place, you got it. That was the broker. You're approved Brandon, congratulations!"

I couldn't believe it. I got accepted! I rode silently back to the office in the back of Sandra's BMW, looking out the window and wondering how the hell I qualified.

We parked back in front of the office and got out of the vehicle. "Well, any decision yet?" Sandra asked as we stood in the parking lot. "Listen, Brandon, I know this is a big step for you, and I really hate to pressure clients. But the fact is, if you like that place you are going to have to move on it quick! It's vacant, and we can probably have the papers signed and have you ready to move in a month or even sooner. The thing is, it's a hot property. There's already two other showings on that unit later today. It's not going to last long."

She was good, I'll give her that. But she was also right; it wouldn't last long, not in today's market. "We really like it Sandra. I'm pretty sure it's the one we're going to go for, but I really need at least one night to sleep on it. I'll have an answer for you in the morning."

Sandra agreed reluctantly, "I can understand that. I'll keep an eye on it, and if anyone else shows interest in it, I'll contact you immediately. Get back to me with a decision as soon as you know."

"Thank you for everything Sandra. We'll be in touch."

There was a lot of pacing that evening. Things were coming at me with the speed of light. Katy didn't intrude on the decision, but I could tell she was sold. I really wanted it for us. I also couldn't stop thinking back to the gym with all the steroid monkeys hanging around her all day.

The next morning, I bought my first piece of real estate. We talked about it all through the night. Considered all the pros and cons, and by the end of the discussion, we had eliminated all the cons. I was confident I had made the right decision.

We spent the rest of the week together looking at furniture. Excited for our place, we never left each other's side. Then on Sunday, we said our sad goodbye as

I dropped her off at her place. During the week, I forced Katy to let me buy her a cell phone so we could keep in touch better. She was hesitant at first because it was me buying it for her. But I explained that it was for the greater good, so that we could stay in touch.

All the way up to Cold Lake I drove. Under me, the little Civic began to cough and sputter. It was hard for me to admit, but the little engine was turning from could to just-didn't-want-to. That would be the next big purchase, a new vehicle. With Steve moving up in the company, he would be gone a lot more. So, I wouldn't be able to depend on him for a ride. I supposed I could ride with Dave or Smokey, but the bottom line was I needed a dependable vehicle.

The drive up was long, especially by myself, and gave me nothing but time to think. *What did you do man? You bought a fucking condo your first week back. Are you nuts? Was it a bad move? Was it all for the girl?*

The thoughts rolled around in my head. It's true, I was making good money, but what if something happened and it all ended? Then what? What I had was my first bout of real-world financial stress. Not the little stuff, like where I would get my beer money for the weekend. That used to be my biggest concern, and at the time it was a legitimate concern. But now, beer money was the least of my worries.

My phone vibrated from the centre console. It was Katy. I took some deep breaths and gathered myself before I answered.

"Hey sexy, miss me already?" I answered happy and positive.

"Yeah, of course I do…" There was hesitation and uncertainty in her voice.

"What's wrong? You sound upset."

"Well, it's my roommates. Apparently, they gave a notice to the landlord a few weeks ago and forgot to tell me, I guess. Anyway, I have to be out by the end of the month. I can't believe they did this to me. Who does such a thing?"

I was furious. How dare those bitches toss Katy out into the cold. I wouldn't have it. "Well, you're moving in with me then!"

"Brandon, I don't know."

"Katy, really, it's no problem. We'll keep it simple. Since it's my place, I'll pay the mortgage. Since I'm out of town half the time, you set up the cable and all the fixins and you can cover those. We'll work out the groceries and whatever."

"Well, I am really stuck for options."

"It'll be fine. I'd feel better if there was someone to watch the place anyway. And if things don't work out with us, then you haven't invested anything into the place and we can just part ways, right?"

"It sounds good, I guess." The hesitation in her tone began to lift.

"Good, it's done then! So, go tell those bitches that you're moving into your new boyfriend's penthouse!"

I hung up, satisfied with the outcome, until the realization hit that my new girlfriend was moving into my new quarter million dollar condo. Teetering as close to a nervous breakdown as I had ever before, I was forced to the side of the road. I was able to open my door just in time to hurl my lunch all over the snow-covered shoulder.

I closed the door and sat silently, gripping the steering wheel. The only noise was coming from the occasional passing semi and the lonely ticking of my right turn signal. It wasn't right. Every instinct told me that I had gone too far too fast. The condo, my relationship with Katy, everything. Really, I hardly knew her. But I gathered my wits. Pulling back into the highway, I convinced myself it was the proper thing. *It's normal to puke your guts out in celebration of your first home and live-in girlfriend.*

35

I pulled up to the Super 8 in the early evening. Dave was there to greet me as I got out of the car.

"Hoooly shit! You drove up here in that? Brave man," he nodded in awe. "Or stupid," he laughed. "Hey buddy, why don't you throw your shit in your room and come over for a beer? I don't have a clue where the other guys are."

"Sounds good to me," I did just that. A beer sounded fantastic after the drive.

Good old Dave, always happy no matter what. As soon as I walked in, a beer came flying at my head. I managed to catch it as I closed the door behind me.

"Whew, cold as fuck out there, eh?" Dave said as he took a drink from his can. "So, young lad, tell me of your adventures in the big city. Enjoying it so far?"

"Yeah, definitely." I pulled up one of the chairs by the small table and began filling Dave in on what I'd been up too. Everything just dumped out like I had been waiting for someone to listen, and he listened really well.

"So, let me get this straight. You met some hot little fox fitness instructor. You two fall head over heels for each other, then you wind up in some love drunk state and end up buying a condo, all in the matter of a month. That my friend, is seriously intense!"

I slumped back in my chair exhaling, filling the room with an air of depression and concern. "Yeah, tell me about it."

"Whoa, dude, why so glum? You like this chick, right?"

"Oh yeah. I mean, she's the coolest girl I've ever met. And her body ... don't even get me started."

"Oh yeah, good body is key Brandon." Dave and I chuckled as he reached down and massaged his less than attractive beer gut. "Listen kid. Let me tell you a story about something I've learned in my lifetime. That's how it works man. You can't plan love. That's what makes it one of the best, most exciting things about life! BAM!" Dave pounded his fist on the table, scaring the shit out of me and making me dump some beer down the front of my shirt. "It just fucking smashes you man. From out of nowhere."

I had spent some time with Dave over the last few weeks. But out on the job site mostly. And after work for some beers. But always with the other guys. I always got the impression that there was an incredibly big kid hiding inside him. Like there was a playful child that he concealed when he was around adults. Sitting there now, I had a couple of beers in me, but man, Dave gave some awesome speeches. He was standing up tall and proud, physically acting out emotions, waving his arms about. He could be one of those big southern gospel preacher guys, except he was drunk, and wearing boxer shorts and a muscle shirt.

"So, let's get this straight, Brandon! You come in here all down and bummed out like the world is ending. What you need to do is take a minute and look at the complete picture here. Number one, you meet this wicked, hot totally cool chick with a rock-hard body that's totally into you!"

I nodded in agreement.

"And she's probably all dirty frisky like, right? She's frisky, right little buddy?"

"Yeah, she is." I was a little hesitant to get into any specific details about our sex life.

"Hoo haa! That is sooo right on! Now, number three! She is so into you and likes getting her freak on with you so much that within a month, she is moving in so she can parade around in little sexy outfits every night like your own private stripper." He mimicked what I guessed to be Katy, prancing around daintily on his tiptoes. Then he stuck his butt out and spanked it. "Oooh yeah, naughty girl. So, you buy your dream place! And in a month, you my friend, are going to have that little honey in that sex pad all to yourself. Right?"

"Yeah," I was actually starting to feel a bit better about my situation. The tension was lifting from my shoulders. Suddenly, two big meaty hands clasped in on either side of my face, squishing my cheeks together the way my grandmother used to do. Except it wasn't my meek old grandma, it was mighty Dave Miller, his big round face right in front of mine.

"So, you know what I want you to do now Brando!" The beer was heavy on his breath and the spit sprinkled my face. "You know what to do!"

"Whuft," I managed through squished cheeks.

"You picture that little honey of yours."

All I could do was nod in response as he squeezed even harder.

"C'mon, man, picture her!"

I tried my best to nod that I was thinking of her.

"How can you be thinking of her when you still got your eyes open looking at me, close your fucking eyes!"

I closed my eyes quickly, tightly.

"Okay, that's good, now you got it. You got her in something skimpy and sexy?"

"Duh uh!"

"Good. Now picture her in that stylish little pad you just bought, out on the deck, with a couple of glasses of wine. You just got home from two cold hard weeks of work. Have you got it???"

"Duh nuh, duh nuh" I nodded frantically. Then just like that, he let go. The blood flooded back into my face, causing my eyes and nose to run.

I opened my eyes with Dave still in my face, smiling enthusiastically.

"So, did you see it Brandon? Was it nice?" He had calmed down and lowered his voice.

"Yeah, I saw it. It was really nice."

"Now, let me ask you this," He paused for suspense. "What the fuck have you got to be depressed about?"

I looked at Dave, in shock of what a fucking lunatic he was. Or maybe he wasn't such a lunatic after all.

Dave smiled as a look of wakening grew on my face. Victory was his. He returned to his seat across the table and took a deep swig of his beer in reward, "Ahhhh."

I looked at Dave in admiration, "Hey, thanks man." I held up my can.

"Anytime little buddy. I'm not the most senior guy on the crew, but I've been doing it long enough to know that a six-hour drive by yourself can sure fuck up a good mood, eh?"

"You got that right."

"See, you got to get your head straight with this job. When you're out here, you're out here to work. Work is all you got out here. In return, we get paid well to be here. But back home, man, that's your time. The reason we're here is so we can have a better quality of life back there. If your quality of life back there sucks, then what the fuck are we up here for?"

"You're a wise man Dave Miller," I smiled.

"Ah, in this job, you'll meet all kinds of people. And let me tell you, some, no, most of the guys end up as drunks. The only loving they get is from paid whores. They're hard into drugs, gambling, drinking, whatever. If you roll like that, this job is most likely the only thing keeping you alive. It's all you got to get off the floor for. You have to have something, man! Buying property with your money is smart, don't even sweat it. There are guys out there who went home this week and burned their whole paycheck on blow and slot machines. I ain't joking, I've seen it happen. You're doing just fine man. Keep that angel back home happy and take care of her. She'll take care of you, and everything will be just fine. Always, always remember your priorities."

With my internal issue dissolved, Dave ventured into his own home life, pulling out a big photo album. He leafed through pictures of his wife, the love of his life, vacationing on houseboats, surrounded by friends and family, and always smiling. His wife was now pregnant, and he was so proud and so excited. She was due in mid-spring. They were expecting a little girl. He spent every minute of his time off getting the nursery ready, of which he had many photos. He couldn't stop talking about it.

I admired the pictures, wondering, "How do you do it?"

"What's that?"

"Leave that to come up here and work? Don't you ever think about calling it quits and finding something else to do back home?"

"Ah yeah, that's a constant battle with the wife. She's always nagging me to quit. But honestly, Brandon, I'm a man of little education. I've been rigging most of my life. It's what I know. I suppose if I really wanted to, I could go home and find something. Framing houses or road construction. I considered it once, but in all reality, you work from sun up till sun down on those jobs, and you're lucky to get a weekend off. So, would I really be home anymore? And the pay and benefits would be nothing compared to what I make here. We'd never be able to afford a holiday. And even if we could, I wouldn't have the time. And honestly, we've

166

grown accustomed to our time apart. I know people who quit to be home every night with their wives, then in a couple months they're filing for divorce. If it ain't broke, don't fix it, I say. Absence makes the heart grow fonder, you know?"

It was getting late and I still needed a shower. I thanked Dave again then journeyed to my room. I had a warm shower, unpacked my things, got some stuff ready for the morning, and then crawled into bed. I found my phone and called Katy.

She was a little pissed at me for not calling as soon as I got in, but she understood that I wasn't quite used to the check in routine. I ensured her that everything was all right and I was excited for her to move in. I was happy. We talked for at least an hour 'til we had to hang up before we passed out.

36

I fell into the lifestyle of a rigger. Gone for a while, back for a shorter while. I spent every day off with Katy. She was more willing to take time off when I was home. No longer having to pay rent, her job turned to more of a hobby.

The thing about working a shift that gives you a lot of days off in a row was that it gave you equal opportunity to spend what you worked so hard to make. Now that I was a real estate guru, I had equity, and a well-paying job. Credit wise, the sky was the limit.

The paper work on the condo went fast, and we were able to take possession in a couple weeks. Then, the new truck, jet-black diesel crew cab. All the bells and whistles, straight off the showroom floor. Now Katy and I were riding in style. I insisted that she drive it, but she refused. The truck was too big for her, and trying to park it would be a nightmare.

But I noticed while I was working out the deal on the truck that she was in the used section checking out a used VW Beetle. The salesman gave me a good deal on it. So I used a healthy chunk of the down payment for the truck, to pay cash for the car. Having them deliver it as a surprise the next day.

Katy was pissed at first. Spending all this money on her was making her pretty uncomfortable. She was an independent girl, and didn't like to have somebody provide for her. I explained that she was still independent. The car wasn't a necessity; it was a gift from me to her. Granted it was the biggest gift she'd ever received. But work was going well for me, and there was a promotion in the near future. I talked her into taking a drive, and we went out for breakfast. She eventually relaxed and let herself enjoy her new freedom after a tour around the city. She even pulled in to a Canadian Tire to pick out air fresheners and some seat covers. Her own personal touch. I didn't push my luck and I let her pay for those.

Christmas holidays came. Katy insisted I take her back to Medicine Hat and introduce her to my friends and family. So, I did. Mom and Dad welcomed her with open arms. She put on her charm and won them over with ease, as I knew she would.

It was the first Christmas ever that I was able to buy presents of any value for my folks. I got Dad an expensive set of limited-edition golf clubs. The card read "See you on the course next year, love Brandon and Katy." Stumped on what to get for my mother, I let Katy take the wheel. She picked out a weekend spa package at the Elkwater lodge. The two women sat down together going over the details like mother and daughter. Christmas with the family was a big hit.

With the parents taken care of, it was time to meet the guys. As usual, we agreed to meet up at Roscoe's pub for some drinks. Everyone welcomed Katy, but Joey seemed a little edgier than normal. Aaron prepared me for it before we arrived. He explained over the phone that good old Joey was going through some tough times lately. Getting frustrated with his job and running out of women to chase, he seemed to be slipping into a depression.

Sitting at our usual table, everyone mingled nicely. Katy had no trouble winning over the guys, showing she could hold her booze just as well as any man. Joey did seem under the weather though, sitting quietly at the end of the table. I noticed he didn't even put his songs on the jukebox. His appetite for alcohol seemed a little excessive, even for Joey. I wanted to talk to him. Maybe lift his spirits a bit. But something about his demeanour told me to just let him be. I suspected all my good fortune might only set him off.

Later in the evening, everyone was good and drunk, and Katy had the guys fully engaged in some story about her friend's mishap at some beach where she lost her clothes. Joey decided to butt in, starting loudly from across the table.

"So!" He slammed his glass down on the table, demanding attention. And he got it—from everyone in the bar. "Look at you, big man!" He turned to me. "All this shit, big fancy truck, your big flashy big city roller life, with your little playgirl thing there."

He sat there smug and fully drunk. His tone laced heavy with sarcasm. The tension around the table confirmed that nothing good was to come of this.

"C'mon Joe. Don't do this man," Curtis leaned over, talking softly.

Joey simply pushed him back in his chair out of his way. "What, Brand? Huh? You think you're something fucking special? Think I couldn't do what you're doing? It was handed to you man. You're not fucking special. It was handed to you!" He swayed slightly in his seat, the contents of his glass sloshing violently from side to side. "Fuck man, if I had a cousin that got me that job I could be doing all this."

Curtis leaned over again attempting to calm Joey down, but again he was pushed back, and ended up wearing a bit of Joey's drink.

"You shut up Curtis, just shut the fuck up!" Joey's anger grew with the volume of his voice as he stood from his chair. He leaned closer to me over the table, which teetered under his weight. "I told you man, it'll never work. You'll come back. You're nothing better than the rest of us. You'll fuck up your big shot job, and her!" Joey directed his focus to Katy who leaned back in her chair, lengthening her distance from Joe. "You think she's real man? You're stupid. She's just taking your money man! You honestly think someone like her is actually interested in you?" He laughed. "Fuck, you're stupid. Look at her!" He leaned in farther over the table and examined Katy closely. "She's nothing more than a paid slut!"

That was it. I jumped to my feet right in front of his face, causing the rest of the guys to react and try to separate us. "Is this what you want man?" I yelled back, furious with my once long-time friend.

"Look at you, you're the fucking fuck up. You fucking drunk. what happened to you man? You've just turned into a fucking waste!"

Joe stumbled slightly, suddenly looking very ill. He wobbled, then burped chunkily. Placing his hand to his mouth, he took off, fumbling down the hall toward the bathroom.

Relieved the scene had ended, the guys jumped up, wiping up the mess from the conflict. All of them apologized to Katy repeatedly.

"It's not your fault guys. Shit, why'd he have to do that?" I told them. I shook my head while assisting with the cleanup. I turned to Katy who was still sitting back in her chair stunned. "You all right babe? Don't listen to him, he's just drunk."

She snapped out of her daze. "Yeah. No, I'm all right, I just better go freshen up." She stood from her chair and kissed me lightly on the cheek before heading to the washroom.

After finishing the cleanup, we settled back in our chairs. "Jesus, Brand, I don't know what's gotten into him. Don't take him literally, he doesn't mean it. He's just had a rough go the last little bit," Aaron consoled.

"Yeah, I know, it just sucks, right. Maybe this whole get together was a bad idea."

We talked some more. The minutes ticked by. Katy had yet to return from the washroom, so I excused myself to go check in on her. As I rounded the corner to the bathroom hall, the night went from bad to worse. Joey, who I'd assumed had passed out in a pile of vomit in a bathroom stall, had found Katy in the hall. He had her pressed up against the wall, forcefully groping her. "C'mon, you filthy slut, you like it rough?" I heard him growl in her ear.

Katy struggled to push the big man off. I ran up fast and pulled him off her, throwing him against the wall. "Oh hey, Brand." He smiled wickedly. "What? You got something 'bout sharing with your friends?" He spit in my face then cocked his hand back. He was too late as mine was already loaded, and I let it fly landing square on his nose. Blood spattered the wall behind him as his nose popped and he buckled to the floor. I paused and looked at him. His crumpled, lifeless mass. Some of the good times we shared in high school flashed through my head. I didn't even recognize him anymore.

We returned home the next day. Katy seemed oddly quiet since the incident at the bar. I did my best to comfort her, explaining how Joe had just been going through some hard times, and he really was a decent guy. She said she was all right, but something in her had changed. She seemed detached.

We got home, unpacked, then curled up together on the couch to watch a movie. It had been a long stay at my father's house, and Katy decided it best to refrain from any type of sexual indulgence while we were guests. Now that we were back home, we were free to partake as we pleased. As we snuggled closely on the couch, that tingly sensation returned to my manly parts I wasted no time hinting my intentions to her. I ran my hand up her leg past the bottom of her shorts, kissing her neck seductively. She reached down and pushed my hand away.

We had been together for a while now. I'd heard all the stories about the magic drying up in relationships. But she had never, up to this point, ever refused my sexual advances. She always welcomed them with open legs. I was under the impression that I had found the perfect girl who would forever tend to my sexual wants.

Maybe I just read it wrong. She just had an itch, maybe. I returned to my horny intentions placing my hand back to its rightful spot to pick up where I'd left off. Again, she pushed it away.

She turned her head back to me, "Not tonight honey. I'm tired."

"Tired? Oh, come on baby. Just a quickie, huh. It's been a long week," I proceeded with the groping.

"No Brandon!" She pushed my hand away again, with some serious force this time. "Not tonight."

Something just felt wrong. What was behind this sudden change in our lovemaking? What did I do? It was like lying beside a total stranger. Maybe Dave was right. I'd been home too long. She was losing interest. She was usually an animal, and after the long drought I really, really wanted some. She continued watching the movie, but I couldn't concentrate on it. What exactly is a guy supposed to do with his hands in that situation, if petting time is cancelled? I behaved for the rest of the flick. Hoping the reverse psychology would change her mind, but it never did.

It didn't change that night, and more depressingly, it didn't change for the rest of the week. Things were different with Katy. She didn't even seem happy when I wasn't trying to pry her pants off. I tried to talk to her a few times, but she insisted nothing was wrong and everything was fine. I wanted to believe her but there was no mistaking things between us had changed. I had girlfriends before, but I had never lived with any of them. I'd heard some of the older married guys at work talk about their wives and their hormonal stuff and how their mood can change on a dime. I figured I was finally getting my first taste of this phenomenon. It seemed strange she had never displayed it before, but then again, I was out of town a lot. So, maybe the timing had just always worked in my favour.

Sunday morning came and I was due to leave for another shift. I packed my stuff and set it by the door. I found Katy in the kitchen cleaning up. I wrapped my arms around her playfully and spun her around, searching her eyes for something positive. "Hey, sweetie. I know something's been bugging you lately, but I won't push it anymore. If you need to talk, I'm always here for you. I have to leave, but I'll give you a call when I get there. In a couple of weeks we'll do something special, okay? This could be a big week for me, I could hear something about the promotion." I smiled, poking at her ticklish spots, hoping for a smile.

She just nodded and gave me a big hug. I didn't get her. Here I was on the brink of a promotion that would increase our cash flow, and she didn't seem to care. Anxiety crept in. I had to figure out how to get her back on track. I couldn't help but blame all her issues on the incident with Joey.

Cruising down the road in my new truck was a lot more comfortable than driving the old shit box. But it did lack the character. I couldn't stop thinking about Katy. It was the first time in our relationship where I didn't want to leave. Not just because of the sex, but because she really seemed troubled.

I needed to concentrate on something else, so I picked up the phone and dialled Steve.

"Hello?"

"Steve, what's up man? Long time no talk."

"Hey, Brand, what's going on? You on your way up?"

"Yeah, you bet. So, what's new? Where are you?"

"Oh, I'm up at the rig still. Didn't get to the Christmas thing this year."

It was a surprise to hear that he had worked all through the holidays. I was sure operations were supposed to be completely shut down.

"No holidays? Shit man, that's rough! So how many days have you had off this fall?"

"Four dude. Four days." There was cockiness to the comment, as if he were bragging about it.

"Wow, only four, eh? What they got you doing?"

"Like I told you before, the company's expanding. Brian's moving up start of the New Year, and I'm taking over his job right away. Making the big bucks now buddy!"

"Well, good for you man!"

"We haven't forgotten about you either. You're going to be moving up as well. You'll start training here this shift."

"Really? Wow, that's awesome."

"You know it. But I got to let you go man. If I don't see you tonight at the hotel, we'll see you at the morning meeting."

"Right, see you then."

Big expansion, eh. Interesting. My mind was racing. I was going to start training for a new position right away, that's what he said. What were they going to train me for? What was going to happen to all the other guys? My foot grew heavy on the pedal. I was excited to get up to the hotel and talk to the other guys. Maybe they knew something. My thoughts of Katy took a backseat.

37

I arrived at the hotel slightly after dark, which was at about 4:00 pm that time of year. I pulled into the parking lot. Smokey and Dave's vehicles were already there.

I knocked on Dave's door. Him and Smokey were bullshitting over a couple of beers.

"Hey Brand, come on in," Dave held the door for me. "Say, is that your new ride? Fucking sweet dude, love the new Fords."

I went over to the fridge pulled out a cold one, then I popped the question. "So, what the hell's going on? Steve's all excited about some big expansion and people moving up the ladder."

"So, you heard, eh?" Smokey said, shaking his head slowly.

I sensed disappointment. Judging by the overall feeling in the room, I sensed neither Smokey nor Dave were happy. I took a seat on the side of the bed in front of the table.

Smokey swallowed the last sip of his beer, "Yeah, expansion all right. I've seen it happen before. Good for the company, but not always for the guys."

"But I mean, it sounds like more money, right? Steve said they'd start training me for a new position right away."

"Well of course they are Brandon," Smokey continued. "They have no choice. It works like this. Big Johnson started out small, with just a couple of rigs. They offered good pay and benefits, and in return attracted the better hands. So, the product Big Johnson's been providing to clients is top-notch, for a decent price.

Because they're smaller, they have less overhead, so they can offer better rates to the clients. Now the price of oil is through the roof. Big Johnson's been around long enough. They're starting to attract bigger clients, so they've decided it's time to expand. Not just a little expansion either."

"That's right kid," Dave interrupted. "They just got back from the States. Bought a whole shitload of used equipment. Enough to double their current production. So yeah, Steve's all excited about taking over Brian's job, but truth is, he's taking that job and then some. He's going to be managing three rigs all by himself. Now, he's young, and although he's been in the game for a while, he still doesn't know much about the business side. Buying the equipment is the easy part."

"Yeah, but finding the skilled men to run it, that's the hard part," Smokey cut back in. "So right now, Steve's found out that he's going to be looking after all this shit. And like a rookie dumb ass, instead of looking at the big picture, he's blinded by the dollar signs and the fancy title. What he doesn't see is one, we're getting a bunch of used equipment. No one knows when the last time it was run, or even if it was run. Two, if it can run, who the fuck is going to run it? Alberta's dry man. All the skilled labour's taken. Like I said, I've seen it before, more than once. This type of move usually spells disaster, for us anyway, sometimes for the whole company."

"Ah, don't get too bent up about it Brand. Smokey's just turning this into some big doomsday event. It can't be that bad."

Silence filled the room. We sat, considering what had been said. I figured the guys were overreacting. What could be so bad about expansion and more money?

I broke the silence. "So, what do you think is going to happen? What positions do you think we'll be getting?"

"All we can do is wait for the meeting and find out tomorrow." Dave took another sip of his beer, slumping back in his chair with his usual "it is what it is" look.

I didn't feel much like sticking around. I was actually excited about moving up in the company. But I didn't feel this was the right environment for a "go team" speech. I finished up the last of my beer, then headed back to my room.

I considered the possibilities as I made my way down the sidewalk. I began to get more excited. I had to call someone and tell them what was happening. I opened my door, turned on the lights, and went straight to the shower.

I finished in the shower, quickly dried off, and called my old man. I didn't even give him a chance to talk, spilling the whole story in one breath.

"Well son, that's great! I'm really proud of you. But be careful up there, and take care of yourself. Don't get too run down. And don't forget about Katy either. Be sure to make time for her."

"I will Dad, thanks."

Katy. I still hadn't called her with the good news, and really, she should have been the first to know. Something told me it would scare her more than excite her, but it was really no big deal. Higher position, higher pay, that was all. I lay back on the bed and considered calling her. Then I just simply thought about her. The way we were not so long ago. We seemed so much more in love then. I was still. We were just in a lull. That thing with Joey unsettled her. It unsettled everyone there. Absence makes the heart grow fonder, that's what Dave said. After my stretch at work, she would remember how much she loves me, and everything would be normal again.

Eventually, I buckled and placed the call. She was the most important person in my life. It would be wrong not to share my exciting news with her. But just as I feared, she didn't share the excitement.

"You're getting a promotion?" She made an effort at support but there was no doubting her true feelings.

"Yeah. I don't know what position yet, but it sounds like I could move up pretty fast."

"Well, is that what you want Brandon?"

"Well, yeah. Of course that's what I want. I'm up here anyway. Might as well make as much money as I can."

"What about your shift? Are you going to be working the same shift?"

"Yeah, I guess. They haven't said anything for sure, but I think so."

"Well, that's great. I'm happy for you" Her words said she was happy, but there was no enthusiasm in her voice. "I'm pretty tired Brandon. I should get to bed. I have some early classes at the gym."

"Oh, okay, I guess." We had never ended a conversation short like that before. We always talked until we couldn't hold the receiver any longer. I just couldn't figure out how to make things better between us. Ever since the holidays, she just seemed to slip into depression. I would do anything to bring her back. But I didn't have a clue how. "Hey, babe, how 'bout with all the new money, we do something special to celebrate? Why don't we take a trip? I've never been anywhere tropical before. What about Mexico?" Surely this surprise would brighten her up.

But even that didn't seem to fix things. No matter what I said or offered, it seemed like she wasn't even paying attention. It was like she was in a totally different place.

Leaving her like that left me feeling uneasy. I tossed and turned in bed trying to figure out how to set things right. This trip idea seemed good, just a couple of weeks alone on a beach should reignite the fire. Steve was going to be running things. Surely he'd have no problem giving me extra time off.

38

I was pumped up like a little kid on Christmas morning. I was up extra early, fed and watered myself, and went off to the site in record time to get a front row seat for the morning meeting.

It wasn't long before the rest of the crew arrived. I guess everyone was a little anxious that morning.

The few minutes that passed felt like a lifetime. Then we heard the trailer door close and around the corner came ... Steve?

It was Steve all right. I had to look twice to make sure; he looked like shit. His posture was slumped, his complexion pale, complimented with large bags under his eyes. The extended time on the road seemed to have taken its toll.

His first brilliant speech to us as our newly appointed manager started with an awful hacking cough. Once he had collected himself, he began.

"Good morning guys." His voice was hoarse, like he was ill. "As I'm sure you're all aware, I've taken over the position of rig manager. Big Johnson is currently in the process of expanding to a point that will in the end, double their production. With that, there are going to be some changes with personnel. With me gone, the rig is in need of a driller. The only person in this crew who is capable right now of filling the position is you, Smokey." Steve looked up from his clipboard at a disgusted Smokey.

"Aw, c'mon Steve. I'm happy doing what I'm doing. I've been driller before and I don't want it!" Smokey shot back.

"Listen Smokey," Steve defended. "I know how you feel about drilling, but for now you're the only one who can do it. It's not forever. We'll switch you back as soon as you get Dave trained up."

Then Dave erupted, "Uh-uh, no fucking way am I taking on that job. I know what I know and that's where I'm staying!"

Steve blew out, frustrated, looking back down at his clipboard and scratching his head. "All right then, there's only one other option." He looked up at me this time. "Brandon, you want to train up for driller?"

Caught completely off guard, I figured at most I'd train up for Dave's position, which was probably the original plan. "Well, Steve, I don't really know anything about drilling."

"Our back's against the wall Brand. We need you to step up. You won't be alone; I'll have Smokey train you up. You'll be busy. There's a lot to learn, and you need to learn it as fast as you can. But there's a fifty percent rate increase to start, and more as you progress. It's the fast track."

Everyone in the room turned to me with raised eyebrows. Somewhere in the room, a pin dropped.

"Well, if no one else wants it, why not?"

"Fine, then. This is going to be a bit trickier of a move, but if everyone pulls together, we can make it work." Steve scanned the room, making sure everyone acknowledged the challenge. "So then, Dave, Brandon can't be drilling without knowing all the processes. You're going to have to learn him up on your part when the drilling work is slack. When the drilling's on, Brandon will be in learning from Smokey. Got it?" Everyone nodded again, though I couldn't help but notice Smokey shaking his head in disbelief. "So, with that, we are going to be shorthanded on the low end of the totem pole. We're all going to have to pitch in when needed, and for the time being, we've brought in an extra set of hands."

Into the room from behind Steve walked in a young man with shaggy blond surfer looking hair, slightly tanned, with a big happy smile. He pulled up a chair in the middle of the group.

"Guys, meet the new addition to the team. This is Ryan." Ryan stood up from his chair and politely made his way around to all of us, shaking hands and introducing himself. "Ryan here is Brian's nephew. He has some oil patch experience, but can only fill in until summer when he has to return to his other job. So, everybody watch out for him until he learns his way around. Now to finish up, it's probably needless to say we are going to be stretched pretty thin with the man power until we get some new guys hired and trained up. This means that we need all of you to put in a little extra. This could mean some longer hours and sacrificing some of your days off, just until we get caught up. But in return, it's going to be an excellent opportunity for all of us to make a shitload of money. I won't take up anymore of your time. You all got your assignments, so let's get at it." Steve nodded with a smile then turned and left.

Everything was flipped upside down just like that. As soon as Steve left, I expected the guys to go ballistic. But only one thing filled the room: silence. Complete and utter silence, with a side of bitterness.

We finished donning our gear, then Smokey walked by and slapped me on the shoulder. "Well, come on kid. You heard the boss, let's get at it."

It was a long day trading back and forth between Smokey and Dave, wherever I was needed. Ryan did well. He had worked roughneck jobs before. So once he became familiar with the site, he was a lot of help. He was mostly pretty quiet, but he was always smiling and easy enough to get along with.

The drive back to the hotel was long. I was exhausted both physically and mentally. There was a lot to learn, and after my first day at it, I felt overwhelmed.

After my nightly shower, there was a knock on my door. I opened it to find Ryan standing there with his usual smile and a six pack. "Hey bro, got time for a beer?"

"Uhm, yeah. Sure Ryan, c'mon in." I reached over to the table side chairs, clearing room for him to sit. Ryan found a spot and handed me a beer.

"Hey, thanks man."

"No problem. Brandon, right?"

"Yeah."

"Sorry man, I've had so many new names thrown at me in the last couple of days."

"Yeah, I bet. No problem."

"Anyway, sorry to intrude on you and all, but I could really use a beer, and drinking alone is, well, depressing," he chuckled. "I figure we're about the same age, so we could probably relate a bit better than the old timers. Besides, those other two seem a little too cheery for me." He raised a sarcastic brow.

"Oh yeah, Smokey and Dave, they're a little upset at all the new changes. Can't blame them, really."

"Yeah, I heard. Big things happening, eh?"

"Yeah, lot of changes. We'll see how it works out."

"Well, congratulations to you man Moving right up to the big show."

"Thanks, I'm pretty nervous but I'd be stupid to turn it down. So, you're related to Brian, huh?"

"Yeah, good old Uncle Bri. Truthfully, I don't know him all that well. Don't think he cares for me that much. But he gets me work from time to time when I need it. So cheers to my favourite uncle." Ryan laughed.

"Steve mentioned you're just filling in till you can get back to your regular job?"

"Oh, haha. Yeah, right, my regular job." He mocked.

"I don't get it."

"Dude, this is about as regular a job as I get."

"You mean there's no job in the summer?"

"Summer work? No way man. Summer is for play only! That's just me, it's how I roll. I settle down for a bit, find a job that pays decent, one where I can work my ass off for like six months, then I'm out."

"So then, what do you do?"

"Whatever I want man, whatever I want." Ryan leaned back in his chair and cracked another cold one. "I like to travel, you know, Australia, Europe, wherever I can get the best deal on a flight."

"Really?"

"Oh, for sure dude. What about you, you travel much?"

"Well, no. I'm from Medicine Hat, down south of here. I got a job with these guys, so I moved up to Calgary, and that's about it."

"Oh man, you are missing out." He looked on, eyes wide in disbelief.

"Yeah, I guess. What do you do when you travel?"

"Everything. It's just me and my backpack and whatever fate throws at me. I meet all kinds of people, most of them real friendly. Some took me diving on a reef. One time, I spent like a month skydiving. It was a blast. Last trip, I stopped off in Thailand on my way to New Zealand, and this guy got me hooked on this new sport. Hey, just wait, I'll be right back." Ryan jumped out of his chair and ran out the door.

He was only gone for a few seconds. I waited patiently, curious where the hell he ran to. He returned just as quick as he'd left, rushing into the room and slamming the door closed behind him.

"Holy fuck man, it is cooooold out there!" He reclaimed his spot, then from inside his jacket, produced a crumpled magazine and spread it on the table.

I glared down at the wrinkled mess. The publication looked well-travelled. On the front cover was a guy riding on some sort of wake style board across nice turquoise water, the Caribbean I supposed. I couldn't make out what was propelling him. Surely he couldn't ride a wave on a board that short, and there was no sail, just a bunch of lines strung out from his waist. The title on the cover read Kiteboarding Magazine.

"Kiteboarding" I looked up, disoriented. "What's that?"

"Ohhh man, this is it, that's what it is! It's a new sport, kind of like windsurfing but with a huuuuge kite dude. Here, take it, look at it!"

I took the magazine and began leafing through it, and it was just what he said it was. Kite boarding? Every page filled with various large colourful kites like I'd never seen before. As I flipped through the pages, I became increasingly convinced that Ryan's drug experimentation had vastly exceeded my own. "So, how does it work?"

He was waiting for the question. Like a tensioned spring, he jumped from his chair, eyes bulging with excitement, mouth almost foaming. He went into this big physical demonstration on how these gigantic kites could be controlled when attached to a bar that's hooked to your waist. He was running back and forth across the room, leaning, jumping on and off the bed, 'til finally he fell back into his chair out of sheer exhaustion. He was teetering on the edge of insanity.

"Wow, Ryan. It sounds really neat."

"Yeah man. It's like nothing else ever! Some of these guys I rode with could get like thirty or maybe even a hundred feet of air, like nothing!"

"Really, a hundred feet, eh?" It sounded right off the wall; the life expectancy of a kite boarder couldn't be all that good. But Ryan was just nuts about this stuff, lending support to the theory that acid truly did impair a person's judgment.

"But the best thing about it, dude, is when you are out there. There's nothing else. Your mind is clear, and all you can do is concentrate on the kite, the wind, and your board. It's total freedom—no gas gauge, no mechanical shit." His shoulders relaxed and a look of serenity flooded him, as he drifted into a trance focused on a single point a long ways from the hotel.

When he explained it like that, it didn't sound that crazy. I looked back at the heavily creased magazine photos. All the models seemed to be enjoying themselves. No one seemed scared for their life.

Ryan snapped back from his session in the tropics. "Yeah, so this trip I am dedicating strictly to the sport. It's my new religion. It, and partying." He leaned ahead with a new sparkle to his eye. "Hey Brandon," he said while lightly tapping me on the knee with his beer. "You gotta check out some of these places, like outside North America, Mexico, or somewhere. We are trapped here dude. Too much politics and rules. The rest of the world is free man! Anything goes. You want to drink, drink. You want some drugs, get some drugs. You want to get fucked, get fucked! Sex is nothing down there my friend." He leaned back chuckling.

I chuckled along with him. For as far out as Ryan seemed, he sure was a good salesman. There could be something contagious about his youthful, carefree ways. I'm quite sure I was younger than him, but next to him I felt … older. Tied down?

Ryan calmed down after a while, and we changed the subject. We ended up spending a couple of hours bullshitting and finished off all his beer. Turns out he was a pretty cool guy, with a lot of neat stories. He just had a zest for life. It was something new for me, meeting a guy like him.

With the beer gone, we realized how late it was and threw in the towel. Ryan left back to his room, insisting on leaving his magazine there for me to look at.

I lay in bed with the lamp on, looking at all the cool kite gear. Some of the riders did look like they were getting some big air. It seemed pretty neat, but you'd have to be fucking crazy to try it. I finally tired of the magazine, so I set it on the table then turned off the light and went to bed.

It was the first night away from home that I totally forgot to call Katy.

39

The shift dragged on and the work got more intense. We were all taking crash courses in everything. To make matters worse, Steve started sending us down the road to help out on the other rig when it went down. Twelve hour shifts turned to sixteen hour shifts. Everything outside of that small, contained area slowly began to fade in my mind, and it quietly began to consume us all, like a cancer.

Finally, the time came for days off. I had my stuff already packed in the truck, and I left for home right after shift, driving through the night. I pulled into the condo in the early morning, hit the shower, then crawled into bed beside Katy. Snuggling close to her, all the fighting and issues from before didn't matter. I was home with the woman I loved, and I wasn't going to let any second go to waste.

I kissed her neck softly. I was so glad to be back. The sweet smell of her soft skin began to dilute the poisons I had been breathing for the last couple of weeks. She buckled at my advances and we made love that morning like we had back in the beginning. It was the perfect way to come home, like the problems from before never happened. Magically mended by absence. We never discussed the past arguments or the fact that I hadn't called her one night. Our smiles returned and my license to grope was renewed. A couple of shitty weeks on the rig could make you really appreciate home and the ones you love.

The weather broke that day and a Chinook wind had blown in overnight, warming the air to a spring-like illusion. It was a beautiful day, and with our renewed love we made plans to enjoy the outside. Go for lunch on a patio, then down to the park for the afternoon.

Riiing! Riiing!

I scrambled for the phone. Steve's name scrolled across the screen. He was the last person I wanted to talk to. I flipped it open. "Steve, what's up?"

"Brandon, where are you?" He was panicked.

"I'm at home. Why?"

"You got to get back up here right away!"

"What? Steve, I'm on days off." I lowered my voice so Katy couldn't hear.

"Yeah, well, they've been cut short. I'm calling everyone back today. One of the rigs is down."

"So, when do I have to be back?"

"Right fucking now Brandon. Pack up your shit, throw it in the truck, and get the fuck back up here, now!"

I looked back at Katy who was busy blow drying her hair and getting herself all sexied up for our special day together. It had been so long since I'd seen her smile. *Sonofabitch. Why now?*

"Brandon. Brandon!" Steve shouted into the phone, waiting for a response.

There was nothing I could do. New house, new truck, gotta go to work. "I'm on my way," I hung up the phone.

I couldn't even look at Katy. Above everything else right now, I needed time with her. The morning started out so perfect. But what else could I do? I was trapped. I hung my head, went back into the bedroom, threw my duffle bag onto the bed and started packing up.

I heard Katy at the door behind me, "Who was that on the phone?" I didn't have to look back. I knew she'd noticed me packing. I could picture in my mind the instant devastation on her face, as her heart was broken once again.

There was no argument from her, nothing said at all. She just turned around and headed back out the door to the main room.

It only took a couple of minutes to pack; I never really had the chance to unpack. Knowing there was no easy way to leave, I grabbed my bag and headed out of the bedroom. I found Katy silently sitting on the couch.

"I've got to head back up to work," I began. "There's an emergency. I'm not sure how long it will take to fix it. Maybe we can get it done quickly and I'll be back tomorrow."

"Well, it's your job." She seemed surprisingly supportive. She stood from

186

the couch and walked over to me. Looking in my eyes with a forced smile, she hugged me and gave me a kiss. She didn't seem that mad, which took the stress off me somewhat. She really was a great girl. "When I get back, we'll do something special, all right?" I gave her a wink and another kiss with a complimentary bum squeeze.

Driving up, all I could think about was how I left her. Such a strong girl, one of the good ones, she deserved everything I could give her. It was tough times at work right now, with all the changes. But in the end, I'd have lots of money and we'd be free to spend it on whatever we wanted.

Back up at site, we did manage to repair the rig fairly quick, but there was no going home. Steve had us there and he wasn't about to let us go. Not with all the chaos. We worked for the remainder of our days off into our next shift.

"Just think boys. Double time all week. Think of all the money you're making." It was Steve's way of making us feel better. "Lots of money."

We did end up getting some days off, one at a time. At first, I would drive all the way home after a twelve hour shift. I'd get home early in the morning, sleep 'til about 10:00 am, then get up and spend what time I had with Katy, before making the drive back up late at night. It was exhausting for me, and I wasn't a lot of fun to be around. Soon, Katy just stayed at work for the day to let me get as much rest as I could. Eventually, I just stopped going back.

Winter began to lighten its grip. The days gradually got longer and warmer. In late spring, we had only four or five days off since Christmas. I hadn't been home in over a month. My calls to Katy became fewer and shorter, maybe every second night. The conversations were dull. She had stopped asking when I would be home next, because I never had an answer.

Steve turned from my cousin to my worst enemy. He'd pull up to the site at random, get out of the truck and yell some bullshit at us, then hop back in his truck and take off. He wasn't just pissing me off; he was pissing everybody off. His health had really gone downhill. He'd recently picked up the smoking habit. I couldn't remember the last time I'd seen him without one in his mouth.

Dave was a proud new father, but he missed his child's birth cause of work. His mother-in-law went to stay with his wife for support when the due date drew near. It drove him nuts because he couldn't stand the woman, and she would get to hold his new born baby before him. She emailed some pictures of his new 8-pound baby girl to the office and he called us all in to show her off. They named her Adeline. That had been a couple of weeks earlier, and he still hadn't been home to see her. I questioned how much more he could take. One night, I found him in his room broken down to tears. Not the silent manly tears, but the big, sloppy bawling his eyes out tears. I couldn't blame him. All he wanted was to be home with his family. He needed to make a living just like the rest of us, but at what price?

40

From March, time seemed to skip right through April and into May. Nobody spoke anymore. Anything we had to say had already been said. We all knew our jobs by now, so communication seemed more of an inconvenience.

That particular spring morning, it was cold. Although we were approaching the beginning of summer, there was a snowstorm warning in effect. The wind picked up and a freezing drizzle had begun. The site was muddy and once the chill had set into your bones, it was impossible to reverse. Wind, rain, snow, nothing fazed us anymore. Those kinds of physical discomfort only affected the living.

I was busy cleaning up some tools left out from a job we'd just finished. A semitrailer loaded with drill stem pipe blared its horn as it entered the yard, beckoning assistance. Dave slowly made his way across the boggy lease to relieve the truck of its burden. I continued on with my task.

A sudden crash thundered across the yard, calling everyone's attention. On a rig, there are a lot of loud crashes and bangs. For no other reason than shear instinct, this one stood my hair on end. Dave had been there as my mentor the first time I had to unload drill stem. The chains that strap the load to the deck are tensioned unbelievably tight, but despite that, the load can shift during transport. Before I released the binders, Dave gave me a strong word of warning.

"Don't you ever stand in the way of that load when you release those chains Brandon. If that load shifted, it'll be like a fucking avalanche. It'll kill ya, sure shit!"

Somehow, when I heard the crash, I just knew. *Dave. Shit!!!*

I ran at top speed. The mud sucking and clinging heavily to my boots. I eventually abandoned them as the eerie silence swelled the fear in my chest.

I rounded the corner past the storage container. The confirmation of my fears hit me like a load of pipe rolling off the back of a truck. My face flushed so fast a rolling sound of thunder filled my ears and tears flooded my eyes. For those last hundred yards, I ran so hard and so fast the mud and water never touched my feet.

I screamed for help, pushing every last drop of air from my lungs. I dove into the mud to where Dave lay pinned beneath the pipe. I lifted his head from the slop and rested it on my legs. Thousands of pounds of steel had settled on him. No part of his body was visible below the rib cage.

I looked down. His eyes were open, but I could tell that shock had set in. I immediately placed my two figures on his neck. Thankfully, I found a pulse. It was weak, but it was there.

Ryan came flying around the corner next. "Hey Brand, what—" His eyes fell upon the gruesome scene. "Holy shit! Holy shit! Holy shit! What? How?" He ran over, pulling on the ends of the pipe and trying to free Dave from his cage.

"No, Ryan don't!" I yelled. "We can't take the pipes off. He may be severed or something. Just get to a phone, get Smokey. Get an ambulance! Hurry!!"

Ryan nodded and took off as fast as he could, scraping for traction in the mud.

A hand reached up and grabbed the collar of my coveralls. I looked down at Dave who seemed to have regained some strength. "Dave!" I looked down, happy to see he wasn't dead, my face flooded with tears. "Hold on Dave. Hold on buddy, we're getting help. Help's coming!"

His eyes locked hard into mine. He fought hard to overcome the shock, but he was losing. With surprising strength, he pulled me down toward him. He wanted to say something.

"Yeah Dave, what is it buddy? Talk to me. Stay with me."

"Brandon … tell my wife and my baby girl that I love them."

I cracked, crying hysterically. "No, fuck you Dave! Fuck you man! You hold on, don't you let go! Your baby girl's waiting for you buddy! She's waiting!" I tried everything I could to make him hold on. But as the minutes passed and the reality of the situation settled, I felt I was also slipping into shock.

Dave pulled harder. A small trail of blood trickled from the corner of his mouth and down his cheek. "Don't … don't do it Brandon. It's not worth it." His head rolled back and forth slowly. Tears glazed his eyes. "It's not worth it … go … get out of here. Go back to her and just … I'm so fucking stupid Brandon."

"Okay Dave. Okay buddy, whatever you say. We'll get you fixed up, then we'll get the fuck out of here. Just hang on." The trail of blood grew thicker, darker. "You just hang on!"

Dave trembled and his head fell back on my lap.

"No Dave!!! No!!! You get back here man! Don't you fucking … Oh shit … Dave!!!"

The rest of the crew came running around the corner carrying blankets and tarps, working quickly to shelter us from the elements. I too had passed into shock, rocking slowly back and forth, staring blankly on the horizon. The ice-cold rain washed down my cheeks. Dave's lifeless head rested on my lap.

I could hear the soft thumping of an approaching helicopter in the distance.

41

The paramedics arrived, and with help from Smokey and Ryan, they forced me to leave the scene. Within half an hour, I watched from the lunch trailer as the chopper lifted into the air. I bowed my head and broke into tears again. The table below the window still littered with the printed photos of Dave's newborn baby girl.

Steve had a meltdown. Accidents on rig sites were a big fuck up, especially if there were fatalities. He was forced to report the incident to his superiors, and before we knew it, Occupational Health and Safety representatives were on the scene, along with local media.

The rig was shut down completely. We were forced off the site and ordered not to return until a complete investigation was performed. Even though he had turned into an asshole over the last six months, I couldn't help but feel sorry for Steve. As I drove from the lease, I saw him being escorted into the office by the health and safety representatives, followed by the RCMP.

I returned to the hotel and went directly to the shower. Leaning against the wall, the hot water washed over my head. I prayed for it to wash away the memories. But some stains never wash.

Various scenes flashed in my mind. Dave's lifeless, severed body, the blood streaming from his cold lips, his family, and his last words. I crumpled to the bottom of the tub, sobbing.

After a while, I calmed down and all the emotion seemed to run dry for the moment. I turned off the shower. As I was towelling off, I heard a knock at the door.

"Just a minute," I yelled, and rushed to throw on some clothes. It was Ryan. He had his backpack slung over his shoulder. He was ready to leave.

"Hey Brand." It was the first time I'd seen him without a smile. He seemed much less interesting. "Listen, sorry 'bout what happened to Dave, Man."

"Thanks Ryan, but it's not your fault."

"I know, but what the fuck is a guy supposed to say?"

"Yeah." My chin quivered as I fought back tears.

"Anyway, I spoke to my uncle Brian. He doesn't figure anybody's going to be back to work anytime soon. I feel sorry for him, and your cousin Steve. They're in some shit. I guess the safety guys are all over them about working their men too many hours and spreading them too thin. It's only right though. Roll the dice you pay the price, right? Well, someone pays the price, I guess. Anyway man, I just came to say good bye. I've made more money than I expected. Figure I might as well just take off now."

"Oh, well, good for you man." I smiled as best I could. "It was awesome meeting you Ryan. Thanks for your help. Sorry it had to end like this."

"Yeah, sure, we're all sorry. That shit should never have happened." He paused for a moment, then held out his hand. "Well, man, it's been a pleasure. Take care of yourself."

We shook hands, then he turned and walked away. I stood at the door and watched him go down the walkway, around the corner and out of sight.

I closed the door. Knowing now that the rig was officially shut down 'til further notice, I considered making the drive home. It was late and dark, but there was no way I'd be getting any sleep. So, I might as well be making some miles. I peered out the window. It appeared as though all the others had already left. It was finally time to go home.

I did a quick cleanup of the room, placing the beer bottles by the door. Then I packed my bag the going home style, grabbing and stuffing. When I was done, I did one last scan of the room, then turned off the light and closed the door.

The ride home was long. It'd been a couple months since I'd been back. It was crazy how much time I had lost. Alone with my thoughts, I'd realized just how fast the spring had passed. The snow-filled ditches were now replaced with flowering plants. New leaves were budding on the trees, and the air was saturated with the smell of rebirth.

Katy. I hadn't talked to her in a couple of days. I wasn't going to call her though. I'd surprise her when I got home. Grab her in my arms and hold her so tight she'd have to pry me off. She'd be so happy to hear the rig had been shut down. I would focus all my time and energy on setting us straight. Maybe I'd even look for a job in town, or closer to town anyway. I had rig experience now, and there were a lot of rig companies. Surely there'd be some around town. Dave was right. I had to get my priorities straight. My thoughts returned to the night in Dave's room when he cheered me up after I bought my place, and my chin began to quiver again. A six-hour ride by yourself can sure fuck up a good mood.

I arrived home at ten in the evening. I figured Katy would be sleeping. I opened the door a crack. Sure enough, all the lights were out. I crept inside, closing the door silently behind me. I felt my way through the kitchen and found the light switch for the small light over the sink, so I could find my way carefully through the main room. I gently turned the knob of the bedroom door and pushed softly. The hinge squeaked slightly. I waited, then poked my head through the opening. There was no movement from the bed. I walked over to the edge and stretched my hands across the cover to her sleeping body, only to find there was no sleeping body. I searched a little farther, pressing slightly harder to every corner of the bed. Nothing. My heart skipped a beat and I rushed to the wall and flicked on the light.

Sure enough, there was no Katy. I sat on the bed for a moment, weighing the options of what could have happened. Maybe she was in an accident. I pulled my phone from my pants and dialled her number.

"Hello," she answered on the second ring.

"Katy! Oh, thank God you answered. You had me scared for a minute."

"Brandon, what ... where are you?"

"Where am I? I'm at home babe, where are you?"

"Oh ... what are you doing back? How come you didn't call?"

"Well, there was an accident at work, so we got shut down. I thought I'd sneak home and surprise you. Looks like I'm going to have some extended time off. I'll explain it to you when you get back. So ... where are you?"

There was a long pause then a heavy sigh, "Listen, Brandon." Her voice had a nervous tone that didn't sit well with me.

"Yeah, what is it? Everything all right?"

194

"Brandon, it's … it's over. I'm leaving you."

As stupid as it seems, I had no clue how bad things really were. "What? No, Katy … why? Listen, I know things haven't been great with work and all. But I have some time off now, and I'll set things right. I'll talk to Steve. I'm sure our hours will be reduced after this. If not, I'll … I'll just stay home. Just come back, it'll be better, I promise."

"No, Brandon. It's not just that … I don't know how to say it. I'm with someone else." Another slap to the face. I fell down on the couch as tears filled my eyes.

"What? No, no. Katy, why? Don't do this, please. Not now." It was too much, too fast. My whole world had fallen apart.

"I didn't plan it Brandon. It just happened. I mean, you were gone so much. What did you really expect?"

I leaned back, trying my best to hold it together. "Who Katy? I mean, do I know him?"

"Brandon, don't. Just let it go."

"Well, come on, I deserve to know. At least give me that." I had trouble detaining my growing anger.

She sighed heavily. "It's Brad."

"Brad? Who the fuck is—" my mind quickly searched for which, if any, friends she had introduced me to. There weren't many. "Brad? Your boss, Brad? Oh, shit." The reality hit even harder when I was able to put a name and face and muscular physique to my nemesis. "But Katy, he's fucking married! He's got a family. You told me not to worry. That nothing would ever happen."

She sobbed into the phone. "It just happened, okay. It's not like either one of us planned it."

"But his wife, Katy!" I yelled back, no longer able to keep my emotions at bay.

"He's leaving her!"

"Ah c'mon, you believe that shit! So what, where are you staying? One of his kids' bunk beds?"

"No. He has a vacant rental place that he's letting me stay at 'til he gets his personal things straightened out."

"Oh, right, right. Big muscle boy with lots of money. That's what it is with you, eh? All about the money. I'm up there risking my life to get you what you want and you don't even give me a chance. The first guy comes along flashing some cash and you're gone. You bitch!" The line fell dead. "Katy! Katy!"

I hit the speed dial, but it was too late. She'd shut off her phone.

42

No address, no contact number, no nothing. I just wanted to find her, hold her, bring her back and never let her go again. Or punch her in the face. I was sorry for what I'd said on the phone. But then, I also wasn't. My emotions switched back and forth as I pictured my smiling girl naked in bed with that hulk. *SONOFABITCH!* I couldn't let it end like that. I had to find her, but how? A thought crossed my mind. Email!

I sprang off the couch and ran to the laptop on the kitchen table. I poured my heart out to her, telling her I was sorry and if she would just come back, we could make everything work.

It went through. *Thank God!* Now all I could do was wait. *Might as well have a drink while I wait. Been a long fucking day.* I searched the pantry where we kept the booze. We never really bought any, but there was a full bottle of spiced rum still sealed. A Christmas present from my parents. I found some mix and returned to the couch, making sure I had all the phones for when she called. I waited. And drank. And waited. And drank. And waited 'til sunrise. I was hammered. I stumbled onto the deck. The warmth of the morning sun felt good on my skin, with no coveralls to shield it.

I returned inside and flopped down on the chair in front of the computer. I hit the send and receive button again. Nothing. I hit again. Still nothing. I paced the floor, waiting. Then I passed by the bedroom and noticed that the covers were all messed on the bed. Images of Katy and hunky Brad rolling around naked and doing all those things flashed in my mind. I checked the time. It was already 7:00 am. I knew Katy's classes started at 6:00. A devilish plot formed in my wasted mind. I grabbed my keys and headed down to my truck.

Drunk and enraged, there was no way I should have been driving, but I had nothing else to lose. I drove to the gym and parked out of sight from the windows. I sat for a minute scanning the parking lot. It was still early, but there were vehicles at the gym. Including Katy's VW that I bought her, and the shit head's silver Mercedes. I had the whole scene planned out in my drunken mind, and I'd been drinking up the courage to do it all night.

I stumbled slightly getting out of the truck. I braced myself against the hood for a minute then began walking to the door. As I walked, visions of Katy and the good times we spent together replayed in my head. And then I thought about Brad. It was fuel for the fire that was burning in me that moment. With each step, my anger grew. Using the key in my hand, I dug deep into the side of the silver Mercedes, running it the full length of the passenger's side.

I reached the door to the building and stormed in, searching for Katy. Still dressed in my grubby work clothes and stinking of booze, it didn't take long for me to draw attention. Katy was nowhere to be found. I checked the weight room, then I followed the music to the training room. Still no Katy. But at the front of the class with his microphone headset on, shouting instructions to the class, was Brad. The techno music was blasting. He was ignorant of my presence. It wasn't the way I had planned for it to go down, but I was willing to improvise. I used the element of surprise and charged him from the side. Unfortunately, I left my quick attack footwear behind, and my ninja assault was handicapped as I tripped and clunked along in my untied work boots. With the mirror-lined walls around him, Brad had plenty of warning about the coming storm. I threw back my arm, fist clenched, and hurled it forward with every ounce of power I possessed. I leaped high with the full intention of killing him in a single blow.

Alas, even without the lack of sleep, and the drunkenness, and the restrictive clothing, the chances of my success were slim. Brad darted quickly to the side then countered with a right cross to my eye that sent me straight to the ground. I landed hard on my back. My spine went limp and my head slammed hard on the floor. I lay there for a minute, hand over my eye, stunned from the blow. I looked around at the class, mostly females, a lot of them hot. Their hands covered their mouths as they took in the sight that was me, broken on the ground. I gathered

198

my wits and pushed myself up to my feet. Brad stood, ready for another attack.

"Brandon, just think about what you're doing here. Don't be stupid. I know you're upset and all, but this isn't the way to go about it."

"Shut up, you fuck head!" I yelled over the music. I contemplated my next move. Another physical attack seemed useless. I had lost the element of surprise, and my first attack just about killed me. I had only one option left: I told on him, like a kid in the schoolyard. I pointed at him just to make sure everyone was up to speed on who I was mad at. "He fucked me!" I scanned the crowd, making sure I had their attention. "He fucked my girl. The sonofabitch! He's married! you know that?! married with kids! And while I'm out of town working, he's fucking my girlfriend!"

"Brandon, that's enough!" He yelled back.

It was the reaction I was craving. I'd hit the sweet spot. If I couldn't beat him physically, I'd embarrass him in front of his clients. "She's over ten years younger than him. Cradle robbing asshole!" Some of the older female clients seemed very interested in what I had to say. They looked at Brad in disgust.

"Brandon, I'm going to tell you one last time, you better shut up now and leave." His face turned a deep shade of red. Veins popped out of his neck. He was losing his composure, fast.

"Where is she Brad? Huh? I see her car's outside."

"Brandon!"

"Hoho, why so worried Brad? What's the concern? You did tell her you were leaving your wife, right? Got her set up in a little love nest." My fans in the crowd wanted more. They hung on my every word. "Katy, you all probably know her. The trainer that works here." I was cut off mid-sentence. I had pushed it too far. Brad seized my arm, twisted it behind my back and promptly marched me to the front door and threw me out on the street.

"You really fucked up this time!" He was so furious, holding back every urge to pummel me mercilessly on the pavement. "She'll never go back to you, you fucking loser!" He was so very upset he couldn't even come up with the words. He turned around and stormed back inside. I leaned up on an elbow and managed to laugh as he left. It definitely didn't go the way I planned. But I managed to deal some damage.

Then Katy appeared, and I stopped laughing. She stared down at me through the glass door. She was beautiful as always, dressed in her tight workout gear. But her smile was gone. She stood motionless, with a blank expression. Just looked at me. Finally, Brad appeared from behind, grabbed her by the arm and pulled her away. Maybe I should have gone after her, but I was out of fight. Tired and battered, I picked my sorry ass up from the parking lot and started back to my truck. I lifted my swollen face to greet the warm morning sun.

I woke again later in the afternoon to my phone vibrating on the table. I scrambled for it frantically, hoping it was Katy. It was my father.

"Brandon, how are you son? You sound a little sick."

"Yeah, well, I've been up all night drinking and waiting for Katy to call."

"Why, what's going on? What's wrong with Katy?"

I poured my heart out to my father like the lonely drunk sitting at the bar. I told him everything about the rig, Dave, Steve, and Katy, and how it was all falling apart. "I'm all fucked up Dad. What do I do?"

He sighed heavily. "That has got to be the worst couple of days I've ever heard of. I really wish I could make this all better for you son, but truth is, I can't. It's what life has thrown at you, and you need to deal with it. The only good thing I can tell you is that I don't think it can get any worse. I hope."

"Yeah, thanks for the wisdom!" I scoffed.

Dad chuckled. "Listen, son, you're still young. There's going to be a lot of these days coming your way, maybe even tougher ones. The only real advice I have for you is, don't ever let someone else choose your road. The only one who knows what is best for you is you. I'm always here when you need someone to talk to."

"I guess that's just as good advice as any. Thanks Dad."

"Take care Brandon, I love you. One thing is for sure: time heals everything, if you let it. Even this. Keep in touch, and don't kill anyone."

I felt a little better after talking to him, but everything was still a mess. I needed to sleep the rest of the booze off before I faced anything more. I flopped back down on the couch.

My cell phone rang again and I dove to the table. "Hello?"

"Brand."

"Steve, is that you?" He was the last person I wanted to talk to.

"You bet little buddy," he sounded surprisingly chipper, despite the recent events.

"What's up?"

"Well, I got some good news, and some bad news. Which one do you want first?"

I was in no state to make any decisions, not even the simple ones. "Whatever man. What is it?"

"Well, you probably already guessed, but Dave didn't make it. That's the bad news. But the autopsy on the body found drugs in his system. Nothing big, but it's enough to take the blame off the company!"

I couldn't believe what I heard. "What … what do you mean? They found what?"

"Well, it wasn't that bad. It's some kind of pharmaceutical. An anti-depressant or something, but he was way over the prescribed dosage. Plus, he was careless with the procedures for unloading the truck. If they can prove that the company wasn't at fault, then we'll be good to go. We should be back up and rolling in a couple of weeks. So, get rested, get your rocks off, and get ready to go again buddy!"

The pleasure Steve was getting out of making Dave look like an ass, was bringing my blood to a boil. "But his family. If they put it on him, what about his insurance?"

"Don't panic. Brian says they'll still get some, just not all of it. What can I say man? It's a bitch, but it's business. He should have been more careful. Anyway, if you want to go to the funeral, it's tomorrow down at the Heritage Funeral Home."

43

It wasn't something I was looking forward to, especially in my present condition of being a complete mess. But Dave was a friend, and friends seemed few and far between those days. So, I decided to go.

It took a bit of searching, but I managed to find the place. As I stepped out of the truck, a clap of thunder erupted in the distance, and the rain fell instantly, as if some prop operator had flipped a switch. It fit my mood perfectly.

By the time I reached the entrance, my flower bouquet and I were both completely drenched. I stood just inside the door, taking a moment to let the excess water soak into the welcome mat and searched the crowd for a familiar face. I was hoping Smokey would show, but I figured funerals just weren't his thing. So, I really wasn't surprised when I couldn't find him.

I had never actually met Dave's wife, Sandy, but I had seen many pictures. It didn't take long to pick her out of the crowd. I simply followed the line of mourners waiting to offer their condolences. She stood at the end, holding her daughter. Their daughter. I took my spot and waited for my turn. Small puddles trailed behind me on the once spotless floor.

My turn came. I suddenly felt stupid and out of place. I didn't know anyone; this was a time for close family and friends to mourn their loss. I dreaded the awkwardness of holding up the line to explain who I was and how I knew him.

Adeline lay quietly resting on her mother's shoulder as Sandy looked up at me—a scrawny ragged kid soaked to the bone and leaving a mess on the floor. She instantly wrapped her free arm around my neck and pulled me in tight, so very tight. I melted. I don't know how she knew. Dave always liked pictures.

Adeline stirred from her slumber, whining softly as Sandy whispered in my ear. "Hello Brandon. Thank you so very much for coming. Dave talked about you all the time."

The smell of newborn innocence tickled my nose as my lips brushed the top of Adeline's soft head. She looked up and I saw Dave in her eyes. I wrapped my arms around them both holding them tight. Sandy's body shuddered in my arms as she wept. I clenched my jaw hard, but there was no stopping the tears.

She held my hand through the whole ceremony, keeping me by her side always. The service was fitting. Many people stood with praise for Dave; he'd have been proud to hear them. We had a final hug when it was over. She smiled as best she could with tears in her eyes and waved goodbye with Adeline's little hand as I pulled away. I couldn't help but wish that Steve were there. Him and Brian and all the other Big Johnson big wigs, so I could punch them all right in their fucking faces!

Back at home, I went straight to the computer. There had still been no reply from Katy. I checked all the phones. Nothing. I did a few laps, paced the floor, but the day's events had taken their toll. I was exhausted. Katy, Dave, the booze, and only a couple hours of sleep. My body was due to shut down at any time. I grabbed what was left of the rum and sunk back into my dent on the couch. I sipped slowly, looking out the window to the setting sun. My life had been flipped. No work, no Katy. What was left? Sit on the couch and get drunk.

44

I woke the next morning on the couch in an upright position. The bottle of rum I held in my hand tipped during my slumber and spilled the remainder of its contents onto my lap. The room spun violently as I pushed myself from my seat. Stumbling and weaving, I made it to the bathroom just in time. I stuck my head into the toilet and bucked out what remained in my stomach. It was pure liquid. I felt like shit. I couldn't keep on going like this, but I had nothing to stop for. No job, no woman.

After an hour of cleansing, I felt stable enough to stand. I looked in the mirror and didn't even recognize myself. My eyes were bloodshot, the left one darkened where Brad had connected. I couldn't even stand the stink of me anymore. I returned to the couch disgusted, and rested my throbbing head. I raised my feet to the coffee table, accidentally knocking a pile of papers to the floor. I leaned forward to gather the mess, and there, lying by itself on the table, was Ryan's crumpled up issue of Kiteboarding Magazine. How it got shoved under a stack of papers on the coffee table was beyond me. I couldn't remember bringing it back, but there it was. I picked it up and sat back. Leafing through it slowly, I recalled how Ryan had described it and how excited he was.

"When you're out there, your mind is clear. There's nothing else!"

I leaned up from my seat. Resting my elbows on my knees, I continued flipping the pages and admired all the happy times the kiteboarders were enjoying. It was crazy, but at that moment, I was an easy sell for anything with a smile.

Especially if it got me the fuck out of my slump.

The cab ride was long, and I wasn't much in the mood for conversation with the driver. He tried to spark up some topics, but I stayed silent, looking out the window in disbelief of what I was talking myself into. We pulled up at my destination. I threw the fare plus a tip at the driver, then stepped inside the Calgary International Airport.

I had no idea where to go or where I was going. I walked up to the first available desk I could find, the Air Canada Travel Information Desk.

"Good morning sir. How can I help you?"

I approached the nice attendant, unsure of how this all worked. I still hadn't showered, changed clothes, brushed my teeth or even combed my hair. My clothes were badly wrinkled from sleeping on the couch and my left eye remained blackened from the encounter with Brad. I had no luggage at all, not even a backpack. Just a crumpled up magazine in my hand. "I'd like to take a trip."

"That's great sir. May I see your tickets and itinerary please." The lady's expression remained surprisingly neutral despite my condition. She had been well trained.

"I haven't got any."

"You haven't any tickets, sir?"

"No, I … Well, can I get tickets here?"

"Well, yes, sir. I'm sure we can help you out." She reached over to her computer and prepared to type in my information. "All right sir, where is it you'd like to go?"

It was a question everyone in an airport should be prepared to answer, but I had yet to think about a destination. I was aware of the fact that I may seem odd to her, but I was also still a little too drunk to care. I rolled out the crumpled magazine on her desk and quickly flipped to the back pages where I had previously noticed the advertisements for the kiteboarding resorts.

I scanned each one quickly but carefully, making sure I chose the place that best suited my current skill level of borderline suicidal. And there it was, ranked the number one destination to learn or improve your skills. I pointed to the ad.

"There, I want to go there."

I turned the magazine so the attendant could read it properly. "Oh, my. Well, it's definitely not one of our major stops, but let's see what we can do."

She busied herself typing away. A couple of "hmmm's" and "oh my's" later, she had come to a conclusion.

"Okay sir. It took a bit of research, but I think I got it figured out. It'll work out a lot better than I thought, and since it's last minute, I managed to save you some money. The best route to get there this time of year is down to Houston from here. I can get you on a flight that leaves at noon."

I nodded.

"You'll have a two-hour layover, then you will fly to Miami. There you'll only have a one-hour layover before you take off for your final stop, the beautiful Caribbean island of Bonaire. Have you been there before?" she asked.

"I've never been outside Canada before."

"Well, this is very exciting. I'm sure you'll have a wonderful time. I've never been there myself, but I've heard of good things. So, should I go ahead and book it for you?"

I hesitated. Booking it sounded pretty final. And I still wasn't convinced I should be making a decision to fly across the world after a twenty-four-hour drinking binge. "Yes, please do!" I heard myself say.

I handed over my credit card. She tapped a few more clicks on the keyboard, and it was done. She handed me my tickets and itinerary and instructed me to the gate.

I followed the procedures and suffered a lot of staring and pointing, but I managed to clear customs with little issue. I had two hours 'til take off. So I thought it best to get coffee and something to eat to sober up a bit, or they may not let me board the plane. I pulled up a stool at a table by the window. I loved watching the planes take off.

I sat quietly, sipping my coffee and picking at my muffin. Sobriety was slowly beginning to return, and with it, the realization that I was sitting in an airport about to get on a flight to I had no idea where. Bonaire. It sounded made up.

Brandon, what the hell are you doing? This is nuts. You don't even know where this Bonaire place is. What about work, your family, your responsibilities? This isn't you man. You don't do wild shit like this. You're not a kiteboarder. Have you even flown a kite before? Just get up and head home. Sleep it off and start over tomorrow. This is fucking crazy.

The inner battle with my subconscious raged. One minute I wanted to run back home, crawl into my warm safe bed and pass out. Then memories of my warm bed with Katy sleeping soundly and the smell of her in the sheets flashed back. Then Brad—the asshole! With her, in his bed. Then Dave's head in my lap as I sat in the mud, freezing rain pelting my face. And Adeline's silky hair brushing my cheek. By then, I couldn't decide which direction scared me more. Going across the world into the unknown, or going home.

I fought off the urge to flee and handed my boarding pass to the stewardess. She reviewed it quickly then ripped off the stub and welcomed me aboard.

I found my seat in 12A by the window. I took of my jacket and got comfortable.

Looking out the window of the plane to the runway reminded me that I had never flown before. I was pretty excited about it—until the owner of the seat beside me arrived. I was sure I'd heard something on the radio once about oversized people having to pay for two seats on some flights. This guy could have bought the whole isle.

The comfort level in my seat diminished as I was reduced to one arm rest because skinny next door had to flip them both up to fit. So, I squished myself up tight to the window, looked out to the runway below and began to mentally teleport to a happier place.

We taxied out to our designated runway where the plane stopped momentarily before the pilot put his foot to the floor and I was sucked back in my seat. I watched the yellow lines on the runway increase in speed, then we slowly lifted into the sky. Calgary grew smaller as we climbed to the clouds.

Up, up, up. We flew right into a cloud bank that blocked the view like a heavy fog. Then shortly after, we broke through the top, and spread before me was a spectacular sight. Towering mountains and deep valleys of white fluff. The sun was so clear and brilliant it forced me to neglect my doubt.

45

After the initial awe of flight, I managed to pass out 'til Texas, where I was crudely woken by a rumbling quake in the seat, followed shortly by a nasty stench. I realized the disturbance came compliments of my neighbour.

After landing in Houston, I got directions and made my way to the connecting gate. The airport was huge, but I managed surprisingly well, just in time for the first boarding call. Then I was off to Miami.

After touchdown in Miami, I was beat and ready to find a nice bed. But Miami had enough live entertainment to revive my spirits, with all the Latino women parading around in skimpy tops and short skirts. My head almost snapped off its hinges. It was a bad time to be sporting the strung-out junkie look.

I only had an hour to make the connection, so I had to move quickly. I had never heard of the airline before. The desk was small. I actually passed it a couple of times before I realized that was it. I pulled up to the Antilles Air counter with precious minutes to spare.

A large black woman tended the counter.

"Hi." I puffed and handed her my tickets. I guessed she didn't speak very good English because all she did was motion and grunt. She scanned my pass then her head nodded to the clock.

"What!"

"Too late, is gone."

"It left already?"

She nodded, "Yes. Gone."

Fear gripped me. I didn't have a clue what happened when people missed a flight. But there was still time left. The plane couldn't have left already.

I pleaded and begged "Please, Ma'am …."

She huffed and rolled her eyes, then waved me down to the small boarding gate. I ran at top speed, turned a sharp corner, and slammed on the brakes as I found the end of a long line of people still boarding.

Out of all the planes I'd been on up to that point, I wondered why the aircraft with the duct tape patch on the wing got to fly us over the open water. Nevertheless, the old clunker took off with no issue.

I looked out the window. The scenery was awesome. Turquoise blue water as far as the eye could see, freckled with specks of brown and green. I doubted if one could see sharks from that height but I could have sworn I did.

My vast knowledge as a world traveller suggested that the flight should have taken no longer than half an hour. All the Caribbean islands were just off the Florida coast. I was sure of this, until the pilot announced we had four hours to arrival.

Four hours? Either this plane is really slow, or Bonaire is in Australia.

I relaxed and settled in for another long plane ride. Bonaire wasn't a very popular summer destination, so there was some room to stretch out on the plane. Looking in the forward seat pocket, I found some reading material about the island. I thumbed through it. All the hotel ads reminded me that I didn't book a room. Landing on an island at night with no place to go. It was no big deal. *Idiot.*

Turned out Bonaire is in the Caribbean, the deep Caribbean. A small desert island just off the coast of Venezuela. Only 112 square miles in total area, the island was famed for scuba diving.

With excitement of reaching my destination, the time passed by quickly. The pilot came back on the speaker to announce our final decent, adding that the night time temperature was 32 degrees Celsius.

46

The plane landed, signaling the end of my long trip. The small airport didn't have an official jet way. Just a portable set of stairs leading to the tarmac. I had never been exposed to a tropical climate before. Even though it was nighttime, the hot humid air was almost suffocating.

There I was, in May, on a desert island just north of the equator, dressed in my jeans, long sleeved shirt and a fleece jacket. In hindsight, it would have been smart to wear my maple leaf embroidered toque, so people wouldn't mistake me for a local. After a few steps into the small terminal, my jeans began to stick to my legs like saran wrap. But what was done was done. I was already there, so I would have to make the best of it. Priority number one was to find a place to get some much needed rest.

The terminal was decorated quite differently from back home. The walls were painted with bright yellows and blues. There was a welcoming committee waiting anxiously for their guests to arrive, holding signs with the hotel logo's and the names of the guests to be picked up.

I was unsure about what type of language barriers I would encounter. The brochure on the plane said most residents spoke English, so I approached the person who looked the most likely to do so. Off to the right of the exit was an average height, slim built Caucasian man wearing tan, knee length shorts and a black button shirt with a floral print, unbuttoned half way down his chest. He had blond, shaggy, shoulder length hair and bright blue eyes. I tagged him as a surfer sport enthusiast.

I smiled, letting him know I was friendly, as I was aware that my attire suggested I enjoyed such pastimes as sleeping in gutters and eating from dumpsters. *Okay, Brand, speak clear and loud and use some hand gestures.* I cleared my throat, "Excuse me, sir." I waved casually.

The smile faded from his face as he looked me up and down. I could only guess what he was thinking. But he was quick to recover his professional manner, and his welcoming smile returned.

"Hi, yes. My name is Pieter." He seized my hand in a friendly shake. "Are you a member of the Steadman group?" He asked, pointing toward the hand written name on his sign.

"Oh," I straightened, surprised at how good his English was. He did have a slight accent, which I guessed to be Dutch. Another tip I picked up in the airline brochure. "No, sorry, I'm not. But I wish I was."

"Ah, well, how can I help you?" His smile held, but he seemed less interested.

"Well, I'm wondering if there are any taxi's on the island."

"Taxi's? Well, yes, there is a taxi. But I don't see him here right now. Would you like for me to call him? Where are you going?"

"Well, you see, I don't really know. Can you recommend any nice hotels in the area?"

The man looked me over again, eyes wide with curiosity. "Hotel? What type of hotel are you looking for?"

"I'm not picky. Something clean with a comfortable bed would be nice. A toothbrush would be a bonus."

The man paused for a moment, suspicion still on his face. "Where are you from my friend?" he asked politely.

As polite as Pieter was, his tone indicated that he had no intention of helping me out, and was simply humouring me in fear that if he told me to fuck off, I might attack him physically. My head hung in defeat, and my tone turned to a sorrowful drone as I replied, "I'm from Canada."

"Canada? This is a long way from home for you. We do get Canadians down here, but mostly in the winter."

"Yeah, I guess it would make more sense, eh. I know the season isn't right, but I've had a hard couple of months. Had to get away for a bit. Kind of a last-minute decision. But I'm sure you guessed that."

"Yes, well, everyone in here is looking at you with the impression that you are an addict of some type. It's quite common on the islands you know. I also thought that maybe you were suffering from drugs or alcohol. But I consider myself a good judge of character. Now I'm thinking that maybe you are not what you seem. Have you travelled much?"

"No, not internationally, and never on my own like this. And honestly, I am a little hung over."

"Your choice of clothes makes your story believable. I don't know where one could even find a woolly jacket like that in these parts. And you surely wouldn't need it here, even if you were sleeping in the streets." He faced me. "There is an honesty in your eyes. What is your name my friend?"

"Brandon."

"Very nice to meet you Brandon. We happen to have some extra rooms available back at our place. The beautiful Kon Tiki Hotel. Just the place to mend your wounds. Come, I fear the Steadman group has most likely missed their flight. It happens more often than not here on our beautiful island."

"Well, you can blame that on the attendant in Miami." I replied as I followed my new guide.

We left the terminal into the small parking lot. Pieter led me to a small white VW van and held the passenger door for me.

Off into the deep island night we sped, no hills, no winding turns, but quite bumpy. The surrounding landscape remained a mystery veiled in darkness. Not one street light lined the road. Pieter knew exactly when to swerve to avoid the major potholes. Out the passenger seat window, I noticed a faint glow on the horizon. I suspected it was a city or town, but we didn't appear to be heading that way. The only thing on the path ahead of us was darkness.

Paranoia set in. *Brandon. Where are you Brandon? Who is this guy, really? Did you look at his ID? His guest just suspiciously pulled a no show and you fell for it. He's driving to the darkest part of the desert. There are no lights. No hotel in sight. He's going to kill you, and do other stuff to you probably. Nice vacation, idiot. We should really do this more often.* The boost of inspiration from my subconscious prompted me to get some answers.

"So, Pieter, where is this hotel exactly? The Cal-tic-"

"The Kon Tiki."

"Yeah, right, the Kon Tiki."

"It is a very nice relaxing place in the middle of the island's wildlife preserve."

"Wildlife preserve?"

"Yes Brandon. Here, look!" He pointed ahead of the van.

I followed his direction, and to my relief, there it was—the Kon Tiki Hotel. A small cluster of lights in the distance, an oasis in the night.

After a few minutes, we pulled up in front of a small hut with a grass roof, which looked just like those in the movies. Pieter put the van in park and said, "Stay here a second Brandon. I will be right back." He hopped out and hurried inside.

I scanned the area. It was dark, but there were lights scattered throughout the yard. I could make out faint silhouettes of the surrounding complexes. It looked nice. Dead ahead sat a group of houses, and one main building of what appeared to be townhouse apartments.

Within a minute, Pieter had returned and tossed a small travel sized shaving kit in my lap.

"Take that. We always keep some supplies on hand out here. The airline sometimes loses our guests' luggage."

I opened the zipper and found inside a welcome surprise: a toothbrush, toothpaste and a bar of soap still in the original packaging. "This is awesome Pieter. Thank you very much!"

"Don't mention it my friend. Now come, I will walk you over to the apartments."

We got out of the vehicle, and walked across the gravel lot to the large apartment building of about twenty units. He stopped in front of the door marked 103, pulled a key from his pocket, opened the door, then reached inside and flipped on the lights.

"Here you go Brandon. Go get yourself cleaned up and get a good night's sleep. When you wake in the morning, come to the restaurant. I will wait for you and take you to town. I have to run there for supplies, and I will take you for a tour."

"But the room, isn't there some papers to sign, do you want some money?"

"We can worry about that in the morning. Just relax Brandon, and get some sleep."

I locked the door behind Pieter after he left, then toured my new place. It was nice, a lot homier than I expected. The living room floor was completely tiled.

There was a separate bedroom with a queen bed, a full bathroom, and even a kitchen. I couldn't believe my luck. So far, the island hospitality was phenomenal.

I glanced out the patio windows. There was little to see but darkness. Exhausted, I turned on the shower and took my time rinsing off. The water felt fantastic. As I soaped down, my mind travelled back through the day's events. All the way back home … then I stopped. I reminded myself that I was here to forget about home for a bit. Soon, I would return to face the problems. But right now, I needed to reset.

I finished up in the shower and brushed my teeth, twice. I felt great, human again, ready to take on the bed. I pulled back the fresh covers and crawled inside. Even with all of the excitement of this new land, what I had done had not yet set in. I would have to sleep off the booze, and deal with it all in the morning.

47

Knock, knock, knock!

I was awoken from my slumber by the banging on the door. I jumped out of bed and stumbled slightly. At first, I had no idea where I was, then pieces of the puzzle started to settle as I found my way to the source of the noise. I opened the front door. A wave of hot sunlight flooded into the room. Pieter stood there smiling.

"Well, good morning. I was wondering if you were ever going to get up."

"Pieter, hi. Uh, good morning. What time is it?"

"It's nine o'clock my friend. I couldn't wait any longer. I have to head to the market and get supplies for the restaurant. I thought that maybe, if you like, I could give you a ride as well. I also brought you some clothes of mine for you to borrow. They are much better suited to the climate. Don't worry, they're clean." He winked.

"Oh, thanks Pieter. You didn't have to."

"It's nothing. Now hurry up and get dressed. I will be waiting in the restaurant."

"Okay. I'll just be a minute."

I closed the door and hurried back to the bathroom where I cleaned up and put on the clothes Pieter had brought me. Some more tan shorts and a straight white button-up shirt.

They were nothing fancy, but a lot cooler than my winter attire. They would do 'til I found a clothing store.

Not that it mattered what I looked like, or so I kept telling myself. I was down here for one reason. To find that sense of euphoria. The thing Ryan spoke of so passionately. To find that point in life where nothing else mattered but saving myself from being dragged out to sea by a giant kite. Ryan's portrayal was more appealing. I was there to learn how to kiteboard, to forget about all the bullshit; work, Dave, and women were strictly off the list. It had been a long adventure down here so my mind could find time to neglect the painful images of all the good times, and now all the bad ... or Brad. It was frustrating that no matter how far I physically travelled, my mind could return home in a fraction of a second. Yet I would fight it off and remind my brain that I would have no use of those memories 'til after my vacation.

I stepped out the front door and checked to make sure it locked behind me in case someone tried to break in and steel my long sleeved shirt and fleece jacket. I took a step down the sidewalk and the small brush on either side shuttered threateningly. I looked down. In front of me on the cement walkway frozen like small garden gnomes were hundreds, maybe thousands of lizards, ranging in various sizes and colours. Some no bigger than my pinky finger, others as big as a small house pet. I froze in panic. The only time I'd seen a lizard before was in an aquarium with a good solid piece of glass separating us. They reminded me of the raptors from Jurassic park. Small, but deadly in vast numbers. I stood perfectly still watching them. They stood perfectly still watching me.

Common sense told me that surely these couldn't be man eaters, seeing as Pieter had just walked back to the Kon Tiki down this exact same path. At least, I was pretty sure he made it.

Something from down the path drew their attention, and like a wave through a crowd, their heads all turned in the opposite direction, then they scattered off to the leafy foliage.

"Goedemorgen." I looked up to see a young woman approaching down the path toward me. She wore a drab sweat suit that must have been sweltering in the morning heat. Her hair was tied back and she was covered head to toe in dirt. I figured her for one of the landscaping staff.

With the lizards gone, I quickly adjusted from my frightened little boy stance to my casual, yet sophisticated man of the world pose. Although she was not much to look at herself, I decided it would be all right for her to want me.

216

"Do not worry for the lizards, they are harmless." She said shortly, and continued on past with little more than a friendly smirk.

I brushed it off as a whatever. She was likely intimidated by my button shirt. Why would I care what she thought anyway? Girls were off the list. Usually my penis would recruit assistance from my imagination, brush the dirt off her, get rid of the sweat suit and make the best of a below average situation. As unbelievable as it may seem, my actual brain seemed to be holding my penis at bay. Maybe they had both learned a lesson. It was liberating in a way, but also disturbing. A young male with no hormones is similar to a horse-drawn cart with no horse.

It was a short walk to the restaurant, but I began to sweat after the first couple steps. I'd experienced heat before. Medicine Hat has a desert climate, and it can get hot in the summer. But this here was a whole different planet. It was like standing in the sweltering hot desert sun while someone held a blow-dryer on you.

The front of the restaurant was wide open, which was a neat change from Roscoe's dank interior. I looked inside to a dark mahogany bar with rattan furniture. Decorations littered the roof and walls, polished up items one would find on a sunken ship. There were some shells and pottery. A windsurf board hung from the roof, and spread out on the corner was a kite, just like the ones from the magazine.

The place was empty, aside from Pieter and a woman working the bar. I approached with a friendly smile and pulled up a stool.

"Ah, there he is. Brandon, please meet my wife Marion."

We greeted. She, like her husband, was also blond haired and blue eyed. She had a very nice curvaceous figure.

"Marion, it's very nice to meet you." I gently shook her hand.

"You as well Brandon. Pieter has already told me much about you."

"Oh, really?" I looked up at Pieter in confusion, wondering what all he told his wife, as he really knew very little of me.

He smiled guiltily, then gently pushed his wife off to the side, who laughed playfully in return.

Pieter set a bowl in front of me filled with a shrimp concoction. "Here, try this out. It's a new recipe I've been working on."

I popped a piece of shrimp in my mouth. I wasn't much of a seafood eater, but I was starved. I couldn't remember the last time I'd eaten.

"So, Brandon," Marion intruded. Pushing Pieter back out of the way, she set down a glass of juice for me. "What brings you here?"

"Well, my girlfriend …"

"Yes, yes, we have already guessed at your love problems. But why specifically the island of Bonaire?"

"Oh, yeah," I was relieved to hear they were not going to pry into my recent history. "I met this guy back home. He does a lot of travelling. He told me about this sport he tried out. He loved it, kiteboarding."

"Ahhhh," Marion rolled her eyes.

Pieter quickly pushed her aside again.

"Yeah, kiteboarding, like you have hanging from the roof there." I pointed to the kite. "Pieter, you must kiteboard. I mean, you live here."

"Correction, Brandon. I used to kiteboard. And windsurf also."

"Used to? So, you quit? But I heard it's an awesome sport."

"There, you just said it. Sport. Hockey, Brandon, hockey is a sport. Kiteboarding is a way of life. What you seek is not just a pastime. Beware of the power of the wind, my friend. Its power is relentless. Attempt to harness it, and it will pull and tear at your world until it carries you away completely." The look in his eye was serious as he polished one of the glasses with a hand towel. He stared off to the horizon with a small grin on his lips. He was somewhere else, on the wind, sifting over the blue water, carving some waves, boosting some air. Then he came back to polishing his glass. "Just be warned, Brandon. What lies out there can change your life."

It was the same look Ryan had on his face back at the hotel. I'm sure kiteboarding was a lot of fun, but all the dramatic life changing stuff seemed a little cheesy. "Yeah, well, I'll try to remember that." I turned my head and rolled my eyes.

I was quick to finish up my fancy breakfast. Pieter collected the dishes and took them through a swinging door to the kitchen, leaving Marion to wipe down the bar.

"Excuse me, Marion. Do you have a computer here?"

"Yes, of course Brandon. Just over in the corner." I followed her direction to a corner of the room where a bamboo room divider was set up for privacy. "Use it whenever you like. There is no charge." She smiled.

I went to the computer and logged into my email. I didn't want to waste a lot

218

of time, but I thought it best to let someone know I was still alive.

There was a message from my father.

Brandon, I've tried calling your home and cell phone a couple of times and left a few messages. Where are you Son? Please contact me as soon as you get the message.
Love Dad

Reply:
Dad, sorry to have worried you. I'm all right, alive and well. But things got a little crazy over the last couple days and I decided to get away from it all. So, I'm on my first solo vacation on a small island called Bonaire in the Caribbean. Bet you weren't expecting that. I just arrived last night, but so far everyone is really friendly. I don't know much about what's going on with work right now, or with Katy. All I know is I need a little me time. Don't worry, I'll be fine and I'll keep in touch.
Love Brandon

The name on the second email made my heart pound.

From Katy:
Brandon, I'm so confused, you were crazy the other day. I can't believe you did that. You sure stirred up a lot of shit at the gym. I won't get into it right now, but I miss you and I'm worried about you. How come you won't return any of my calls? I know you're mad Brandon, but please give me a call when you can. I'd like to get together and talk.
Thinking of you, Katy

Reply:
Katy, sorry 'bout all the shit at the gym. I was just really pissed off, and pissed drunk. I haven't returned any of your calls because I don't have my phone. I've left town for a while. Sitting around and waiting was killing me, so I had to get out. I'm on a small island in the Caribbean. I'm all right and I'll be back in a couple of weeks. You still got a key to the place, so if you need anything just go grab it. I'll call you when I get back and we'll talk then.
Take Care, Brandon

"All right man, grab your stuff and let us go," Pieter called from the bar as I hit send.

48

The drive was short, but even in the short distance the wildlife was abundant. Pieter drove slowly, pointing out the donkeys, which the island is famous for, and the flocks of flamingos. I also noticed some of my small lizard friends sporadically squashed to the pavement. Geckos, Pieter called them. They were not man eaters, or poisonous. And apparently not as fast as they thought.

Off to the right of the van, the endless blue ocean stretched on to the horizon.

Pieter slowed as we approached a couple of huts alone on a beach that bordered a lagoon. "This is Lac Bay," Pieter announced. "The best place on the island to learn kiteboarding."

The first hut had no signs and was heavily shielded by leafy trees and a tall fence that encased the lot and stretched out into the bay for a distance.

"Is that a kiteboarding place there, the one that's all fenced in?"

"No, no, Brandon. That is the nudist resort."

"The what?"

"Nudist. You know, naked. Don't be concerned. They keep to themselves. They are just as scared of you as you are of them." He nudged me with his elbow and chuckled.

I peered harder through the window as we passed by slowly, hoping to spot one of those ladies who like to walk around naked all day.

The next two huts were kiteboarding shacks. One was named Bonaire Wind Sports and the other Air Bonaire. Sure enough, high in the sky over the bay were a few lone kites decorating the breeze with their brightly coloured graphic designs, swooping and diving in the wind. It looked like a lot of fun. They were a lot bigger than they seemed in the magazine. I swallowed hard. *Maybe I can go bird watching instead. I heard there's some beautiful species down here.*

"Would you like to still come to town with me? Or should I drop you off here so you can get started?" He was sitting forward in his seat even more excited than I was to see me get going.

"No, not today. I have some things to take care of first," I replied. I did have important things that needed tending to. One was to build up the courage to go kite boarding.

Within fifteen minutes, we had navigated our way down the long, straight desert highway and pulled into the market on the south side of Kralendijk, the capital city of Bonaire.

I followed behind as Pieter made his way through the store. He knew everyone and happily greeted them all in Dutch.

Outside on the docks, Pieter gossiped with the local fishermen and carefully examined the wares before making his selection. He thanked the man, then lead me back toward the van.

He opened the side door and tossed in the supplies, then looked over at me. "Well, Brandon, I apologize my friend. I would like to show you around more, but you slept in late and I am out of time."

I turned and looked down the main street. It looked very inviting. The quaint shops lined the right side. To the left, a colourful brick walkway overlooked the ocean. Boats were moored wherever they deemed fit. I turned back to Pieter, "Thanks. I think I'll manage." I smiled and watched as he got in the van and pulled away into the desert.

The sun was hot. The walk was scarcely populated. Many of the shop owners were out sweeping the street in front of their businesses. Most of them waved and shouted greetings, but I could only understand a few words.

Pieter had given me directions to the bank as I came down with very little money. The air-conditioned building was a shock from the warm street.

As I suspected, getting funds for me down there was not going to be as easy as back home. I had a few papers to fill out with my branch information. After they got the necessary papers, they promised any future transactions would be less time consuming. Until then, they advanced me a thousand dollars from my credit card and told me to check back in a couple of days to see if they could gain access to my account.

Back out in the warm sun, I found a suitable clothing store down one of the side streets, and I purchased a couple of decent shirts and shorts. That was all I needed to get done. It took a small portion of the time I expected and I had many daylight hours left. So, I decided to check out the local establishments.

I made my way down the walk, looking out over the bay and all the fancy boats. I found the traffic surprising for such a small island.

"Good day my young friend." I looked across the street to the voice. A lone smiling bartender leaned over the bar and waved casually.

I returned the gesture, uncertain of the man himself and his seemingly random interest in me.

He persisted, "Hey, come here friend." He straightened himself and beckoned me over like a game vendor at a carnival. "Yes, you. Come."

I was hesitant, but I crossed and stepped up to the bar.

"Hello my friend. I am Braam. I do not recognize you. Are you new to the island?"

"Well, I … I'm here on vacation."

His faced scrunched slightly. "It is May, not really the season for tourists." He wasted no time getting to the chitchat. "Welcome to Braam's Bar By The Bay. I am the owner, Braam." He shook my hand.

"I know it's the off season, but I really want to learn how to kiteboard. The magazine ad said this place is the best. I'm staying out at the Kon Tiki."

"Ah yes, the kiteboarding. Well, it is the perfect time of year for that. This is when the wind is at its strongest." The newfound piece of information did little to boost my confidence.

Braam continued. "So, you are staying at the Kon Tiki with Pieter and Marion. It is a fine establishment. They are very good people. And today you are touring the fine city of Kralendijk? What do you think of our little island so far?"

"Well, I just arrived late last night, and I came a little unprepared. Pieter gave me a ride into town this morning so I could do some banking and get some necessities."

"Ah, very good. It would be an honour to be the one to serve your first beer on the island, if I am not too late? It is on the house." He smiled and pulled a beer from the cooler. He popped the cap and placed it in front of me.

It was a little early to be popping caps, and I was just beginning to appreciate sobriety after my binge. But I was on a vacation, and a cold beer would be a welcome relief from the heat of the day. I took a long draw from the frosted bottle and thanked my new friend.

The afternoon passed by, and with every drink, I grew more comfortable in my seat. Braam rambled on about the island, introducing me to other residents as they came and went. Everyone was friendly and welcoming. The hospitality was as warm as the climate.

The sun peaked, and began its decent. Dinnertime drew near, and the main street became more populated as the people completed their daily adventures and came in search of sustenance.

An older gentleman dressed in bright white casual wear pulled up the stool beside me. "Braam!" he yelled, as he held his hand high in the air.

Braam stopped tending to his other customers for a moment and looked over to my new neighbour, then smiled. "Hey, Bernhard. How are you, my friend?" He approached us, stopping by the cooler on the way to grab a beer for his friend. "Here you are Bernhard. How was your day?"

"You can never please everyone Braam. Remember that." Bernhard frowned.

"Ah, one of those again?" Braam replied.

"It's nothing," Bernhard smiled and drank his beer. He was a short, portly gent. The film of sweat on his face and the large stains beneath his armpits suggested Bonaire was perhaps not the best latitude for him. "A small price to pay to live in paradise," he laughed, then held his bottle up in salute and nudged me in the arm.

"Oh, Bernhard, this is my new friend, Brandon." Braam began with the introduction. "He is visiting from Canada, staying out at the Kon Tiki. Pieter's place."

Bernhard shook my hand graciously. "Welcome Brandon. The Kon Tiki, it is a very good place. Pieter and Marion are clients of mine."

"Yes, Brandon, Bernhard here is the island accountant. Takes care of most of the businesses on the island."

Satisfied that we had each other to keep us company, Braam left us to tend to his other customers.

"Well, Brandon, how do you like our island so far?" Bernhard seemed well practised at mingling with strangers.

"I love it. But I guess I really haven't seen much of it yet. I just got here late last night."

"Really, so this is your first time in our fair city? Then let me welcome you by taking you to dinner."

"Oh, that's nice, but—"

"You can't refuse," he interrupted. "I'll never eat alone, and if you refuse, I will have no one to join me. Therefore, I will starve. You don't want that on your conscience now, do you?"

I chuckled. "I guess not."

"All right then. Let's move from the bar and find a table. The food here at Braam's is second to none."

We found an empty seat at the back of the restaurant and we were promptly greeted by an attractive waitress. Bernhard waved away the menus, then placed an order for some fancy dishes and some specialty wine. It was a couple of plane rides off from my usual palate of beer and wings.

He looked over at me as he sat down. "I hope you don't mind, but I ordered for the both of us. It really is a fabulous dish."

It was odd to have someone order for me. I wasn't much of an adventurous eater, but I didn't want to be rude. "Not at all, I don't have a clue what to order down here anyway."

"Haha. Indeed, young Brandon. Relax and let me act as your guide for the rest of the night. You will not be disappointed."

I listened to the stories of his life, and he had many. He liked to talk, which worked for me, as I was not much interested in visiting my past. The wine came. We finished the bottle before the meal arrived. I wasn't much of a wine drinker but I was already quite drunk. Then the meal arrived. It was as I feared—some sort of fish dish. Being from the prairies, fancy fish dishes were a rarity that I hadn't yet acquired a taste for. But the presentation was exquisite enough for me to actually think of a word like exquisite.

After supper, we polished off another bottle of wine, followed by more beers. Bernhard introduced me to mostly everyone that visited the establishment. He was indeed a perfect tour guide to a perfect first night in Bonaire.

Then, as quickly as the crowds came, they diminished. Bernhard checked his watch and rubbed his belly. "So, you are staying at the Kon Tiki? How is it you are planning to get back, young lad?"

"I'm not sure. I was hoping there would be a cab around somewhere?"

"Yes, there is one, but I myself wouldn't trust him. By this time, he has had more to drink than either of us. Come, my car is just down the road, I will drive you."

"No, Bernhard. It's all right, really. You've had way too much to drink."

"Ha, nonsense my boy," he put his arm around me and pulled me along. "No one cares if we've had a little too much to drink. Besides, there's nothing to hit on Bonaire." He laughed heartily then drug me out to the street and bid farewell to his friends.

We walked down to his car. I paid close attention while he walked to see what kind of condition he was truly in. He seemed aware enough, but I still wasn't overly excited about getting in the car with him.

We pulled away from the curb and made our way through town. I had no idea where we were. Blackness engulfed the vehicle as we pulled away from the safety of the city lights. I kept my eyes trained on the road ahead to make sure we stayed on the path, but he kept a surprisingly straight line.

A very sudden blinding flash lit up the midnight sky, momentarily illuminating the desert surroundings. It was followed shortly by a familiar crack of thunder. It was a brilliant spectacle with no trees or hills to impede its beauty. There was only the surrounding ocean to enhance its raw energy.

"Beautiful, isn't it?" Bernard fell silent, looking into the dark sky.

I nodded and stared unblinkingly, not wanting to miss a single second of Mother Nature's majestic performance.

"I remember my first lightning storm on the island. It far exceeds the ones back home on the mainland." Bernhard started to hum softly to a tune I didn't recognize.

As I leaned forward in my seat to get a better angle at the sky, I felt a sudden uncomfortable intrusion, as Bernhard's arm reached over and began to caress my upper back. His humming grew instantly louder at the first touch. My eyes shifted from the sky back to the road ahead as my mind searched for an innocent reasoning for his actions. His hand moved quickly from my back to my neck where his fingers flirted with my hair.

I remained silent and dead still, unable to find a fitting excuse to his invasion of my comfort bubble. I couldn't look at him from embarrassment, but my polite nature prevented me from refusing him any fondling. After all, he did buy me dinner. He must of mistook the lack of refusal as an invite to the next base as he grasped the back of my neck and leaned over in attempt to start a make out session. Dinner was nice but I wasn't that easy. I resisted, blocking his advance with my elbow braced against his chest.

"Ah, Bernhard, you should really concentrate on the road man. I increased the pressure to his chest hoping to get the point across. But he was committed and pulled me harder 'til I could feel his breath on my ear, then a whisper.

"C'mon Brandon, it's all right. There's some dirty magazines in the glove box."

"What! No! All right Berni, pull it over." I shoved hard pushing him violently across the cab, causing him to swerve on the road. He thankfully let go of my neck and brought the car to a grinding halt. I jumped from the vehicle before he could get hold of me again.

"Brandon!" He called from the car. "C'mon Brandon, don't be silly. I'm sorry. Please get back in." The excitement seemed to have sobered him enough to grasp the realization that I wasn't the type he had hoped me to be.

"It's all right, I can find my way from here." I tried my best to act casual and create the illusion that what had just happened wasn't a big deal for me, like it had been already forgotten.

He paused in silence, looking at me through the window with an expression of heavy regret. Then, without a word and with his head bowed in drunken shame, he put the car in gear and drove back in the direction from which we came. Another blinding flash reflected off the back of his car, then darkness again as the taillights deteriorated into the distance. Then another booming crack of thunder broke the dam into an instant torrential downpour.

Drunk, soaked, lost, and violated. I stood in the middle of the desert, in the total blackness. I thought about the events that brought me here. My inebriated mind was having a difficult time grasping the reality of being felt up by a man who bought me dinner. And now left standing in the middle of a dark desert island in a monsoon, with no direction. My adventure on the little island had certainly taken a hard turn. I tried to convince myself that the whole trip including that very moment was all a dream. But it wasn't. And not so deep down, I knew it wasn't. As the rain poured on my head, I felt like I should be more pissed off than I was. But the truth was, I wasn't pissed off at all. I had gone to the island to get away. To take my mind off things back home. To have an adventure. And although things weren't the way I had expected, I had gotten more than my money's worth so far. I started to chuckle, then I laughed. It was funny, and it was the first time for a while that I had honestly laughed. The first time since … Dave. I reminisced back to the time in his hotel room after my long drive. My laughter turned to tears I looked to the sky and let the rain wash my face. I knew he was up there, and he was watching and he was laughing his ass off. I dropped my head and a smile returned to my face at the memories of my friend.

I turned a full circle and found one point of light, a small glimmer on the horizon. We had been travelling for a while in the direction of the Kon Tiki, or so I'd hoped. Either way, it was all I had to go to.

After what felt like hours of hiking, the rain had stopped. I sloshed into the yard of the Kon Tiki. All was thankfully quiet. I wasn't in much of a social mood and craved a warm shower. I fumbled with the lock on the door then a motion to my left drew my attention. I turned my head, remained silent and watched. It was the girl from the morning. I didn't recognize her at first because she was cleaner and had changed her clothes. It seemed strange for her to be out at that hour. As curious as I was, I was in no mood to trade stories about our evenings.

I turned back and fumbled frantically with the lock. Finally, it gave and I quietly slipped inside and closed the door softly behind me.

49

The next morning, I stood at the patio doors and looked out over the desert landscape as I pieced together the events from the previous night. It didn't seem quite as funny then as it had been when I was stranded in the dark downpour. I was concerned that Bernhard had gone back to town and filled everyone in on his side of the story, whatever that may be. How could I go back there? People would stare at me and whisper. And what if I ran into Bernhard? It would be awkward, and awkward was a situation I wasn't looking for on my vacation. If I did go to town, it would have to be a quick in and out. Judging by the lack of Bernie's physical condition, I guessed that one of the safest places on the island would be at the kite beach.

The wind was up as I watched the palm trees bowing and waving in the breeze, taunting me to come out and play. Today was the day.

I made my way over to the restaurant, and to my surprise, sitting at the bar visiting with Marion was the mystery girl that I had seen wandering the resort.

"Brandon!" Pieter busted through the swinging door. "Good morning. How was your time in town yesterday? I didn't hear you come in last night. Must have been late." He smiled excitedly waiting for details.

"It was good. I met Braam and … Bernhard." I spoke quietly and quickly, hoping to kill the momentum of the subject.

Pieter's smile faded at my lack of enthusiasm. He seemed to have caught my hint. "Well, that's good. I'm glad to see you made it home all right. Come, have a seat and I'll fix you some breakfast." He motioned to the bar stool beside the mystery girl.

Marion and her friend turned their heads. "Yes, Brandon, please come and join us," Marion pleasantly insisted.

I took the chair beside the girl and gave her a timid smile. "Brandon, have you met my niece yet. She is staying in the same building." She pointed to the young woman. "Aleida, this is Brandon. He is visiting us from Canada."

We shook hands. I was surprised at how well she cleaned up. Without the hat, her long blond hair was free to rest on her shoulders. Her eyes were a sharp blue and she had a natural smile that never faded. The dirty sweat clothes were replaced with a nice set of khaki shorts and a tank top that complemented a very feminine figure, full breasts, and slender tanned legs. Most unusual to me was the lack of makeup—no lipstick or cover-up, just a natural, confident glow.

"Brandon, so that is your name," she smiled. "I apologize for the other morning. If I would have known where you were from, I would have spoken in English. It is not the usual season for the North American tourists. I am happy to see you made it past the geckos without injury." She giggled. "It is very nice to meet you."

I blushed, hoping she hadn't noticed my cowardice state that morning. "It is very nice to meet you, too." She was beautiful, but I was still making an effort to detach myself from the opposite sex.

Pieter seemed as if he was putting in an effort to keep things flowing between us. He'd slip me a quick wink in secret as if he were doing me a favour. "Yes, Aleida, Brandon has come down to our island to study the art of kiteboarding."

"Ohhh, yes, kiteboarding. I watch them down on the one beach where I work. It looks dangerous."

I nodded, chuckling, "So you work at the kite beach?"

"No, no, I am on the other side of the Lac Bay."

Pieter cut in again, filling in all the gaps, "Aleida is a marine biologist. She is down here to study the sea turtles."

"Oh, wow, sea turtles." I showed a mild interest in effort to be polite. Again, I had a goal and finding love wasn't it. I already had a taste of Bonaire romance the night before.

"Yes. The turtles are in much danger in the Caribbean. Bonaire is one of the few safe places left for them to breed."

230

As much as I tried to avoid getting too interested in her, it was quite difficult not to. After all, it wasn't every day back on the prairies that I got introduced to a sexy marine biologist studying sea turtles. "So, you're a marine biologist, that's very interesting. It must pay well?" I figured a big dollar paycheck must have been her true motivation; a fifteen-letter title like that must pay out.

She laughed, softly leaning over the bar. "No, unfortunately it doesn't. We go to school for a long time and the title is sophisticated but the pay is not. Maybe if you write a paper perhaps. But I have sponsors and they pay for my travel. Some supplies and rooms are donated. I love to travel and I love working with animals. It seems it is all I need, for now." She looked up at the time. "Oh my, Brandon, I am sorry but I have to get to the beach. Please excuse me. It was very nice talking with you. We will see each other again I'm sure."

"Sure. We know where each other lives," I grinned.

"Thank you," she lifted her hand to Pieter and Marion. "Thank you for breakfast. I am going." She waved and headed out the door. I watched as she unhitched her donkey, complete with loaded saddlebags from its post.

Pieter was quick to get my thoughts, "So, what do you think?" He smiled eagerly.

I continued watching her walk away as I sipped on my drink, "She's…nice." I turned back. "So, she walks all the way to the other side of Lac Bay?"

He worked on polishing a glass, "Yes, she has always walked. She has her Shrek with her, that is what she calls her donkey." He chuckled. "She is a very independent young woman. She did have a partner once, a man. They were involved, and then for reasons I'm not sure of, he left. I have never asked and Marion has never talked about it. So anyway, my friend, today is a good day for the kiteboarding yes?"

"Yes, today is the day!" I pounded my fist lightly on the counter.

"Okay. So, you would like for me to drive you?"

I paused and looked back over my shoulder. Aleida had disappeared from sight. "No, no. I'm going to walk."

"Oh, Brandon, it is very hot," he frowned. "I know that Aleida can do it, but she has been here for a long while and has adjusted to the climate. Please let me drive you."

I stood from the bar and walked to the door. "Don't worry Pieter, I'll be all right. Thanks." I didn't give him a chance to protest as I disappeared around the corner with a smile and a wink.

About half an hour into the journey, I realized just how hot it really was as I observed the waves of heat throbbing from the road ahead. I decided to accept Pieter's offer for a ride, next time.

Then, like a God sent, from behind me squawked a toy like honk one would hear at a circus. It was followed by the familiar whine of a lawn mower being pushed beyond its limits. I turned around to see a lone, blond, shaggy haired surfer dude coming up behind me on a scooter, honking and waving. He skidded to a stop beside me.

"He-heey man, where you headed?" He smiled then bumped his fist on his chest twice rapidly followed with an odd type of three fingered hand gesture.

"I'm going to Lac Bay to try out some kiteboarding," I replied, shielding my eyes from the sun as I tried to get a better look at the dude.

"Awesome. I'm going there as well. Hop on, I'll give you a ride."

I looked over the small 50cc chariot, then the pilot. Another Dutch judging by the accent and the long shaggy blond hair. I'm sure it wasn't safe but I was more than ready to get out of the sun. "Yeah, sure, what the hell," I mounted on back the scooter. The little engine groaned as the dude pinned the throttle. I had to assist by running with my feet 'til we got up to speed.

The ride took only a couple of minutes, thankfully. It was bumpy and the driver didn't really help things out as he bounced up and down on the front, convinced he could pull a wheelie with my added leverage.

We pulled up to the Lac Bay, Air Bonaire hut. I thanked my chauffer and he bid me good luck. He pointed me around the side of the building and told me to ask for Gregoreo, the best instructor on the island.

I rounded the corner to the back of the hut where a dark-skinned man was busy sweeping the patio. He greeted me with a beaming smile and a strong handshake. "Good morning, my friend!" He bellowed joyously. "Welcome to Air Bonaire. I am Gregoreo. How can I help you today?"

"I'm Brandon. I'm visiting from Canada and I came down to Bonaire for one reason, to learn how to kiteboard. I heard you're the best, so I would like to pay for lessons and equipment rental up front for two weeks."

The dollar signs flashed in his eyes, but he resisted and advised me to hold off paying the full amount. "Yes, Brandon, my friend, but maybe you should just try it today and see if you like it. You may not want to go every day."

"I appreciate the warning Gregoreo, but this is what I came here to do. I'd like to pay for the full two weeks. And I guess I'll need some board shorts."

Gregoreo shrugged his shoulders. He escorted me back to the hut and got me fitted with some new shorts. I paid him the full amount.

I changed into my new gear. Admittedly, I liked the surfer look. I applied some sunscreen, then followed Gregoreo around to the side where sat a storage container with an assortment of kiteboard gear.

"So, Brandon, have you ever flown a kite like these before?"

"No, never."

"Okay then. I will teach you the basics of kite flying with this trainer kite." He grbbed a small bag from a shelf and tossed it at me then led me out to the beach where we found a suitable place to lay out the equipment. "The wind is good today. You must get to know the wind for kiteboarding. Feel it, the consistency, the power. It is a good day to learn."

In the bag was a small trainer kite. Gregoreo explained about the different types of kites. The one I had was a small two-line kite. It didn't require inflating the leading edge, which had to be done with some of the larger kites. He rambled on about C's and SLE's and stuff that was way over my head. "But you will learn about all that stuff as you go, Brandon. Right now, we have to get you feeling the wind." He winked.

We laid the kite out on the beach, then unrolled the lines from the ski bar contraption, walking upwind of the kite. After we straightened the lines, Gregoreo gave me some quick instructions on how to fly the kite. Hooking up the lines to the kite was quick and easy. We went through the steps. I picked up the bar and he grabbed the kite. He then walked it to the edge of what he called the wind window. Then, as if the kite were as light as a feather, I steered it out of his grasp and high into the sky straight overhead.

He explained the whole theory about the wind window and how the 12:00, 3, and 9:00 positions were where the kite had the least pull while straight down at the 6:00 was the high-power area. It was only a matter of minutes before I had the kite climbing and streaking through the air. Gregoreo complimented me on my skills and said I caught on fast. He motioned me into the water a short distance up to my knees. He then left me to practice while he attended to other clients.

I continued for an hour. The kite was small enough that I could overpower it, but even at that size, the straight down wind still gave it a surprising pull.

Gregoreo returned, this time with bigger gear. He landed my kite and brought me back to shore where he had me put on something called a harness. It was basically a pair of molded padded shorts with straps all around for tightening to your body and a round metal hook jutting out right below my naval. They felt fine, but the metal hook made me nervous.

He tossed a hand pump on the ground and rolled out what was a six-metre, four-line inflatable kite that was three times the size of the one I had just flown. It was quite an aggressive step up, I thought. He demonstrated the process of inflating the kite. At only six metres, It wasn't that hard. But I got a feeling about the work involved to inflate some of the bigger models.

Bigger kite meant more lines and more power but it used the same basic principles. The steel hook on the harness, I found out, was used to connect the kite to your body, which added a whole new level of excitement.

With the kite in the air and the loop from the bar secured to the hook on my harness, Gregoreo guided me out into the water till I was waist deep this time. Since I had landed in the island heat, I had always thought a cold dip in the ocean would be refreshing. But I found the water surprisingly warm, like a bathtub.

With more instructions, he had me diving the kite. However, this kite had more power than I could hold. Instead of trying to stand and resist the power, Gregoreo had me body drag behind it. He followed close behind in a small, motorized inflatable boat, shouting instructions along the way.

It was a little rough at first, diving the kite to aggressively would cause it to yank hard on my body. That would cause me to panic and send the kite crashing to the water. This forced me to relaunch the kite solo while floating in the water with a kite pulling me downwind. It was exhausting and frustrating. I was flailing my arms and legs, trying to keep my body straight while taking in water hacking and coughing. It was more than enough to make one quit. But I didn't, repeatedly telling myself it was what I came to do. Then, about halfway across the bay, I began to get the hang of it. I got the feel for the power of the kite, the wind. My body drag became smooth and consistent and I crashed the kite less. At the end of the bay, Gregoreo deflated the kite and wrapped it up, then collected me on his way back to the start beach.

We sped along the water in the boat, the salty spray of the water sprinkling on my face. In the sky, the sun had begun its western descent.

"Well, Brandon," Gregoreo yelled over the whine of the motor. "you've done very well today. The next step tomorrow will be to get a board on your feet. It shouldn't take long now to get you up and riding."

"Tomorrow?" I yelled back. "But the wind, it's still good. We have plenty of daylight left. Why can't I try it right now?"

Gregoreo looked at me in disbelief. After many hours of wrestling with the kite, he must have expected me to be exhausted. I'm sure most beginners would have thrown in the towel long before that point. But I was on some type of personal mission that enabled me to push through any physical trauma. There was a determination inside me that insisted I ride that board, and tomorrow was behind schedule. I looked over the bay and only a few kites remained in the sky. Most people had packed up for the evening. It was a perfect time for me, an empty bay all to myself.

"Listen, Gregoreo. I know you're probably ready to close at this time, but look." I pointed to the empty bay. "It's the perfect time for me. I'll do all the set up. You won't have to lift a finger. I'll pay whatever price you ask. I need this Greg."

He looked at me apprehensively, then to the sky, then back to the pleading desperation on my face. "All right my friend. We will try it, we will try." He forced a smile.

We returned to the hut and Gregoreo handed me the big one, a twelve-metre. By the time I had it inflated and launched, the sun was sinking lower, casting an orange hue across the bay. But the wind was still strong and consistent. I walked slowly into the water with the massive kite lofting overhead. Gregoreo puttered along beside me in the boat.

"Okay, Brandon. Just sit down into the water and then put your lead foot into the strap. Then when you feel the time is right, push the board out quickly and place your other foot in the back strap."

It was frustrating. Every time I took my eyes off the kite to look at the board, it would shift a little in the sky and pulled me out of position. I had to scramble and collect my board and start all over. As the sun continued to sink, my body grew weaker and I began to feel my strength deplete. I drew in a deep breath and regained my focus. No matter what the cost, this was going to happen today.

Slowly but surely, I began to master the technique of getting the board on my feet, while retaining control.

"Okay Brandon, good … good," Gregoreo shouted happily. "Now when you are ready, dive the kite hard, straight downwind and push hard on your lead leg."

Okay, board on feet. Wait ... wait ... Now!

I twisted the bar and the kite dipped toward the water, jerking hard on my harness. I pressed hard on my leg then came up briefly out of the water, and before I could think how incredible I was, I was yanked clear of the water with incredible force, and smashed back down to the surface face-first. I drug lifeless for a bit then I came up, coughing and sputtering the salt water burned in my lungs and sinuses.

"That's it. I'm done Greg. Let's pack up."

It was now Gregoreo's time to prod me along. "Brandon, you are so close. Just give it one more try. Concentrate. You have to dive the kite, dive it straight for the water, Brandon, do not be afraid of the power. Dive it as hard as you can then push on your lead leg. You can do it, my friend."

I stood in Lac Bay just Gregoreo and I. The sun was nothing more than a half ball floating on the ocean. I had done so much that day. I had everything to be proud of already, but the thought of surrendering and letting the world beat me, kept me going. I owed it to myself and to Greg to give it one more go, give it everything I had.

I took another deep breath and pushed back my fatigue. "All right Greg. One more try."

I sat down in the water again and looked up to the kite high overhead swaying back and forth tauntingly. I got the board on my feet and managed to keep the kite under control. I closed my eyes and reviewed the instructions then envisioned myself riding the board. *Dive the kite, deep this time, chicken shit. Then just push on your right leg. Simple. Just do that and you'll be up.*

I opened my eyes and looked back overhead to the giant wing in the sky, waiting for my command. Another crash would be the end of me. I pressed back the fear. I drew long, deep breaths to calm my nerves and regain my composure. I felt the bar in my hands, the board on my feet, and the wind on my neck. Everything around me fell silent. I even blocked out Greg. I concentrated on the kite tipping left to right, then the wind picked up ever so slightly and the kite stiffened. I held the bar perfectly still, just for a moment. *Now!*

I pulled in hard on my right arm at the same time thrusting out with my left, twisting the bar a complete ninety degrees. The kite stalled for a millisecond waiting for my command to travel down the lines, then it tipped right side wrong

236

and shot straight toward the water. My pulse switched to rapid fire, but I didn't flinch, did not even blink, as it picked up speed, faster and faster. Then the sound, the scream of a fighter jet shooting from the sky, and the bar began to resonate in my hands. Raw adrenaline pounded through my veins, everything I had left. I whispered my challenge. *Bring it, fucker!* And it did bring it, and then some. Halfway down to the water, the mighty hand of Mother Nature reached to my waist and pulled me from the water like nothing more than a leaf on the breeze. There was no puff of smoke or roar of engine, just an invisible force, powerful enough to alter the very face of the earth.

I stiffened my right leg and came up onto the board. I had to react fast. As the kite neared the surface, I switched the direction of the bar. Pulling now with my left and pushing with the right, the kite instantly changed from dive to climb. Its wingtip lightly grazed the ocean surface. It continued to pull, blasting hard into the sky and giving another strong pull at my waist. I turned my board slightly downwind to counter the force. Finally, everything relaxed. The board planed out. I stroked the kite up and down like a master puppeteer. It heeded my every command. *You did it. You fucking did it man!, Look at you!* I relaxed and leaned back in my harness resting my weight on the kite.

The sound of the motor boat at high throttle came up behind me.

"Look Brandon, you are doing it! Go man, gooooo!"

"Woooooo hoooooo! Fuck ya!!! Fuuuck yaaaaaa!!!" I screamed at the top of my lungs, shooting a fist in the air.

I cruised out into the bay then headed back to the shore. I didn't want to quit, but it would be dark soon. I looked back over the bay. I was exhausted but thrilled at my accomplishment. Once I was able to control my fear, it all just came together.

I landed the kite on the beach and collapsed on the sand behind it, every last ounce of energy spent from my body. After a minute, I sat up and looked out over the bay. The water shimmered with the light of the setting sun. The waves lapped gently on the shore. The salt breeze ruffled my hair and the warm sand squished between my toes.

I sat and reflected on the day. Sucking in the ocean water, coughing and hacking, struggling furiously as the kite constantly pulled at me, being slammed so hard to the water over and over. But I never quit, and in the end I did it. It was like nothing I had ever done before. I never wanted to stop.

Then I thought back to the first night on the rigs when I helped fix the pump—all the cold, the dirt, and the pain. For what? For a big paycheck. All those guys up there working huge shifts risking their lives for the companies—it now seemed like such an ugly world. Katy, Steve, Dave, all of it seemed so far away. The ocean water had finally washed away the stubborn oil stains that had permanently set into my elbows. I was cleansed, and for the first time since I could remember, I felt free. I looked to the sky where the stars began to replace the sun's rays, and I felt my friend Dave smiling down. I accomplished something beautiful that day.

50

The next morning, I woke refreshed and reborn as a kiteboarder. Nothing could take the smile from my face. It was a fabulous day, and I was anxious to get back on the water. That is, until I attempted to move from my bed. Something vicious had happened during my slumber. Every joint and muscle in my body ached. Having avoided any type of serious physical activity since the start of puberty, I was caught unaware of the consequences of such pastimes like kiteboarding. I squeaked and groaned myself to a sitting position on the side of the bed. I leaned over and slowly moved all my limbs to get a full tally of the damage. My back, shoulders, arms—not one inch was spared from punishment. Even my hands and fingers creaked from holding the control bar. Large blisters had formed in spots and the tops of my feet were very badly burnt.

After I sat for a bit, I was able to force my battered carcass to the shower. Despite my physical pain, my ecstatic mood never faltered. I got dressed quickly, wanting to get to the restaurant. Somewhere in my subconscious I hoped to run into Aleida at breakfast. She could look upon me for the first time as the warrior I had become. But when I arrived at the restaurant, neither her nor Shrek were anywhere to be found.

Pieter picked up on my surveillance, "I'm sorry, my friend, but she has already left." He chuckled.

I blushed, not realizing how obvious I was. She wasn't really my type, but it was nice to have someone my age to talk to. She was interesting, and now I was also interesting, no more fix pump stories for Brandon. Now I was the master of the wind and sea.

"So, you look a little beat up and quite burnt. Did you have a good day kiteboarding?" He smiled because I know he had been through the same experience at some time. And despite my beating, he knew I had a great time.

We talked over breakfast. I filled him in on my accomplishment and he congratulated me, laughing and shaking my hand.

"That is fabulous Brandon, good for you. So, what for today, are you going to return for more kiteboarding?"

"Oh," I let out an exhausted sigh. "I would love to Pieter, but my body really hurts today. I had such a good day yesterday, but I think maybe it would be best to rest and heal."

"Yes, it can be very physically demanding when you are first learning." He slapped his hands together, rubbing frantically. "All right, I have the perfect thing. Today I have the day off. There is this awesome band in town tonight. You will love them, and then I can give you a proper tour of the town."

I was backed into a corner. Having already explained how I was too exhausted to kiteboard, I couldn't fall back on the excuse now. And really, sitting in town enjoying some cold beers and taking in the local talent sounded pretty right on. I feared the awkwardness of running into Bernhard. But what would really happen? He was the one who made an ass of himself. I couldn't let him ruin my whole vacation. "All right Pieter. Let's go."

"Excellent," he slapped me on the shoulder. "I'll get my things."

Bouncing back along the dusty highway toward the city, I stared out the window, nervously pondering the possibility of an encounter with my dirty old friend Bernhard. But as we drew closer, I grew tired of thinking about it and decided that I would deal with it as it came. I was a new man, after all.

We got to town and I went to the bank first. They had access to my account so everything was good. Pieter walked me through town, pointing out different areas and shops. It really wasn't that big for a capital city.

By mid-afternoon, men and women dressed in colourful Caribbean attire flooded Braam's restaurant and a large crowd had gathered on the street out front. Pieter introduced me to all the patrons, many of whose names I couldn't pronounce. They were all very friendly.

"Hey, Pieter, my friend," A young Spanish man, darkly tanned with dark,

240

wavy, shoulder length hair approached Pieter and slapped him on the back. Pieter turned and hugged his friend.

"Leo, it has been a long time. It is good to see you. How have you been?"

"Busy as I like to be. Working in the restaurant and teaching the dancing to the beautiful ladies." They laughed. Leo looked at me quickly through the corner of his eye.

"Oh, I'm sorry," Pieter looked back. "This is my friend Brandon. He is visiting from Canada, came down to learn kiteboarding. Brandon, this is my long-time, good friend Leonardo, or Leo works just fine."

We shook hands. "Brandon, it is very nice to meet you. So, kiteboarding hey. Those mother fuckers are crazy!"

I chuckled, "Yeah, I thought so at first, but it's actually not as bad as it looks."

Pieter stepped in, "Brandon, you stick with Leo here. He is friends with everyone, especially the local women." He winked and nudged my shoulder.

"Yes, Brandon. Come, my friend, I will introduce you." He turned to the crowd and held his hands in the air yelling something out in Spanish, or Dutch, I really couldn't tell. The crowd parted slightly as everyone turned to listen to his announcement. The men laughed and the group of women in the back cheered and called out his name as he began to shake his hips in a sultry fashion. They begged him to join them.

"Come, Brandon, let's party." He grabbed me by the arm and dragged me along.

It was fantastic. Finally, there was someone my age who was acquainted with the local ladies. Not that I was looking. Leo knew everyone, pretty well, and anyone he didn't he was quick to get introduced. He was a local dance instructor on the side and he had taught most of the island women. He took his turn bumping and grinding with them. I was surprised and thankful to see all the boyfriends laugh it off as no big deal. Leo seemed to have that same ability as Nate back home. Some guys can just get away with that shit.

I spent the rest of the afternoon with Leo, meeting the local lovelies dressed in their sexy sundresses. Then he noticed the clock and announced it was time for him to leave for his job at a restaurant down the street. The crowd booed the news.

I was also bummed at the news. I was really beginning to have a good time with Leo. With him gone, I would be left to return to Pieter. It was fine, but he was married and not so much into wheeling and dealing the ladies. Not that I was looking.

I felt a tap on my shoulder. "Brandon, why don't you come with me?" Leo invited.

"What, go to work with you?"

"Yes, it is just another restaurant down the street. The chef prepares a meal for the workers before it opens. The rush only lasts a few hours, and then we will be free to return here to the party. If Pieter needs you, he will know where to find you."

"Oh, I don't know Leo."

"C'mon, Brandon, it'll be no trouble at all. I insist." He again dragged me by the arm from the crowd.

The restaurant wasn't far, just down the main street overlooking the ocean. It was called The Flying Fish. A quaint place with rattan furniture tastefully decorated in island colours. A chain blocked the short flight of stairs that led up to the establishment to indicate it was still closed to the public.

Leo casually unhooked the chain and waved me through then hooked it back up. We made our way up to the main floor.

Everyone turned to greet us. Leo held his arms open wide with a joyous announcement. "Youp, Don, everyone, meet Brandon, my new friend from Canada. He will be joining us for supper tonight."

I leaned over to Leo, "Supper? Leo, you didn't have to. I really don't—"

"Nonsense, Brandon, come sit down."

Leo made the rounds through the group and introduced me to everyone. Youp and Don were the owners. Both of them from Holland. They had taken a risk and invested their life savings into the restaurant. They were both quite tall, over six feet, with slim athletic builds. No one ever said for sure, but I guessed them to be brothers. Youp had long spiralling blond hair while Don had a shorter brush cut.

"Hi Youp, Don, thank you very much for … Leo said I could, but I really didn't …"

"It is our pleasure, Brandon. Any friend of Leo's is a friend of ours. Please sit and enjoy the feast our chef Alex has prepared."

The supper happened every night before the restaurant opened. All the staff would gather for a complimentary meal. Understanding this, I was expecting scraps left over from the previous night. That would have been fine. But instead,

242

the plate placed before me held a meal fit for royalty. It was not just a meal, but a work of art. The chef took great pride in presentation. It was even more splendid than the decorative Big Mac cartons back home.

It was delicious, whatever it was. Alex explained the venture as we helped ourselves. We ate a special cut of beef shaved paper thin with assorted vegetables. The sauce combined the groups in a festive harmony in my mouth.

Bellies full, the staff busied themselves cleaning the mess, then changed into their appropriate attire for the coming shift. I offered to help, but they insisted instead that I take up a stool at the bar before they opened. Youp mixed me a tasty rum concoction with fresh mint leaves.

The chains were opened and the tourists filed in to their tables. It was a busy environment. The staff worked well together and provided top-notch service. I sat on my stool talking with the staff when they would stop at the bar to fill an order.

The sun slowly extinguished into the ocean, turning the sky over to shine a brilliant starlight display. The supper crowd thinned as quickly as it filled. The attendants one by one removed their aprons and joined me at the bar. Leo mixed some experimental drinks he had been working to perfect, then we filed out to join the party on the street, which was a regular occurrence for the islanders.

Crowded with people, the street was alive with excitement. At a small bar, nestled on a peer about a hundred feet into the bay, a small stage had been prepared for one of the bands. The bassist struck a deep chord to signal the beginning of their set. The sound echoed a wave across the surrounding ocean. They played good rock, mostly European, but stuff that was still familiar from back home.

I snuck off to the side and separated from the group for a bit to take a breather. I'd had a few drinks already, and was a little cautious about getting too drunk. Scared that Bernhard may appear and start to circle around me, sensing another opportune moment. I leaned over the railing that bordered the ocean and stared in awe out over the water. The stars were amazing. I had never seen so many. Then, out on the horizon shone a halo of light, like a star had fallen into the ocean.

Leo checked into my shoulder and disrupted my hypnosis. It wasn't hard to tell that he was well into party mode as he stumbled slightly. Then he did something unexpected but welcomed. He pulled out a big fat dubie, placed it between his lips, and lit it ablaze. Small embers floated out over the water. He lit it right by the crowd. He didn't give a shit about being seen. My luck was getting better and better. I was glad I had gone to town. Although I had only just met Leo, I could tell we were going to be good friends.

He coughed out a large cloud then offered the joint over to me, "You smoke?"

"You kidding? I'm from Canada man. We grow the best shit around." I accepted the offer, and took a big tug, grateful for an alternative to the booze. The weed hit smooth and hard instantly, forcing my eyes to slits and my smile to my ears. Life was good. Just when I thought the island couldn't get any better.

"This is fucking awesome man, thanks."

"For suuure, dude." We laughed.

"So, Leo," I struggled to continue through small bouts of laughter. "you're from Venezuela, right? How did you end up out here?"

He stopped laughing and his smile faded. He looked down at the water. "Well, I had a fight with my father. It was stupid, really, but he's a stubborn man. So, I just left. Hopped on a boat that was heading over to Europe. They stopped here for the night and I stayed. Didn't make it very far, did I?" He nudged me and his smile returned.

"Shit, man! I'm sorry."

"Forget it, my friend." He placed a friendly arm around my shoulder. "It is in the past."

Feeling stupid, I searched for a quick change of topic. "Hey, what the hell is that out there?" I pointed to the mysterious halo on the horizon.

He stretched to his full height, keeping hold of my shoulder for support. "Ah, those lights way off there, that is Curacao. Another island off the coast of Venezuela."

"No shit! Man, we must be really close."

Just then the band struck up a tune I recognized immediately. As the strong bass guitar began into the familiar riff, Zombie, by the Cranberries, came to life. I never would have considered that song for that moment, but they played it just perfect, better than perfect. I turned slowly, taking in the entirety of the surroundings. Everybody was laughing and cheering. I had found new friends, a new passion, a new life on a tiny island a million miles from my roots. A million miles it seemed, from anything. It was surreal. If I could have picked a point in my life to stay and exist only in that moment, it would have been then.

244

51

At the kite beach the next morning, I was back up on the board immediately. Back and forth across the bay, my new focus was to practice my turning transitions and staying upwind. It took a bit. Gregoreo had to collect me from the far end of the bay a couple of times. But later into the afternoon I found myself consistently able to return to my starting point. After learning to ride the board, it was quite easy to advance in the sport. My next challenge would be to jump. I studied the others as they launched effortlessly into the air—over ten feet easy—and float back down to a soft landing. They made it look easy, but for the time being, I decided I was comfortable with my board on the water.

The sport had consumed me. It was all I thought about, even when I was away from the bay. At supper, at breakfast, even in my sleep, I mentally retraced my moves from my daily session. What I did wrong, and what technique I would focus on next. I understood now why people who had experienced it, would express themselves so passionately about it. I couldn't help but wonder though, if it was solely the sport that had possessed me, or a combination with a need to escape the past. Whatever the explanation, it had my full attention, and I was more than willing to let it blow me where it willed.

One time, toward the end of the day, I took a long ride down to the end of the bay and stopped in the shallows for a moment, before I began my long trek upwind. I looked out to the waves of the open ocean breaking on the distant reef then to the opposite shore, and there, although I had to squint to make her out, was Aleida, moving along hunched over. She seemed to be studying the ground. I may not have recognized her if it weren't for her loyal mule Shrek following close behind.

I stood with my kite fluttering high overhead and tried to make out what she was doing. She seemed to dig in the sand for something, deposited it in one of Shrek's saddlebags, then grabbed his rope and began to lead him back in the direction of the Kon Tiki.

I couldn't help think how strange a specimen she was herself. Maybe someone should study her? I decided she was right; it was getting late and packing it in seemed like a smart idea. It had been many hours for me in the sun. I collected my board and powered my kite then made my way back to the beach.

I packed up my gear and headed back to the Kon Tiki, just in time to see Aleida close the door of her upstairs apartment.

I decided it would be nice to have a rinse off and remove all the salt and sand from my cracks and crevices before heading down for supper.

Returning to the restaurant, I grabbed a beer at the bar and took some time at the computer to check my emails.

From Dad:

The Caribbean! I'll admit I didn't see that one coming. It's good, I guess. As long as you're not on a giant bender to end all benders. Take time to clear your head and rest up. Have a good time and things will be better when you come home. Please be careful, and make it home in one piece. I love you son.

P.S. Katy called, I didn't tell her anything.

Reply:

Hey, Dad just checking in again. Life is great down here. I've learned to kiteboard. It's awesome. The people are awesome, the whole island is awesome. Don't worry, I'm not drinking hardly at all, and all the things back home are far away for now. I'm just living the moment. Sorry for the late reply but emails aren't a high priority right now. Take care and say hi to Mom if you talk to her.

Love Brandon

The next email was a surprise.

246

From Joey:

Brand, it's been hard for me to find the courage to do this, but since the incident at Christmas I kind of did some adjusting. I got some professional help with the booze. I've been clean now for almost six months. I still see the guys, but not as much. I stay away from the bars now, best not tempt it. Since my dry out, I've been promoted at work. Now I just drive around doing P.R. work with the clients. Life is good so far on the dry side.

I ran into your dad the other day and he filled me in about the accident at work and he mentioned that Katy had left. Listen, Brand, I'm really sorry for what happened. I didn't mean any of it. I hope it wasn't what caused the breakup. I feel like a shit about the whole thing, I was just in a bad spot at the time and I took it out on you. I hope you can forgive me. You've always been a good friend.

Your old man also mentioned you'd fucked off to the Caribbean? That's fucking crazy! I wish I were there with you. Don't let the shit back here get you down man. You take care of yourself.

Love Joey

P.S. I have to say love. It's about being honest with my feelings or something, part of the therapy.

I laughed to myself and tears welled in my eyes. It was good to have my friend back.

Reply:

Joey, good to have you back buddy. No hard feelings. I hate to admit it but you were right, she's a bitch. Glad to hear you're figuring things out. Someday you and I will take a trip like this. I'm down on an island called Bonaire, look it up. I've taken up this kiteboarding thing. It's awesome, and there's tons of chicks down here. Take care buddy. I'll come see you when I get back.

I like you too, Brandon

And last and least from Katy:

Brandon,

Things didn't work out with me and Brad. Turned out after you made that big scene at the gym, well half the clientele came forward and claimed he was screwing them, and two of the other trainers. He's an ass. His wife found out and she's leaving him. Taking all his shit too. Anyway, I was wrong. It was stupid of me to go for him. I guess I was just lonely. You were gone so much. I want to give it another chance. Please call me.

Love Katy

It didn't sting as much anymore to hear from her. I wasn't even sure if I was still angry at her. I could understand her point to some extent. I was gone a lot, and she's a sexy girl. I was stupid to think someone wasn't going to move in on her. I began to accept it for what it was—a fuck up on both our parts. A powerful realization hit me as I sat there contemplating how a few days before, my whole world had been crushed. I had nowhere to go and no hope on the horizon. Time had healed the wound. I sat there trying to get angry about what she had done, but there was nothing, not a hint of emotion. It had happened, and now what was happening was kiteboarding, and nothing else mattered.

Reply:
Katy, I'm sorry to hear that things didn't work out for you and Brad. He seemed like a good guy, I guess.

I apologize for the way I reacted. I see now that the whole thing was as much my fault as anyone's. I was at a really bad point in my life. Maybe I'll tell you about it sometime. Right now, I'm too far away to really care. It's totally fucked up crazy, but it's exactly what I needed.

I considered my options for an ending. She said the word love, so did that mean I was obligated to do the same? Finally, I just got tired of thinking about it.

Keep in touch, Brandon.

Done with the emails, I logged out and headed back to the restaurant where I found Aleida sitting by the bar. She waved me over to join her. "Hi Aleida. How are your turtles doing?"

"Hello, Brandon." She smiled. "The turtles are doing very well. In fact, I have to return tonight. I am expecting to see some breeding on the beach."

After my recent closure with the Katy thing, I thought Aleida's suggestion of breeding on the beach sounded quite chafing, but I could probably be persuaded "You're really busy. I saw you out there earlier. I was in the bay kiteboarding."

"Yes, the kiteboarding. How is it working?"

"It's going really well, thanks. I'm already turning and stuff."

"That is great. You will be riding the professional competitions soon." She smiled.

Pieter and Marion watched silently as Aleida and I drifted into conversation about our adventures on the island, laughing and joking with each other. It took shape so naturally, I didn't even realize. There was no awkward sexual tension. It seemed we just played the part of two people thankful for some company.

When we finished our meals, the sun outside was barely enough to cast a faint glow in the sky. I sensed her urgency to get on with work, so I thought it best to leave. I stood from my chair. "Well, thanks for the company Aleida. I guess I'll let you get off to work."

She smiled, then hesitated before she popped the question. "Brandon, seeing as I kept you company through dinner, it only seems fair for you to return the favour."

I looked down, confused. "Yeah, sure. What did you have in mind?"

"I have to go back out to the beach tonight. It will be a long evening and I would enjoy a companion, other than Shrek of course. Would you like to join me and learn about the turtles? It may not be as exciting as the kiteboard, but …" She scrunched up her shoulders and applied the puppy dog eyes. The seductive side of her caught me off guard. I would never have pegged her for the type that would resort to such measures.

She was cute and what the hell, I had nothing else planned for the night. There had to be something to those turtles for her to be as nuts about them as I was about kiteboarding. "Sure, why not?"

She jumped from her seat and clapped her hands tightly in front of her, inadvertently enhancing her cleavage.

"Good. Well, we should hurry." She stood up and turned to look for Pieter.

He was standing quietly in the shadows and sprang over to us as soon as she stood. "Oh, Pieter. I guess we'll be needing—"

"Already packed and ready, sandwiches and water … for two." He smiled and held up two large, brown paper bags.

Aleida blushed brightly, and giggled softly. It was a state of insecurity I never expected from her, and strangely, I found her more attractive for it.

We accepted the bags and went outside where she packed the supplies in to Shrek's travel bags. She gathered his pull cord and we made our way off into the twilight.

It was a long walk. Thankfully, the sun was down and the nighttime temperature was bearable. Despite the distance, we never once lacked for conversation. We talked about our homelands and how we grew up. Coming from very different backgrounds, we had an endless list of questions.

The night was full when we arrived at the beach. The sky was clear and the stars again were incredible.

She immediately went to work, rummaging through a saddlebag and producing a headband with a small spotlight attached. She then grabbed my hand and led me across the beach in search of her turtles.

It didn't take long to find them. They were out in a busy abundance, building nests and laying eggs. I followed her as she searched the beach, stopping to examine certain specimens and different nests. She documented the turtles by the different markings on their shells. I found it surprisingly interesting, both the turtles and Aleida.

Her lengthy detailed research took us into the early morning. Satisfied that she had collected all the information she could, we found a comfortable spot on a sand dune and brought out our paper bag lunches. I admit the turtle inspection was harder than it looked.

I examined my sandwich before taking a bite. Making sure it was a food group familiar to me. "So Aleida, this is quite a big project to take on by yourself. Usually when I watch stuff like this on television, there's like a group of scientists." I was curious about the male partner Pieter had mentioned to me earlier.

She remained silent for a moment while she finished her mouthful, then she took a drink. I suspected she was using the time to outline a reply. "Yes, well, I had a partner when I first started. He was a mentor, really, from home. We met in school. He tutored me through some of my subjects. He was considerably older than me, by ten years. He'd travelled a lot, to many amazing places. It was stupid, really. We got involved romantically, which is not very professional. But you can't pick who you fall in love with."

I nodded. "So, what happened? Where is he now?"

"I don't really like to talk about it. But now that I know, things that happened in the past make more sense. It is neither of our fault. We just realized that we were not meant to be. So, he took off on his next adventure and I stayed here in Bonaire to continue the turtle research."

"I'm sorry, I didn't mean to intrude." I said. "I have a story that is way worse than that if it will cheer you up." I figured it only fair, seeing as I had pried and made her depressed.

It worked. As I finished my painfully drawn-out story of shame, we both burst into laughter.

"Really Brandon, that is so sad." She placed a hand on my shoulder. "What a horrible woman this Katy. You really went into the gym after her and her big muscle man?"

"Yeah," my laughter dampened. I turned to her, looking in her big blue eyes, slight tears of laughter hung on her cheeks. "I was really drunk."

"I'm sorry, I should not laugh. It is a horrible story."

"Nah, it's nothing. Now that I look back on it, we were doomed." I looked down to the beach. "Thanks for listening Aleida. I haven't told anyone that story. I really needed that."

"I'm sorry to hear that this Katy left you for another man, but really, can you blame her?"

I turned to her a little shocked at her bluntness, and the way she continued to smile.

"When I hear the story, Brandon, I am wondering if she left you for another man, or if you left her for a job that you didn't even like. Working up in the cold with these ugly machines, with these corporations that put you in danger. That is the way you have just described it to me."

"Well, yeah but. … yeah." My shoulders slumped as I realized how I described what I once considered a dream job.

"It really doesn't sound like you enjoy your work very much. Yet you leave this girl you say you were in love with for very long times. Why?"

"Well, for the money."

"Yes, the money, it is nice, but what about you? You see, I am having a hard time understanding this working so much at something you hate. This, what I do here is something I believe in and I may never make good money. But I am helping a good cause, and I am happy and healthy. There is not much chance of a turtle exploding or something falling on me. How does one put a price on placing themselves in danger so much? It is your life Brandon."

I picked up a handful of sand and watched it filter through my fingers and fall back to the beach where it piled, just like at the bottom of an hourglass.

"I guess it's all I know. All the guys back home want to work the rigs."

"Maybe you are not all the guys back home. Maybe you are Brandon." She looked at me innocently, like the conversation had me dancing a thin line between anger and revelation.

I wasn't upset, not at her. I was confused. She was right. No matter how many safety courses a person completes, accidents happen. If they didn't happen, there would be no safety courses. Control was an illusion. So how do you put a price on your own life?

I turned my focus from the sand up to her eyes. We both felt it, the moon, the beach, the gentle waves, the emotion and the mystery sandwiches. It was romantic as hell.

As we looked in each other's eyes, we began to drift inward. Our lips pulsed softly, then I stalled, only for a second, but it was enough to break the spell of the moment. We pulled back and turned away, finding other places to focus.

I couldn't be sure, but I sensed a hint of disappointment in her. "Well, I am finished here for tonight, and it is very late. We should head back." She stood and brushed the sand from her shorts.

52

The next day, I continued kiteboarding. I had advanced to the doorstep of the jumping phase. Gregoreo filled me in on the basics, and I began to test my new wings on the water. Just small at first. I'd steer the kite overhead and feel it climb into the air and pull on my waist until my feet became light on the board. I lost my board the first few times, but I wisely stuck to the shallows so I could walk back and retrieve it. It was fatiguing, and after a couple of laps I landed my kite, found a shaded chair on the deck of the hut, and relaxed with a cold iced tea.

Sitting at the table, I looked back as a growing rumble announced the coming rally of vintage vehicles. They pulled up in front, all polished and sparkling in the tropic sun.

The men and women of the rally parked their vehicles and made their way to the deck of the hut. Dressed in their Sunday's best, they were all laughing joyously. As they rounded the corner to the deck, a tingle in my spine straightened the hairs on the back of my neck. Bernhard.

At first he laughed along with the rest, until he noticed me sitting at the table. Then his laughter stopped as his eyes dropped nervously to the deck. The group lined up at the refreshment stand one by one and got their orders. Most of them moved down to the beach to take in the action. I expected Bernhard to follow his friends and avoid me. Instead, with his group otherwise occupied, he took the chance to pull up a chair at my table.

His eyes remained trained on the table while he gathered himself. Then he looked up at me. "Hello Brandon." He smiled meekly.

I smiled back in an attempt at politeness, but the rest of me felt rank with irritation. "Bernhard, how are you?"

"I'm good, thank you. Listen, Brandon, this is very hard for me, but I really want to apologize for the other night. I had mistaken you for something that you are not. It's just, you are down here alone. Usually when we get young male travellers to the island they are … Anyway, it doesn't matter. But if you could please … I have many clients on the island, and if some were to find out …." There was sincerity in his eyes, and a pleading in his voice.

I was relieved to find that Bernhard was as anxious to keep this as quiet as I. Now having addressed my fears, my nerves were eased knowing the secret would be locked in a vault and we could forget all about it. My tension faded. "Don't worry Bernhard. I haven't told anyone, and I don't plan to."

He exhaled a heavy burden. "Oh thank you Brandon. Thank you so very much."

"It's all right. You were drunk, I was drunk, and no one was hurt. Let's forget about it." I smiled and held my glass up. It felt good to get the whole dreaded encounter over with. Now I could fully relax and enjoy the rest of my vacation.

He smiled as his glass connected with mine. "Thank you my friend." He took a sip of his beer and looked down to the beach. His friends were beginning to regroup for their departure.

Bernhard stood from the table. "I'm glad we got this chance to talk. You are a good person, Brandon. Take care." He waved goodbye as he disappeared around the corner and reunited with his friends.

53

I took a break from kiteboarding the next day and returned to town. I met up with the gang at The Flying Fish by mid-morning. Some were just sitting around. Others were in preparation mode for the evening rush. I sat down for coffee and they took turns updating me on the local events and quizzed me up on my kiteboarding experience.

"Brandon," Leo announced excitedly. "My roommate has lent me his car for the day. Have you seen all of the island yet?"

"I don't know Leo. I've been to the Kon Tiki and the kite beach and here. Is there really that much more to see?"

"Oh yes, there is the whole north side of the island. Come, there are still things you must see before you go." He disappeared behind the bar and returned with a six pack in hand. "Guys, I am taking our friend on a tour. I will be back in time for work."

They wished us well as we walked down the street, where I followed Leo around the corner to an old blue, late seventies Datsun station wagon. "It is not sexy but it is perfect for the island terrain," he joked. "Get in."

We sped through town. Leo drove his way through the streets with ease using his own mental map of the pothole locations. Then the city faded from view as we headed off into the hot arid plains, toward the north end of the island.

I was surprised to see some hills covered in lush vegetation. There were some small shops where we stopped in for a couple of drinks. Leo knew everyone on this side of the island as well. So we had many people to visit.

Finally, Leo brought the blue stallion to a grinding stop, producing a cloud of dust that engulfed the car. When I got clear of the haze, I found we had parked in front of yet another small hut placed in a shaded cove of leafy green trees.

Leo came up from behind and slapped me on the back. A lit joint hung from his mouth. "These are the mangroves. They are beautiful, right?" He squinted at me with a raised eyebrow.

I took the joint from him. "Yes, it's awesome." I smiled back, taking a big pull while scanning the area and nodding slowly.

"Bob! Hey, Bob!" Leo called out as he walked toward the hut.

A dark-skinned man came out from behind the hut planting a machete-like blade he was carrying in a stump. He pulled a rag from his back pocket and wiped the sweat from his brow. He smiled and greeted us in a language unknown to me. Leo walked over to him and they hugged and rattled off into a conversation I had no hope in understanding.

After a minute of listening to their babble, Leo shook his friend's hand again and waved me over and introduced me to Bob. He seemed like a decent dude, when he wasn't wielding a machete.

"Bob has agreed to let us use his kayaks for as long as we want. Come, let's go."

I thanked my new friend Bob as best as I could in English, then followed Leo back past the hut down where two kayaks lay upside down by a pristine lagoon.

Leo found it funny that I had never kayaked before. So he took a minute to give some basic instruction, and away we went.

The weather was perfect for exploring the mangroves. The sun was strong yet the surrounding shade from the trees was abundant whenever we needed a break.

It was a decent substitute for kiteboarding. I felt a lot more relaxed as we paddled casually through the emerald canals. I couldn't let myself go completely though, as the kayak demanded a little more care and attention than a canoe.

We drifted along side by side. Leo would pass around a joint about every half hour, or half-dozen beer. The whole experience was quite intoxicating, literally.

Leo turned out to be quite the guide. For a bartending dance instructor, he surprisingly knew a lot about wildlife. He was quick to spot large iguanas camouflaged in the canopy, which I would have easily missed. The large parrots and many types of colourful fish he drew in close to the boats with an offering of bread crumbs.

We stalled for a while. I lay out flat on my back to soak up in some rays. It was tricky to get positioned without tipping the boat, but I managed. Leo reached over and lightly tapped my shoulder and held a finger to his lips. He pointed to the water below the kayaks. I sat up slowly, suspecting another school of fish, and it was. Sharks! Three large grey masses gliding swiftly and silently below us. They were the first sharks I had ever witnessed outside a television. And there was less than three feet of water separating us.

I panicked only for an instant, but it was enough of an instant to tip my steed. I was completely submerged and my life blurred before my eyes. My feet thrust down hard in search of a foothold. I hit ground and pushed with all my might. Grabbing the boat, I heaved my body back to the surface. On my way up, I screamed in horror as the silky firm skin of one of nature's most skilled predators slid between my legs.

Unscathed other than my pride, I lay flat on my stomach on top of the overturned kayak. Leo was laughing hysterically, holding his gut, coughing and choking. I laid motionless and thanked God and everything holy for life and the trees and lizards and the air. It took a couple of minutes for my heartbeat to slow down and my breath to return to normal. Combine the adrenaline rush with the beer and marijuana, and I could barely move. Leo was still laughing. He would give an honest effort to stop, but when he looked over at my limp mass, he would burst out again.

"Are you crazy?" I finally managed to blurt, unable to lift my head from the boat. "How can you laugh? I could have been killed!"

He laughed even harder, slapping his hand on his boat. "You should have seen your face!"

"Well, yeah! There's fucking sharks down there!"

"They were sharks?" He mocked. "Those were fish, Brandon, fish that may someday become sharks. They were little, maybe two feet long." His laughter continued. "Look!" He pointed back down.

I was terrified to move as I was afraid of tipping again, but surely they were monsters. I very slowly slid my head over the edge and peered down into the realm of Jaws. At first, there was nothing. Then the trio made another silent pass beneath us, moving in complete unison like an elite force of fighter jets. They were lucky if they were two feet long.

"Son of a bitch!" I relaxed. I could have sworn they were man eaters." I shook my head, embarrassed of my cowardice. Leo burst back into laughter once again.

"You should have seen your ..." He pointed at me, hand still clenched to his gut.

I was trying to maintain my anger, but Leo was having such a good time that I couldn't resist and joined in, laughing along. "Shit man! It's a good thing sharks aren't attracted to the smell of piss. I'm sure they got a mouthful."

"Yes, yes! It is fine. Piss, it is only the water." He smiled.

After taking a moment to muster the courage, we both jumped into the water. My fearsome man-eating sharks scattered like frightened goldfish. Leo helped me set my boat back properly then we lit another joint and made our way slowly back to Bob's hut.

The festivities were already underway when we finally made it back to the city. I sat at the bar while the crew tended to the guests. Leo waited on tables and Youp tended the bar where I found my regular perch.

"So Brandon, are you enjoying your stay on our little island so far?" Youp asked.

"Yes, it's been amazing. Everyone has been so friendly, and kiteboarding is awesome. I will definitely come back."

Youp grinned the grin of a man with something on his mind.

"What?" I asked.

"I was just thinking. Maybe you should consider staying a little longer." He shrugged innocently.

"What do you mean?" I shot back as if he had just suggested something illegal.

He laughed, "Why go? Why wouldn't you stay? You enjoy it here. You get along well with everyone. Have you ever thought that maybe you should just not go back? You could work here at The Flying Fish. Or maybe at that kiteboarding place?"

I smiled, "Yeah, sure. It's nice here and all, but really I have to get back to ..." I paused.

Youp cut in, "To what? To that job that you hate?"

I remained silent. The thought had never crossed my mind to possibly not return. It was absurd. Surely, one couldn't just do that. There had to be laws. "Well, that would be great Youp. I mean, this place is great right now cause I have lots of money, but what happens when it runs out? Bonaire's great. This trip has been amazing and so have all of you, but a person can't honestly ..." I wanted to say that a person couldn't honestly live like that but the evidence was all around me that people were living just like that. "I've worked really hard to get where I am back home and there's no way I could make that kind of money down here. No big deal. I'll go back and work a couple of months and then come down again for another vacation. I guess this would be good for those people who are soul searching and trying to find themselves and all, but eventually a guy's just got to grow up."

That last comment soured Youp. His tone changed as he continued with his chore. "Yes, of course, you should go home and grow up. This is just for us who are confused or immature, who will never find a place in society." He leaned over the bar, his face mere inches from mine. "Tell me Brandon. Look at me. How old do you think I am?"

I had secretly contemplated the age of some of my Bonairian friends during some of the earlier gatherings. I figured Youp was older than I, but not by much. "I don't know, thirty?"

"Oh wow, thirty. Would you be surprised to learn that I am considerably older than that?"

I shrugged my shoulders, not knowing how he wanted me to respond.

"Forty-five. I am forty-five." He stood back up and began to wipe down the bar. "So now, grown up Brandon, do you know any men my age back where you work in the oil field?"

"Yeah."

"How many of them do you look at and estimate their age at fifteen years less than the actual?" He pressed out his chest with a hint of arrogance.

That was a question I had indeed not considered. I thought back to the Big Johnson crew. Brian definitely looked his age, and he wasn't much fun. Smokey, he looked well beyond a person ten years his senior, his body crippled after years of hard labour. Steve just looked like shit now. And Dave. I bowed my head as I recalled my lost friend, then I looked around the restaurant at Leo and the workers. They were all smiling. None of them owned a house or a vehicle, but there they were enjoying life.

Then I looked up at Youp, he was well tanned and had nice hair and clean clothes. He looked especially good for his age. I couldn't remember ever meeting a happier guy. I slowly nodded as I began to see where he was coming from.

Youp started up again but the bitterness was gone and happy Youp had returned. "I am not ignorant to your oil business Brandon. The oil industry has filled my pockets just as it has yours. I used to work in a big office back on the mainland for IBM. I made lots of money—but the stress! I had to take a leave from it and I found myself here, like you. I loved it, the island and its rhythm. This place was for sale, so I cashed in everything I had back home and here I am. I am not making as much money but I have yet to take stress leave. I get up in the morning and I am happy. I am surrounded by great friends. I want to do this for the rest of my life. Who cares about retirement? How many guys where you work enjoy their job as much as I do? Even with all the money they make, how many of them are set up for a good retirement?" He smiled knowingly. "Now you tell me Brandon, in your opinion, which man is more grown up? The one who lives to work, or the one who works to live?"

Youp was a great guy but when motivated, he could sure make a guy feel stupid, as I did right then.

The last of the diners made their way down the steps to the street. Leo linked the chain behind them to make the official close. We gathered at the bar. Some shed their formal work attire for a more casual option. We toasted to another successful shift.

That night, the main street was not as busy with celebration. There was no band playing anywhere. So we hung around the restaurant where the drinks were cheap. I had trouble getting into the spirit that evening. I kept to myself mostly and just watched the others. They were all from different walks of life, but here together, they were one happy family. It was a totally different attitude from back on the rigs, where finding the oil and making the money was the driving force. Even after death, they just kept on pushing. Dave would have loved it on Bonaire.

Leo noticed my distance. "Brandon, what is wrong? You do not seem quite with it tonight. Is everything all right?"

"Yeah, I'm all right, just tired. I'm still not totally adjusted to all this Caribbean sun." I smiled.

"Yes, right, you are probably tired from wrestling the killer sharks?" He joked and slapped me lightly on the back. "It is not really a party here tonight anyway, if you would like I can take you home."

I felt bad ducking out on the party, but like Leo said, it wasn't much of a party anyway. Besides, I would make sure and set some time aside to return one more night before I left. "Okay Leo, thanks."

Up and down we bounced along the dark desert road toward the Kon Tiki. Leo spoke of his many adventures but it was only background noise to me then. I was lost in my own thoughts as I looked out the window into the darkness.

The clock ticked on and my time on the island was growing shorter. Thoughts of home began to interrupt my vacation more frequently. Reality was knocking on my door to remind me that my time in Neverland was limited.

The lights of the Kon Tiki came into view, "Hey Leo, do you want to come in?"

Leo glanced over with a look of surprise, "What, to your place?"

"Yeah, come on in. Check it out. It's not that late. Let's smoke a joint?"

"Oh, yes, sure. I will come in and see your place." Leo was acting kind of odd to the invitation.

All was quiet at the Kon Tiki. I did a subtle sweep of the area, but there was no sign of Aleida or Shrek.

We got inside and Leo asked to use the bathroom. I directed him down the hall, and handed me a joint on his way by.

Back in the kitchen, I found a lighter. I heard the sound of the toilet flush and made my way around the corner of the counter going to the living room. Leo came around the corner from the bathroom at the same time. As we bumped into each other, I smiled at my friend. I held the joint up in one hand and the lighter up in the other. Then I saw something really different in my island companion as he smiled back. He was flushed and acting somewhat bashful.

Leo wrapped his arms around my shoulders and ran his fingers through the back of my hair. He tilted his head slightly, closed his eyes and pressed his lips full and tight against mine. It happened so fast that I had no time to respond or even consider what was happening. Both my hands were still occupied by the joint and the lighter.

I remember thinking how impossible it could be that I was caught in this situation with Leo. He was a stud, the ladies loved him. He was good-looking, dressed to the tens and a dance instructor. Then it dawned on me: all the ladies loved him but he never ever took any home, and none of the guys cared when he danced with their girls. And he was good-looking and dressed to the tens and he was a dance instructor.

Just when I felt the light bulb flick on, his lips began to part and I felt the tip of a tongue tickle its way across the centerline.

The joint fell to the floor and I pushed him back. I held a hand up to ensure he didn't come in for more and wiped my mouth on my arm. I'm sure the look of shock and disgust on my face said more than I needed.

Leo's face instantly flushed and tears gathered in his eyes as he absorbed my reaction. His hand shot to his mouth. "Oh, shit! Oh shit!" And he ran out of the apartment into the night.

I didn't move. I just stood in my spot as I heard the car peel away and spray rocks through the parking lot. I stood dumbfounded. My mind traced back to the times I had spent with Leo. How I could have been so fucking stupid?

I closed the front door, then reached down and collected the joint and the lighter. I sparked it up and inhaled long and deep. I made my way toward the patio doors and released the plume into the warm night air. I forced the incident from my mind.

The sky was clear and the stars were out. The wind was strong and steady, it called to me. Tomorrow I would go kiteboarding.

54

The next morning, I was up early. I didn't bother to stop in the Kon Tiki for breakfast or to say hi. I didn't even look for Aleida. I walked the road to Lac Bay, all the time in deep thought as I looked over the landscape.

I finally made it to the bay. All was quiet. It was still too early for the shop to open but Gregoreo was there, preparing his equipment for the day ahead. He looked up in surprise as I rounded the corner.

"Brandon, my friend, you are early." He smiled nicely. But then noted the serious expression on my face, and his smile faltered.

"Hey Greg, sorry to get here so early, but I need to get out on the water."

"Ah, Brandon you look troubled," he smiled sympathetically. "I will guess it is woman problems?"

"No, why would you say that?" Women were the farthest thing from my mind.

"Oh, it is nothing," he quickly dropped the subject.

"So anyway, the wind is good. I know you don't open for another hour, but can I head out? I'll pay extra."

"No, Brandon, you have been a good customer. You go ahead. I already have the 9.0 inflated." He pointed to the kite.

"Thanks Greg," I managed a small smile.

I hit the water hard and pushed the weight of my frustrations into the board, carving deep into the water. The slice of the board through the chop, the pull of the wind—life was good out on the bay, easy. There was no misinterpretation; the wind was the wind, and the water was just what it seemed. Then there was me.

Questions rang through my mind first about Katy and how she had betrayed me. Then there was that guy Hanso, then Bernhard, and now Leo. It was hard for me to deny that I seemed to have some specific quality that attracted homosexual men. Maybe there was a special wave or signal that I was ignorantly flashing around. Or maybe I possessed an alluring aroma. Whatever it was, the attraction was becoming more undeniable, it seemed, with every passing week. Maybe there was something to it if I did swing that way. I could have access to a harem of options. I definitely wasn't hitting it big with the ladies.

It was a stupid thought. I may not have been a stud with the women, but what I did have was good quality, and the sex, I really enjoyed the sex. Sex with a guy, that would be …

It was too much thinking and it was beginning to get confusing. I countered the negative energy with positive and dug the board hard into water and carved slightly upwind to build resistance to the kite. Then, void of thought, I cranked hard on the bar shooting the kite straight overhead, and instantly I was airborne. Ten, maybe even twenty feet, no problem. My biggest yet by far. I had mentally envisioned the moves repeatedly and worked the kite just as I had been told and gently floated back down to a smooth landing.

Then I smiled as every thought, every doubt or concern had all been blown from my mind. It was my first real jump and it was fucking awesome. If I had been addicted to the sport before, I had just progressed to full blown junkie.

I sailed for the rest of the morning into the early afternoon, making pass after pass in the bay, jumping and carving. Then as I was making a run by the beach, she came down the white sand and laid a towel out near the water. Dressed in a skimpy bikini top and short shorts, Aleida looked out and waved to me. I was due for a break anyway, so I parked the kite. Gregoreo rushed out to grab it and congratulated me on my newly acquired skill.

"Aleida, you came to watch?"

She laughed, "Yes, well, you spent a whole night with me and helped with my turtles. I thought that I should come and see what you like to do." She leaned in close and rested against me as I pulled up a spot on the towel.

"Well, this is it," I pointed out over the bay now populated with a flock of colourful kites diving and climbing through the air.

"I see you out there. You are very good."

"Yeah, not bad for a couple of weeks, eh? I just started the big jumps this morning. It was one of my goals before I leave."

"You are leaving soon?" I was selfishly happy to see her disappointment.

We sat quietly for a while. As I relaxed, my action-packed adrenaline surge depleted. I gazed out over the bay and watched the other kiteboarders carve thick lines through the water. Then my draining thoughts of Leo and my return home climbed back on my shoulders. I scooped another handful of sand and let it fall through my fingers.

Aleida recognized my sign of distress. "Brandon, what is wrong? I don't know you well, but well enough to know that look."

I pressed my hands hard to my face and rubbed up through my hair. "It's nothing." I corrected my posture for a poor attempt at concealing the obvious.

"You should tell me. Why wouldn't you tell me? You will leave soon and you can just leave it behind." She nudged me coaxingly.

"It's just the friends I've met on the island. Well, one in particular."

"Leo?"

My gaze snapped over to her. "Yeah, you know Leo?"

"Brandon, I have been on the island for a while now. All the people at The Flying Fish are well known to many. I know Leo and Youp and Don. I saw Leo drop you off last night." I noticed a slight smirk on her face as she watched her feet stir through the sand. "He seemed quite upset when he left."

I nodded grimly and looked down at the beach. "He …" Aleida waited for my explanation with a prodding smirk. "He kissed me. He kissed me!"

Her jaw tensed and she nodded. "Yes, he is gay you know."

"I do now. I don't know how I didn't pick up on it before. He's a good guy. I like hanging out with him."

"Yes, they are all very good people."

"What do you mean they are all good people?"

She laughed at me. "The guys at The Flying Fish. Youp, Don, they are lovers. Then Leo, he is gay also. There are many on the island who choose that lifestyle." She laughed and nudged me again. "You really didn't know?"

I paused and reflected on my time spent with The Flying Fish crew. "No, I didn't even consider it. I thought Youp was Don's brother. But now that you mention it, it all makes sense." I shook my head. "How could I be so stupid? It's crazy. It seems like ever since I left Medicine Hat, I've attracted homosexuals like a homosexual does. Every time I turn around, some guy's trying to get in my pants." We both couldn't help but start laughing.

"You will find that many people from all over the world come to these small islands to escape, or maybe find themselves. They just want a place to start over and live the life they want to live. Imagine what it must be like to want something so badly but to have to resist it because it is not accepted by others."

"So, what does that mean for me? Maybe I'm gay? Maybe all these guys are picking up on something I haven't realized yet? Maybe that's why I came here?"

"Honestly, Brandon, I was also wondering if you preferred the men." She raised her eyebrows. "You have been on the island now for over a week. I am staying right upstairs from you. We had an incredible romantic night on the beach and you pulled back."

I opened my mouth to protest, but stopped. I turned back to the water and realized she was right. She was right there, all the time. A beautiful, exotic woman. We got along great. The other night on the beach was one of the most romantic nights … no, it was the most romantic night I'd ever had. I'd never even attempted anything with her. Maybe … ?

She jumped to her feet and grabbed my hand, pulling me up with her, "C'mon."

"What? Where?"

"Just come with me. Let me help you figure you out."

I got to my feet and let her drag me along with little resistance, "What are you talking about?"

She led me out past the hut and around the corner, down the road and past the forbidden fence. The one that extends out into the bay to separate the kiteboarding area from the nudist place. Then she turned down the path leading to the resort.

I resisted hard. "Aleida, do you know what this is?"

"Just come with me Brandon." She pulled harder, giggling.

The trees and brush were thick around the front of the resort to provide total privacy. The path rounded a large tree out of sight of the road. We pushed through a set of swinging saloon gates. I started to panic. There was no way I would have suspected Aleida would come to a place like this. I was still convinced she didn't have a clue what went on in there.

Beyond the gates was a thatched roof bar. Everything was well shaded by overhanging vegetation up to the beach where the sun beat down on to the well-manicured white sand.

"Hello Magda," Aleida smiled and waved to the elderly naked woman tending the bar.

"Aleida," Magda smiled. "I have not seen you for so long. The turtles must be very busy? Who is this new friend of yours?"

Aleida dragged me over and found us a seat at the bar. "Magda, this is my friend Brandon. Brandon, this is Magda. She and her husband own the resort."

"Hello Brandon." She smiled pleasantly and very casually. Considering she was completely naked.

"Uh, hello." I managed uncomfortably.

Aleida laughed, "This is all quite new for my friend Magda. He may take a little time to loosen up."

Magda winked at me. "A first timer, huh? Well, do not worry Brandon. We are all friends here. Take your time and move at your own pace."

I slowly surveyed the resort, while Aleida ordered up a couple of beers. It really wasn't very busy—ten, fifteen people maybe. But every single patron was naked. Completely naked. It wasn't the ultimate male fantasy I imagined a nudist resort would be. Most of them were couples, and at least half of them were elderly. There were no orgies happening anywhere. People were just talking and visiting as they would in a normal establishment. As if they were among the clothed.

Aleida handed me a beer and took a big swallow from her own. "Okay Brandon, enough looking." She grabbed my hand again and pulled me down to the beach.

"Uh, Aleida, I don't know if I'm ... I mean, you can't be serious."

As soon as we reached the sun, Aleida dropped my hand and without the slightest hint of self-consciousness, she removed her top. She did not even attempt to shield or conceal her stuff. Then she reached down and unbuttoned her shorts, letting them fall to the sand. She pulled the silk string of her thong panties down past her hips to fall with her shorts.

There she was, standing right in front of me, without a stitch of clothing. The tiny beads of sweat on her golden tanned skin sparkled in the rays of the hot sun. The lack of any lines suggested that Aleida was not as conservative as I suspected. My eyes started at her top and groped down slowly, taking in every last curve, dimple and freckle—and her only reaction was a teasing giggle.

She backed into the water slowly with a daring smile on her face. She held up her hand and beckoned me with a curled finger to follow her. "C'mon Brandon. Come play. You will regret it if you don't."

This was big. Thirty minutes ago I was lost in the world of kiteboarding. Then I was in a moral debate about my sexual orientation. And now I was standing in the middle of a nude beach with a beautiful naked woman begging me to play in the water with her. The little island of Bonaire just never stopped surprising!

I attracted enough attention being the only fully clothed guest. Now, as Aleida called and taunted me from the water, everyone had literally stopped what they were doing to watch the action. All eyes were focused on me and I could actually feel the shade of red in my face. I watched Aleida frolic in the warm, knee-deep water. Bending over and splashing water at me. Her breasts bouncing playfully with every motion. It was so crazy, but looking out at her, my only choice was to join. I would never forgive myself if I walked away.

I took a deep breath and pushed out my chest, then I ripped off my shirt and threw it on the ground. The small crowd of onlookers held their breath in suspense. I hesitated. I could just run in there and leave my shorts on, but I knew she wanted it all or nothing. This was a test. My mind raced back and forth. Shorts, or no shorts? Then something clicked. Or maybe it was a snap? My mind just shut down. It was my body's way of dealing with the situation. Don't think, just do. I reached down and grabbed my waistband, closed my eyes, and let them drop.

The crowd erupted in applause. I nodded and raised my hand with a gratuitous wave, radiating an aura of insecure confidence.

Assured that everyone had an equal opportunity to cop a peek at my wares, I took a casual stride toward the water. Maybe it was the breeze or the sun, but most likely it was Aleida's boobs. Whatever the reason, I felt the blood begin to move and the familiar tingle that normally preceded a stiffening of sorts. My casual stride turned to a hard sprint and I dove into the shallow water.

I surfaced beside Aleida. She reached over and wiped my wet hair from my face. Then she wrapped her arms around my neck and pulled her naked body close to mine. She was so beautiful—her eyes, her smile, and so much more.

"Aleida," I spoke softly as her lips brushed my cheek. "Whoever that guy was that left you, he was an idiot."

She smiled. "Brandon, that other guy left me for another man."

My head jerked back in shock, "Sonofa—"

She laughed and pressed her lips passionately to mine before I could finish my comment.

There, naked in the water, our bodies wound tight. There was no chance of me hiding how I felt about her sexually.

"Well, Mr. Brandon," she whispered. "I would say we have answered that question of which sex you prefer." She giggled, as she reached down to my undoubted erection.

After a much shorter time than I had hoped of exploring in the shallows, we joined the rest of the patrons in a shady patch on the beach. One of the old men lit a big fatty and passed it around the group. With naked Aleida nestled between my legs, I watched my new friends tell of their worldly adventures as the brilliant blue bay sparkled in the background. We were naked, all of us, not a shred of clothing. On some small island in the middle of nowhere. Naked and high as a kite. It was a beautiful thing I experienced that day. I wondered if I would ever experience anything as great as that again.

Bristol, the old portly retired man, drove us home. Aleida and I got dressed before we left, but not Bristol. He said he was too old to waste time with clothes. So, he drove us in his old rusted jeep with no roof, no doors, and no clothes, down a very bumpy road. We both kept our focus on the scenery outside the vehicle.

I opened the door to my room and turned gentleman-like to escort the lady as she passed the threshold.

"Thank you very much for today Brandon. I had a lot of fun." She smiled innocently, gave me a light peck on the lips and started to walk away. "I will see you in the morning."

My jaw fell off the bottom of my face. Was she joking? After splashing around naked in the water all afternoon? We were naked, both of us, no clothes!

"Aleida!" She stopped and turned. "I thought ..."

She laughed and came back to me and placed her hands on my cheeks. "Brandon, I know. Maybe it was wrong today, what we did? I'm sorry, but you are leaving soon. It is best we don't get too involved." She kissed me again, then turned and walked upstairs to her separate room.

I stayed outside and listened for her door to close in the hope that she was only kidding, and she would return. But she didn't.

ALTERNATIVE ENERGY

You're fucking kidding me!

55

I awoke the next morning to find that my blue balls had thankfully returned to their normal colour. I reviewed my mental list of the things I had left to accomplish on my trip, then I headed over to the restaurant. Aleida sat at the bar eating breakfast. She looked uncharacteristically stressed. I pulled up the seat next to her.

She fumbled with her teacup then looked over to me. "Brandon, I am very sorry about—"

I stopped her mid-sentence. I didn't want to waste time on unnecessary apologies. "Aleida, listen. You don't have to apologize for yesterday or last night. It was fantastic, probably the best day of my life. Except for the blue balls."

Her face screwed. "Your wha— Your balls?"

"Yeah, don't worry about it. Anyway, today is my last day here. My plane flies out tomorrow. There are some things I have to do before I go."

"Like what?"

"Well, kiteboarding."

She rolled her eyes. She probably expected something a little more romantic. "Of course, kiteboarding."

"Yes, but then I have to head into town. The guys were going to throw me a farewell bash, but with what happened with Leo, I don't know if that's still on. Either way, I have to find him and try to patch things up. I'd like you to go with me for support, and I'd like to spend my last night on the island with you. So, will you come?" My stern expression relayed that no was not an option.

"Of course."

"Right on." I reached across. Putting my hands on her cheeks, I pulled her in for a big wet smooch. She turned red and looked around to take note of all the witnesses. I smiled wickedly as I headed for the door. I was on top of the world that morning. It was my last night, and I didn't give a fuck who had seen what.

I hitched a ride to Lac Bay and sat with Gregoreo a bit before he opened the shop. For my last day, he had a beer with me at nine in the morning. On the house.

"Wind looks good today Greg."

He studied the sky with concern. "Yes. Yes, it is good. But there is a change coming."

No matter what Greg thought, it was a good day on the water where I was alone with my thoughts. The time to return home had come. I spent a small effort to mentally prepare for my return. Katy, and everything that was my life. The sound of the board in the water and the feeling of weightlessness as I soared through the sky made it hard to take anything serious.

I rode well for my last session. Carved hard, and jumped high. I wondered when I would be able to do it again, if ever. Then the wind gasped and sputtered. I had to work the kite hard to keep it in the air and keep it aloft on its own momentum, but inevitably it crashed into the water. I pulled hard on the rear lines, trying like hell to relaunch but it would not lift. It was bizarre. I had never suspected the wind on Bonaire would ever fail. It was just always there. Just like that, my final kiteboard session ended.

In the distance, I heard the lonely purr of Gregoreo's motor boat pushing across the bay to my rescue. He first went to the kite, deflated it and gathered the lines, then circled around to me.

"I had a feeling Brandon. Something was not right this morning. I am sorry my friend."

"Ah, there's nothing you can do about it."

"Come, I will take you back and we'll have another beer."

I considered my situation, then looked to the far shore across the bay. Aleida was there, looking all sexy in her short shorts and white shirt towing her Shrek. She was also sporting a gigantic set of green headphones and held a multi-pronged antenna high in the air.

272

"A beer sounds good Greg, but I've got a tight schedule today. Can you take me over there?" I pointed.

Gregoreo squinted against the sun and scanned the far shore 'til he zoned in on my target. He turned to me and smiled. "Ah my friend," he nodded with approval, "she is quite the woman Miss Aleida. Come, of course I will take you to her."

We skimmed along the bay in the small inflatable boat. I laid back against the side and watched the various shades of blue water pass beneath us, then turned my face to the warm Caribbean breeze.

The boat skidded to a stop on the sandy beach. We hopped out and I walked over to my friend and embraced him with a pat on the back. "I don't know how to thank you Greg. I'll never forget you man."

"You can thank me by coming back someday, Brandon. It was a pleasure to meet you." He turned to the beach and nodded toward Aleida. Her head was just visible over the next dune. She was oblivious to our arrival, focused heavily on her transmitter. "Now go get her man."

We shook hands, then I launched him off back into the bay. He pulled the motor to life, turned back for home, and waved goodbye.

I turned my attention back to Aleida who still hadn't noticed me. I crept quietly over the dune and waited as she turned to her left then snuck quickly in behind her, shooting my hand around her waist, "Ha!"

She turned fast, too fast, and smacked me square on the side of the head with the butt of her steel antennae. I hit the ground hard and my hands covered my head as I cringed in pain.

"Oh no! Brandon, what are you doing here? Why did you do that?" She knelt down beside me in a panic to survey the damage.

I moaned, "I was trying to be romantic."

"Oh my God, you are bleeding."

The blow had opened a decent gash on the backside of my head. She ran back to her Shrek and returned quickly. She pressed a towel to my wound.

"Oh, Brandon, I'm very sorry. Are you all right?"

She dabbed lightly at my head. "What are you doing here anyway? We were supposed to meet at the Kon Tiki later."

I waved a hand at the sky. "My last day and the wind died. I saw you here waving your thingy there around so I got Greg to bring me over."

She stopped with the dabbing and examined my scalp carefully. "I think maybe the bleeding has stopped. You are going to be all right." Relieved, she sat down on the sand beside me.

We both sat looking over the mangled antenna lying on the beach.

"I'm sorry I broke your alien transmitter. What the hell do you do with that thing anyway?"

"It is for the turtles. The ones I have tagged. I am trying to locate them, but I'm not having any luck. The equipment is old and it doesn't work very well." A sullen look crossed her face. She turned her head from me and stared out over the water. She pulled her knees in close and hugged them to her chest. "It is very frustrating to be here. All I'm trying to do is help, and sometimes it seems like no one wants to listen. Nobody cares about the turtles. Sometimes I feel like there is no hope for us people."

I couldn't let it happen, have Aleida slip into depression. Not on my last day. But I could see her point. Really, what was she really going to accomplish down there? How do you get people or corporations to fund something that is only going to pay out with more turtles? There may be a saying like "He who has the oil controls the world!" But he who owns the turtles just has a lot of turtles.

"Let me see if I can get it to work." I jumped to my feet. It was just that little bit of hope that got Aleida back into good spirits as she followed. I picked up the different components and placed the headphones around my neck. I grabbed the antenna and turned it in my hand, examining all the bits and pieces.

"No Brandon, not like that. You have to—"

"Listen, Aleida," I looked at her smugly, "I do have a bit of a way with electronics."

She backed off as I placed the headphones over my ears, positioned the antenna in the air, and fiddled with the little electrical box thing. And then— "Goddamsonofa!" I screamed, backpedalling frantically before landing on my ass. I sat shaking my hand from the vicious shock.

"I was trying to tell you about that." She looked down at her now totally destroyed contraption, then back at me sitting on my ass and rubbing my hand. She laughed, "Yes, you definitely have a way with electronics. I have never seen anyone get electrocuted with it before."

She offered her hand and helped me back to my feet, then collected her equipment from the beach. The sun had begun to set and we had a fair hike back to the Kon Tiki. I followed her over to Shrek and helped pack away her gear.

I felt really bad. It may have been a piece of shit, but at least it was something she had. "Aleida, I'm really sorry for breaking it."

"Do not be sorry. I'm glad you came today. I needed some company. We will manage, me and my turtles." She picked up Shrek's towrope, then wrapped her arm in mine and gave me a soft peck on the cheek. "Let's go celebrate your last night with all your boyfriends." She laughed.

"I'll let you get away with that because I broke your turtle tracker." We made our way arm in arm in the setting sun across the tropical desert.

Back at the oasis, we separated to our own showering facilities. I instructed her to put on her extra fancy attire because I was taking her out for supper. We met up out front. She did look incredible in a white island dress that hugged her figure perfectly. It brought back sweet memories of our naked frolic in the bay.

56

Pieter gave us a ride into town, smiling all the way as he drove and subtly pried in to our relationship. When we got there, I let Aleida pick the restaurant. She led me to her favourite five-star establishment. At least she thought it was her favourite, as she explained how she hadn't actually eaten there yet as it was way too expensive.

It was the perfect last supper of the trip. Aleida's lustrous smile flickered by the candlelight. The sound of the waves lapped against the peer and the moon was perfectly mirrored on the black ocean surface. I dragged it on as long as I could, chewing slowly and keeping up the conversation. I needed the time to build courage for the coming confrontation with Leo. It would have been much easier to hide out there and spend the evening with only Aleida. But for some reason I had to try and set things straight.

The Flying Fish was down a couple of blocks. We walked along the pier hand in hand, watching the water.

"Are you nervous Brandon? You look nervous."

"Yeah, I don't know. I hope he's all right. But if he's all bent out of shape, then I guess you and me will just go do our own thing tonight. Tomorrow, I take off and I won't have to worry about it anymore." I was really tired of the whole situation, but in a way it was good. At first, Bonaire was this magical paradise. But over the time of my stay, it began to show its little imperfections. Like any other place in the world, It was nice to visit.

We inched closer to our destination. I could see the welcoming lights of The Flying Fish. The place looked packed as usual. I kept my head up and focused on my goal. There was a decent chance they'd toss me out on my ass. If they did, then Aleida and I could just continue on with our night.

We crossed the street and climbed the stairs out of the darkness and into the light of the restaurant. Youp was behind the bar, the girls were busy tending tables, but there was no Leo. A slight sweat broke on my forehead as we reached the crest of the stairs and turned to the bar. I held my breath. Youp turned and flashed a big welcoming smile.

"Brandon! And Aleida, what a nice surprise." He opened his arms wide and motioned to some bar stools.

We took our seats. Not wanting to beat around the bush, I jumped right to the point. "Thanks Youp," I leaned over the bar and lowered my voice. "Where's Leo?"

The expression on his face said that he had heard the whole story. "He is here Brandon, helping in the kitchen. We had a sudden rush of customers."

"How is he? Did you hear?"

"Yes, yes. He told me all about it. He was very upset, but I wouldn't say he is mad at you. He is just very confused." He fished for the appropriate description.

"When he met you, he was very excited. You both got along so well and he … well, we all just assumed that a young man travelling on his own, you know." He tilted his head and raised his brow.

"I know, I know. Lots of gay people come to the Caribbean. I feel stupid because I didn't even consider it. I'm ignorant to these things. I mean, I actually thought you and Don were brothers."

Youp chuckled, "Don't feel bad, Brandon. It is not a matter of whose fault it is. It is just one of those unfortunate things. Leo has been without someone for a long time now, and when you arrived, he was very excited. He was very quick to fall for you."

Some of my mouthful of beer seeped out my nose as I choked on his last comment.

"It is very strong of you to show up Brandon. None of us thought that you would."

"Whatever. Leo is as a … well …" I was tongue tied. Youp smiled understandingly. "It just is what it is. Leo is a good friend to me and I still consider him one. If he is mad, then at least I tried."

"I don't think he is really mad Brandon. Just disappointed. And his pride is hurt. But you are right, it is what it is." Youp suddenly drifted from the conversation. I noticed his glance focus on a point behind me and caught a quick jerk of his head.

I turned to see Leo standing behind me over by the kitchen entrance. He paused. He first looked at me, then to Youp, then Aleida. His jaw clenched tight before he dropped his head and walked very swiftly toward the stairs and out into the dark street below.

I jumped from my stool and chased after him. "Leo, Leo!" He continued on across the street and stopped by the chain posts that bordered the bay. I stopped short behind him. "Leo, I'm sorry." I realized that I never rehearsed what exactly I was going to say if I ever got to that point.

"Yes, good!" His voice crackled. "That is fine then. Thank you for coming." He kept his head down and his back to me. His tone was laced with a thick sarcasm.

He was hurt, there was no mistaking that, but what was I? I didn't deserve to be handed the guilt trip; I didn't do anything wrong. I dropped the apologetic approach and just gave it to him straight up. "Listen man. It took a lot for me to come here tonight. It would have been a lot easier to just say to hell with it and get on my plane tomorrow. But you are a good friend, and I figured I owed you better than that. What happened was shit, but I can't change it. If I had known, I would have told you. But you could have also maybe mentioned something to me." I paused, hoping for a response, but he said nothing. "Well, I tried. It sucks to leave it like this, but at least I tried. So, thanks for … whatever." I turned and walked back to the restaurant. He didn't stop me and he never followed.

I claimed my stool back at the bar. I needn't say anything to Youp or Aleida. I had the telltale look on my face and there was no Leo with me. Aleida reached over and softly rubbed my back as I sat down. Youp served me up a fresh cold one.

It wasn't long 'til Youp made another jerky motion toward the stairs. Aleida found an excuse to go to the bathroom, and Youp quickly tended to some patrons at the other end of the bar.

Leo took a seat on the stool beside me. He had dried his cheeks, but even so, I could tell he had been crying. "Brandon," he looked me in the eye, "you are right. I apologize for the way I acted just now. It's just—"

I cut him off. "That's it, that's all I need. If you want to go through a whole speech, buddy I'm more than happy to listen. But it's not needed on my part. We both know the reason this whole thing happened is because I'm fucking sexy!" His eyes grew wide at the arrogance I delivered without so much as a flinch. But I could only hold it for a second before my smile told the truth. "And you're pretty fucking sexy too buddy." We both laughed then put down our drinks and hugged a big man-on-man hug. He truly was a good friend.

With my small Bonaire family reunited, we laughed and partied the night away in true Bonaire fashion.

Then, much too quickly, the night grew tired and the crowd began to thin. One by one, my island friends would stop to say goodbye on their way out. Leo was smashed. He gave me a big drunken hug and a slobbery kiss on the cheek. I promised to return. But as I watched my friends disappear down the walk, I knew the reality was more likely I would never return. It was just how it was.

Aleida and I bounced down the road in the cab. I stared out the window at the total blackness. My last drunken ride through the nighttime desert. Time had passed so fast that the whole excursion seemed more like a long dream. Only, I could never dream up a place like this little island.

Back at the Kon Tiki, Aleida walked me to my door. Full of courage, I grabbed her around the waist and pulled her in for a soft kiss. "You're not getting away that easy tonight," I whispered. It was my last night on the island. I figured I should at least swing for it.

She rested her hand on my chest and smiled that shitty denial smile. "Brandon, I like you very much, and I always had a wonderful time with you. But you are leaving tomorrow and it is better we don't get any more attached. Neither one of us needs to get hurt again." She kissed me again, softly and sensually and held on way longer than she should have. I released her and she turned and walked away. My balls throbbed with her every step.

57

The next morning, flight 436 flew out over the island of Bonaire, destined for Miami. My mind congested with thoughts of home as I watched the plane climb high into the clouds from Aleida's second floor balcony. She had a way better view than my main floor suite. I looked at the airline ticket in my hand, then tore it into small pieces and let the Bonairian breeze carry it away.

When I could no longer see the plane, I returned to the bedroom and crawled back under the sheets and softly kissed Aleida's naked back. She was beautiful, and I was in love, with everything. I ran after her that night, spun her around and took her in my arms. She melted, and I stayed.

I was awarded the title of turtle research funding guy until my money ran out. Our first order of business was to go into town that morning and order a new turtle tracker. The best money could buy and fuck me, we were going to find some turtles!

I emailed my father later that day so he wouldn't worry. I wondered what would happen to my place and personal belongings if I failed to return after too long. But they were a million miles away. Katy, Steve, the rig—if they wanted me, they were going to have to wait. For the time being, I was trading in all my oil stocks. Down on this little desert island in the Caribbean, I'd found an alternative energy.

To be continued…

www.ingramcontent.com/pod-product-compliance
Lightning Source LLC
Chambersburg PA
CBHW061615190726

48288CB00007B/2334